COPYRIGHTED MATERIAL

Copyright © 2012 by S. M. Boyce, L. L. C.
Cover and art copyright © 2018 by Amalia Chitulescu
Book design and layout copyright © 2012 by S. M. Boyce, L. L. C.

This novel is a work of fiction. Names, characters, places and incidents are either products of the author's imagination or used fictitiously. Any resemblance to actual events, locales, or persons, living, dead, or undead, is entirely coincidental.

All rights reserved.

No part of this publication can be reproduced or transmitted in any form or by any means, electronic or mechanical, without permission in writing from S. M. Boyce, L. L. C.

www.smboyce.com

2nd Edition

BOOKS BY S. M. BOYCE

The Grimoire Saga

Lichgates

Treason

Heritage

Illusion

The Misanthrope

The First Vagabond: Rise of a Hero

The First Vagabond: Fall of a Legend

The Demon

The Fairhaven Chronicles

Glow

Shimmer

Ember

Nightfall

Standalone Novels

Ari

STAY CONNECTED

Boyce posts official artwork, updates, and random things that will make you laugh on Facebook, Instagram, and Twitter.

Boyce also created a special Facebook group specifically for readers like you to come together and share their lives and interests, especially regarding the Grimoire Saga novels. Please check it out and join in whenever you get the chance! Everyone in there is amazing, and you'll fit right in.

https://www.facebook.com/groups/Grimoire-Readers/

Sign up for email alerts of new releases AND exclusive access to the Grimoire Saga Fandom Encyclopedia: the official guide to Ourea exclusively for the Grimoire Saga's biggest fans. The encyclopedia is

ONLY available to Boyce's VIP email tribe, so sign up now to get access:

https://smboyce.com/email-signup-pages/grimoire-saga/

Enjoying the series? Awesome! Help others discover the Grimoire Saga by leaving a review at Amazon: **http://mybook.to/treason-by-boyce**

TREASON

BOOK TWO OF THE GRIMOIRE SAGA

S. M. BOYCE

BOOK DESCRIPTION

Kara Magari ignited a war when she stumbled into Ourea and found the Grimoire: a powerful artifact filled with secrets. To protect the only family she has left, she strikes a deal that compromises everything she believes in... but things don't go as planned.

To survive this world of death and darkness, Kara can't just overcome the evil knocking at her door... she must become it.

Welcome to Ourea, where only the cunning survive.

Buckle in & experience the beginning of a timeless epic fantasy adventure with this second installment of the Grimoire Saga. If you enjoy Lord of the Rings, The

Wheel of Time, or Eragon, you'll love this breathtaking epic fantasy adventure with a modern twist.

Warning: this story contains adventure, action, and mild cussing.

CONTENTS

Chapter One	1
Chapter Two	15
Chapter Three	34
Chapter Four	48
Chapter Five	57
Chapter Six	70
Chapter Seven	82
Chapter Eight	88
Chapter Nine	105
Chapter Ten	116
Chapter Eleven	129
Chapter Twelve	136
Chapter Thirteen	148
Chapter Fourteen	158
Chapter Fifteen	170
Chapter Sixteen	183
Chapter Seventeen	193
Chapter Eighteen	207
Chapter Nineteen	219
Chapter Twenty	236
Chapter Twenty-One	251
Chapter Twenty-Two	260
Chapter Twenty-Three	266
Chapter Twenty-Four	280
Chapter Twenty-Five	291
Chapter Twenty-Six	306
Chapter Twenty-Seven	315
Chapter Twenty-Eight	325
Chapter Twenty-Nine	341
Chapter Thirty	359

Chapter Thirty-One	371
Chapter Thirty-Two	386
Chapter Thirty-Three	397
Chapter Thirty-Four	407
Chapter Thirty-Five	419
Chapter Thirty-Six	428
Chapter Thirty-Seven	436
Chapter Thirty-Eight	451
Chapter Thirty-Nine	456
Chapter Forty	474
Chapter Forty-One	483
Chapter Forty-Two	492
Chapter Forty-Three	499
Chapter Forty-Four	513
Chapter Forty-Five	523
Chapter Forty-Six	531
Chapter Forty-Seven	545
Chapter Forty-Eight	567
Chapter Forty-Nine	578
Chapter Fifty	590
Chapter Fifty-One	618
Chapter Fifty-Two	627
Chapter Fifty-Three	639
Chapter Fifty-Four	647
Epilogue	662
Important Characters and Terms	677
You're Missing Out...	689
Books by S. M. Boyce	691
Acknowledgments	692
About the Author	693

For Mom and Dad.
Better parents don't exist. Thank you for supporting and
loving me through every twist and turn.

CHAPTER ONE

KARA

In the hidden world of Ourea, there are too many beautiful places to name. Rose-covered cliffs tower miles over the valleys and forests below, cities thrive in submerged ecosystems beneath the sea, and the dragons that once ruled volcanoes are now but fossils in a cave. The creatures of human myth flourish in Ourea. Trees are this world's skyscrapers. Magic is its currency. And while the rest of Earth forgot what it meant to dream big, Ourea kept alive its wonder.

At least, that's how Kara saw it.

She sat on a ledge in a cave, a dozen feet or so above an indoor river littered with rapids. Sunlight poured through a crack in the ceiling, its rays tinted green from the branches that blocked her view of the sun. The light danced across the river, illuminating the white foam that splattered into the air as the water rushed by below.

Kara dangled her legs over the edge, listening to the chorus of water roaring through the cave. Her perch served as a catwalk through the cavern. Several more lined both sides of the cave, but she hadn't yet figured out how to get to them. She stared up at the rocky shelf ten feet above her, her eyes followed the natural walkway until she came across a missing chunk a few yards off. Maybe she could climb that someday, but all she wanted now was to relax.

Her ledge wound around a bend in the cavern wall and toward a waterfall that fed the river. Behind the waterfall was a flight of stone stairs leading to a dirt trail, which curved through a forest for about a mile before it opened out into the Vagabond's village—her village. And there, somewhere in the myriad of empty houses and vacant rooms, Braeden had probably realized she'd ditched their sparring practice for the day.

Kara eyed her satchel, which lay empty against the cave wall. Flick—the red, teleporting ball of fur that he was—was out and about exploring the cave. The Xlijnughl—she'd spent an hour with the Grimoire before she could pronounce it properly as *Zyl-LEYN-guhl*—could find trouble anywhere, so she hoped he would stay close. She would have to keep an eye out for him.

Her stomach growled. She glanced through the

tree branches above to take a guess at the time, but she couldn't even see the sun through the leaves. As much as she wanted to believe Braeden wouldn't find her little haven, she knew better. Braeden could track anything. That prince could track a month-old trail if he wanted. There was no escaping him, not that she would ever really want such a thing. Not after all he'd done for her.

She sighed and leaned her head against the cave wall. Pebbles broke off as she pushed against it, so she grabbed one as it fell and chucked it over the edge.

Braeden had guarded her while she'd visited the yakona kingdoms. He'd helped her bring them together, in a loose sense of the word. He'd saved her life when she'd fled Hillside. She shuddered—her brush with Gavin had been too close. He'd tried to trick her into wearing a poisoned tiara that would have made her his slave.

She scoffed. None of this even sounded real. This *world* couldn't be real. She would wake up from her coma any day now. That had to be it. A secret world hidden beneath the human race's collective nose couldn't be real. Right?

"You scrunch your eyebrows when you're lost in thought."

She blinked her eyes back into focus. Braeden sat next to her, even though she hadn't heard him on his way across the ledge.

He watched her with that half-cocked grin of his. Black hair framed his face, longer now than when she'd first met him a couple months ago. A few beads of sweat rolled down his temple, tracing his olive skin in a pattern she wanted to mimic with her finger. His dark eyes caught her in their gaze, and she forgot how to breathe for a moment.

"No, don't stop. It's cute," he said.

She laughed and punched his shoulder. He teetered and reached for her, grinning as if he was about to pull her over with him, only to scoot a little closer once he righted himself. Though he would never throw her off a cliff, Kara pulled her feet onto the platform all the same when he laughed, too.

"You shouldn't push people who are sitting on ledges, you know," he said with a wink.

Kara smiled. "You'd heal instantly."

He nudged her shoulder. "Doesn't mean it wouldn't hurt."

"Well, I'm sorry, then."

"Ungracious apology accepted."

She laughed. She couldn't help it. Even if her mind had created Ourea as some elaborate defense mechanism, she would stay just to be near him.

But Ourea was real. She'd escaped armies, decapitated shadow demons, and had too many scars for it to not be real—and the gravity of her dangerous new life sent bile into the back of her throat. The people vagabonds loved, died. Every time. Thus, why she couldn't have Braeden.

"You all right, Kara?"

She forced a smile. "Yep."

He narrowed his eyes as if waiting for her to crack under the pressure. She wouldn't. She wanted what she couldn't have. It was as simple as that.

A noise like a dove cooing echoed through the cave. A small, red ball of fur about the size of a squirrel jumped onto Braeden's shoulder, but the prince didn't flinch. The creature's long tail batted his face.

"Hey, Flick," he said, scratching the creature's ear.

Flick purred, rubbing his cheek against Braeden's neck. Kara shook her head. Her pet said hello to Braeden first.

Furry little traitor.

Flick jumped onto her shoulder and gave her the same welcome. She scratched his ears, unable to resist the little thing, and swung her bag over her shoulder before pushing herself to her feet. Flick crawled into her satchel, his tiny nails digging into her clothes as he scampered into the bag.

"Shall we go, Braeden? We should probably make our way back to the mansion," she said.

"Nope."

"What do you mean, 'no?'"

"You wanted to learn to fight. We haven't trained today. We need to spar."

She groaned. They'd been sparring for days. She'd healed dozens of bruises and even a broken finger, all evidence to the fact she was barely able to react to a sword coming at her face in time, much less a magical technique. She simply wasn't a very good fighter.

"But—"

He laughed. "You'll never get better if you don't practice. Come on."

He drew his sword.

Her stomach twisted. "Right here? Seriously? On a ledge? Those are rapids!"

"Yes. Today, it's all about controlling your opponent's movement and fighting in difficult terrain. Since you aren't strong in this environment, drive me back up the stairs and to the forest where you have more room to move. Also, you should never be without a sword."

"But I don't have one!"

"Exactly my point."

"Shouldn't I practice one lesson at a time?"

In answer, he swung his sword at her arm. She pressed her back against the cave wall, ducking the blow seconds before the blade cut the air. Goosebumps crawled up her neck.

Braeden laughed. "The best way to learn is baptism by fire. Let's go!"

Kara ducked another swing and looked around, but she had no tactical advantage. Braeden blocked her way to the stairs. She couldn't run past him or… she glanced over the ledge at the tumbling river below. Nope, she was not jumping. Her only escape was the nearby hole in the ledge above. If she could—

Braeden shifted his weight onto the balls of his feet, apparently ready to lunge and end this whole bout before it began.

No time to think. Just go.

Kara sprinted away, toward the gap. Braeden followed, and Kara jumped for the ledge seconds before he lunged. She grabbed the walkway, the splinters of rock digging into her arms as her momentum lifted her legs out of Braeden's passing reach.

His fingers brushed her ankle, sending a shiver up her leg. She resisted the impulse to smile at the tingling sensation his touch left behind. It made her think of his hand on her back, of their kiss—

"Clever!" he said.

Focus, Kara.

She pulled herself onto the ledge and wished she had a witty response, but she'd learned that lesson the hard way during an earlier match. She had distracted herself by talking, instead of distracting him as she'd hoped. Braeden had tripped her and knocked her clean onto her back. Dialogue was yet another weapon, one that required practice. Better fighters banter. Lesser fighters focus.

Kara got to her feet and raced along the upper

pathway toward the waterfall, her satchel bouncing against her back while she ran as fast as she could. Braeden would be faster, but she had to try.

The shelf curved around a bend in the cave. Her feet pounded against the rock, sending shards of cave wall sprinkling to the ground below. The walkway likely hadn't seen action like this in its lifetime. She hoped it wouldn't crumble.

Braeden's steps echoed from under her as the edge of the catwalk came into view. It would end about ten feet before the stairs, so she picked up her pace. She couldn't slow down, or Braeden would catch her.

Five feet away now.

Two feet—

Jump!

Kara kept her eyes where she wanted to go, as Braeden had taught her the last time they'd sparred. She'd tried to jump from a tree and wound up in a bramble bush.

Instinct, and a dozen failed attempts in prior matches, told her to tuck her head, curl onto her shoulder, and let the momentum propel her forward. She grabbed her satchel and hugged it close. Flick's body heat seeped through the fabric as she landed and rolled.

Rocks dug into her neck and shoulder before pushing against her back, but nothing stung. Flick giggled from the bag. She rolled onto her feet and took off again, not daring to look behind for Braeden. She would probably trip if she did.

She grinned, adrenaline numbing her fingertips as she ran. She had no earthly idea how she would do it again, but to hell with it. She'd finally rolled!

Kara followed the path as it curved and disappeared behind the waterfall. The water misted along her neck, blocking all light as she passed behind it. She let her feet find the stairs as she bolted up two at a time. Braeden's light breaths came from somewhere in the darkness behind her.

At the top of the stairs, green sunlight cut through a thick canopy of trees in the forest beyond the cave. Brown blurs came into view—bark. There would be a root right when she rounded the last stair, so she had to be careful not to—

Kara's foot hooked on the root anyway.

She shot forward and skidded along the dirt path, shifting the satchel onto her back as she fell so Flick wouldn't get hurt. He barked in gratitude.

Sticks left gouges in Kara's arms. Her cheek stung. She wiped her hand over her face, but it only made the stinging worse. Blood stained her fingers when she pulled them away.

A sword glinted in Kara's peripheral vision. She sprang to her feet. Braeden stood a short way off without a scratch on him. He grinned.

"Falling was an interesting tactic," he said.

"Cute." Kara rolled her eyes and brushed dust off her clothes.

"We're not done yet, so don't get comfortable."

He lunged. Light glinted along the blade as it missed Kara's head by inches. She ducked and rolled beneath a nearby tree, losing a few strands of her hair to Braeden's sword as he swung again for her neck.

Flick stirred in her satchel at the sudden movement, chirping his disdain that she was moving too much. Honestly, she couldn't understand why he stayed with her during these matches, but she was grateful for it nonetheless. She didn't want to let the little guy out of her sight.

She glared at Braeden and focused her energy into her hands. Pearl blue light congealed over her fingers until it formed the shape of a sword. This technique had taken her hours to manifest and still longer to control, which was unnatural for her; she had gotten used to picking up magic quickly. The light blinded opponents and made her attacks stronger, which she always needed. She had about as much muscle as a plank of wood.

She gripped her sword even as it pulled its energy from her. The drain was a slow one, and she should be fine for this sparring match. This was supposed to be practice and all, but Braeden's attack had been too close. Way too close.

"I don't need bangs, Braeden!"

He laughed, and she used the moment to roll farther out of his reach. She was really getting the hang of rolling now that she had adrenaline and a small success under her belt.

"Tuck your head more when you roll!" he called.

She stood and chuckled. "Yes, sensei."

He raised his hand without answering, even though Kara was pretty sure he didn't know what a sensei was. A wind shot through the trees, rustling Kara's hair on its way to Braeden's palm.

Crap. He was summoning blades from the air again.

Light bent around the air gathered in his hand as he aimed for Kara's face. She ducked, the blade of air missing her head by inches. It landed with a *thunk* in the tree next to her and dissolved, leaving behind only a pale scratch in the bark.

"Hey!" she snapped.

"No one is going to be generous in a fight, Kara. Pay attention."

The prince twirled his sword and ignited a gray fire in his hand. The flames burned and crackled, hovering above his palm as he poised for his next strike.

Who was he kidding? Of course, he was going easy on her. He could heal instantly and change his appearance at will. This wasn't even his natural form.

Braeden could have ended their sparring match the second it started.

A smile played on his lips, curling into a smirk as he shifted his weight and crouched. Kara's heart fluttered, both from excitement and fear. He had spent his life training to fight, and she'd only found the hidden world of Ourea, with its magic and demons, a few months ago. Summer was bleeding into autumn, and she only had the barest understanding of how she was even still alive at this point.

"Pay attention!"

Braeden's sharp command pulled her out of her daydream. She blinked. He was a good ten feet closer now and gaining ground at a full run.

She leaned backward just in time. His sword cut the air in front of her face. A burst of wind blew her hair out of her eyes. The gray flame in his hand sputtered and grew as he prepared for the follow-up attack.

Kara did not want to heal another burn wound.

Her lips twitched. She needed to harness all her energy for this, so she mentally broke her tie to the blue sword in her hand—it dissolved with a shimmer of light like a mirage. Heat pooled in her fingers. Sweat tickled her wrist. Weight settled into her shoulders, and she took a deep breath as she flexed her still-new ability to control magic.

When she wasn't sparring or exploring the village,

Kara studied. The Grimoire, with all its lessons and articles on magic, had told her about a new technique, one even the first Vagabond hadn't mastered in his time a thousand years ago: a red spark that could either heal or destroy, depending on its creator's intentions. In a heartbeat, the spark could heal someone on the brink of death or disarm nearly any opponent. It could sometimes even kill, depending on how much emotion the creator employed. Kara had only ever been able to create a single *snap* as the red spark blinked in and out of her palm, but maybe a rush of adrenaline was all she'd really needed.

Heat bubbled through her arms and neck as she focused. Time slowed. The world dimmed around her as she stole light from the very air, focusing it in her palm. Red sparks crackled between her fingers. She grinned—

—and a wall of gray flames barreled toward her.

She cursed and ducked out of the way, her red sparks fizzling away with a *pop*.

Braeden groaned. "Don't try new techniques in the middle of a fight, Kara. You know that! It requires focus you should be directing toward your opponent!"

"I almost had it!"

"Hardly! You're on fire."

A trail of smoke wafted across Kara's face, carrying with it a scent of charred thread that burned her throat. She coughed and glanced down. Sure enough, orange embers glowed on the edges of her sleeve. She patted them out, her palm searing as it grazed the burning fabric, but she let loose a relieved sigh as the last of the ash fell to the ground. At least, that was until Braeden raised his palm and aimed another gray flame at her head.

CHAPTER TWO

KARA

Okay, time for plan B, Kara thought.

As her duel with Braeden raged on, the woods' energy thrummed through her veins, beating as a pulse separate from her own. Time slowed once more as she focused. Dirt shifted beneath her boots. As Braeden's second wall of flame roared to life, creeping toward her at half-speed, she raised her hands and pulled with her the top layer of earth.

The ground rumbled. Dirt blotted out the sky. The fire dissolved midair, and Braeden disappeared in the dust and crumbling soil. Kara coughed and covered her mouth to keep the dust from her lungs.

As the sun began to flit through the falling dirt, illuminating the layers of mud on her clothes, Kara stepped back into the forest; that way, she could catch sight of him first when the dust settled.

She slipped behind a tree and crouched. Flick stretched in the satchel, making the strap slip a little over her shoulder. She corrected it as the dirt cloud dissolved.

The clearing was empty.

"Nice try." A hot breath rolled along her neck, leaving goosebumps in its wake.

Kara turned a second before Braeden backed her into the tree she had, only seconds before, used as cover. He raised the sword to her neck but kept his distance. It was a signal for her to forfeit, not a threat, so the sword never touched her throat.

No way would she give in that easily.

She reached into her satchel, brushing Flick's forehead. They'd only had marginal success with teleportation, and they hadn't yet worked out how to control it. Flick had only been able to teleport them once—when Carden had nearly ordered Braeden to kill her. Panic and necessity had fueled the teleportation then; maybe it could work again now. This was as good a time as any to try.

Braeden grinned, and she visualized standing behind him. Flick chirped, and Kara smirked. This match wasn't over yet.

A *crack* broke the air. In the blink of an eye, she stood behind the prince who'd previously had her cornered. He turned. His grin dissolved.

Kara pushed him back into the tree with one hand

and summoned her pearl blue sword once more. She raised the blade to his throat, as he had done to her moments before. She focused on the wind as it tore through the trees and borrowed a bit of it, drawing it into her palm to create a second blade of air sharp enough to slice skin. She held this over his heart.

"Cheater," he said, grinning.

"I prefer the term 'resourceful twit.'"

"I'll use that from now on, then."

"So, do I win?"

He laughed. She took that as a yes.

Kara stepped back and released the second blade of air in her palm, which hissed as it dissolved. Braeden stood and brushed the pearl blue sword aside with an ease that could only mean he'd let her push him back into the tree.

She huffed. "One minute, you're giving me a haircut for not paying attention, and the next, you let me win? You're the worst tutor ever."

"I was genuinely caught off guard. That was a good move, using Flick. I hadn't known you'd been working on it."

"I haven't."

He groaned. "Dang it, Kara! You don't listen to anything I say, do you?"

"I listened to the bit about tucking my head when I roll. Doesn't that count?"

He rubbed his temples. "Well, using Flick was still

quick thinking, and improvisation is what I really wanted to work on today. I think we're done with sparring."

Kara resisted the impulse to dance for joy. "I mean, if you're sure..."

Braeden shook his head. "You're so transparent. So, what was that red sparking technique you tried back there?"

She shrugged. "Something I found in the Grimoire. It's supposed to be a versatile technique, one that can either heal or disarm, but not even the first Vagabond mastered it."

Braeden took a deep breath and shook his head. "So, you decide to try it when I'm about to shoot fire at your face?"

Kara laughed. "It seemed like a good idea at the time."

"Well, stop it. Work more on teleporting with Flick before we leave and don't try that red sparking technique in a fight until you have a better grip on it."

She chuckled and bowed with a flourish. "As you wish, oh great master."

He smiled and stepped closer as she stood. Her heart did that fluttering thing again. Her breath caught in her chest, which made him grin even wider.

"We only have a day left in the village, Kara. We have to go back to the real world tomorrow and—"

"'Real world' is a relative term," she said, the

butterflies in her stomach making her a little light-headed. She cleared her throat, trying to look anywhere but at him.

Braeden laughed. "You know what I mean. Before we go, I'd like to discuss our—um—moment from when we first got here. You've been skillfully avoiding that."

"By moment, you mean kiss." It wasn't a question.

He nodded and closed the final few inches of space between them. She should have stepped back, really, but he smelled like oak and spices. His cologne melted her feet into the ground. All she wanted to do was lean into him and close her eyes, but she took a deep breath instead.

"We've been over this, Braeden. This—us—it won't work. I'm going to get you killed. That's what happens if vagabonds care about someone. They die."

"Kara, I've lived a lie for the past twelve years. I'll lie to everyone until they discover the truth, and then I'll probably be killed for treason anyway. I accepted a while ago that death is coming sooner for me than most. It doesn't mean much to me."

She frowned. "It should."

"There's something more you're not telling me, Kara."

"No, there isn't."

"You're a terrible liar."

"I'm a fine liar."

"You really aren't."

She grumbled. "Leave this alone, Braeden."

"Why won't you give me a real answer?"

"Braeden, stop—"

"No! Not until I get a real—"

"The people I love die!" she snapped.

He stepped back, his eyes narrowing.

But Kara couldn't stop. "When I care about people, they die! I killed Mom when I tried to get her to a hospital. I killed Dad when I was trying to keep him safe. I don't even have a picture of either of them, Braeden! I have nothing to remember them by. That's what happens to the people I care about! They die and disappear without a trace. I can't lose you, too!"

His eyes softened. Regret panged in Kara's stomach. Her cheeks flushed. She wanted to hit her head against a tree trunk and vomit at the same time.

Did I really say all that out loud?

Braeden grinned. "So, you do want me!"

"You're so frustrating!"

Kara turned on her heel and plodded into the forest, leaving Braeden at the edge of the clearing. He didn't stop her.

How stupid. Love was too strong a word at this point, but yes—she wanted him. She wasn't supposed to let him know that she'd enjoyed every second of the kiss or that she'd thought about it daily and wanted more.

But the Vagabond had ruined the kiss entirely. While she had closed her eyes and savored the tingling trace Braeden's lips left behind, the first Vagabond had manipulated her mind. He'd forced her to relive the bloody image of his own lover's corpse. He'd elicited the memory of Helen's death to remind Kara of what happens to those the vagabonds love: they die.

The first Vagabond later told Kara to push Braeden away if she cared. She was a vagabond now, and that meant being lonely.

"Are you all right, Kara?"

The deep voice pulled her from her thoughts. She looked up to see the Vagabond's ghost standing on the dead leaves nearby, his face shrouded in the darkness beneath his hood.

She gasped and gritted her teeth, closing her eyes until her heart settled.

"Don't surprise me like that, Vagabond."

"I apologize," he said.

She looked him over once more. The trailing edges of his cloak drifted on the breeze, transparent enough to show the dirt and dead leaves littering the ground behind him. Though she couldn't see his face, she knew what he looked like: tanned and blond, with gray eyes and a long scar on his cheek. That scar was a constant reminder of the lover he'd lost to his cause.

"You did not handle him well," he said.

"I don't know how it could have been handled well, Vagabond."

"To begin, stop implying 'yes,' when you tell him 'no.' It is quite confusing for a man."

She sighed and sat beneath a tree. Dried leaves crunched beneath her pants.

"Do you love him?" the Vagabond asked.

"Don't start."

"It's a simple question. A yes or no will suffice."

"We're not discussing this."

"Suit yourself. Shall we discuss the gala instead?"

The gala. The reason she and Braeden had to leave tomorrow. All summer, she had travelled to the various kingdoms in Ourea, asking the kings and queens—the Bloods, as they were called here—to see reason and unite against Carden, the tyrannical Blood who was also Braeden's father.

Dang it. She was thinking of Braeden again.

"The world didn't stop spinning because you stepped off for a while, Kara. The gala is supposed to be a meeting of peace and unity, yet one of the Bloods tried to manipulate you and control you barely a week ago. It's not safe to go."

She sighed. "Yes, what Gavin did with the tiara was stupid. But I was the one who brought them together. At least, for the most part. What would happen if I didn't show?"

"They would likely quarrel as to whose fault it is

you didn't come. Then, they would likely go their separate ways or make secret alliances to undermine the treaty they'll be signing."

"Guess I'm going, then."

"If you were to choose strong fighters who will be in attendance and make them vagabonds, they can mingle in the crowds and protect you should something go wrong."

"This again?"

He still wanted her to make a vagabond army. He had a hundred grimoires identical to hers sitting on a shelf in his old mansion—well, it was her mansion now. And this was her decision.

"You must make more vagabonds, Kara. You're weak if you don't. You can't trust anyone with a blood loyalty, and that includes Braeden."

"I'm trying to show you that I learned from your mistakes, Vagabond. I'm not budging on this. You became a threat to the Bloods of your time because you made more vagabonds. You took their people and their power. The peace in this world is fragile enough without me throwing more wood on the fire."

"My vagabonds weren't killed because I made them. They were killed because I couldn't choose them over Helen."

"No, that's not why you were all rounded up and chained like criminals. You were prisoners because the Bloods felt threatened. Their power is in their people.

If you take away their people, you take away their power. You took away their power, Vagabond, instead of simply sharing your knowledge like you claimed to."

He sighed and crossed his arms. "We vagabonds must sacrifice ourselves for the many. I failed because I could not sacrifice my lover for the lives of hundreds."

"I won't make your mistake, Vagabond."

"I'm not convinced."

"What do you mean?"

"I wish you could see the way you look at Braeden. You cannot get close to anyone—especially not him—because those you love will become leverage to be used against you."

"Love isn't a weakness. It's not leverage."

"So, you love him, then?"

She sighed and rubbed her eyes. "It's a little early for that, don't you think?"

"Kara, that isen, Deidre, already has leverage over you because she stole your father's soul. I know you still want revenge, so don't give such power to anyone else. If you truly care about Braeden, you have two choices: reject him or never let anyone know. Neither is fair to him, but one option is safest for you both."

The first Vagabond had already beaten the rejection option into her head, so she dwelt on the thought of hiding a relationship from the world. Everywhere she went, she would be watched; she could never hold his hand or touch him in public. She could never maintain his gaze for too long or smile wider when he came into the room. She didn't know if she could control that for more than a second or two, much less stop it altogether.

The Vagabond leaned against a tree, the lines of its bark visible through his ghostly torso. "I can see it's futile to discuss this further. At least you are better prepared for what lies ahead. The boy is a good tutor. I will grant him that."

He was right, too. She'd learned a dozen new techniques thanks to Braeden's teaching, including how to control vines, add thorns to any solid surface, and even a way to create smoke from the air to confuse and disorient her opponents. And now, thanks to the epiphany from the sparring match, she and Flick had finally begun to understand teleportation.

In her time at the village, the Vagabond had taught her much, too. He had focused mostly on willpower, and in doing so taught her to control her ability to read another's most influential memory—a control that meant she no longer had to wear gloves. Beyond that, though, he hadn't taught her much that was useful. Most of the time, he'd just lectured her like he was doing now.

She sighed. "The gala will be tense, but nothing

dire will happen. I've learned to be careful around all of them. I won't let my guard down."

The Vagabond shook his head. "At a minimum, you should pick a sword to take with you. Though you can create the blue sword from the light around you, it's better not to exert your energy on a weapon. Energy is better saved for techniques."

"I'll do that."

Silence settled between them, so Kara glanced through her fingers to examine her mentor. His shoulders hunched, and he stared at the ground. It was as if he'd given up.

"We can do this," she said.

"I know, but this treaty is not enough. Even if they unite and kill Carden, the feud will continue. We must come up with some way to maintain the peace when the war is over."

"We will."

"It's far easier said than done."

She sighed and poked the satchel, which rose and fell to the tune of Flick's tiny breaths. Flick squeaked and shimmied out of the bag. Kara stood and brushed away the beads of dirt clinging to her palms, but when she looked up, the Vagabond was gone.

She rolled her eyes. "Bye."

Flick crawled up her arm and sat on her shoulder. He nuzzled her neck, brushing his soft fur along her throat. She suppressed a giggle.

It would be interesting to see how far he could teleport. She might as well practice. Besides, she wasn't ready to face Braeden yet.

Kara thought about all the places she'd wanted to visit: New Zealand, Germany, maybe a Mayan temple. She thought of her home in Tallahassee or the rental where Deidre had stolen her dad's soul.

Her throat tightened at the thought of his soul still trapped in Deidre's body. She tightened her fists. The Vagabond was right—Kara did still want revenge, but she couldn't think about that right now.

As for practicing teleportation, she and Flick needed to start small. It was probably best to teleport to the road outside the Amber Temple.

She brushed Flick's head and thought of the leaf-covered cobblestones leading to the temple. In her memory, the dark trees hunched overhead like a tent. The wind howled by, whistling through the trembling branches.

Crack!

Kara opened her eyes. Though she wasn't in the forest any longer, she also wasn't on the cobblestone road.

She and Flick stood in front of the only lichgate she and Braeden had discovered in their time at the village: a stone arch built into the back of the Vagabond's tomb. Its rose stone met the base of the tomb's windows, which were above the sarcophagus she couldn't see from the ground. The entire tomb conformed to the lichgate, as if it had been built around the only known entrance to the dead man's village.

The portal never failed to amaze Kara, even for all the times she'd seen it or come to simply stare. Whereas most lichgates revealed a diluted view of the world on the other side, this one showed only the night sky. Stars glittered like the gold flecks in the lapis map that had led Kara to the village. A comet streaked across the dark blue night, leaving an imprint on her vision.

Beautiful as the lichgate was, she shouldn't be there. It wasn't the cobblestone road. She walked a little closer to the portal out of curiosity. She'd done something wrong but didn't know what.

Flick growled from his perch on her shoulder. His tail twitched, batting her in the ear. He climbed onto her head and stared into the lichgate.

"Let's try again," she said.

She envisioned the cobblestone pavement once more, focusing on the chill of the wind that should be rolling over her right now.

Crack!

Again, she opened her eyes to stare at the lichgate. This time, though, she stood in the same spot she'd appeared in the first time.

Weird.

Flick had teleported on command during the sparring match she'd had with Braeden but couldn't leave the village. That must mean he couldn't teleport past a lichgate.

To test her theory, she envisioned her study in the Vagabond's mansion. She wanted to appear at his window, staring down at his desk—

Crack!

Kara opened her eyes to see the Vagabond's old desk waiting for her in her study. Flick jumped onto the empty surface and barked, apparently pleased with himself.

So that was it—Flick couldn't teleport through a lichgate. Kara sighed. Well, that would complicate things. She patted him on the head and headed out the door. She would let him rest, but she had to see to getting herself a sword.

Kara headed down the stairs and into the Vagabond's war room, which Braeden had turned into an armory on their first day. Swords, maces, and other assorted sharp things now adorned the walls, all of them freshly polished and mounted for display. She hadn't seen him on the way into the room, but he would be back soon. He was probably off realizing what a terrible girlfriend she would make.

Kara scanned the weapons, and one in particular caught her eye.

A thin sword hung at the far end of the room,

framing the head of the table with its shining silver. The blade was about the length of her arm. An ornate hand guard curved over the hilt in thin flourishes. As she stepped closer, an etching of the Grimoire clover flashed along the base of the blade.

She lifted the sword from the wall to examine it, but it didn't weigh down her hands at all. Light as it was, though, the sharp edges still glinted in the midday sun streaming through a window.

"There's a sheath for it, if you need one," Braeden said from behind her.

She turned and offered a thin smile, but he was already heading for a trunk in the far corner. He rifled through it for a few, silent minutes before he pulled a scabbard from the heaps of leather, walked over, and offered it to her. The leather was smooth in her hands when she reached for it.

"Thanks," she said. The sword whistled as she slid it into the scabbard.

He nodded and opened his mouth but closed it as quickly without saying anything.

Kara toyed with the belt buckle on the scabbard. "I'm sorry about my outburst earlier. It was inappropriate."

"Hardly."

"What?"

"It's exactly what I needed to hear." He glanced out the window to avoid her gaze, and she couldn't quite tell if he meant that in a positive or negative way. She wasn't sure which was better.

"Oh," she said.

They stood there for a while without talking. Kara waited for him to speak, though he no doubt wanted her to break the ice.

"I hope I—"

"Could you—"

They laughed. The icy chill of their silence faded.

"I'll do my best to respect what you want, Kara. I only want to be nearby. Someone has to catch you when you fall."

She chuckled. "Thanks, I guess."

๑

KARA

The day's final hours passed more quickly than Kara could appreciate them. Before she knew it, the moon rose from behind the windowpanes of the Vagabond's study. She sat on the floor, resting her weight on her palms as she stared into the bookshelf that housed the one hundred grimoires she was meant to simply give away.

It was ludicrous. It would get her killed, and the dead man in her own grimoire just couldn't see it.

The door scraped along the rug. An old floorboard

creaked. Kara's heart skipped a beat at the sound, but when she turned, Braeden froze in his retreat from the room.

"You're still up?" she asked.

"I wanted to leave these keys on the desk before I forget them again and accidentally take them to the gala," he said.

He opened his hand to reveal a blue orb and a slab of stone with a rose carved into it: the keys he'd used to gain entry into Losse and Kirelm. Only citizens of each kingdom were supposed to know what they looked like, and even then, only a select few ever had the privilege of owning one. If the muses hadn't given him those keys, he wouldn't have been able to stay with Kara as she toured the various kingdoms.

Kara whistled. "Good idea. You wouldn't want anyone to ask you where you got those or why you even have them."

"Exactly."

"Why didn't you leave them with the muses when you were training with them?"

"Adele was too busy beating me senseless in our sparring to ask for them. I was too busy healing myself to remember."

"Oh," Kara replied. There wasn't really a suitable response to something like that.

He set the keys in the first desk drawer and sat

next to her. He leaned against the desk's oak base and stretched his arms as if asking for a hug.

"Come here," he said softly.

"Braeden—"

"Don't think about it."

She sighed. Sleep played on the corners of her eyes, and he would probably make a comfortable pillow.

Sure. That's why she wanted to oblige.

Carpet fibers rubbed along her palms as she readjusted herself and leaned back into his chest. He wrapped his arms around her, and the warmth from his forearms chased away her fear.

He rested his head against hers. "This is the last peaceful moment we'll have for a while."

She nodded, eyes drooping from the warmth and comfort that came from touching him. The gala was tomorrow, and the growing war would come shortly after. But for now—for what was left of the moonlight—they could just be.

CHAPTER THREE

BRAEDEN

A blinding ray of sunlight woke Braeden.

He had fallen asleep against the desk with Kara in his arms. A flood of excitement flurried in his gut—she was still there.

Kara had curled into him in the night. She'd tucked her knees under her chin and leaned her left side against his chest. She nuzzled against him as he moved, and he smiled. Her soft hair pooled along his neck, so he ran a hand through it without thinking.

She stirred. His heart fell. The peace was almost over.

"What time is it?" she asked, rubbing her eyes.

"Time to pack up, I'd imagine."

She didn't let go. They sat there, looking everywhere but at each other.

Kara cleared her throat. "I found out that Flick

can't teleport through lichgates, so we have to travel on foot until we're outside the Amber Temple. Once we do, though, can you show Flick where to go so we can teleport to the gala?"

Braeden hesitated. He could, sure. He simply didn't want to. He wanted to steal every last second he possibly could from the tranquility. The moment they reached Ethos, their peace would be gone. Worry and doubt and fear would return. Kara would pull away.

So, he lied. "I don't want to risk it. What if I have him teleport us over lava or something by accident?"

Kara laughed and shook her head. "Let's take the giant wolf, then."

Her gray eyes caught him in their gaze, spurring on the tingling feeling in his gut he used to hate. He swallowed hard. She paused, watching him, and seemed to force a smile even as her real one faded. She kissed the line of his jaw before pushing herself to her feet and walked from the room.

He meant to get up and follow her, but he needed a moment. His knees gave out when she looked at him that way.

The door shut with a *bang*, probably harder than she'd intended. Braeden didn't care. He knew she wasn't mad. She was frustrated, like him. Kara had lost people she loved, and apparently thought Braeden was next. He could appreciate why she wanted to push him away, but that didn't make him want her less.

Braeden sighed and pushed himself to his feet. When he died, it wouldn't be because of Kara. In time, she would realize that.

He walked into the hall and headed for the stairs, trotting down to the echoes of his own footsteps ringing around the vacant hall. The village was primed and ready for life it would never see. Well, not as long as Kara had any say in the matter.

Either Kara had to make more vagabonds, or she had to play by the Bloods' rules. Braeden didn't know the right answer, even after a lifetime of military training. Sure, more vagabonds would mean more allies, but at what cost? Kara was right. Stealing the Bloods' subjects would turn them against her. She didn't have much of a choice but to trust them—and it was a choice he hated. Besides Aislynn, there wasn't an honest royal among them. He didn't even trust Aislynn's niece, Evelyn.

He cringed. What Gavin saw in her, he would never know. Of course, he couldn't exactly ask his adoptive brother, either. Both Gavin and Evelyn thought they were being secretive in their affair, despite the fact Braeden had often covered their trail to keep nosy maids from discovering the trysts.

"Whoa. What are you thinking about? You look angry."

Braeden looked up to see Kara a few feet away. She watched him, a pack weighing down each of her shoulders. They sank low across her back from the weight of whatever was in them.

"Sorry. It's nothing. What do you have there?" he asked.

"A ways back, Gavin mentioned that I needed to find presents for all of the royals. Apparently, it's part of the ceremony. So, I grabbed a few things from the treasure room. I put blankets and food in the other bag."

He glanced across the hall to the treasury—the only room in the mansion with no doorknob. It had sat open during their week's stay, but it was now closed. It was yet another sign they were really leaving.

"Do you need help with those?" he asked.

She smiled and slid the packs into his hand. The weight pulled against his grip, but he wasn't about to let her see. How she'd carried them at all was beyond him. Their training must have had a greater impact than he'd thought.

"So, when are we leaving?" he asked.

"As soon as possible, since the gala is tomorrow night. I let us sleep in because I hadn't counted on having to travel there on foot, so we're a little short on time. Ryn should be fast enough, though, depending on where it is."

"Well, the gala is supposed to be tomorrow, but it will be delayed."

Kara stopped in the doorway and turned around. A breeze played with her hair such that it framed her pinched eyebrows. Braeden's jaw tightened on its own as she caught his eye.

"Why?" she asked.

"Yakona are always late, Kara. It's our way."

Kara laughed. "I guess there's no rush, then. Let's just chill here for a bit longer."

Braeden inched through the door, stopping when he was directly in front of her. The crackled musk of leaves wafted from her hair, and he wondered what she would do if he leaned closer.

He grinned but kept as much distance as was possible for sharing a doorway. "Bloods can be late. We cannot. We should leave now, but we can take our time getting there."

They stood in the doorway, neither moving. Braeden waited for her to do something, to relent maybe. To let him explore what it might be like to love someone, whatever the word truly meant.

"Well, let's get going," she said.

She headed down the steps. A short ways off, Ryn turned in welcome as she approached. The giant wolf leaned into her as she patted its head.

Braeden sighed, but the disappointment flared for only a moment. It had been a long shot.

He trotted down the stairs, still holding the heavy bags, and walked toward the giant, black wolf Kara so loved. It eyed him, watching him even as Kara rubbed its face.

"Why don't animals like you?" Kara asked.

"I don't know," he lied.

"Is it because you're Stelian?" she asked, looking away.

She was trying to be coy, he could tell—to offer the suggestion as if it was nothing. He lifted one of the bags onto Ryn's back and shrugged.

"Perhaps. I do radiate evil, I suppose." He smirked to cover the sting from the truth in his statement.

Kara laughed. "You're hardly evil, Braeden."

"Many would disagree."

"Enough of that. Come on. I'm sorry I brought it up. Let's just get going."

Ryn knelt to let her hop onto his back. Braeden draped the last pack over Ryn's shoulders, in front of Kara, and jumped on behind her. He reached for the fur on the wolf's shoulders, wrapping his arms around her as the beast stood. He didn't need to do it, of course. Usually when he rode a drowng or a horse, he didn't even need a saddle or reins. He only wanted to be close.

The ancient wolf stood then headed toward the lichgate behind the Vagabond's tomb. In minutes, they stared into the portal's darkness. It was unlike any Braeden had ever seen, and he still couldn't understand why it didn't show the other side like any other lichgate.

Ryn trotted forward on some silent command from Kara Braeden had missed. Kara's body tensed as they neared the gate, and it was all Braeden could do to not hold her. She had a lot to fear: Gavin, the gala, the other Bloods. He wished he could steal her away from it all.

Moving through a lichgate had two signs: a flare of blue light and a jolt that passed through the body. But this portal was different. Instead of blue light, a kaleidoscope of color broke across Braeden's vision, and instead of a kick to the gut, warmth spread through his body, soothing every muscle.

The spattered colors dissolved into pure white, which faded away to the green glow of a forest brighter than the one surrounding the Vagabond's village. A dirt path curved through the trees, disappearing around a bend.

"What the hell was that?" Kara asked.

"I haven't the faintest idea," Braeden answered.

"Was that—the colors—?"

Braeden laughed. "I really don't know. You should ask the Grimoire later."

Kara nodded and urged Ryn on with a small tap of her heels.

They travelled for only a few minutes before they found yet another lichgate. It was normal, though, built from two branches that twisted away from their trees and met over the path in an arch. Through the gate, a platform carved from solid amber housed an hourglass in a hole at its center. Grains of sand drifted to a small pile in the hourglass' bottom chamber.

Beyond the platform, the muted darkness of a temple cast a sharp contrast against the bright glow around them. Columns faded away into the depths of the dark shrine.

"Think they're really gone?" Kara asked.

"Those shadow demons?"

"Yeah."

He hoped so. The demons had guarded the temple, which housed the only lichgate into the Vagabond's village. Kara had gone alone, and Braeden had only barely made it in time to help her. How the Vagabond had expected his successor to go alone and face the demons was beyond him.

Kara nudged Ryn again, ushering him through when Braeden didn't respond.

Blue light flared in Braeden's peripheral vision, and a kick to his gut meant they'd passed through. A chill raced over his body until the hair on his arms stood on end. Ryn's shuffling footsteps echoed through the vacant hall, leaving Braeden to wonder if daylight ever touched the place.

"Ryn disappeared the first time I came in here," Kara said. Her voice echoed.

Braeden shrugged. "The hourglass was empty, then. Maybe the effect is part of its magic."

"Maybe. I don't know. I don't like this place."

"I don't either."

They trotted past the hourglass and down the stairs leading to it. Ryn kept his eyes trained on the door, but Braeden couldn't help glancing around. The columns dissolved into a dark haze. He leaned into Kara, silently urging her to hurry. They shouldn't stay in the temple any longer than necessary. Whatever the Vagabond had invited here—or whatever had been here before the Vagabond—was truly evil.

The temple doors opened as they neared, the iron hinges creaking as the doors came to a stop and beckoned them to the warm air outside. It was still dark, but Braeden and Kara sighed together as Ryn walked down the steps and onto the leaf-covered cobblestones meandering away from the shrine.

"How lovely! You both survived," a voice said from behind them.

Braeden turned, one hand already on his sword, when he saw a creature the size of a tiger and the color of ditch slime lounging on the small roof over the door. The beast's orange eyes glowed with a light of their own. Sharp teeth curled through the thing's lips even when its mouth was closed.

"It's good to see you, too, lyth," Kara said, nudging Braeden in the gut.

Braeden turned to her. She nodded to the sword in his hand and shook her head. He slipped the sword back into its sheath but didn't let his hand stray too far from its hilt. He didn't like this thing.

"What is it?" he mouthed to her.

"The lyth protects the village, Braeden. Though if he didn't appear when you came to the temple, I guess he's not that good at his job."

The lyth let out a few rasping breaths in what was either a laugh or a sigh. "I knew you'd be fine but figured prince charming over there would help you out. That's why I let him in. I do hope that was all right."

"I was kidding. Braeden is always welcome," Kara said.

"Wait, what is going on? Why do you protect the village?" Braeden asked. He'd never seen this thing or anything like it before in his life.

The creature stretched its long legs and yawned. "We all need a purpose. Don't you agree, yakona?"

Its glowing eyes trained on Braeden with a knowing glare. Braeden suppressed a shudder.

"Should we take the lapis map, since we're leaving?" Kara asked, apparently having missed the creature's glare.

The lyth chuckled. "Not unless you want to fight all of those demons again. The Vagabond wanted to add an emergency failsafe, so removing the key resets the hourglass and awakens the demons. They happen to have excellent memories, by the way, and will recall your last visit. Besides, is an immortal lyth not enough protection?"

Kara shook her head. "I guess we're leaving it, then. Take care."

"Stay well, Keeper," the lyth called. It jumped from the roof and, as it touched the cobblestones at their feet, dissolved into smoke.

"That thing is so weird," Kara mumbled.

Braeden resisted the impulse to agree, as much as he wanted to. It was probably still listening.

Ryn trotted down the path, but Braeden kept an eye on the temple as they left. The world darkened, the light fading as they moved away.

Sunlight flared around them, forcing Braeden to close his eyes in the sudden glare. When he opened them again, light streamed through thin gaps in the rows of trees lining the path. Their branches leaned over the road, creating a canopy that rustled in the midday sun.

Braeden looked back over his shoulder. Nothing remained of the temple but a wall of darkness between the trees. Though the light should have illuminated the temple, or at least, the cobblestone road leading to it, the darkness held. It was as if they'd passed through a sheet of solid gloom.

"Why did the Vagabond choose such an evil place?" he asked.

Kara eyed the darkness. "I don't know for certain, but I have a guess."

"Which is?"

"If you had Ourea's most powerful beings after you, where would you hide? I'd go to the one place they themselves would never want to go."

Braeden nodded. It made sense. As beautiful as the village was, he certainly didn't want to have to go through the temple any more than he had to.

※

CARDEN

Deep in the caves beneath Ethos, Carden held his hand tight over a Kirelm scout's mouth as the young man struggled to get free. The guard elbowed him in the gut, but Carden held fast. The Kirelm spread his wings, no doubt trying to shake Carden off, his muffled gasps barely audible even in the quiet tunnel as they fought.

The fight didn't last long.

With a deft swing, Carden ran his dagger across the guard's throat, and the muffled voice became a desperate gurgle for breath.

The Kirelm's body fell to the ground as the last of

the life drained out of him, the dull thud indiscernible from the soft footsteps of the Stelians waiting for Carden's signal. He nodded into the shadows behind him, and three dozen of the Stele's best assassins continued down the corridor, ready to pick off the other scouts one by one.

Stealthy and silent as a ghost, the assassins' Captain appeared beside Carden, pausing as he waited for Carden's next orders. Without a word, Carden motioned to the three side tunnels ahead. Seconds later, the boy was off, ready to serve his purpose to his Blood—to kill.

It should be Braeden. Carden wrinkled his nose in disgust at his son. Captain of the Assassins was Braeden's role, his birthright, his *duty,* and yet Carden had been forced to give the position to some commoner. A decent fighter, sure, but not the Heir, and the break from tradition boiled his blood.

No matter. He would break the boy's spirit one way or another.

Kara, Carden thought. *Break the girl, and I'll break Braeden.*

His grip tightened around his Sartori as he continued through the hall, the sharp pain in his injured hand a constant reminder of his failure against the Hillsidian Blood. Killing Lorraine had been harder than he'd intended, but he wouldn't underestimate the others. This time, he would be smarter—he would let them kill each other.

In the darkest shadows beneath Ethos, Carden couldn't help but sneer. Soon, he would have his bloodbath. Though he wouldn't get to the surface before his troops were detected, he would get close.

Close. It was all he would need.

CHAPTER FOUR
BRAEDEN

Time crawled by—and Braeden liked it.

He and Kara had already travelled for twelve hours and still had about three left in a trek that should have taken eight. Ryn ambled, walking barely faster than they could have on their own. But Braeden wasn't in much of a hurry and allowed himself to enjoy Kara's company. They'd adopted an odd question-for-question game with only one rule: they had to answer.

"Favorite food?" Kara asked.

Braeden grinned. "All right, so when we go back to Hillside, you have to try these. There's a chef who makes the best fruit tarts you'll ever eat in your life. She adds honey, cream, sugar, butter, and cinnamon, and there's something else she adds to the dough, but she won't tell me what it is. I think it's nutmeg. They're amazing."

Kara laughed. "Is there any fruit in those fruit tarts?"

"You name it—mango, strawberries, blackberries, raspberries, grapes, kiwi, even oranges."

"That sounds like too much."

"Not at all. You have to try them."

Kara laughed. "I will. Okay, your turn."

"Where in the human world do you most want to travel?"

She paused. "Europe. I've always wanted to see Stonehenge or Neuschwanstein."

"What's Neuschwanstein?"

"It's a stunning, German castle. I've always wanted to visit."

"Then we'll go someday."

She turned and grinned. "You'd let me drag you—a prince—around a tourist attraction?"

He laughed. "I've allowed you to drag me around Ourea, haven't I? What's a few tourist traps?"

Kara smiled. "Okay, my turn. I hope this isn't too forward."

Braeden winked. "Uh, oh."

"So, have you—um—you know what? Never mind. I'll come up with another."

"Not a chance. I want to hear this question now."

"No, it's rude."

"I don't mind."

Kara sighed. "Fine. Have you ever dated anyone? I can't decide. You grew up as a prince, and I remember the way those girls in the market were flirting with you when you first showed me around Hillside. But you're so against letting anyone get close to you, and I understand why. So, which is it?"

He laughed. "My, aren't these questions getting personal?"

"See! That's why I didn't want to ask. I'm sorry."

"I'm kidding. Yes, I have 'dated,' as you call it."

"Well, what do you all call it?"

"Courting. There were a few girls I met when I was younger, but obviously nothing ever came of it. I haven't courted anyone in years, simply because of how close the last one came to finding me out."

"How so?"

Braeden's cheeks flushed at the memory of lips pressed into his neck. Her name was Eloise, and she'd pushed him beyond his ability to control himself. She wanted more than teasing kisses, and the temptation had nearly cost him control of his form before she could even pull him into his bedroom.

Intimacy was a risk, one he'd promised himself he wouldn't take again. His heart panged with guilt, and he caught Kara's eye. Was this freedom why he wanted her? Because she knew what he was, and because there was no risk?

"It's okay," she said.

He swallowed. The way she'd looked at him—it was like she'd read his mind. He doubted she would be so calm if she had.

"What's okay?" he asked.

"You don't have to tell me. I shouldn't have asked. To be fair, I'll answer it, too. I've only had three boyfriends, all jerks, but that's ancient history now."

Jealousy panged in his stomach, and he hated himself for it. She wasn't even his, so it was childish to be jealous of the boys she'd dated. Still, images flared in his mind of her leaning into a stranger, reaching her arms around his neck and—

Kara glanced around. "I'm sorry I made things awkward. Here, ask me another question. Anything."

He took a deep breath, happy she'd pulled him away from those thoughts. He wanted to ask her something to get her talking and make her laugh. Her smile could distract him from anything.

"What did you want to be? You know, before you came here."

Kara's jaw tensed, and she turned away. Braeden cringed. He shouldn't have brought up the past—it would remind her of her mother, her father, and everything she was forced to leave behind.

"I guess it's my turn to apologize. I'll think of another question," he said.

She shrugged. "It's fine. I wanted to own an

outdoor recreation company. Take people hiking, white water rafting, that sort of thing."

"It sounds perfect for you."

"Well, I have a different job now."

Silence settled between them, leaving Braeden to mentally kick himself. They'd been having fun, but he'd gone and asked one of the worst questions possible.

The sun sank deeper into the horizon. It would be dark in a few hours. While they should probably keep going, since they were making terrible progress, Braeden didn't want to go to the gala. Arriving would mean an end to his time with Kara. He would have to be on guard again, constantly watching what he said.

"We should probably camp soon," Kara said. Her voice flatlined, as if she were trying not to feel the guilt and remorse no doubt plaguing her.

"Kara, I lied earlier when I said I was afraid of messing up the teleportation. I didn't want to leave. I didn't want to go back."

"I figured."

"You did?"

"Braeden, you're highly intelligent. I'm sure you'd figure it out fairly easily. I guessed you just want to enjoy the quiet a little bit longer."

He nodded. Close.

She pointed to a small clearing beyond the forest

trail. "Anyway, how does this look for a camp? Unless we're close and should just keep going."

They were about three hours away at their current pace, but telling her the truth would mean sacrificing his last night alone with her.

Braeden glanced around. "Walk me through your choice."

"What?"

"You don't get to stop training because we left the village."

Kara laughed. Braeden's shoulders relaxed at the sound.

"Okay, okay. I chose it because it's hidden from the main path, has flat ground, and if you listen, you can hear a brook nearby. We'll have to make sure it's clean, but we can probably use it for drinking water."

"Excellent answer." He nodded and dismounted, offering a hand to let her down. She took it and slid off, but Ryn shifted his weight as she did. The added momentum threw her into Braeden's chest.

He wrapped his arms around her out of instinct, pulling her close, and for a split second, neither of them resisted. Impulse told him to lean down, to kiss her, but the moment passed and took the opportunity with it.

"I'll lay out the blankets," Kara said. She pulled away and reached for the bags on Ryn's shoulders.

Braeden lifted the packs off the wolf's back before

Kara could reach them. He turned and headed for the clearing without giving her time to fight for them.

"Hey!" she said with a laugh.

"I'll set up camp. Would you go check the creek?"

"Well, aren't you bossy?"

He grinned. "You like it."

She shook her head in a painfully obvious effort to hide her smile and grabbed a water bottle from one of the packs. Her boots crunched along the grass as she walked into the forest, the sound softer than ever after their week of training.

Braeden had to hand it to her—the girl learned fast.

He set to work. The main reason he'd grabbed the bags was to set up the beds close to each other. Kara would have separated them, no doubt still embarrassed by her question about his courting experience, but he preferred to be near her. This was their last night to just relax and enjoy each other's company.

When he finished, he set out a small feast of apples, pears, and a cluster of grapes. He refrained from grabbing something even as his stomach growled. He would wait for Kara.

They'd only managed to find fruit in the village, so they would have to bring back cured meat or learn to bake bread if they returned. Braeden had stumbled onto a kitchen while they were exploring a few days ago, but only the pans remained. It was as if the village had been cleared of all life long before it had been tucked away.

The crunch of Kara's footsteps sounded before Braeden could see her, so he sat on his blanket to wait.

"That stream is actually a lot farther away than I thought," Kara said as she came into view.

She sat on her blanket and set her bag on the ground before reaching for an apple. Flick crawled out of the satchel and eyed the grapes on Braeden's blanket.

Braeden didn't have a response, so he grabbed a pear and bit into it. What he really wanted was some ham or maybe turkey—he didn't care what kind so long as he had meat. Living off fruit left him hungrier, but he didn't have much choice. He could hunt, but he doubted Kara would want to watch him skin and cook something. He could eat fruit for one more night.

The sun dipped beyond the canopy, and dusk drowned what light remained in the forest. Flick settled back into his satchel as Ryn curled up at Kara's feet, his eye on the woods. Braeden figured the wolf would be sentry enough; he'd never seen any of the creatures from the Grimoire sleep. Neither he nor Kara would have to stand watch.

Kara stretched out on her blanket and closed her eyes. "Good night, Braeden."

"Night."

Braeden lay down, too, and listened to the forest

for a while. Kara's breathing mingled with the chirp of the crickets. An owl hooted now and again. The fluttering of wings passed overhead on occasion. Flick shifted in the satchel on the grass beside Kara, and the bag rolled with him.

Something nuzzled into Braeden's side. He looked down to see Kara, sound asleep, curled against his shoulder. Her hands slid beneath her head like a makeshift pillow.

He wasn't sure what to do. Guilt and excitement churned in his stomach, shooting adrenaline into his fingertips. Finally, he wrapped an arm around her shoulder and closed his eyes, too.

CHAPTER FIVE

BRAEDEN

Sunlight poured through Braeden's closed eyelids, blurring everything into one large, orange glow. He stretched without wanting to wake.

"Rise and shine, prince of darkness," Kara said from somewhere nearby.

Braeden opened his eyes and squinted as the sun poured around the trees. Judging by how bright it was, he'd slept in.

"How long have you been up?" he asked, rubbing his eyes.

"Not too long. The packs are tied and ready to go when you are. I just need your blanket."

Not far off, Ryn dug at the dirt, already laden with the bags. Kara wore her satchel, though Flick rested on her shoulder as she busied herself with tying the bags. Braeden wondered if she'd woken up still pressed against him. If so, she didn't seem interested in discussing it.

"All right," he said.

He stood and rolled his blanket. A few loose circles of dirt marked where Kara had probably buried their apple and pear cores from the night before.

Kara pulled herself onto Ryn's back and waited, so Braeden stowed his blanket before he followed suit and sat behind her. He reached into the forward pack for an apple, since he hadn't eaten yet. Kara tensed as he leaned to put an arm around her.

"Everything all right?" he asked.

"Yeah," she said without looking at him.

She tapped Ryn, and they trotted off at a quicker pace than before. Ryn's gait was smooth no matter how fast the wolf ran, which made eating possible. But Braeden couldn't ignore Kara's mood. Something had upset her. Waking up in his arms couldn't be so horrible.

The idea made his gut twist so much he couldn't eat. Guilt and frustration churned in his stomach, and bile burned the backs of his teeth. He threw his untainted apple into the woods. Hopefully something else was hungry.

They travelled almost completely in silence, for which Braeden quickly became grateful. Soldiers lined the trees, beginning almost ten miles out from the gala entrance. He saw glimpses here and there—dark brown boots matching the bark, green tunics only a shade or two off from the trees. They hid their faces, but a few did nod silently to him as he and Kara rode beneath. He nodded back.

Kara watched the road ahead, apparently oblivious to the sentries. Braeden resisted the urge to sigh. Hillsidians were stealthy, far more so than any other kingdom could even realize. They were trackers, hunters, and they could always hide. The fact made Braeden want to hold Kara closer, but such a protective gesture would give him away with all these guards watching.

Kara cleared her throat. "Braeden, I have to—"

He was about to interrupt, to ask her to save whatever she wanted to say for when they were actually alone, but Braeden's old friend Demnug jumped from the forest's thick underbrush on the back of a drowng.

"Master Braeden!" the captain said.

Braeden smiled. Demnug was only a few years older and had always been Braeden's favorite sparring partner in the Hillsidian training rings. The captain had taken Kara to the Kirelms all those weeks ago when she was called to visit the other Bloods.

Demnug trotted to them, and Braeden bit back his laughter when Kara's lips parted in gaping shock. She'd apparently thought they were alone.

"It's good to see you both safe and well." Demnug

sniffed the air around them. "And it's particularly wonderful that neither of your souls were stolen by isen. Blood Gavin would like to see you, Vagabond."

"I'll join them," Braeden said.

"He asked to speak to her alone, Master Braeden."

"A private meeting is not going to happen. And you know I don't like it when you use my title, so stop it."

Demnug shook his head and turned around. He started down the trail, but not before he sighed and muttered under his breath so that only they could hear. "You are more stubborn than Blood Gavin, my friend. As you wish."

Kara rolled her eyes and patted Braeden's shoulder. "My hero."

"You're welcome."

Kara nudged Ryn again with her heels, and the wolf trotted after Demnug. The trees ended after a bend in the path, revealing a mountain slope with a giant fissure in its face. A thin line of Kirelm soldiers tucked their wings in as they walked through it and disappeared into the crevice. The mountain towered overhead, the crack in its rock several hundred feet tall by the time he and Kara stopped beneath it.

Braeden patted Ryn on the neck and dismounted, offering a hand to Kara. She ignored him and slid down on her own. He shook his head and walked through the fissure ahead of her, but not before he saw her scratch Ryn's ears. The wolf dissolved into dust at her touch, no doubt disappearing into the grimoire pendant around Kara's neck to wait to be summoned yet again.

A cluster of stable hands manned the entrance, and one of them turned to lead Demnug's drowng to one of the hundreds of stalls in an adjacent stable carved from the stone. Demnug bowed as they walked in and gestured to a pathway on the left. Hallways rose overhead, crossing over one another in curved bridges connecting the dozens of floors above. Flick stuck his head through the edge of Kara's satchel and chirped as he looked around with wide eyes.

Demnug led them down a hallway to the left and up a dozen flights of steps. Several of the rooms' doors stood open, the beds inside remained untouched as their occupants had apparently not yet arrived. Each room Braeden passed contained a mirror, dresser, and even a robe draped over each bed. If it hadn't been for the deep gouges in the walls or occasional missing handrail, Braeden would never have guessed the city had been lost to the world for thousands of years.

Kara stopped a few feet in front of Braeden, which made him snap out of his reverie. Demnug knocked on the last door in the hall and waited for an answer, but the entry opened on its own. Braeden looked through to see Gavin peering out of a window, his hands behind his back. The Blood turned to face them, but his eyebrows rose when he caught Braeden's eye.

Gavin took a few steps closer. "Are you well, brother? You were gone quite a long time."

"I've been better."

"We weren't sure if you would make it for the gala, but Richard prepared a suit for you, just in case. It's on your bed, though the gala has been delayed until tomorrow because some guests have yet to arrive."

Kara chuckled, and Braeden resisted the impulse to smile. Yakona were always late.

"Thank you, Gavin. I haven't heard any rumors of the gala at all, so I wasn't prepared," he lied.

Gavin smiled. "That's good, then! Security is doing its job. We've been patrolling this location for a month now. There were some scares early on, but for now, we're certain it's safe. But if you'll excuse us, I would like to speak to the Vagabond privately."

"She already told me what you did, Gavin. I'm not leaving."

Gavin sighed. He pulled out a chair and sat at the table in his study, even though a messy array of parchment adorned with trees and cliffs and gorges littered its surface. Kara took a deep breath and crossed her arms, eyes on the Blood. She raised an inquisitive eyebrow, and Braeden braced himself. Between Kara and Gavin, one hot temper was about to ignite.

Kara spoke first. "Gavin, you're the one who asked me here. Let's not just sit in silence."

He waved her comment away with a lazy hand. "I will explain. I'm simply hunting for the right words."

Bags lined Gavin's eyes, and the king's shoulders slouched a bit. Braeden's gut twisted. He barely recognized the prince he'd grown up with. He couldn't imagine the stress of being Blood; he certainly didn't want the responsibility. He glanced at Kara.

Gavin finally took a deep breath. "I'm sorry, Kara. I don't know how you found out about the tiara, but I'm actually glad you did. Please forgive Twin, as she was acting under my orders. I hope the two of you will remain friends."

"I do forgive her, but I'm not as certain I'll forgive you. Where did this sudden remorse come from?" Kara asked.

"I may be the Blood, but I still have a father who freely speaks his mind."

She nodded, as if his words were enough. "Good. I hope he chewed your head off."

Gavin nodded. "He did. I've tried so desperately to keep you with us. I wanted Hillside to be your home because it's the safest place for you to be."

"That's what Frine said when he tried to kidnap me. I barely escaped then, too," she said.

Gavin turned to face her and narrowed his eyes.

Kara continued. "Starting a war to get revenge on Carden for killing your mother isn't the right reason to go into this peace treaty, Gavin. It won't last when it's over."

"We all have our own agendas, even you. Don't act righteous," he spat.

"Don't even start with me." Her eyes narrowed dangerously, considering who she was talking to, and Braeden tensed as she continued. "I'm not going to live in Hillside, no matter what you do or say. I'm not a weapon in your arsenal. And if you ever try to control me again, I just won't help you at all. Are we clear?"

Gavin looked back out the window and let her question settle, unanswered, on the air. Braeden wanted to add something, to drive the point home, but he kept quiet. He hated the fact that Kara kept him at arm's length, but he understood her reasons. Gavin would no doubt interfere if it became clear that Braeden cared for her as more than the Vagabond.

Gavin gestured toward the door. "I would like to speak to my brother, Kara. Twin is outside. She will show you to your room."

"You didn't answer me."

"You've made your point clear enough, Vagabond. I don't feel more discussion is necessary."

Kara hesitated, but turned and caught Braeden's eye for a moment before she opened the door. Twin stood waiting in the hallway and smiled at him as Kara slipped past. The door closed.

"I know those maps," Braeden said when he and Gavin were alone. He lifted one from the table. It depicted a dark gorge where mists played in the shadows and snow touched everything in sight.

Gavin nodded. "Suspected locations of the Stele, yes."

"You weren't even listening to her, were you?"

"Why are you so concerned with the Vagabond, brother?"

"I'm not. I'm worried about you," he lied. "I don't even recognize you anymore. Becoming the Blood has changed you."

Gavin ran his hand along his jaw. "For the better. I see the world a little clearer, now. Braeden, there is more at play than you realize. You have no idea what's going on, and you must remove yourself from this."

"It's obvious what's happening, Gavin. You're trying to control the Vagabond, and that's borderline insane. Why bother? The tiara trick failed. If you're still trying, it means you haven't learned anything."

"That's enough!" Gavin stood. His voice boomed in the study, and the echo reminded Braeden very much of his father's voice. The similarity floored him, and for a moment, he simply couldn't speak.

"Look, Braeden," Gavin said, his voice dangerously low. "You need to trust that I will tell you more when we return to Hillside. I respect you, brother, but you should not get close to her. She is not one of us and should not be treated in such a way. There are hundreds of Hillsidian women who would kill to have you. What happened to—what's her name? Eloise? Find her. Or pick another woman but stay with your own kind. Leave Kara out of your life."

"But Gavin—"

"This conversation is over, Braeden. Prepare for the gala, and try to enjoy yourself."

Braeden gritted his teeth and forced himself to bow before he stormed from the room.

A guard ushered him into a bedroom nearby and left just as quickly. The mattress dipped under Braeden's weight as he sat on the edge of his bed and wondered how power hungry his brother had become. A resourceful Blood like Gavin could find a way to take anything—and anyone—he wanted. Kara would never be safe so long as she remained close to the Hillsidian Blood.

Braeden reached a hand into his pocket and fiddled with the small talisman he'd brought with him from the Drenowith caves where Adele had trained him. The muse had discussed several matters with him, including one he'd never wanted to speak aloud: the fact that, after all these years, he still kept the key to his father's kingdom. It was a small, black carving, its design comprised of several black jade thorns interwoven in a small square. Though it had nothing to do with Carden's hold over him, keeping it confirmed what he subconsciously knew: someday, he would want to go back to the Stele.

A thought pulled on his mind, buzzing like a fly just out of reach. This sensation only ever plagued him whenever he thought of the Stele or sensed Carden's presence. How annoying. It would disappear if he could only ignore it.

He rolled out of his bed and looked through the window as the red sun set beyond the vast forest. His room loomed over the ground, much higher than he'd expected.

In the rooms above and below him, representatives from four of the five remaining yakona races bustled and prepared for the gala. That the kingdoms were even here proved miracles could happen, but a treaty was only the first step. If Gavin made another move to control Kara, everything she had worked for would dissolve from under her.

Braeden ruffled his hair and opened his door. He walked down the hall until he found a guard and asked for Kara's room. She was evidently upstairs.

He took a staircase and walked toward her room, trying to uncover the missing puzzle piece in Gavin's intentions. The Hillsidian had tried and failed to control Kara, but he knew nothing of limits or restraint. A cursed tiara was no doubt the first of many deceptions.

GAVIN

Gavin groaned and sat at his desk, slumping against the chair as he finally let himself relax. Rubbing his eyes, he wondered if he was still doing the right thing.

"Of course, I am," he mumbled to himself. He brushed his thumb over the stubble on his jaw. "Kara belongs to me. I need her power, whether Braeden likes it or not."

And he most clearly did *not*.

Frustrated, Gavin pushed himself to his feet and paced his makeshift study. Braeden was clearly more involved, more devoted to the Vagabond than was appropriate. The girl had obviously begun to twist Braeden's mind, seducing him away from his kingdom and his loyalties. A pang of jealousy hit Gavin hard in the chest, but he didn't entertain it for long.

She's mine.

Kara had escaped him, sure, but Braeden had brought her back. Whatever was going on between them, Gavin could use it to his advantage—for the moment, at least.

His first plan to win her loyalty had failed, but only barely. He wasn't worried. Gavin always had a backup plan, and he suspected that not even *she* would figure out what he was up to until it was too late.

Satisfied, Gavin leaned against the windowsill, scanning the forests below as he nodded to himself, lost in thought. Hillside needed the Vagabond's magic, and even though it would mean taking the woman his brother seemed to be so fond of, Braeden didn't have a choice in the matter.

Gavin sighed, not entirely happy about what he had to do next. But Braeden would forgive him… eventually.

CHAPTER SIX

KARA

Kara sat on her bed. The plush comforter reminded her of Hillside, which simultaneously soothed and terrified her. She would have to return there eventually, but she would postpone that as long as possible.

Twin left almost as soon as she dropped Kara off, mumbling something about how Kara could use some time alone. And, after the week she'd spent with Braeden, she could definitely use some time to think.

She sighed. He'd wrapped an arm around her in his sleep last night.

The door opened and shut before Kara could even look up. Gavin stood by the entrance, his hands behind his back.

"Normal people knock, Gavin," she said without getting up.

"Normal people also bow when in the presence of a Blood, so I suppose neither of us is normal."

Kara shook her head and resumed her stare out the window.

He cleared his throat. "I came to apologize for the incident with the tiara. It was arrogant."

"It was many things, none of them nice. Therefore, you'll need a bit more than that to make up for it."

He walked around to the edge of her bed and set something on the blanket behind her. He crossed to the window and leaned against it, blocking most of her view. With such a relaxed stance, he looked more like an athlete than a king. He folded his arms across his chest and looked down at her, three feet away and too close for comfort.

Kara wanted to turn and see what he'd put on the bed, but a small part of her already knew she wouldn't like it. She caught his eye and almost instantly regretted it. His stare made her throat tighten. Her heart raced. He gave her a smolder, a look that had no doubt broken many a heart in his lifetime.

Her face flushed, and she hoped he couldn't see it, but his grin told her he had. She wanted him to leave, but it didn't look like that would happen anytime soon.

BRAEDEN

Braeden neared Kara's door. Voices bubbled through the stone. He paused. One voice definitely belonged to Kara, and the other could only be Gavin's. The thick door muffled their words.

With a quick look down the hall, Braeden confirmed he was alone. He leaned in, managing to make out a phrase here and there, and he grew angrier with every word he caught.

KARA

Kara resisted the urge to scoot away from Gavin, choosing instead to stare through what bits of the window his body didn't block.

Gavin smirked. "You're a puzzle, Kara. Did you know that? I can't understand you, and it's driving me crazy."

"You're crazy all right, but I don't think it's my fault."

He laughed. "I have to admit, women don't usually deny me anything. And yet, that's all you've done—tell me no."

"You don't really ask. You just demand. It's annoying."

"It's what rulers do, Kara. We don't ask for respect or power—we expect it. Deep down, you crave it, too."

"Not everyone wants power."

His smile faded. "Perhaps not, but it's what you need. The Vagabond's cause won't survive this war if you continue what you're doing. You need my power to show the other Bloods how serious you are."

He stepped forward, but Kara refused to move. She caught his gaze, glaring at him as he came closer. He was probably trying to prove his point by making her inch away from him. Sweat beaded on her palms, but she wouldn't give him the luxury of knowing that her body tensed more with every step he took.

He didn't stop until he stood in front of her. He grinned.

"I'm impressed," he finally said.

"Get to the point, Gavin."

His expression softened, and he took a step back. "I find you mesmerizing. You're stubborn, proud, confusing, beautiful... and you don't want me. I don't understand."

"Good lord, you're arrogant."

He shrugged. "Enlighten me, then. Is there someone else?"

Kara bit the inside of her cheek. There wasn't supposed to be anyone else. If there was, they would become leverage, just like the Vagabond told her back in the village. But there was someone else.

"Braeden?" Gavin asked.

"Just stop it. You're about to sign a peace treaty, for heaven's sake. You need to focus on what's important!"

"I am," he said. His eyes never left hers.

Kara groaned. She looked around the room for inspiration, and her eyes settled on the familiar black box now sitting on her bed. That must have been what Gavin had hidden behind his back when he came into the room.

"Is that—?"

"Before you get upset, hear me out," Gavin interrupted.

"That's the tiara, isn't it? The one you tricked Twin into giving me?"

"It's a peace offering. I removed the curse. It's nothing but a crown anymore. It's a priceless heirloom, and I can't make myself look at it for what I've done, so I want you to have it. Wear it to the gala as a token of forgiveness."

"I'm not wearing that tiara!"

Gavin crossed his arms. "This is all a misunderstanding. Please, take it with my apology."

"Do you think I'm stupid enough to wear it?"

"Not stupid. I simply wish to rebuild our trust by proving to you the curse has been removed."

Kara sighed. "I don't want a crown. If you want to prove anything to me, then don't unite with the other

Bloods to get your revenge on Carden. Do this out of a true desire for peace. That's all I want."

He leaned in but glanced to the door and paused. Kara followed his gaze. The door hadn't opened or anything. When she looked back to the king, he reached for her hand. She tensed, but he simply bowed and kissed it.

"Enjoy your stay, Vagabond," he said without looking at her.

He headed out the door without looking back. It shut behind him. For a moment, she heard voices, but they trailed off even as she strained to hear them.

Kara eyed the black box on her bed for a moment before she picked it up. She didn't open it—there was no need. She knew what the tiara looked like. But even if she didn't see the barbs on it any longer, she couldn't bring herself to trust Gavin.

She opened the drawer in her nightstand and threw the box inside.

BRAEDEN

Braeden pulled back and darted down the hall as footsteps shuffled for the door. He hid in the alcove of another entry as Gavin left the room. Gavin's footsteps stopped as soon as Kara's door closed.

"Brother, I thought I told you to stay away from the Vagabond," the king said.

Braeden sighed and slid from the doorframe to face the Blood. "I'm just trying to keep you from making a mistake. What are you trying to do? Seduce her?"

"She's off limits, brother. Don't worry yourself with why."

"It's not your decision to make."

Gavin sighed. "I'm sorry to do this, Braeden, but I forbid you from spending any more time alone with her. She is poisoning your mind."

The Blood's intense glare said more than his words—he was trying to control Braeden, to force a mandate. Carden had never been so kind as to verbally warn Braeden when he delivered a direct order, but Gavin's threat held the same intent.

To disobey the mandate would only hurt Braeden's cause—either Gavin would think Kara had broken the blood loyalty of the king's adopted brother, or he would discover Braeden wasn't Hillsidian after all.

"The queen never forbade me from anything in all the years I lived under her roof," Braeden said.

"Times have changed. Leave."

Gavin guarded Kara's door, motionless. Braeden bowed and walked away, going nowhere as fast as he could. This wasn't a fight he could win.

When he rounded a few corners and Gavin was

out of sight, Braeden slowed. His fingers grazed the wall as he passed. Gavin had given him a direct order. A command. This was yet one more thing to look out for among his growing pile of complications.

That Gavin had been kind enough to verbalize the order was a relief, though; Braeden hadn't been so lucky in Losse when he'd changed into his Lossian form to join Kara in the sunken kingdom. There, Blood Frine had forced him into the throne room to test his loyalty, giving Braeden a silent order he couldn't have hoped to hear, much less obey. It had proven he didn't have the Lossian blood loyalty. Luckily, Frine had believed it was because Kara had turned Braeden into a vagabond. No one there had ever suspected what Braeden truly was: a Stelian.

But Gavin had spoken the command aloud, which proved Gavin still respected him and had no suspicion Braeden was anything more than a Hillsidian his parents adopted. It meant there would be no tails or spies watching him, since a direct order was the undeniable end of it.

It would have been, at least, if Braeden were Hillsidian.

He needed a plan. He couldn't leave Kara to fend for herself, especially not now. His admittedly confusing feelings aside, he needed to help her. She didn't have anyone else.

There weren't many options, but he did settle on

one: once the gala ended and everyone went home, Braeden would feign isen hunts. If he said he was trying to find a guild, it would be impossible to prove he hadn't actually gone. He could use that as a cover and keep an eye on Kara from a distance.

In the meantime, Braeden needed to find a place to meet Kara in private. He had to explain everything before it became difficult to find her.

Gavin hadn't said anything about being around Kara in public—an intentional loophole, no doubt. It would be suspicious, not to mention rude, if the king's brother suddenly stopped speaking to the Vagabond. The others would notice.

Braeden walked aimlessly, lost in his thoughts, when his fingers brushed something in the wall.

A wooden ladder jutted from the carved mountain hallway, bolted to the wall with rusted screws. As Braeden looked up, he saw a small door in the wall about twenty feet in the air. He climbed just to have something to do, and when he finally reached the top, he opened the door to see an overgrown garden.

Dusk cast shadows over the terrace as he pulled himself onto the weeds. Several large windows lined the mountain to the left of the overrun space, their light spilling out along the grasses. Braeden looked in. A hundred or more feet below, figures darted through a grand hall where the gala would probably be held. Tables cluttered the floor, and several yakona from every nation set each table with linens and dishes.

Braeden turned back to the garden and brushed aside some of the lilacs as he sat on a stone flowerbed. The scent stung his nose, but he resisted the impulse to draw his sword. He doubted isen could find their way here—no one could stumble across this corner of Ethos, not with all the guards in the trees.

He ran his hands through the crowded weeds, trying to shrivel them to let the more vivid flowers bloom so that the garden would look presentable. He laughed—he'd gone crazy. Here he was, a prince living a lie, gardening to impress a woman. He'd lost his mind.

Instead of giving the flowers more room to bloom, though, the weeds thickened at his touch and the lilacs wilted. He cursed under his breath. Not only was he terrible with animals, but he apparently couldn't garden to save his life.

Kara would have been able to do it without even trying.

He glanced around, abandoning the flowerbed. Night crept in around him. A wall protected the garden from the sheer drop beyond, and the moon shone full and low on a purple horizon. The stars glimmered in the blanket of darkness above him, and as he watched, a meteor blinked across the sky. The forest swayed in a breeze.

Braeden reached into his pocket and pulled out the talisman. He turned the Stelian coat of arms over and over in his hands, examining every detail. Adele had nearly punched him when he'd told her he still had it. She'd even made him dig it up. She wanted to see him destroy it, but he never got the chance. Not long after he'd unearthed it, Adele's amulet had told her Kara was in danger.

In training, Braeden had thought of Kara more than he cared to admit. At first, the anger of what he was had been enough to make him stand after taking a hit from Adele. When the anger faded, he relied on the hope that he could somehow overcome his blood loyalty to Carden without the help of the Grimoire. When that hope faded, he'd had nothing but memories.

He focused first on what he could recall of his mother, hoping the anger would reignite at seeing the pain Carden had caused her. That didn't last long. No memory did—until he recalled his hands around Kara's neck and how the life in her eyes had flickered as she'd gasped his name.

The rage smoldered in his chest again, but he quelled it.

She had given him enough fire to continue. Carden had controlled him, forced him to nearly kill Kara, and his guilt at obeying his father never faded, even when everything else had. He built upon the anger with more memories. At first, he had focused on how clear Kara's gray eyes were. How her hair always turned a little red in the sun. How, when she laughed, her face lit up and glowed with the sound.

She was the only person who knew what he was and didn't care.

He stood. The garden would work as a meeting spot. He stuck his head through the door leading to the ladder, glancing around to make sure no one walked along the corridor below. After a few silent minutes of listening for footsteps that never came, Braeden climbed down and shut the door on his way.

He landed on the stone floor with a *thud* and turned back the way he'd come. He would go to his room and try to sleep, but he knew he wouldn't have much luck. All he could think of was Kara nestling against him as they camped in the forest or the warmth of her body curled against his in the Vagabond's study.

It terrified Braeden how one person could bring him such peace, and he couldn't imagine what would happen if anyone took her from him.

CHAPTER SEVEN

KARA

Kara sat against her bed's headboard, feet propped on a pillow as Twin's head lay on her stomach.

Twin shrugged. "All I'm saying is you should consider the fact that Braeden is head over heels for you."

Kara's body tensed at the thought, but she managed to keep her face expressionless. Leaning back and pretending to relax seemed to help. She shook her head. "Don't be ridiculous. We just ran into each other on the way here. Either that, or he found me because he was keeping an eye on me for Gavin's sake."

Kara hated lying to Twin—just hated it. But there was no way around it, not so long as Twin had the blood loyalty to Gavin. The girl could be controlled at any time or forced to tell Gavin Kara's secrets. At least Braeden wasn't around his Blood all the time. He wasn't constantly susceptible.

Twin smiled. "You want him. I know you."

"You're my friend, but I don't think you know me that well yet."

"I do."

Kara peeked through an eyelid and grinned. "Oh?"

"Yes. Every time I say his name, you tense your stomach. Why do you think I'm lying like this?"

"You little sneak!" Kara grabbed a pillow and whacked Twin in the head.

Twin giggled. "You had it coming. You can tell me!"

"Look, just let it go. Okay?"

"Why?"

"Because I asked nicely. Isn't that enough?"

Twin huffed and lay back down, hugging the pillow to her chest. "You're no fun."

"I'm insanely fun. You're just never around to witness it."

"Well, if you won't gossip, what do you want to do?" Twin asked.

"I don't know. What is there to do here?"

"Explore, really. It's all in ruin."

"Let's go, then!" Kara stood, ushering Twin to her feet. She would do anything to get the girl to stop talking about Braeden.

They meandered for hours, crossing hallways and

passing guards. There wasn't much they could still access, considering that most of the upper hallways were caved in or blocked off with doors no amount of magic could unlock.

Twin's eyes finally drooped too much for her to feign interest any longer, so Kara walked her back to her room. Kara, however, continued through the hallways, passing guards and nodding hello as she ambled. There was so much to see that Kara didn't imagine she would ever go back to sleep. Even if she explored only this one, small, section of Ethos, she doubted she would find all the rooms during their short stay.

She slipped through the upper hallways, which were lit by sconces along the walls. After a short distance, the guards disappeared. Kara guessed it had something to do with the lack of guest rooms in these upper halls. She passed open doors, the rooms within filled with shelves and food, but there wasn't a soul around to protect it.

She shrugged. They were in Ethos, miles from anything. Scouts had lived here for a month before anyone arrived, apparently. No war would break out; as much as no one seemed to like each other, everyone she passed seemed to agree that Ethos was safe.

So, Kara continued along the empty halls, staying up most of the night. Her exploring led her closer to Braeden's garden without her even realizing where she was going.

BRAEDEN

Braeden's ear twitched. He was half-awake. The red glow of the sunrise bled through his eyelids. The door handle scraped as somebody turned it from the outside.

Someone was trying to get into his room.

He pushed himself upright, smoke consuming his hand before he was even fully awake. He aimed the spell for the door, ready to fire the same fuming curse he'd used against Deidre when he'd first met the isen. In his half-asleep stupor, he would take no prisoners.

"*Bloods*, Braeden! It's me!" a woman said.

The spell dissolved from his palm. He rubbed his eyes with his non-smoking hand and finally opened them fully.

Twin froze midstride in the doorway, a suit draped over her arm. "What is wrong with you? You could have killed me!"

"I—I'm sorry. I've been on edge lately."

Twin watched him out of the corner of her eye, but her lips twisted into a cool smile. She laid his suit on the edge of the bed and set a piece of paper beside it.

"Could your mood be because of a certain Vagabond?" she asked.

He furrowed an eyebrow. "There's only one Vagabond."

Twin laughed. "That joke just doesn't get old."

He groaned, apparently missing the punchline. "Thank you for bringing me my suit, Twin. Now, may I have some time to myself?"

She sat next to him. "You're welcome, you grump. But before I go, I have to tell you how you'll walk into the gala. You're in the Hillsidian procession, obviously, so you'll walk in with Gavin. Make sure to be in his study in an hour. Kara is walking in alone. Braeden, just wait until you see her! I did her hair myself. She's stunning."

Braeden wasn't sure how he should respond, but he couldn't imagine Kara ever looking anything less than stunning.

"There are rumors about the two of you, you know," Twin continued.

"You Hillsidians have nothing better to do than gossip, do you?"

"Don't be a hypocrite! I'm sure you gossip just as much."

He clenched his fists in frustration, hiding them beneath the covers. He'd slipped. He needed to calm down.

"Twin, you need to remember gossip is a waste of time. There's no truth in it. She's not interested."

Twin shrugged mischievously. "From the way she

talks about you, I'd have to disagree."

"What?"

"I'll leave, just like you wanted." She laughed, shrugging again as she slipped back into the hall. When the door clicked shut behind her, Braeden hurled a pillow at it.

He reached down to the edge of the bed and grabbed the paper she'd left on his clothes. It was a program, written in elegant script. Ink coated the page, most of it curves and swirls from the uppercase letters. All in all, it was a great waste of ink for how little was written.

Braeden scanned the page and groaned. Speeches started after noon, followed by toasts, the signing ceremony, performances by each kingdom, gift exchanges, more speeches—it went on forever. Only afterward could everyone eat dinner and dance. He hoped there would at least be rolls or fruits on the table to keep appetites at bay. It wasn't wise to get between a Stelian and a meal.

But the dancing—his stomach twisted. Maybe he could lure Kara away from the gala for a dance in the garden. He could tell her he wanted a chance, a real one, and that he no longer cared about the consequences. He couldn't let her slip away.

He pushed himself to his feet and walked toward the bathroom. He needed a distraction from his thoughts, sure, but he needed a bath more.

CHAPTER EIGHT
BRAEDEN

Braeden managed to calm the rising nerves in his gut after he bathed and dressed, but he still needed something to distract him. He'd already written directions to the garden on a small sheet of paper, which he intended to slip into Kara's hand at the gala. That hadn't taken nearly as long as he expected. He'd wanted to tell Twin to pass along the message but doing so might mean Gavin would learn about the rendezvous. Too risky.

He left his room and headed for the garden. Maybe he'd try his hand at gardening again—he didn't know. But he needed to prepare what he would say when he pulled Kara aside later. So far all he had was, "Meet me in some garden I found."

He retraced his steps, nodding as Hillsidians passed him and acknowledging the forced smiles from the other nations with a broad grin of his own as he came across them. For all the claims of security, Braeden had expected more guards—he passed only a handful on his way. He reasoned the rest must be in the forest outside or waiting out of sight in case something went awry.

About ten minutes after he saw his last guard, he found the ladder to the garden again. He glanced around to be safe and climbed the ladder when no one appeared in the hallway. Once at the top, he pushed the door open.

Someone in the garden cursed—a woman from the pitch of her voice.

Braeden peeked through the door to see a blonde standing by the wall, one hand over her mouth as she sucked back laughter. Her red dress spilled onto the overgrown grasses.

"You scared the crap out of me! Why didn't you use the stairs?" Kara asked.

Braeden pulled himself into the garden, but he couldn't answer. He could only stare. Kara's hair rested in pinned curls on her head, though a loose curl or two splashed onto her shoulder as she moved. Her skin glowed, and her gray eyes had an almost blue tint. Her neck and shoulders peeked from the blood-red gown, which pushed the boundaries of his self-restraint.

"You look beautiful," he finally said.

"Well, thanks. You look quite dashing yourself."

He didn't have an answer, so they stood in silence. Braeden couldn't quite put together words. Kara's cheeks burned red. She looked out over the trees.

"You're staring, Braeden."

"Sorry." He cleared his throat and stared at the trees with her. He cheated, though, and looked back at her from the corner of his eye. He couldn't help himself. Twin had been right. Stunning was the perfect word.

"So, I repeat—why didn't you use the stairs?" she asked, nodding back to an open door at the opposite end of the small garden.

"Oh. I didn't know about a stairwell."

"It's a bit easier than—is that a ladder?"

"I had to be secretive, but maybe I overdid it," he said with a laugh.

"Secretive? Why?"

He sighed. "Gavin issued a blood order for me to not be alone with you. I can't let anyone see us together."

"Wow. How did that happen?"

Braeden shook his head. "I don't want to talk about it. You need to stay away from him as much as you can. He's up to something."

"Yeah, I figured that one out."

"What did he do?"

"Don't worry about it, Braeden. Let's just try to enjoy ourselves tonight."

"Kara, if he hurt you—"

"He didn't."

Braeden sighed and leaned against the wall again. She could be so frustrating.

"So, have you seen the program yet? I just skimmed over it," Kara finally admitted, apparently trying to break the silence.

"You didn't miss much. It'll be hours of listening to people talk before we can eat."

"And dance." Kara wrung her hands.

"You've fought shadow demons and survived two run-ins with Carden, but you're scared to dance?"

"I didn't do those other things in front of people. No one noticed when I messed up."

"Well, I'm not really looking forward to it, either. We can stumble through the steps together, though, if you save me a dance."

It was a lie—he'd been taught to dance at fourteen, as was tradition for all members of the royal family—but he didn't want Kara to be alone in this.

She laughed. "That sounds good to me if you don't mind me stepping on you."

"Not in the least." He inched as close to her as he could without being painfully obvious about it. The sun worked its way across the sky as they both simply watched. Braeden was happy to just stand there. In the peace, he spoke without thinking. "You know, you sort of ruined my surprise."

"What do you mean?"

"I was going to invite you up here during the gala. I even have a little slip of paper ready with directions to the garden on it and everything. It was going to be quite romantic." He laughed, but Kara watched him with a strange blur of emotions he couldn't read. Her smile lit up her eyes, but her eyebrows twisted as if she were sad or maybe disappointed. Panic spread through his chest.

"Braeden—"

"Hear me out."

She leaned against the wall, slouching her shoulders as she leaned closer. "The Vagabond told me I can't get that close to anyone. I'm sorry. He's wrong about some things, but I think he's right about this. I couldn't live with myself if I got you killed, too. Not after all you've done for me."

"But you want this. There's something more than friendship here."

"Shouldn't that have been a question?"

"No, Kara. I see it, but I don't understand why you think my life isn't already dangerous."

"Of course, I understand that. It's not that at all. It's—"

"Kara? Braeden? Are either of you up there?" Twin's voice echoed up the stairwell.

Braeden turned in time to catch a shadow moving against the stairway's wall. He tensed—no one could see him with Kara.

"I'll keep her out of the garden. Hide," Kara whispered. She nodded to a ledge over the door.

Braeden wrapped his hand around the small of her back and pulled her toward him before she had time to tense or resist. He kissed her forehead.

"Think about it," he said.

He pulled himself onto the overhang as Twin's foot rounded the corner. He crouched on the ledge, out of sight.

Kara grinned into the stairwell. "How are you doing, Twin?"

"There you are! The gala is going to start soon, and you need to be at the procession line. Are you ready?"

"Sure am," Kara said with a nod.

Twin's voice continued from the stairwell. "Have you seen Braeden, by chance? We can't find him anywhere."

"That's weird. No, I haven't."

Braeden studied Kara's expression—her face remained perfectly smooth, without even a twitch in her lip to give away the lie. She could have even convinced him.

When did she learn to lie?

Kara smiled again at Twin and disappeared into the stairwell without another glance upward.

Braeden sat on the overhang and sighed. Her ability to lie shouldn't have bothered him so much. Of course, she knew how. She'd hid the truth about what he was, and no one was the wiser. She'd kept her real reason for pushing him away a secret, too—for a while, at least. How she could let herself be lonely because she'd lost her parents, he couldn't fully understand.

He groaned. How hypocritical. Of course, he could understand—he simply didn't want to.

He picked up a few pebbles from the mountain beside him and passed them through his fingers since he didn't have any grass to rip apart. Well, at least none he could reach without moving. He needed to get to Gavin's temporary study to prepare for the procession, but it was more important for him to wait a while longer and give the girls a head start. He couldn't risk someone knowing he'd been alone with Kara.

After ten minutes, he jumped off and trotted down the stairs, his eye peeled for Hillsidians. The upper levels remained empty, though, and he descended to the lower levels without a moment's hesitation.

He retraced his steps to Gavin's study, to the best of his ability, but had to stop a passing guard for help in choosing the right corridor. Another fifteen minutes went by before he made it to his adoptive brother's office.

Braeden opened the door to find Gavin sitting at the desk.

"You're late," the Blood said.

"I am. Where's Richard?"

"I told him to wait in his room," Gavin said with a nod to the hallway.

"Why?"

"So that I could talk to you alone for a moment."

Braeden's fist tightened instinctively. Gavin knew. There was no other reason for his wanting to speak alone. He must have discovered the truth somehow. Maybe he'd ordered a spy to track Kara or had simply seen the two of them in the garden. Or—

"At a minimum, are you going to apologize? It's inconsiderate," Gavin said.

Braeden paused. Inconsiderate was not the word he would have chosen for twelve years of lying and deception. Come to think of it, Braeden would already be in poisoned handcuffs if Gavin knew the truth. This was about something else entirely.

"What am I supposed to apologize for, exactly?" he asked.

Gavin smacked his desk and stood. "*Bloods*, Braeden! What happened to you? Your mind is always somewhere else. You don't talk to me or Richard anymore. You've completely changed! And for what, some human girl?"

"Don't speak about K—"

"I am your Blood, and I will speak however I please!"

Braeden clenched his jaw to bite back the scathing rebuttal that would have ruined everything.

Yes, he'd changed since he met Kara. He was on edge now, constantly afraid he would be discovered. But it wasn't her so much as the truth—the Grimoire couldn't break his blood loyalty to Carden—that had changed him. All his hope for freedom had disappeared the night the Grimoire became useless to him.

"People change, Gavin. You're proof of it. You're greedier than ever, hung up on revenge and the vain hope that an old book will solve your problems!"

"No, not the book. Its master," Gavin snapped. His jaw tensed, and he closed his mouth, but it was too late. He had evidently said too much.

"Are you sharing part of what you planned to tell me when we returned home? You're going to use Kara? You've already tried, Gavin. It didn't work."

"Please, just trust me," Gavin softly said. He stared at the floor, shoulders bent as if he hadn't slept in ages.

"No."

The only person in the world Braeden could trust was Kara. She knew the truth, and he had begun to care for her in a way he'd never thought possible.

Gavin fell back into his seat and rubbed his eyes. "Braeden, you used to spar with me before the Vagabond reappeared. You and I would hunt, talk about strategy and war and philosophy and women and love. You've never believed in love, but I can see you are falling for Kara. You're almost always out hunting, but when you are home, you're not mentally with us. You're thinking of her, always. I know it. I see it. I understand it, I do. She's beautiful. But you can't lose yourself to her. She doesn't want you. She's using you. She needed a bodyguard, and she took it too far. Just look—"

"ENOUGH!" Braeden's tone startled even himself. Rage pumped through him: the aftermath of nearly losing control. Twelve years of denying his royal heritage had surfaced in that one word. For the first time in his life, he'd spoken like the Heir he was.

It was a miracle he hadn't shifted into his natural form.

"You will never speak to me like that again," Gavin said in an even tone.

"You may be the Blood, but I'm still your brother. You cannot treat me as a lesser."

Gavin frowned and leaned back in his chair. "Brothers. Yes, let's discuss what it means to be brothers. When we were growing up, I always thought of you as equal. I shared everything with you, trusted you. I could have treated you like an orphan, Braeden. I could have wondered why my parents would adopt a child when any family in Hillside would have taken you with a single request from Mother. Why did she choose you? I never asked. I never cared. So, yes, Braeden, until the Vagabond lured you away, you were my brother. I wish you would remember yourself."

Braeden shut down. It was all he could do to keep from screaming, from shifting and telling the arrogant Blood the truth. His face hardened, and all he could do was examine Gavin with an icy stare, which was neither interested nor hateful. "You're the one who has lost his way, Gavin. Not me."

Gavin set his fingers against one another and leaned his hands against his face. He stared at Braeden as if he was dissecting something, or maybe trying to piece together some greater puzzle. "I want my brother back."

"Then stop trying to control me." Braeden tensed. He'd said *try*.

Gavin, however, continued without a moment's hesitation. Braeden suppressed a sigh of relief. "I don't want to control you, Braeden. I'm trying to help you. The Vagabond is a weapon, and she knows that. She has to be playing you."

"She's not."

"How could you possibly know?" Gavin asked.

Braeden didn't answer.

"I want to fix this, Braeden. I want you to have faith in me again. I don't even know when I lost your trust, but I am right about this whether you like it or not. If time is what it takes for you to see the truth, so be it. I will not remove my order. You are not to see Kara in private. I hope you will someday understand why. For now, though, we must head down to the ceremony."

Gavin got to his feet and walked around the desk, but Braeden stood in the doorway as he approached. Braeden wanted to remain, to make the king walk around him, but he knew what would happen. Gavin would likely issue a wordless command to move. If Braeden didn't obey, the last shreds of normalcy in his life would unravel.

The Blood stopped short of him, and Braeden moved aside to let him by. He didn't know how much longer he could submit to the man who had once been like a brother, but who was now quickly losing his mind.

The door opened with a wave of Gavin's hand, the stone groaning as it slid across the floor. Richard stood in the hall beyond, his back to them. He turned as they came closer and raised his eyebrows when Braeden caught his eye. He gaped as if Braeden's glare had scared him.

Braeden followed but kept his distance from Gavin. Richard joined him behind the king and nudged his side.

"You look ready to kill," Richard whispered.

Braeden shrugged. He *was* ready to kill.

Richard nudged him. "You must relax. This isn't a

party—it's a political arena. If the Hillsidian Blood's brother looks murderous, it will reflect poorly on all of Hillside."

Braeden sucked in a deep breath. He wanted to explain, to tell Richard what Gavin was doing, but he couldn't possibly have spoken low enough for Gavin to miss their conversation. Instead, he shook his head, hoping his adoptive father would understand his anger and leave it alone.

Richard put a hand on Braeden's shoulder and squeezed. "Have faith, boy, and trust everything will work out for the best."

They rounded a turn in the hallway and began down a curved flight of steps. The stone stairs angled into the grand hall below, where hundreds had already gathered. Musicians sat in chairs on a platform at the far end of the hall, their fingers strumming across the strings of their instruments. Their notes swelled into the rafters and washed over Braeden, thanks to the room's acoustics.

Hundreds of guests, sitting at the dozens of tables below, stood as Gavin headed down the stairs with Braeden and Richard in tow. A wave of applause swelled among the Hillsidians and carried out into the other guests until the light patter of hands clapping together became a mild tsunami.

The applause settled as Gavin led Braeden and Richard farther into the hall, toward a raised platform with a long table. The other royal families sat in their places, having left the center seat and three to its right open. Gavin took his place immediately beside the center chair, and Richard took the next. Braeden had no choice but to sit between Richard and the princess Evelyn, which left the center open for Kara. He wouldn't be near her, nor would he be able to look at her without Gavin noticing.

Braeden cursed his brother under his breath. The man even controlled the seating placement. Braeden sat and gave a sharp nod to Evelyn. She returned the gesture without looking at him.

A few boxes lined his plate, but only one caught his eye—a twelve-by-three-inch wooden box with the Grimoire clover carved into its lid. The clasp was nothing more than a metal hook tucked away in an eye, and it was all he could do not to open it right then.

He grinned. Kara hadn't forgotten him when she'd brought along presents for everyone. He'd seen the village's treasury but couldn't begin to guess what she'd chosen for him. It wasn't like he needed more weapons.

A series of gasps spread through the crowd like wildfire, followed by applause much louder than had been given to Gavin. Braeden looked up and caught his breath.

Kara had begun down the steps, her feet slowly

following each other. Though he'd already seen her, he couldn't help himself; he stared. Her pale hair almost had a red tint in the hall's warm light.

Her cheeks flushed at the room's reaction to her arrival, which made Braeden grin. That girl couldn't stand attention.

Someone beside him chuckled, the sound too quiet for many others to hear. He turned to see Gavin smirk and lean back, eyes fixed on Kara as she entered. Braeden's grip on his armrest tightened, his knuckles bleaching from the effort.

Gavin wanted Kara's power, but the glint in the king's eye hinted that he perhaps wanted something else as well.

So that was it—Gavin wasn't trying to protect Braeden from what he believed to be a manipulative, political player. He wanted Kara for himself, and Braeden was in the way.

Those sitting at the head table with him stood, but it took Braeden a moment to figure out why. He pushed himself to his feet as he saw Kara nearing them. An attendant pulled her seat out for her, and the rest of the table sat with her.

Kara glanced at Braeden as she took her seat. He smiled. She grinned back. He was about to mouth a quick *thank you* for his gift when Gavin leaned forward, blocking Braeden's view. The king set his elbows on the table and leaned just slightly over his plate, turning his head enough to catch Braeden's eye. Gavin frowned and turned away but didn't move.

Braeden sat back in his chair. This was going to be a long night.

Gavin stood and spread his arms to address the table, but he faced the throngs of people sitting at the tables below the platform.

"My friends and neighbors, this is an exciting time. Here, in the once-powerful halls of Ethos, we have gathered to celebrate the beginnings of a new era of peace and unity. The world is broken, my friends, but together we will fix it!"

Evelyn sighed, the sound so quiet Braeden barely heard it. He glanced farther past the princess to see Aislynn watching Gavin with a tense smile. Farther down the table, Blood Ithone leaned back, his wings flowing over his seat. He sat still as a statue, but his daughter Aurora kept moving the silverware beside her plate. Ithone's wife stared off into the crowd, her eyes clear but empty. With a start, Braeden realized he didn't even know her name. The Queen of Kirelm had never even been mentioned in his presence.

He studied the other end of the table but couldn't see past Gavin's frame. He assumed they were equally as unengaged in whatever the king said.

Gavin continued his speech, but Braeden stopped listening. He wanted to roll his eyes. He wanted to laugh, to scream that this was a façade. A joke. None of the other Bloods were even listening. This was a charade, a formality they were all eager to end.

Braeden glanced out over the throngs of yakona sitting beside each other. At the first table, Twin watched Gavin with a forced smile from her place next to a Kirelm woman, who eyed Gavin through narrowed lids.

With a small sigh, Braeden leaned back. He rubbed the small, black talisman in his pocket and let his mind drift again to Kara. He would still ask for at least one dance, with or without Gavin's permission. That way, he would at least be able to enjoy one last moment with her and not have to think about what would happen once they left Ethos.

CHAPTER NINE

KARA

Kara should have been paying attention to Gavin's speech, but she was mostly focused on how much she wanted to look at Braeden.

"Yakona!" Gavin said, still talking. "For the first time in over thirty thousand years, the kingdoms have been brought together under one roof to celebrate a new era of unity and peace."

Gavin continued, but Kara tuned out. She'd tried. She tried to listen, but Gavin just went on and on. He spoke like he had no time limit. It was all Kara could do to sit up straight. Now and again, her shoulders would hunch, or her eyes would snap in and out of focus as a bug crawled across the tablecloth. On one such occasion, she looked up to see a group of Hillsidians sitting at the nearest table, scowling at her. They leaned into one another and whispered when she caught them staring. Kara looked back to Gavin, who rambled without hesitation.

"...but that was ages ago, and this is a new era. We will not fall prey to what we once were, but look to the future..."

Nope. She wasn't forcing herself to listen to that.

The room erupted into applause, which Kara joined without questioning. Gavin sat back down beside her, and she suppressed a sigh of relief. Finally—they could get on to the ceremony and then dinner. Her stomach growled. At least—

Ithone stood and addressed the table in much the same way as Gavin. Kara's shoulders drooped. Her mouth hung slightly open.

But I'm so hungry!

Movement in her peripheral vision made her glance again at the first table. Twin caught her eye and pointed to her lips before smiling.

Kara closed her mouth and sat up straight. Twin was right—Kara needed to get over it. She was a political figure now, as much as that sucked.

She watched Ithone but didn't force herself to listen. Braeden snuck a look over his shoulder to her. He grinned, which made her smile back—that grin of his was too infectious to resist.

His eyes shifted to Gavin, but Kara couldn't see the king's face from this angle. Braeden's smile disappeared, and he turned away with only one quick look back to her. Whatever was going on between them, Kara didn't like it. They were two powerful yakona—if they didn't sort this out soon, their spat wouldn't end well.

Something scampered up her leg, and Flick curled onto her lap. His ear twitched, and he settled down to sleep as if she had simply forgotten him in her room.

She hadn't forgotten—Twin had told her she shouldn't bring him. She'd set him up with a feast, which had distracted him as she left. However, it seemed his food hadn't lasted as long as she'd intended.

She ran her fingers through his fur. He purred. Gavin looked at the furry creature and frowned, but Kara shrugged. She wasn't going to make her pet leave. Besides, she wasn't much good at controlling him anyway. She settled back into her chair in an effort to find a balance between comfort and grace. This was only the second speech of several—she just hoped this would all be over soon.

KARA

Kara was two seconds from taking off her shoe and throwing it at Blood Frine of Losse. His great big, blue head was a beacon of long-winded loquaciousness. She'd vacillated between a couple words in the hour he took to tell everyone how great his kingdom was, but loquacious seemed to suit him best.

Two and a half hours of speeches were enough. She needed food. Flick whined from his place on her lap, so, apparently, she wasn't alone, even after the giant spread she'd left him earlier. She rubbed his head, but he batted at her hand with his tail and glared up at her.

Braeden's occasional smile and Twin's constant reminders to not look bored were all that kept Kara sane during the speeches. Frine was the last to speak, and he needed to stop. She was going to break something if he didn't just stop.

The hall erupted into applause as he finished and bowed, Kara admittedly clapping much louder than she would have if he hadn't been the last to speak.

But instead of food, two Hillsidians in ornate, green suits brought out a long, rolled piece of parchment and a quill. Kara should have read the program Twin had given her earlier. There was no telling when actual food would be involved at this rate.

Each Blood stood, crossed to Gavin, signed the treaty,

and clasped his hand firmly before sitting back down to murmur with their nearest family member. When Aislynn—the last of the Bloods to sign—sat, Gavin rolled up the fully signed parchment and set it back on the table. His hands hovered over the scroll until it gleamed with brilliant, green sparks. With a snap and a dust of smoke, three more appeared on the table. He handed each Blood a scroll, and the hall erupted in applause yet again.

Kara glanced back at the first table out of habit, looking for Twin, but no one sat in the chair.

The hundreds of candles lining each wall dimmed. Kara tensed, wishing she'd brought her sword. Panic shot through her chest. Carden had found them. The gala had been a mistake—it was the perfect place for Carden to attack everyone at once. He must have broken through, must have found—

Lights shone from somewhere overhead, focusing on a cleared area maybe a dozen feet from the head table. A group of Hillsidians in bright costumes posed, Twin at their lead.

Drums played from somewhere above, and the ladies in the group moved their hips in sharp time to the beat. A second chorus of drums joined in, and a third; each line of drums bred new movement from the group.

Kara sighed. She leaned back, shaking her head. It was a performance, not an invasion.

"Are you all right?" Gavin asked, his voice entirely too close.

Kara nodded, leaning back when she realized his face was barely a foot from hers. She turned back to the performance without answering. She leaned her cheek on one hand to give herself a better distance from Gavin. It was an unbecoming way to sit, but she doubted anyone would see her in the dim light.

The dancing intensified, the music and curves of the dancers' movements growing stronger and stronger the longer they danced. Their choreography hypnotized Kara—they moved with a primal passion but spun with a grace she would never master in her life. And Twin led every movement as if she'd choreographed it herself.

The music raced to a crescendo, the dancers spinning and jumping as the racing beat made Kara's pulse skid out of control. They paused—some in midair—as the song ended.

The room burst into applause. Most of the noise came from Hillsidians, but Kara saw a few Kirelms nodding to each other as they clapped. Anyone could appreciate the skill required for such a passionate dance.

Twin bowed as the rest of the dancers retreated into a door behind the sloping staircase. "Thank you! Next, we will be hearing the lovely voices of the

Kirelm singers. Please give them as kind of a welcome."

Four lines of Kirelms walked from behind the very stairs where the Hillsidians had disappeared. As they spread out across the floor, Twin bowed to them and left. The singers now had the room's full attention.

Each Kirelm snapped their wings open in the quiet hall and took off at a different time, heading for the otherwise inaccessible rafters. As they flew, a low hum began. It resonated in the hall's acoustics, brewing as they flew. The sound blended with the beating of their wings, growing stronger the longer it lasted, until the first landed on a walkway high in the rafters. The humming split apart into lyrics Kara didn't understand as the Kirelms sang a sweet tune, its somber lines dipping in the perfect blend of the singers' harmonies.

Kara settled back in her chair, hunger forgotten. Even Flick set his paws on the table to get a better look.

At an unseen cue, the somber melody broke into a racing thrum. The song had no instruments, yet some of the singers managed to create a deep bass rhythm that held the troupe together like a drum line. The song raced away, a vocal epic that kept Kara on the edge of her seat.

The song built, growing in power until Kara leaned forward, waiting for the end but not ever wanting it to finish. Goosebumps raced across her arms. The vocalists held the last note, a cliffhanger, even as the room erupted into applause.

"That was beautiful!" she said to whomever would listen.

"Wait until you see what's next," someone said beside her.

She turned to see the Lossian prince. He had been so quiet throughout the speeches that she hadn't even looked over to realize he'd been in the seat next to her. Come to think of it, she'd never actually heard him speak before.

"Is Losse performing next, by chance?" she asked with a grin.

He smiled. "Perhaps."

One of the Kirelm singers flew toward the head table and hovered in the air as he came near.

"Next come the Lossian dancers, who pride themselves on performances that perfectly balance art and war," the singer said. He bowed to the table and flew off into the now-empty rafters. Kara wondered where the other singers had gone.

A mist rolled out into the crowd from nowhere in particular, weaving through the guests' feet as it consumed the floor. The fog swirled in the room's center, growing thicker. A Lossian woman appeared from the mist, even though there was no way for her to have even crawled through the thin fog without being seen.

The Lossian performer stood on one leg and rested the other on her knee. She held a sword just in front of her face, eyes closed, and did not move. The room settled to watch.

A harp played, though Kara couldn't see it. Its gentle notes hovered over the mist. In response, the Lossian dancer waved her sword in small arcs, her arm the only part of her body that moved. Wherever her sword pointed, another Lossian appeared, already mimicking her movements as they rose from the haze. In a matter of minutes, perfectly spaced Lossians covered the floor.

"How are they doing that?" Kara asked, leaning toward the Lossian prince.

He grinned. "There are some water techniques we will never share, even with you."

So, they had manipulated water somehow—a method used for war, no doubt. She shook her head and turned back to the performance. She would have to figure it out later.

A drum joined the harp's chorus in a combination Kara would have otherwise thought to be, well, strange. But as the two instruments blended together, the Lossians spun their swords and moved in unison, always with a gentle grace that rivaled even Twin's dancing. The drum increased its tempo, pulling the dancers along with it until they were jumping and flipping across the floor as one.

The drum slowed, its notes fading away until only the harp remained. The dancers, in turn, slowed as well until they stopped altogether. Just as the original figure had summoned them, she now dismissed them. They sank into the mist one-by-one until she was alone on the dance floor. She paused in the same position she had assumed at the start and bowed once the harp notes faded away with a mournful twang.

The room applauded yet again.

The dancer bowed once more. "My friends, please welcome Ayavel's seers for our final performance."

She dissolved into the fog as it faded away. Two lines of Ayavelians entered, breaking up the mist as they strode through it. They each carried a glass vase with a lid. Inside, a blue orb glowed in its clear prison, its light twisting around with no defined edge.

The Ayavelians bowed to the head table and lifted the lids from their vases. The orbs flew out, each spinning around the others until they became a floating blur that rose into the rafters. The smudge of light darkened the higher they went, turning black as they spun faster and faster.

A boom echoed through the hall as the spinning orbs collided near the ceiling. Darkness spread from the ceiling like dripping paint on a globe—it encircled the room until the last light faded.

Kara held onto her armrest. She didn't like darkness, not complete darkness like this. Gavin's hand found hers, but she brushed it away. She had Flick. She would be fine.

Unless this wasn't part of the performance.

Unless this was Carden, come to finish what he had started back in the Stele.

Kara tensed, heart racing, ready for battle as the long, painful seconds ticked past.

CHAPTER TEN

KARA

A brilliant, white light erupted in the room's center, blinding Kara. It took a few moments to blink away the sudden glare, but Kara gasped when she did.

An Ayavelian man held the light in his hands. It gleamed through his fingers, casting shadows across his face and across the audience members nearest to him. He slowly pried apart his hands, letting the blaze float above his palm and lifting it for all to see. It hovered and swayed to a silent beat. Its tendrils blew away as it moved, dissolving into the air. The man held a ball of pure energy that pulsated with life—Kara didn't know what else it could be.

Oh, thank goodness. Kara slowly relaxed, trying her best to enjoy the show.

More lights erupted around him, each in the palm

of an Ayavelian seer. They raised their hands, offering their brilliance for the audience to see. At once, they released the balls of light, which continued to hover as their masters faded away into the darkness.

The orbs pulsated, each burning brighter the longer Kara stared. They swayed in unison. A humming erupted from them, harmonized into different notes that made Kara's hair stand on end. The sound was at once chaotic and beautiful.

Red light splintered away from some of the wisps, followed closely by blue and yellow. Green light pulled away from others—and purple, and pink, and orange, until ribbons of color littered the room. The trails of color spun and wove around the audience as gasps and laughter rippled through the assembled yakona.

A purple trail made its way to Kara and slipped through her fingers. It wrapped around her hand, prickling her skin. It settled against her palm and hummed, the sound vibrating clear to her chest. Warmth spread through her—peace. Tension faded from her neck, and her spine straightened on its own, stretching taller than she had ever thought it could.

The light healed her, even when she thought herself to be perfectly healthy.

A smile spread across her face, and she looked down the table. All the Bloods and their families smiled, each marveling at the lights coiled around their hands or arms. Even Braeden looked down at his —a wisp of pure white.

Flick chirped. The ribbon slid off of Kara's arm and wrapped around his paw. He giggled, and Kara scratched his head.

Her purple light began to fade, as were everyone else's. The balls of white light dimmed in the room's center until they, too, faded. The humming continued even as the darkness around them pulled away and the room's candlelight returned. The humming didn't stop until the room returned completely.

Applause rippled through the crowd, but the Ayavelians smiled and offered only one modest bow before they left one-by-one in a slow procession. Kara blinked herself awake, lulled as she was into the happy peace the wisp had given her.

Gavin stood beside her and addressed the still-applauding diners. "Eat, my friends and allies! Enjoy yourselves tonight, for it is the first night of a new era!"

The hall erupted into even louder applause at the thought of food. Waiters from every kingdom brought out plates full of meats, breads, cheeses, fruit—the menu seemed endless. Roasts followed plates of vegetables, and servers set out more types of bread than Kara had ever seen in her life.

Flick peeked over the edge of the table as a waiter put an array of cheeses on Kara's plate. The little creature nabbed a slice and dragged it into her lap, where he remained while she slid him bits of bread and sliced apples.

She glanced around the table at the Bloods as they ate. The boxes in front of each setting went largely unnoticed. She wondered if there would be another large announcement when they started to open their gifts. She hoped not. It would be like a televised Christmas, where each person in turn opened all their gifts while others had to wait patiently before they could get to theirs.

Kara caught sight of Braeden again as Gavin leaned back to speak with an attendant. The Stelian stared at her little box at his place setting, eating slowly and without much interest in the food. She rolled a piece of her bread into a small ball and threw it at him. In reflex, he caught it before it hit him.

She rolled her eyes. Of course, he caught it. He looked at her, confused. She grinned.

"Open it," she mouthed, pointing to his gift.

He smiled and pulled the box toward him. He lifted the lid and raised his eyebrows at the contents but beamed when he pulled out the wrist guards Kara had found for him in the Vagabond's vault. He rubbed his thumb over the silver clover symbol embossed in the center of one of them.

"Thank you," he mouthed back.

She nodded. Even if she couldn't turn him, she wanted him to know he was still a vagabond to her.

Gavin returned to block the space between them and turned toward Braeden. "You've started opening presents already? Well, I don't want to fall behind. Bloods, let's ignore tradition in the light of the festivities and open our gifts as well!"

Oops. So, she had broken a tradition after all.

A few boxes crowded the space in front of Kara, and she moved aside her plate to bring each forward. One box was a shell fastened shut and attached with a hinge in the back, and she could only assume it came from Losse. She opened it with that in mind.

A large, opalescent pearl sat on a blue pillow nestled within the shell. Unable to quell the rising memory of her near escape, she cocked her head to the left. The prince smirked as he raised his glass to her, but she couldn't see his parents from this angle. She forced a smile and squirmed.

The prince leaned in. "There's a note under the pillow."

Kara resisted the impulse to sigh and peeked beneath the pearl. Sure enough, a folded piece of parchment separated the pillow from the polished shell case. Kara pulled it gently from beneath the pearl and read it.

We acted while thinking of your safety. We did not mean to offend, as we obviously have, and hope you find it in your heart to forgive us. We do not want you as an enemy.

"Thanks," she said, feigning a smile to the Lossian prince.

"You are welcome," he said.

When he turned back to his dinner and ignored his own presents, Kara reached for the solid silver box she guessed contained Kirelm's gift. Black silk lined the box's interior, and a note covered the gift inside.

May this remind you, Vagabond, that your way is not the only path, nor is it the only option for those around you unless they decide such for themselves.

Kara peered past the note to see a silver pendant lying on the black, satin pillow. The necklace twisted and arched in an abstract interpretation of what she assumed was a sun. She turned to Aurora, who wore the same necklace around her own neck. The Heir smiled and bowed in her seat. Kara nodded back but snapped the box quickly closed.

She reached for an elegant box with four, silver feet that, she assumed, had come from Aislynn. Inside was a single brown seed about the size of an acorn. Kara frowned as she tried to figure it out.

Did Aislynn give me a cherry pit or something?

"Do you know what that is?" someone asked.

Kara turned to see Aislynn standing behind her with a warm smile on her face.

"I'm afraid I don't," Kara answered with a laugh.

"It is a seed for a sanguini tree. When planted with a drop of your blood, a sanguini seed will grow as your family grows. As members are added, a bloom will appear on the tree. As they die, it will wilt and fall off. The tree will only die when your entire lineage also perishes.

"This is the only seed I have ever seen, and I wanted you to have it. I honestly don't know if it will work for you, considering that you have no blood loyalty, but I hope you take it as a token of my appreciation for all you have done."

"Aislynn, I couldn't..." Kara trailed off, her voice faltering at the thought of even holding something so rare, much less owning it.

"You may not refuse a gift from a Blood in a formal setting such as this," Aislynn said with a wink.

The queen walked back to her seat and sat beside Evelyn, who glared into the box Kara had left for the princess. Kara couldn't imagine what the girl found insulting about the simple silver drop pendant inside.

Kara turned back to her pile of presents. A large, familiar, black box that could only be from Gavin hid behind the rest. She didn't bother opening it because she already knew what was inside.

She leaned forward and caught Gavin's eye. He smiled, but all Kara wanted to do was smack him.

"Are you trying to insult me?" she asked.

"What do you mean?"

"Take this tiara away. I already told you the only thing you can give me. How did you even get it? I buried it at the bottom of my dresser."

Gavin sighed. "I know. I had a servant find it and bring it back to me. As Aislynn said, you cannot refuse a present formally given to you by a Blood tonight. However, you don't have to wear it. I would never insult you, Vagabond."

The king bowed his head low, his voice tense and quiet. They avoided eye contact for the remainder of dinner.

The chatter grew louder as partygoers finished their meals. Servants asked some of the yakona in the audience to stand. As they did, the waiters set their hands on the tables in unison. At their touch, the tables, linens, and dirty dishes dissolved into thin air.

Instead of a blank dance floor like Kara expected, someone had painted the Grimoire symbol onto the stone tiles. In each of the four circles of the symbol's clover, the artist had drawn a familiar castle. In the top right crest, Kara noticed a floating city of spires between spaces in perfectly shaded clouds. At the top left, bridges connected five trees painted in rich browns and greens. On the bottom left, a golden dome encircled a towering castle carved from coral and shells. And in the bottom right, a white castle with golden windows filled every inch of available space in the mural.

The musicians returned to their platform and began strumming a chord before they dove into a smooth waltz. Even as the music swelled, though, the floor remained clear of dancers. Kara fidgeted in her seat, ready to stand and get the dancing over with. Flick climbed up onto her shoulder.

"May I have the honor of the first dance?" a voice asked from above her shoulder.

She turned to see Braeden standing behind Gavin, his boot against the chair's foot as if to keep the king from scooting back. Braeden smirked and offered her his hand without looking at the king—something Kara avoided as well.

She grinned and stood. "I'd be delighted."

She walked around the table with Braeden, biting the inside of her cheek to keep herself from laughing as Gavin mumbled muffled curses. She turned in time to see him stand and bow to Evelyn.

Braeden spun Kara and pulled her in close, leaving her with no choice but to look up at him. He smiled and set his hand on her waist. Kara focused on her breathing instead of the fact that her skin tingled at his touch even from under her dress.

"We'll make it up together, right?" she asked him in a whisper.

"Right."

He pushed against her waist, leading her in a circle, and twirled her around the floor. It took all of two minutes for her to realize Braeden had lied. From the way he led her movement, he knew full well how to dance.

Kara cleared her mind, trying not to question the subtle pull on her waist as he directed her in their next swirl or dip. Even when she pulled in reflex against him, tripping on her own feet, he somehow pulled just hard enough to keep her from falling. His grip held her, always certain of the next step, and it wasn't long before she smiled like an idiot in front of hundreds of yakona.

On her shoulder, Flick swayed to the music and twitched his tail to match Braeden's motion. The little creature grinned and chirped, his stomach no doubt full and the rest of him therefore also happy. Judging by Flick's movement, Kara was pretty sure her pet had more rhythm than she did.

The song ended, and a faster one began. Dozens of yakona in the crowd now grabbed their friends and lovers and took over the gaps in the floor, having respectfully watched their Bloods dance the first tune. This new song had a faster tempo, and now Braeden led her in smaller circles at a quicker pace. Despite herself, she laughed as they spun. Flick's tiny claws dug into her shoulder as he held on, giggling harder than ever.

The party guests spun around the dance floor, all laughing and joking. Though all couples she came across were of the same race, at least they were near each other. It was a start.

"I'm impressed, Braeden. Look at everyone! No one's trying to kill each other," she said with a laugh.

She glanced to Braeden's face, only to realize he'd already been watching her. He smiled, carefree, and leaned in to whisper. The music hid his words from prying ears.

"I hear there's a garden hidden on an enclave farther up the mountain," he said.

She shook her head and laughed. "I heard about it, too."

"You wouldn't want to meet me there in fifteen minutes, would you?"

She pulled on the thick fabric of her dress. "Dressed like this? Of course."

Braeden bowed as the song ended and walked away through the crowd. Kara eyed him as he left, never wanting to let the sight of him fully disappear. Farther off, Gavin stepped in front of him and pulled him aside, but they were too far away for Kara to hear their conversation. Braeden just stepped around the king after a few quick words and continued into an empty hallway.

"You two seemed to be enjoying yourselves. Why did he leave?" someone asked.

Kara whirled to see Aislynn standing beside her, but the queen smiled.

"I'm sorry if I startled you," she said.

"It's all right. I—uh—he said something about needing water," Kara lied.

"I see. Well, nothing to worry about, then. May I borrow you? I'm terribly sick of dancing with my generals. They're all left feet, and they keep stepping on me."

Kara laughed. "I don't mind a bit. Will you tell me more about that seed you gave me?"

"Certainly. We have thousands of these trees in Ayavel, all of which came from a single tree planted long ago when our bloodline was new. As long as my bloodline survives, so will those trees bloom and tell me how many of my people are alive and well. Maybe someday you would like to see them? We are sorry to be the only kingdom not to welcome you."

"I would love to come. Maybe after the gala?"

"A visit sounds lovely, Kara. But I must caution you." The queen paused, the first sign of uncertainty Kara had ever seen on the woman. "You should not create more vagabonds. I know you can, but to do so would break what little trust the other Bloods have in you. Please, don't think my gift is a suggestion to take that path because doing so would destroy everything you've created. I do want you to have the seed, though, so perhaps you can see that the life of a vagabond is not so lonely as you might think."

Kara didn't reply—she didn't need to. She simply

nodded. Aislynn smiled and walked off, their conversation apparently over. It seemed like Aislynn had only wanted to share that nugget of wisdom, but Kara took it as her chance to sneak away.

But as Kara slunk away from the crowd, she couldn't help but simmer on Aislynn's warning. *You should not create more vagabonds.* It echoed her own concerns—a fear her mentor did not want to acknowledge.

CHAPTER ELEVEN
KARA

Kara did her best to sneak through the crowd, though in a throng of mostly green, white, silver, and blue dresses, there wasn't much sneaking involved. The hair on her neck pricked, and she turned to see Gavin's eyes trailing her path from his place on the dance floor. She picked up her pace.

Taking the main stairs would have been too obvious—even though it was the faster route, everyone would have known she was leaving. Instead, she wove through back halls and up rear stairwells she had explored during her sleepless night in Ethos, pausing now and again as she lost her way.

Great. At this pace, Braeden would think she had abandoned him.

She rounded a corner and stopped again, retracing

her steps in her mind to figure out where she'd wound up this time. When it came to her, she grinned—she was only a minute or two from the garden.

"Lost?" someone asked from around the bend in the hallway.

Gavin sauntered around the corner and leaned against the wall as he came into view. He crossed his arms, watching her with a smirk that made her skin crawl.

"No, I was just going for some air."

"What a wonderful idea. I'll come."

He pushed off the wall and wrapped an arm around her waist, leading her the wrong way down the hall with nothing more than a light pressure on her back.

"No, thanks," she said. She slipped out of his grip, falling against the wall as she escaped. He stepped closer, giving her no room to move, and put his hands in his pockets.

"Why?" he asked.

"Why what?"

"Why do you push me away? I made a mistake, Kara, and I apologized. Vagabonds forgive mistakes, do they not?"

"I do forgive you. It doesn't mean I trust you."

Or like you, she added to herself.

He chuckled. "I'm not as devious as you seem to think."

"Please, Gavin. I just want some time to myself."

It was a lie, but she wanted him to leave.

His smile faded in an instant. "Then tell me why you're toying with my brother."

"I—what?"

"He's fallen for you, Vagabond, and you should know better than to mess with his mind. If you break his blood loyalty to me—"

She laughed. When his eyes narrowed, she coughed to cover her outburst and spoke in as even a tone as she could muster. "I would never break his blood loyalty to you."

"Leave him be," Gavin said.

His words were neither an order nor a request—in fact, the tone made Kara lean deeper into the wall. It was tender and calm, with a sweetness to it that slowed her breathing.

Gavin inched closer. "To survive this war, Kara, you need a king. Braeden might give you happiness, but I would give you the strength to do what must be done."

Kara had no answer. Her lips parted, useless and without a comeback. Gavin turned back down the hall the way he'd come, his footsteps receding until there was only silence.

Only a dozen feet and a stairwell separated her from Braeden, but Gavin's words made her walk slowly as she mulled them. He had done nothing but manipulate and trick her—there was no way he knew what needed to be done. He understood the arena, sure, but he frequently made as many poor decisions as she did.

So why is he trying so hard to make me want him?

His attention was yet another trick. It had to be. Besides, Braeden was everything she wanted. She fully admitted that—she couldn't deny him any longer.

She rounded the last stair and looked out onto the garden. A woman stood by the wall, the light from the grand hall shining through the windows but falling short of her body. The woman stood in the shadows and watched the forest, alone in the garden.

Kara didn't know who this woman could be or how she had stumbled up here. What bothered Kara most, though, was Braeden's absence.

She hesitated in the stairwell. The woman still hadn't turned, evidently preferring to watch the trees blowing in a late summer wind beneath the basking glow of the moon.

"You clean up good, darling," the woman said.

Kara's breath caught in her throat—she knew that voice too well.

The woman shifted so that the light from the hall below poured over her face. Deidre's perfect brunette curls danced around her pale face. Her fingers tightened around an already-drawn sword.

Deidre strode forward, her face twisted in that terrifyingly beautiful smile.

Kara gritted her teeth. "What did you do to Braeden?"

The isen laughed. "He never made it, I'm afraid. He's got visitors of his own to worry about."

Part of Kara wanted to fight. She probably stood a slim chance against Deidre now that she'd had some formal training, but she panicked at the thought of Braeden in trouble. She grabbed Flick off her shoulder and turned to run, but Deidre lunged before she had the chance. The isen wrapped her arm around Kara's neck and squeezed, dragging her backward into the garden. Pressure closed on Kara's throat. She coughed but couldn't pull away.

Flick barked, but Deidre swatted him to the ground. He landed with a whimper on the overgrown grass.

Anger burned in Kara's chest, despite the pain. "I'm not going back to Carden!"

"Oh, you're not going to Carden, but Niccoli isn't much nicer," Deidre said in her ear.

Kara choked as Deidre's grip tightened. The name rang a distant bell—Niccoli was an isen guild master. An ancient and powerful one, if she remembered correctly.

She pulled at Deidre's grip on her neck. "What does he want with me?"

"You're so much more than you know, and I hate you for it," Deidre said with a growl.

Blood rushed to Kara's head. Spots dotted her vision, but she had to know what she was up against.

"Is he here?" she asked.

"No. Niccoli doesn't run his own errands, but he is impatient. It's time we leave."

In answer, Kara elbowed Deidre in the gut. The isen doubled over, loosening her grip just enough to let Kara stumble away.

Flick jumped back onto Kara's shoulder and barked as Deidre reached out to grab them. Kara focused on the gala hall. She envisioned the mural on the dance floor and wished she was there, hoping Flick would get the message and—

A loud crack broke the silence of the mountain garden.

Kara's stomach flew into her throat. She was falling. Flick dug his claws into her hair as he fell with her.

She fell through the air above the gala hall, just as she had imagined—even though she'd meant to appear on the floor. Flick must have seen the air above the hall and taken her there instead. How literal.

They had a good hundred feet or so until they hit the ground. Without taking in more than the throng of bodies and swinging swords below her, she turned to Flick and tapped his forehead, her thoughts focused on an image of them standing safely on the floor below.

A sharp crack filled Kara's ears again. Her gut lurched, and she saw the ground a second before she landed on her stomach. Pain shot through her arms and neck. She groaned. Her breathing slowed, but the sting faded as she lay there. After a moment, she forced herself to one knee.

Flick brushed his head against her leg, purring and chirping to see if she was okay.

She scratched his ear. "We need to work on that, buddy."

A cursory look around confirmed her fears—she knelt by the wall, in the middle of a battle. Smoking yakona with gray skin fought beside minotaurs, wolves, and the other monsters that had hunted her when she'd first escaped the Stele. The hordes overran the gala, their gray skin contrasting sharply with the colorful garments of the screaming yakona running from the onslaught. The partygoers sprinted in every direction for any stairs they could find, only to be cut down by a circle of Carden's soldiers blocking every exit.

Blood. Bodies. Screams. This was worse than she realized—and based on the carnage, Kara didn't know if she and Braeden were going to make it out of here alive.

CHAPTER TWELVE

KARA

Blood streamed down the main stairwell where Kara had made an entrance into the gala hall earlier that night. It pooled in dips on the floor, the colors of each yakona kingdom's blood mixing until it became brown sludge.

Bursts of gray or green dust appeared here and there, but Kara couldn't figure out what caused them. A wave of Kirelm yakona took to the air from somewhere nearby. They aimed for the rafters as if trying to escape, only to be followed by dozens of smoking gray yakona who changed form and followed them into the air.

Kara took a deep breath. She had to find Braeden. She glanced through the crowd but couldn't see him through all the bodies. She pressed her back against the wall, unsure whether she should run or try to fight.

If she'd been paying better attention, like Braeden always told her in their training, she would have noticed the tall Stelian slip out of the crowd on his way toward her.

"You do look good in red," he said.

A hand grabbed her shoulder and reeled her around. Carden stared down at her, steam pouring from the pores on his neck and shoulders as he wielded a large, black blade with silver engravings in his left hand.

She paused. Her body froze, and words failed her as she gaped at what remained of the hand holding the sword.

The skin on Carden's left hand had puckered in a festering boil that distorted the natural curve of his palm. Thick scars ran from his knuckles to his elbow. Jagged lines in the meat between his thumb and pointer finger implied that something had ripped his hand open—a dog maybe, or a wolf.

He had killed the Hillsidian queen and taken her Sartori sword. If anyone but the Blood or the Vagabond touched a Blood's Sartori, it would burn their skin beyond belief—it had to be what caused the wound. That Carden could still use his hand was a miracle.

Carden grabbed her hair with his other hand and

pulled her closer. Pain tore through her neck as he dragged her nearer. Hair fell over her neck, loosened from the pins Twin had so carefully set earlier.

"I don't like it when people stare," Carden said with a sneer.

Kara grabbed his wrists and pulled against him, but he wouldn't let go. Her fingertips pulsed as her skin touched his. Her body's natural instinct at direct contact was to see his most influential memory, but she resisted. It took most of her newfound control, but she did not want to see what had shaped this man's cruelty. It would undoubtedly scar her for life.

Flick growled. Carden lifted his hands, and a shot of air blew Flick off her shoulder. Her pet yelped as he flew back.

"Flick!" Kara twisted in Carden's grip, but he pulled her closer.

"I don't make the same mistake twice. I remember how that little thing saved you last time, but no one will save you now."

Panic flooded through Kara. Her knees shook, but she had to focus. No, she wouldn't be saved, not in this chaos. She had to save herself, and then she would go find Flick. If anyone stepped on him, she'd kill something.

Kara focused her panic into her palms. She had trained for this. All that sparring with Braeden and time spent with the Lossian tutors was wasted if she couldn't access her magic when she truly needed it, terrified or not.

Heat bounced across her palms as Carden dragged her toward a side tunnel. No—he would not take her.

Purple fire erupted along her hands and spread to his shirt. His sleeves caught in an instant. Flames churned over his arms before he could react. She slipped out of his grasp long enough to focus the stagnant air into her palms. She would shoot first for his heart, even though she wasn't sure if that would kill a Blood.

Carden snuffed the flames with a sharp huff of breath, as if he'd simply blown out a few candles rather than been on fire.

Kara braced herself to run. She had the Grimoire on her side, but that didn't mean she could take on a Blood. She was in over her head. Still, she summoned a blade from the air around her and aimed for Carden's chest, even as he reached again to grab her hair.

"You're mine, Carden!" someone shouted behind her.

Gavin shoved Kara aside moments before she released the blade. The force of his push threw her into the nearby wall. She slid to the floor as Carden, caught off guard, parried desperately for a few moments before he got the upper hand on his inexperienced foe.

Carden and Gavin swung and ducked, which gave Kara a moment to roll away. She peered back the way she'd come and took a sharp breath when she found Flick on the stones near a tunnel. Voices clamored down the hallway.

Kara ran to her pet and lifted his tiny body in her palms. He didn't stir, but his chest did move. At least he was breathing.

She had to find a safe place to hide him, but bodies and broken swords covered most of the floors and stairwells she could see. She glanced back in the tunnel, searching and hoping for—

Yes!

Bricks had fallen out of a section of the wall at waist-level. Kara ran to the niche and cradled Flick in one arm so that she could feel around the hole and make sure it wouldn't crumble further. Satisfied with its safety, she set Flick inside.

"It'll be okay, little buddy. I'll come back for you," she said. She scratched his ear and ran back into the fight before she could question herself.

Kara had to get the Bloods out of there. If Carden killed them, he would kill everyone with their bloodline. She stopped in her tracks, however, when Carden drove Gavin past the entrance to her tunnel. The Stelian grinned as he parried a blow from Gavin and kicked him to the floor.

"Your mother was a better fighter, boy, and look how that ended!"

"I'll kill you!" Gavin yelled. He charged again. Vines pushed from his pores, growing over his skin and shining with a glossy sheen. Carden attacked, but Gavin's new armor deflected most of the blows.

Kara eyed the battle, lost in their fight despite the melee around her. Though he could probably end Gavin in a matter of minutes, Carden never directly attacked. He swung instead with the flat edge of his sword so as not to cut the Blood. If Carden were here to kill everyone, why not get it over with?

A hefty blow to Gavin's jaw from the flat side of Carden's sword sent the young Blood flying onto his back. He skidded for several feet before his head finally hit the wall with a crack. The gash pulsed with green blood, but the skin stitched itself together as Gavin writhed in pain. Carden set his sword against the Blood's throat and stepped on his right arm. Something snapped. Gavin cursed and yelled.

Carden pointed his sword at Kara. "You're next."

The heat drained from her face. She leaned back against the wall and summoned the Grimoire. As it settled into her palm, she ripped it open and grasped at straws as she tried to think of something to ask it. There had to be something in it that could help.

Carden grunted and circled Gavin as the Hillsidian tried to stand. "Your book won't help you, Vagabond, but I might let you live since you've learned a bit more about it than the first time we met."

A dark figure darted past Kara and landed a kick on Carden's chest. The Stelian flew backward and slid across the rock several feet away.

The figure stood and turned to her, and Kara sighed with relief as she recognized Braeden. He recovered from his attack and lifted Gavin, hurrying the now-unconscious king into Kara's hands. He set Gavin on top of her lap and caught her gaze for a second.

She groaned under Gavin's weight. "Braeden, don't set him on me. I can't move—"

"I don't want you to. Gavin will be fine in a minute. Don't let anything near him or all of Hillside will die," Braeden said.

"But—"

"Please, Kara." Braeden paused and cradled her cheek in his hand, brushing his thumb tenderly along her skin. He tensed his jaw and turned to face Carden.

A clamor of metal and screams beside Kara caught her attention, and she twisted her body from beneath Gavin's limp form to see General Gurien usher Aurora into a nearby tower.

"You must run, Aurora!" Gurien's hand wrapped tightly around her upper arm as he dragged her away from the melee.

"I will not run when my people are in danger!"

"You will because your father commands it!"

"Hang him. I will help!"

"Aurora," the general begged.

"No!"

He pulled her in close, even as she glared at him. "In this, I believe your father is right. If you could fight, if you could help, I would let you honor your people. But this is a deadly battle few will survive"—he cupped her neck with his hand—"and our Heir must be safe!"

Aurora's eyebrows pinched, and tears pooled in the corners of her eyes. She nodded.

Gurien sighed with relief and gestured to a group of Kirelms who stood at the ready nearby. "This old tower will take you to the roof. Go! I will hold off the Stelians as best I can, but you must hurry!"

The guards surrounded her, and they ran through the hallway to where scattered moonlight drenched an empty tower. Kara could see the posts of what had once been stairs winding to the roof, but now it was nothing but an empty tower. Windows dotted the wall between the tower and the hall where Kara sat, pinned against the wall, and she was forced to watch the ensuing escape through flashes in the empty frames.

As Aurora entered the tower, the doors opposite the stairwell opened, and a horde of smoking Stelians funneled through. One lunged and stabbed a Kirelm guard clean through the chest. The Kirelm soldier paled, and as soon as he dropped to the floor, bits of dust cracked away from his face. Kara gasped and tried to lift the unconscious Gavin from her lap to go help. Though he groaned as she heard the snap of his arm mending itself, he wouldn't budge.

She glanced back to Aurora, trying to compose the techniques she had learned at Losse into something useful, but the screaming clouded her focus. Panic flooded her limbs. She didn't even know what technique would be useful from such a distance.

Aurora grabbed the fallen guard's sword, spread her wings, and jumped into the air. As she flew, the Stelians nearby changed form and became Kirelms themselves. They stretched their dark wings, reaching for her with their arms. As one came too close, she swung her weapon wildly. The sword sliced his arm clean off. He screamed and fell to his knees, but more soldiers took his place and swarmed after her.

In another flash of movement through the windows Kara could see, a soldier grabbed Aurora's arm and yanked her to him. Another tied a rope around her wings as she tried to escape. A third gagged her. The first soldier wrapped a blindfold around the princess' eyes and took her in his arms, even as she struggled to get free. Carden's army flew higher, still climbing toward the roof.

Kara tried again to push Gavin off her—the royals were disappearing. And not only did Carden not want them dead, but he was kidnapping them. Aurora likely wouldn't have escaped even if she'd made it to the top of the tower.

Gavin groaned as Kara punched him in the shoulder. He leaned his head into Kara's lap and opened his eyes, just staring at the ceiling.

"Gavin, we have to get out of here!" Kara said. She shook him, trying to make him come to.

He caught her gaze and narrowed his eyes, finally seeming to wake up. But instead of nodding, or debating, or saying anything for that matter, he pushed himself off her without a word. He stood and scanned the crowd.

Before Kara could say anything, a familiar voice yelled in agony. She turned out of instinct toward the sound, only to catch Braeden duck a swing from Carden as he backed toward a stairway. The stairs wound up the wall, carved as they were into its side without a railing for all to see. If Carden forced Braeden up there, he would be trapped.

She pushed herself to her feet, but Gavin grabbed her wrist and pulled her close.

"Gavin, what—?"

"This is what I need you for, Kara. Help me kill Carden, and I will give you absolutely anything."

"How am I supposed to do that?"

"You're the Vagabond. Come up with something!"

Carden smacked Braeden in the face with the flat

of his sword and knocked him onto his back. He skidded into the bottom of the stairs and cursed loud enough that Kara could hear it from a hundred or so feet away.

Gavin grabbed her elbow. "I can show you how to use your power. Let me control you."

"Like hell!"

"I know how to manage a battle, Kara. If you take my bloodline and become my subject, I can direct you in the fight. We can end Carden right here, right now. All you have to do is put this on." He pulled from his pocket the tiara she had rejected so many times.

She pushed him away. "I knew it! I knew that was still cursed!"

"That's not important! Right now, you can either wear it or watch Carden kill my brother. He's no match for a Blood!"

Kara glanced back to Braeden. He parried, but the color drained from his face even as she watched him. It was like seeing him realize he would lose. Carden let him keep his Hillsidian form, though Kara couldn't figure out why. Braeden always moved a second or two behind his father's attacks, barely blocking each blow at the last possible instant.

Carden was toying with Braeden.

Kara didn't have many options, but she couldn't take Gavin's offer. If they didn't kill Carden, she would be Gavin's slave for as long as he wanted. And if they did kill Carden, Braeden would become Blood and everyone would find out the truth anyway. He wouldn't be able to hide as a Hillsidian when his body adjusted to the new power that came with being king.

She summoned the pearl blue sword Braeden had taught her to use from the light and energy in the air.

"Sorry, Gavin. We aren't going to do this your way."

"You're mistaken."

Gavin grabbed her wrist and twisted, sending her to her knees. Pain shot into her elbow. The sword shattered and dissolved into the air. Gavin knelt in her peripheral vision and reached for her head. Something in his hand glittered like a diamond in the hall's candlelight.

Not happening.

She shifted her weight and used her own momentum to swipe out his knee. He fell, and his grip loosened. Kara rolled beyond his reach and bolted into the melee, dodging the twisting bodies as she ran toward Braeden.

If this was the end, she and Braeden would go out together.

CHAPTER THIRTEEN
BRAEDEN

Braeden dodged a blow from Carden's sword. He still couldn't fully understand why his father let him fight at all, but he had a guess. His father probably wanted to distract him and would likely wait until his soldiers finished whatever they'd come to do. Carden would no doubt then fully break the gala guests left alive with the grand finale—making Braeden change form to add the insult of betrayal to the injury of losing the battle.

Though Braeden knew what would come, he couldn't decide how to stop it.

A stairwell loomed behind him. If Carden forced him up those steps, Braeden would lose all tactical advantage and be put on display at the same time. He'd tried everything he could think of, but he always ended up near the stairs. Carden owned this battle.

The Blood threw a bolt of dark smoke into Braeden's chest. The blow knocked him off his feet and kicked the breath out of him. He slid into the bottom stair.

"That human girl is your weakness, Braeden. You could have escaped," Carden said with a sneer.

Braeden's heart raced as he stole a quick look to where he'd left Kara, but only an empty wall with a green bloodstain remained.

"It doesn't matter. I'm strong enough to face you," he said.

Carden grinned. "You are by no means strong enough to win this."

The Blood lunged, aiming the Stelian Sartori at his son's shoulder. Braeden parried, and the two struggled up the stairs. Braeden cursed under his breath. He'd already lost.

With a laugh, Carden erupted into black flame as he donned his daru. His skin darkened further as the flames danced across his arms, and his bones cracked as he grew another two feet. His clothes stretched with him, bending to accommodate his new size.

Braeden buckled under the strength his father pulled from him and dropped his sword. His knees shook. His muscles tightened against the strain of another person using his energy. Several moments passed before he could pull himself back to his feet, though he didn't know why Carden would even allow such a thing. Arrogance, most likely. When he stood, most of the Stelians around Carden were on their knees.

"Acknowledge what you are, Braeden, or I will kill you here and now!"

"I won't," he said, barely loud enough to hear.

Carden swung the flat end of the sword toward Braeden's jaw. He ducked the blow, leaning backward as he reached for his own sword.

Braeden spun with everything he had left, but his father easily stepped out of range. Carden swung again, pushing Braeden up the stairs step by step until those in the gala hall below came into view. Mostly partygoers covered the dance floor, rips and stains dotting their lavish dresses or suits. Those without weapons stared at him, eyes wide as he fought for his life. Only a few Stelians remained, and those darted into a nearby tunnel. Carden's massive army had already disappeared—and fast. Carden must have been planning this for as long as Gavin had been trying to secure the hall for the gala.

Carden's influence tugged on Braeden's gut. It wasn't a command—it was a test. The desire to change into his Stelian form burned through him. Justifications spun in his mind about how he would be stronger and more able to fight, but he knew better.

"Stop!" Braeden yelled.

He swung at Carden's face and brushed the king's

cheek. Black blood dripped from the wound even as it healed.

Carden paused, his glare enough to make Braeden forget what his next move had been. He tensed his jaw as he scrambled to look for an opening, but a burning command tore through him.

Change.

This wasn't Carden's influence. It was a direct order—a mandate that no yakona had ever disobeyed.

Braeden fell to his knees and leaned into the stairwell wall as he fought the urge to turn. For a moment, he did. His body twisted to obey, but he kept it under control. His mind pushed against the order, strong enough to preserve the Hillsidian body providing him a home for the last twelve years.

But as soon as the thrill of hope made his heart flutter, his skin began to change color. He cursed as the hope dissolved into panic.

His veins boiled as his skin darkened to a charcoal gray that matched his father's. Even as he watched, it grew darker. Black flames erupted from the pores along his arms and chest. Fury and guilt crushed against his chest and shredded his resilience. In an instant, his lifetime of lying came to light.

The shame within him reasoned if he could kill his father, he might find some redemption, if only from himself. It was his only thought, his only purpose for existing in that second. He let his daru take over—it was too late to hide the truth now. He might as well embrace it.

He swung.

The two Stelians attacked and ducked until Carden twisted Braeden's sword from his hands and threw it into the throng below. Braeden had only a moment to catch his father's sneer before the Blood kicked him in his gut. The blow knocked him off the twenty-foot-high ledge.

As Braeden fell, his father disappeared above him with a crack. Smoke billowed in the space where Carden once stood.

Braeden hit the stones below, and the surface broke beneath him. The stones in the floor bent from the force and knocked the air from his lungs. His body disconnected and wouldn't obey. Pops and snaps echoed within him as he healed, but he couldn't move.

His father stepped into view above him.

But how—?

"You will find your way home to me," Carden said.

A small, black creature with a large head and a long tail crawled onto Carden's shoulder. With yet another crack, Carden disappeared, leaving behind only a thin cloud of smoke.

Someone screamed. Actually, several people screamed. Some yelled, but Braeden closed his eyes. He still couldn't move. Eventually, the voices faded until only a dull murmur echoed through the massive room.

After a few moments, his fingers twitched. He smiled and moved them. He curled his toes in his boots and sighed with relief as they obeyed. Out of instinct, he shrank back into his Hillsidian form. Gasps and murmurs echoed in his mind.

"Traitor!" Gavin yelled from somewhere in the crowd of bodies.

Braeden flinched at the word and opened his eyes. He pulled himself gingerly against the wall as Gavin barreled toward him. Partygoers stood back to let Gavin through.

Pebbles cascaded from the roof as the Hillsidian's voice echoed through the hall. "Coward! LIAR! For twelve years you have lied to me and to my family, and here you will pay your debt for our kindness!"

Braeden could barely move. Gavin donned his daru, and green thorns pushed from his pores as he drew his sword. Vines pulsed over his skin, wrapping around him, shielding him like armor until all that could be seen of the Blood were his blazing green eyes. Hillsidians standing nearby dropped to the floor, unable to stand without the strength he sucked from them.

Gavin cocked his sword over his shoulder. Judging by the angle, Braeden guessed Gavin planned to simply cut off his head. Even though it wasn't a Sartori

—Carden still had Gavin's Sartori blade—it would likely work.

Braeden's wounds still needed time to heal. He didn't stand a chance against a Blood as healthy as Gavin. He could let Gavin end him. He could finally be done with Ourea, with politics, and with all the lies.

A memory of Kara's smiling face flashed in his mind. He wasn't done yet.

He took a deep breath. Turning to his own daru was the only way to defend himself, so he let his anger and his shame take him, too. His skin rippled with heat, and the raw power for which he would never openly admit he lusted, tore through him. He conjured a black sword from the air and gripped it. The thing blazed like his skin.

Gavin swung. Though Braeden couldn't move from his space by the wall, he parried the attack. Metal clanged as Gavin's blade hit the solid energy in Braeden's sword. Bystanders flinched. Braeden managed to parry two more blows before his elbow shook, and the last of his strength dissolved. His sword shattered with a hiss and evaporated into a cloud of steam.

Gavin kicked Braeden in his gut. He doubled over and forced himself to find Gavin's face, but the king wouldn't look him in the eye. Gavin set his sword on Braeden's neck, likely aiming for the final blow.

Braeden couldn't move. He'd pushed his body to its limit, and now it only shook and twitched as he tried to roll away. All he wanted was to escape and find Kara, but the last flame of Braeden's resilience flickered out in a heavy dose of shame. He would always be the enemy. As Gavin lifted his sword, Braeden didn't even put up his hand to block the final strike.

But Kara did.

Gavin stopped mid-swing as Kara stepped in front of Braeden without a word. Her mess of blond hair and the torn shreds of her dress appeared out of nowhere. She faced the Hillsidian, her loose curls and arched back, blocking Braeden's view of the king.

"Get out of the way," Gavin spat.

"No," she said, her voice calm.

"He's a Stelian!"

"I know."

Gavin cursed. "How long have you known?"

"That's irrelevant. The point is killing Braeden would be a mistake."

"He's a traitor. If you don't move, I'll take you down with him."

She crossed her arms. "That's enough! He has always been loyal to you. He saved your life tonight. Carden would have killed you!"

"His father killed Mother!"

Gavin raised a hand to brush her out of the way, but a blue light pulsed through Kara's fingers. It struck him in the chest as he touched her and shot him backward into the growing crowd of onlookers.

Kara arched her back. "Braeden didn't kill her. There's a distinction."

"This is your last—"

"You would never sleep again, Gavin, knowing you killed the brother who has always protected you."

No one spoke. A distant humming echoed in the silent hall. Gavin stood, and Braeden could see the king now—he glared at Kara as if he wished he could kill her, too. She didn't flinch, even as Gavin brushed past her.

Gavin knelt and whispered in Braeden's ear. "Having your life is more mercy than you deserve. I think your shame will be punishment enough until your trial."

The king walked off and signaled into the crowd of nearby bodies, but Braeden didn't realize why until Captain Demnug shuffled forward with a set of spiked shackles.

"Those aren't necessary," Braeden managed to say.

"I must," Demnug said without looking him in the eye.

Braeden's old friend knelt beside him and waited for Braeden to offer his wrists. Braeden sighed. In his state, he couldn't run. If he did somehow manage to escape, Kara would likely become leverage to lure him back. Gavin evidently knew there was something brewing between them.

A broken bone popped back into place somewhere

in Braeden's arm. He stifled a groan but lifted his hands to the captain in surrender.

Demnug snapped one cuff onto Braeden's wrist in a fluid motion. The spikes bit into Braeden's skin. Pain tore through his arm. He flinched and sucked in a sharp breath. Black blood snaked down his arm from the holes around the handcuffs' barbs.

The captain snapped the other shackle into place. The agony doubled. Braeden tried not to yell. His veins burned from the poison in the spikes. Ringing boomed in his ears.

He looked up to see Kara watching him from beside Gavin. She stood so close—only a dozen feet off. She leaned forward, as if she wanted to run to him, but Gavin grabbed her arm and pulled her back. She flinched at Gavin's grip, but smiled nonetheless when Braeden caught her eye.

Despite the pain and humiliation he'd endured in the last few minutes, Braeden's heart lifted the barest inch from where it lay at the pit of his stomach. Kara would be all right, and he had nearly disobeyed a mandate from Carden. He hadn't known it was possible to resist at all. The thrill of hope shot through him again. If he survived whatever came next, perhaps he could find a way to disobey his father entirely.

CHAPTER FOURTEEN
KARA

A Hillsidian guard shoved Kara into her room. She stumbled and leaned against a wall, balancing Flick in her hands. She had pulled her still-unconscious pet from his hiding place moments before Gavin had assigned a man to watch her.

The guard shifted in the doorway. "We leave in a few hours, Vagabond. Pack your things. You are not to leave this room. I will give you five minutes to change, but you are to otherwise be supervised at all times."

He left and closed the door behind him without waiting for an answer.

The Bloods' presents to her littered the bed. Someone must have put them on her bed during the gala before all hell broke loose. Kara sat beside the boxes and laid Flick on a pillow before she buried her face in her hands.

What a disaster. Standing up to Gavin might have saved Braeden's life, but it had been political suicide. She had become a prisoner, an accomplice to the secret Braeden had kept from the world for so long. She hadn't seen the other Bloods on her way to her room, but she could only imagine they would be as furious as Gavin.

She could teleport Braeden out of trouble when Flick woke up, but that wouldn't prove anything. It would make her a fugitive, effectively undoing everything she'd achieved. So, she had to be delicate. She had to do this the Bloods' way and make them see reason.

Kara took a deep breath and forced herself to her feet. She couldn't wallow in self-pity. She had to change, after all—if she waited, she would have an audience.

BRAEDEN

Two guards tossed Braeden into a prison cell beneath the head table where he'd sat hours earlier. Gavin strode through the throng of soldiers gathered at the door.

"Leave," he ordered.

The guards bowed and obeyed. Within seconds, the prison door closed, and Gavin strode deeper into the cell. He knelt and reached for a chain around Braeden's neck—the chain on which Braeden kept an ornate, golden key that could open the lichgate into Hillside.

Gavin yanked on the key. Its chain snapped, slinking into the king's hand, and he stuffed it in his pocket. Braeden's neck stung where the clasp had broken, but he didn't flinch.

"Hillside is no longer your home," Gavin said.

Braeden shook his head. "I've only ever protected Hillside. Why should what I am matter, Gavin?"

The king put his hands behind his back and grimaced. "You lied to my family for over a decade. Of course, that matters! You should be ashamed of yourself, Braeden. And look at you, still in your Hillsidian form. It's insulting. Change!"

"I wish you hadn't found out this way, but I won't change. This is who I am, brother."

"Don't call me brother."

"I've done so for twelve years. Why should it be any different now?"

"Because you're a traitor! Why would you lie to us for so long?"

"Because I knew this is how you'd react!" Braeden's voice echoed through the cell and down the hallway.

Gavin shook his head and rubbed his temples. "The Heir of Kirelm is gone, as is the Heir and Queen of Losse. What part did you play in that? Were you so desperately pushing the Vagabond's agenda in a ploy to get all the Bloods in one place?"

Braeden shook his head, but the movement sent a wave of exhaustion through him. He needed sleep. His legs and neck and arms all ached.

"Stop lying!" Gavin shouted.

"I'm not! Did you forget that I came to Hillside when I was twelve? I was escaping Carden, not working for him!"

"Stelians are dishonorable," the king said with a growl.

Gavin kicked Braeden in the stomach. He fell to the stone floor and curled around his gut, but the agony doubled as the poison barred his body from healing.

"That's right. You don't heal so quickly when you're chained, do you?" Gavin asked.

He laughed and kicked Braeden again. The pain swelling in Braeden's core blocked out all thought in his mind.

"What do you know of this attack?" Gavin asked.

"Nothing!"

Another kick hit Braeden in the side. Ribs cracked.

"What do you know?"

"*Bloods*! Nothing!"

Thorn-covered vines pushed through the rocks at Braeden's feet, bending with every move of Gavin's hands as the king controlled them. They shot toward Braeden and wrapped around his neck, pinning him against the wall. Their spines bit into his skin, and more black blood dripped down his suit.

More of Braeden's energy faded with each breath, but he would use the last of it to keep his Hillsidian form, even if it meant dying. If he died here, it would be as he saw himself.

Gavin knelt. "This is your last chance to tell me what you know about the attack."

"Nothing," Braeden muttered, weak.

The vines unwound themselves and retreated back into the earth. Braeden sighed with relief. Gavin stepped back and brushed the dust from his ripped suit.

"I suppose we're lucky no more were taken," Gavin said.

Braeden suppressed a laugh. "You mean you're lucky Evelyn wasn't taken."

"I didn't say—"

"You don't need to. I've known for years, but I kept your secret because you were my brother." Braeden spat out the word, hating it. "You've already trapped Evelyn, so don't drag Kara into this spiteful pit you call a life! Whatever plans you have for her, stop!"

"You will stay away from the Vagabond," Gavin ordered.

"I won't. You're using her, like you use everyone around you. Leave her out of this."

Gavin knelt again until he met Braeden's eye. "She could never love you. You're pathetic. Your father's stunt has cost the kingdoms what little faith we had in each other—what faith she worked to build. He destroyed us. And the Bloods blame me for their losses. Me! After the month I spent securing this place, the only possible reason Stelians could have gotten through is because you told them where to look."

"I didn't," Braeden spat.

"This last month, you weren't hunting isen, were you? You were helping him. You probably threatened Kara to keep your secret when she found out. Is that right?"

"No!"

Gavin pushed himself to his feet. "We leave for Ayavel in a few hours for your trial. It will be the first judicial act under the Treaty of Ethos and will define this new era as much as your kind destroyed our celebration tonight. Our parents' war is ours now. Don't expect to survive it."

The room spun as the poison dug deeper into Braeden's body. Gavin strode out of the cell, and two guards replaced him.

Braeden closed his eyes, but his head reeled. He

leaned against the wall and waited. Maybe he slept—he didn't know. Pain shot through his body with every movement, diluting his thoughts.

Though Gavin said they would leave in several hours, it seemed like only minutes passed before two hands grabbed Braeden's arms and hauled him to his feet. He didn't try to walk, and he could barely open his eyes. Blurs crossed his vision as the guards moved him. The arms disappeared seconds before he landed on something hard—wood.

Braeden forced his eyes into focus. The first brush of a red sunrise broke through the metal bars of his cage. He sat in a wheeled prison pulled by two griffins with Kirelms on their backs. Mounted guards and foot soldiers lined a long road ahead of him, all shifting their feet as they waited for a signal to move.

Kara sat on a horse a few dozen feet off, her hands tied loosely before her. She glanced back to him. He tried to smile at her through the pain, but he knew she wouldn't see it. Gavin rode up beside her and took the reins from her horse.

"Move out!" he yelled.

The procession stirred to life at his order. The sun rolled across the sky as they trekked on, and Braeden became somewhat lucid despite the spikes that scraped away at his resilience. He focused his energy on maintaining his Hillsidian form during the silent march. Kirelm soldiers flew overhead, probably as lookouts, but only soldiers and a few politicians remained in the company. Braeden wondered if the rest of the survivors had been sent home.

He healed more slowly with the spikes, but he did heal. These cuffs must have been weaker than anything Carden had. With a twinge of disgust, Braeden was grateful for the time he'd spent in Carden's cuffs if it meant he could resist these.

He lay back and stared at the ceiling. The bars' shadows inched across the wood as the day passed, and he eventually closed his eyes. With each hour he lay still, another grain of lucid thought returned.

Braeden didn't look around until a cool breeze dried the sweat on his neck. He opened his eyes in time to catch a cherry blossom tree pass by. He glanced out the back of his mobile jail—the trees lined a paved road and framed a distant sunset. An entire day wasted in a half-asleep stupor. He cursed under his breath. At least he'd healed most of his injuries on the trip.

Dozens of tree blossoms fell off in the growing breeze. Braeden peeked through the front of the cage and over the two griffins to see a white palace spiraling into the sky. Bleached walls topped with golden spikes rose almost to the clouds. He caught his breath despite the desperate chill of his situation.

A gate in the front wall stood open as the convoy ahead of him walked through into the city. As his cage bounced onto the empty streets, Braeden caught glimpses of several stunning, three-pupiled eyes staring from behind curtains of gold-trimmed houses and the glass displays in storefronts. The entire city had retreated indoors, but he didn't have time to wonder why.

Guards yelled. The gate slammed shut, its boom echoing through the streets. The griffins leading Braeden's cage turned away from the main company and hurried down a side road inside the main wall. He looked back, but he couldn't find Kara before the procession he'd travelled with disappeared behind a line of buildings.

KARA

Kara cursed under her breath as Braeden's jail turned down another road, but Gavin grabbed her wrist.

"Don't say a word," he commanded, his voice dangerous and stern.

She pulled against Gavin's grip, but resisted the impulse to light him on fire. Her second instinct to punch him in the face wasn't much better, though. The consequences of doing either would outweigh the satisfaction. She bit her cheek instead.

Gavin leaned into her, and his breath rolled over her neck as he whispered. "I will kill him before the trial if you visit him."

She grimaced. "What are you?"

"A politician. My country is first. Lives are second."

She twisted in his grip out of reflex, and he let her go. For a moment, she thought he would actually give her space. But he dismounted and gestured for her to do the same.

Kara slid off her borrowed horse, and Gavin grabbed her arm the moment she landed. He turned and led her into the palace. They passed through the main doors and into a large hall, where a massive pair of opened double doors lined each of the walls. A hallway stretched on through the doorway ahead of her, its walls lit by fire-filled sconces. The room on Kara's right held the customary three thrones of any yakona throne room. Rows of tables filled the room to her left, and the sweet spices of roasted chicken rolled over her as she came near. Her stomach growled.

Gavin dragged her into the hallway and through the first door he found. They wound up in an office covered with blue wallpaper. Its only furniture was a wooden desk, but Gavin didn't make her sit. He shut the door and let her go once they were inside. She rubbed her arm.

"Listen closely, Vagabond," he said.

Kara tensed, but let him speak. He was a Blood—as

much as she wanted to think she had more power, she didn't. She wouldn't win a fight with him. Even if she did win by some miracle, several more Bloods waited just outside.

Gavin kept his eyes locked on hers as he spoke. "Braeden's trial is tomorrow. He will be found guilty—I'll make sure of that unless you do something for me."

Kara couldn't breathe. This was it. This was everything the Vagabond had told her would happen—Braeden had become leverage.

"He's your brother," she said. The last word slipped out like a hiss.

Gavin continued as if she hadn't said anything. "Publically declare yourself as loyal to me and take my bloodline—the other Bloods would never let me force it upon you, not now. Allow me to control you as my subject. Do it, and I will convince them to let him live. He will never be free, but he won't die."

"But I would become your pawn."

"It doesn't have to be that way, but you would obey me. Yes."

Gavin watched her, waiting for an answer, but this wasn't a choice. This was blackmail. It was the same choice Carden had given Braeden when they'd found the Stelian amulet… "Obey me, or let her die."

"You have until midnight to decide," Gavin said.

The king grabbed her arm and pulled her into the hallway. The rest of the Bloods waited on the other side of the door. Aislynn, Ithone, and Frine all glared at Gavin, no doubt wondering what he'd said or done, but Kara looked down the hall.

She needed to say something, anything to make the insanity stop, but no words would come.

Kara's heart thudded in her ears. So much for her playing by their rules. She might be able to change their minds at the trial without Gavin's help. He might even be bluffing. With any luck, he didn't really have that much sway over the other Bloods.

She blinked back tears as Aislynn turned without a word and led them down the hallway. Everything she had worked for crumbled around her. Her choices were now slavery, renouncing her vagabond cause, or letting Braeden die.

That wasn't a choice.

CHAPTER FIFTEEN
BRAEDEN

Braeden leaned into the bars as his cage rumbled through a street. He could only close his eyes and wait for the jostling to stop. When it did, the door to his cage opened. Guards dragged him out and threw him into yet another dungeon. He pulled himself against the wall and managed to open his eyes.

Demnug leaned over him, eyes heavy with regret as he clamped yet another set of shackles around Braeden's ankles. Braeden couldn't stifle the sharp cry as the spikes cut through his pants to pierce the skin beneath.

"Your trial will be in the morning," the captain said, "and I have been ordered not to bring you comfort of any kind. I'm sorry."

"I understand," Braeden said.

Demnug sighed and followed his men from the room. The cell door closed, and a torch retreated along the dark hall leading to Braeden's prison. Beams of moonlight sauntered through a window near the roof.

Braeden resigned himself to falling asleep against the cold stone wall with the hope that Kara would visit him, whatever the repercussions might be.

§●

KARA

Kara hid the fact that Gavin's grip on her arm stung. His fingers pinched her skin. She would have to heal bruises.

Gavin dragged her through a hallway trimmed with gold molding. Aislynn led him while Frine and Ithone flanked behind. Kara didn't bother looking at the other Bloods. It wasn't as if they would help her.

Aislynn stopped at a door in the middle of the corridor, its red wood and gold frame identical to every other door in the hall. The Ayavelian queen turned the handle and pushed it open, but Kara only caught a glimpse of a red canopy bed.

"She will be isolated enough, here," Aislynn said to Gavin.

"You all are making a mistake," Kara said. She did her best to keep her voice steady.

"Be thankful you aren't chained in a prison cell yourself," Ithone retorted.

Frine nodded. "You knew what Braeden is. You lied to us and are therefore untrustworthy."

Before she could respond, Gavin pushed her through the doorway and caught her eye. He glared at her as if she had killed the queen by keeping Braeden's secret.

Braeden didn't stand a chance if she couldn't change their minds.

"Hillsidians will keep first watch on her." Gavin looked to someone in the hall and nodded into the room.

"You are not as important as you seem to think, Blood Gavin," Frine said.

Several Hillsidian soldiers marched into the room, ignoring the Lossian Blood's remark. Captain Demnug stood ahead of his men, but he wouldn't look Kara in the eye.

Ithone bristled. "Who are you to claim first right? How do we know you won't have them steal her away?"

"Enough!" Aislynn yelled.

No one spoke.

The queen gestured to Kara. "We can stand bickering over who will guard the poor girl, or we could actually do something useful and discuss what we are to do next. Thrones are being built for you three as we speak, so I suggest we retire to my study until those are ready."

Frine shook his head. "But the Vagabond—"

"—will not be leaving," Aislynn interrupted.

Ithone paused at the doorway. "If you insist, my lady."

"I do insist. I don't care which of you sends guards up next. She's not leaving. There is no way for her to escape Ayavel without my knowing."

Aislynn caught Kara's eye and glanced to her satchel, and it was all Kara could do not to sigh with frustration. Aislynn somehow knew about Flick's powers.

"Lead us, then, dear queen," Frine said.

"My general will take you to my study, but I must first see to Evelyn. I will meet you there shortly."

Frine, Ithone, and Gavin disappeared from view, led off by someone Kara couldn't see, but Demnug and his guards remained. Aislynn gestured for them to leave.

"It is entirely unnecessary that you be in here. I'm certain the Vagabond is exhausted and needs her rest. I can't imagine it's very relaxing to have four armed men watching her sleep."

Demnug tensed. "But Blood Gavin said—"

Aislynn glared at him. "You are in my home, and

you will obey me whilst you are here. I have only ever shown the same courtesy while in Hillside, Captain."

He hesitated but ultimately nodded and turned to Kara after a moment, but his eyes fell to the floor. "There will be guards posted outside the window, ready to kill you should you attempt to escape. That's a fair warning, not a threat."

Kara tensed. "Thanks."

The guards filed out of the room, and Aislynn shut the door once they were through, locking herself in the room with Kara. A muffled cry came through the door, and someone tried the handle without any luck.

Kara took a deep breath and braced herself, her hands tightening on the bed's baseboard. So Aislynn had lied about needing to see to Evelyn—she had just wanted to get Kara alone.

Aislynn sighed. "My dear, that was for show. You have nothing to fear from me."

"You're awfully convincing."

The queen bowed. "It's merely a defense. I must be able to control a conversation if I'm to get anything out of it."

"What do you want?"

Aislynn walked closer, lowering her voice to a whisper. "I want you to go to Braeden."

"You do?"

"He needs you now more than ever. I know you two are more than—"

"We're not," Kara said sharply.

Too sharply.

Aislynn narrowed her eyes. "Very well. I meant only that he needs you. You cannot escape Ayavel on your own, and I cannot let you go for fear that the other Bloods would discover us. But you can keep him calm and clear-headed for tomorrow's trial. He will need quite an argument if he's to survive."

"Where is he?"

"The dungeon. I chose this room on purpose. Do you see that mirror?"

Kara turned. A full-length mirror mounted to the wall reflected her frown and tangled hair. Golden vines framed the glass, all wound around a single, red stone inlaid at the top of the structure.

Aislynn continued when she didn't answer. "Push the ruby to open a hidden passage. You will come across a few side tunnels, but do not turn. The straight path will take you directly to Braeden's cell."

"Won't they notice I'm gone?"

"I'll forbid them from entering and take the key. You have only an hour, though, until Frine or Ithone will grow restless and want to send their guards to take the captain's place. They will not wait outside."

"Why are you helping us?"

"So, you and Braeden are an 'us?'"

"That's not what I meant."

"You don't need to say it aloud, though the words might help Braeden."

"Aislynn, answer my question."

"You should not be ungrateful to those who wish to help, Kara. You have an hour."

Aislynn turned without another word and left, closing the door behind her. Metal grated against wood as the lock turned from the outside, sealing Kara in.

She took a deep breath, peeked into her satchel, and lifted Flick from its depths, grateful that no one had mentioned him or tried to take him away. She set him on one of the bed's pillows and curled his tail around him to keep him comfortable.

A plate of food—just bread and some cheese—sat on a tray by the bed. Kara grabbed what she could and slid it into her bag before she crossed to the mirror. She pushed the ruby, and sure enough, the glass slid into the wall without a sound. Kara turned back to the door, but no one spoke in the hallway.

Beyond the mirror, stone steps led away into a curving stairwell lit by sparse sconces. As she had no idea how long it would take for her to get to the dungeon, she needed to hurry.

She started down the stairs. Once she crossed through, the mirror slid into place and the stairwell plunged into near-darkness. Kara ran her hands along the wall for balance and hoped this wasn't a trap.

BRAEDEN

A shuffling sound in the cell pulled Braeden from his frantic sleep. Moonlight sliced through the barred window, casting stripes of shadow across his feet. The spiked cuffs shifted in his wrists and ankles, but as long as he didn't move, he didn't lose blood. Numbness had long ago set into his arms and legs, but now it trickled toward his shoulders.

Despite his best efforts to remain still, he twitched and fidgeted each time he thought of Kara. The political scene was aflame, and she was caught in the middle of the bonfire. He didn't know what would become of her. He stared into the moon, or what shards of it he could see from the dungeon. Craters covered the moon's face like freckles.

The scrape of rock grating against stone broke the silence. A figure loomed in the shadows beneath the window. He couldn't tell who it was. For all he knew, Gavin was back for more information Braeden didn't have. He tensed his jaw at the memory of his beating earlier and prepared himself for his brother's hatred. But instead of thick eyebrows and a general expression of disgust, he saw a beautiful pale face with gray eyes.

"Kara!"

He could barely move or breathe, but the whisper still rang through the empty dungeon in a fierce echo. She shushed him and wrapped her arms around him in a gentle hug.

"How are you holding up?" she asked, pulling a loaf of bread and some cheese from her bag. She broke off chunks and fed him.

"I've been better," Braeden said around a lump of bread. His stomach growled, and he hoped she had more food in her bag.

She leaned on his wrist near the spikes. He winced. More dark blood trailed down his arm.

She flinched. "I'm sorry."

"It's f—"

"Man, I'll never get used to that. Black blood," she muttered to herself.

He didn't answer.

She grabbed the bread. "Sorry, Braeden, that was rude."

"Don't apologize. You're right. I haven't showed you enough of what I am, and I'm tired of running from it."

Kara narrowed her eyes. "What does that mean?"

"I'm tired of denying what I am. I am a Stelian. This isn't my natural form. And though the other Bloods don't deserve it, I want to do what it takes to redeem myself in their eyes."

"You'll never make them happy. It's like they need to hate you. You're a scapegoat."

Braeden laughed weakly. "Thanks."

"I was trying to come up with a way to convince them that you're good, but maybe we should just leave. Aislynn hinted that we couldn't teleport out of here, but maybe I can call Ryn"—Kara sighed and stopped fidgeting with the bread—"but it all feels so hopeless. How can we possibly do anything with everyone in such an uproar?"

Braeden tried to laugh, but a tremor of pain ran through his core and made him cough instead. "It's exactly what Carden wanted. Besides, I'm not out of tricks yet, Kara. Don't give up."

"Do you have a plan to escape?" She eyed the cuffs on his wrist.

"In a way. If we run from them, we have absolutely no allies. We'll have nowhere to hide. I might never get them to love me again, but at least they will protect us. In the loosest sense, we'll have someone to trust."

Kara stuffed a piece of bread in his mouth, though he assumed it was to stop his talking. She kept feeding him bits of the food until the small portions she'd brought were gone and she had nothing else to keep him silent.

She sighed. "The man you grew up with disowned you the second he discovered who you really are. Without a second thought, he threw you in chains and is putting you on a fake trial. How can you ever trust someone like that?"

"You've been eavesdropping on how Blood trials work," he murmured and smiled wryly.

She sneered. "I don't know if I'd call it eavesdropping, but back to the point. You can't trust Gavin with anything, even if you do get out of this your way."

"You're right. I can't. But the rest are trustworthy. And they need you, Kara. They need to believe there's something more to life than bickering."

"I wanted to research and ask the Grimoire what to do. I promise. But I haven't had a moment alone. All of the Bloods are even having me watched while I sleep," she shivered, "and besides, everyone thinks I'm evil because I'm the only one not stuffing you full of pitchforks. They locked me in my room and threatened to kill me if I tried to escape."

Braeden tensed against the shackles, but his rush of anger outweighed the pain. "Who did?"

"Demnug warned me. The rest didn't want me to know, Braeden."

He sighed. "I'm sorry you're in the middle of this. I knew this would happen eventually. I didn't want you to see it."

"You knew?"

"It was only a matter of time."

Kara brushed a bit of hair from his face, but her eyes slipped out of focus. "I wish Adele and Garrett would get here already. They have to know something's wrong."

"We can't rely on them to fix our problems. We have to get out of this ourselves."

He caught her gaze and couldn't suppress a smile. Her freckles dusted her nose like they hadn't wanted to disturb the flawless face when they'd landed. Her eyebrows dipped over her deep gray eyes, and for a second, he wasn't afraid.

"The Bloods will come around," he whispered.

She leaned her head against his and nuzzled into him.

"It'll all work out," he promised.

He brushed her nose with his and leaned down to kiss her again. She pulled back.

He cocked a weak grin. "What, I don't get a last request?"

"No," she whispered. Her lips twitched into a smile, but she couldn't hold it.

"Why not?"

"Because last requests are for the dying. You aren't going to die if I can do anything about it."

She kissed his forehead and disappeared into the shadows beneath the window. Rock scraped against the stone. When she was gone, Braeden's world was silent and empty again.

He should have told her to leave Ayavel and save herself. When the Bloods killed him—because they probably would—she would be their next target. And if she didn't obey, they would kill her, too.

A strong man would have made her leave, spurned her, rejected her—done anything at all to make her stop caring about him. But Braeden wasn't strong. At some point in the last few months, he'd fallen for her. Seeing Kara gave him a renewed faith that his fate was worth escaping.

CHAPTER SIXTEEN

KARA

Kara's mind raced with panic as she tore back up the stairs. She had already gone over her allotted hour, and she wasn't even back yet.

The mirror slid aside as she came to it. Muffled yelling poured through the closed door from the hallway. She could make out Gavin's voice, as well as Frine's. Ithone was out there, too, as was Aislynn. They all seemed to be yelling at Demnug.

"...strict orders not to..."

"...was Blood Aislynn..."

"...no key? How can you..."

"Gentlemen!" Aislynn's voice pummeled through the wood so loudly that even Kara took a step back.

Kara raced to the bed and sat down next to Flick's pillow as the mirror slid closed behind her. She set her satchel under the bed to hide it from view. She also took off her grimoire pendant and slid it beneath a pillow, in case any of the Bloods tried to take it from her. If they asked where it was, she would lie and say Gavin took it already. He deserved as much.

The door unlocked, and a flood of yakona poured into the room. The Bloods crowded closest, their faces twisted with anger as they glared at one another. Only Aislynn stood apart from the mob. She shot the smallest of winks at Kara before she turned back to the Bloods and frowned.

"The girl deserved a good rest, if only for an hour. No one can sleep while being watched! So much for that, though. All of your yelling managed to wake her up!"

"You had no right to leave her alone without discussing this with us first!" Gavin shouted.

"Watch your tone, boy," Aislynn said, glaring.

"I am a Blood! However close you may have been with my mother, you will not address me as a child!"

"Guys!" Kara shouted.

All eyes turned to her. As much fun as it was to watch the melee, she needed them to calm down.

"Your lack of formality annoys me," Frine finally said.

"Bloods," Kara corrected. She resisted the impulse to roll her eyes.

"What, Vagabond?" Ithone snapped.

"Aislynn was just trying to let me sleep. As you can see, I haven't gone anywhere, nor do I plan to. There are plenty of guards watching my window—yes, Gavin, I noticed—and it's not like I can escape a fortified castle. So, if you don't mind, keep your guards out there, and let me go back to sleep. I'm exhausted, we've all had a hard couple of days, and I'm sure I'm the least of your worries at the moment."

Kara suppressed a grin. With as many lies as she had just rattled off without flinching, she wanted to celebrate.

"If she had been able to escape, she would have done so by now," Aislynn added.

"But you said she couldn't escape," Gavin said.

Aislynn sighed. "That was my point."

"Guards will check on you at random intervals, Vagabond," Ithone said, as though the armies of all four kingdoms were at his command.

"Let her rest," Aislynn said with a nod to the door.

"Ah, no, after you." Gavin stood behind the queen, apparently learning from his mistake the first time he'd left the room before Aislynn.

The Bloods and soldiers filed out. Once the door closed, someone locked it yet again from the outside.

Kara leaned against the headboard and released a long sigh. Flick's paw twitched, and he whimpered. Kara smiled and scratched his ear as he blinked his eyes open.

"Welcome back, little buddy," she said.

He squeaked and burrowed back into the pillow.

Kara grabbed her grimoire pendant from its hiding place and slipped it around her neck once more. That had been way too close. She needed the Vagabond's help.

If guards were going to check on her at random intervals, she didn't want them to see her reading the Grimoire. It was a miracle they hadn't already taken it from her—they'd all likely guessed she kept it in her pendant by now. It might have been the frenzy of the last few days or the constant power struggle that had distracted the Bloods, but she didn't want to remind them.

Her best bet of speaking to the first Vagabond was for him to bring her into the Grimoire, as he had in Kirelm all those months ago. Back then, he'd wanted to learn more of her situation. But now, it was her turn to ask questions.

She lay on the bed and took slow, deep breaths. There was no telling if this would work, but she had to try.

Vagabond, we need to talk. Pull me in.

Kara repeated the words in her mind until sleep tugged at the corners of her eyes. Her eyes stopped darting around, even though she tried to move them. Goosebumps raced along her neck. The light from her bedroom dissolved, plunging her into darkness.

It worked!

"What is it, Kara?"

The first Vagabond's voice echoed around her. Mobility returned. She stretched her fingers and sat up, but the bed had disappeared. She floated in a void, and the Vagabond was nowhere to be seen.

"Braeden is in trouble," she said, hoping he could hear her.

"I know," he responded.

She nodded. Of course, he knew. He saw what she saw and probably took a lot more from it than she did.

"What do I do? How can we save him?" she asked.

"I have an idea, but it is risky and may not even work. It also comes with a price."

"What price?"

The Vagabond stepped into view as if he'd simply walked out of the shadows. He glanced over her at first without answering, his skin solid. In her head, he always appeared as he was in life: tanned, scarred, and without a hood. He crossed his arms and grinned.

"Wouldn't you rather hear my plan first?" he finally asked.

"By all means."

"If you allow me to possess you during his trial, your power would be magnified because I know how to use it. I could force them to listen to you. But because you would undoubtedly need to use magic, the possession would take nearly all of your energy and may still not be enough to change the Bloods' minds. I will defend Braeden, but it wouldn't be like the time I saved you from his daru. You would likely faint afterward. You would be unconscious for several days and weak when you wake up. You would need someone to protect you during that time."

"I can find Twin. She—"

"No one with the Bloodline. Because you haven't made more vagabonds, your only hope is for the muses to come."

She ignored his jibe. "That's a pretty big risk."

"Yes. Adele will sense you need her, but she may not be able to come. If they don't, you will be vulnerable. Is Braeden worth it?"

"Of course, he is."

"Why do you want so badly to help him?"

"He protected me. I'm just returning the favor. It's what friends do."

"I know when you're lying, Kara."

She rolled her eyes. "I'm not—"

"Answer me truthfully for once! Do you love him?"

"Just tell me what to do, Vagabond."

"It is a simple question."

"You can't throw that word around! This isn't the time or place to talk about relationships. Be serious for a second and tell me what to do!"

He huffed. "I will, but as I said, it comes with a price."

"And what's that?"

"You already know."

Kara paused, and it took a few moments before it clicked in her mind. "No! I won't make more vagabonds!"

"Then Braeden will die."

"You b—!" Kara cut herself off. Calling him names wouldn't solve anything.

"You don't have much time left to debate your options, my girl. Turn someone you trust. Task your representative to create one vagabond for every grimoire I made. It will be your job to distract the Bloods while he or she creates your army. Do that, and I will help you save him."

"If I don't, you'll really let him die? After all he's done for us?"

"Yes."

Kara cursed under her breath, though loud enough for him to hear.

"This is what I meant, Kara, when I told you vagabonds cannot love. This is the lesson I learned with Helen, a lesson which broke me. Please, don't make me do this to you! Just learn from my mistakes! Braeden is leverage. He is your weakness. If you care for him, if you love him, others can use him to make you do what you otherwise never would."

"You still don't have to sacrifice an ally. Not now, not to prove a point."

"You are too stubborn to learn any other way. Whatever your choice in this matter, I win."

"You're sick."

"I'm not. I tried to teach you this lesson already, but you wouldn't listen. You had to learn it for yourself, the hard way. This is real. This is life or death. This is what others will do to you if you choose to save him. So, ask yourself—is he worth it? There is no escape from a promise you make to me."

Kara took a deep breath and wrapped her arms around herself as she debated her options. She had no plan. She couldn't save Braeden without the first Vagabond's help, but either way she chose, her mentor truly would win—she either had to create more vagabonds or let the boy she cared for die.

Making more vagabonds was wrong. She would only be risking their lives as well as tempting the Bloods to go to war against her. Kara would become a pawn to her dead mentor's will if she didn't uphold her beliefs. But could she really let Braeden die to avoid that?

"Damn you," she said under her breath.

"So, you've decided?" the first Vagabond asked.

"Yes."

Kara took a deep, steadying breath. Regret stabbed at her, but she didn't have any other choice.

CARDEN

Carden strode through the dark hallways in his castle, the sconces on the wall casting shadows along the floor as he made his way to the dungeons.

He scowled, not altogether pleased with how his attack on the Gala had gone. It was good enough, however, and he had what he needed to make his plan work. The Bloods now knew what Braeden was, and not even that vapid Ayavelian Blood could protect him now.

In the end, only that mattered.

With their hatred of Stelians, the so-called united kingdoms would no doubt try to kill Braeden. They would fail, of course, but it would drive Braeden right back home. Carden had taken everything Braeden had tried so damn hard to preserve—and soon, the boy would realize Carden was the only one who wanted him.

And when Braeden asked to return, Carden would break the boy's spirit once and for all. He would become the Heir he was meant to be: ruthless, brutal, and cruel. No one—not even the Vagabond—would recognize Braeden when Carden was done.

Now, all he had to do was wait.

Carden chuckled darkly, ready for a bit of fun after all his careful planning. He had earned a break, and it was time to play with his new toys.

As he reached the end of the hall, he threw open the door to the dungeons below the Stele, relishing the muffled sobbing that echoed up the stairwell. It was soft and feminine, and he could almost taste the girl's fear.

"Who to play with first?" he asked, his voice carrying through the shadows. "Aurora, dear, how about you?"

CHAPTER SEVENTEEN
BRAEDEN

The creak of the prison door opening woke Braeden before he realized he had once again fallen asleep. Light from the brilliant morning streaming through the barred windows of his cell blinded him for a moment. As he blinked away the spots in his vision, a fleet of guards entered the room. Each took slow steps, no doubt unsure of what to expect from a chained Heir.

Demnug pushed his way through the group and knelt, releasing the ankle constraints before he lifted Braeden gently to his feet. Braeden sighed with relief, and the black scars framed by the holes in his pants slowly healed.

The soldiers led him out of his cell and through dozens of halls, likely knowing they didn't stand a chance if he broke free of the arm restraints. But

Braeden walked on, un-prodded and led without even a chain between himself and the captain.

The procession took ages. They climbed stairwells and turned down long halls in an endless labyrinth that reminded Braeden of the maze of tunnels in the Hillsidian castle. Though the poison in his blood slowed his gait and weighed his feet, he forced himself to remain in his Hillsidian form and focused on staying calm.

They passed a cluster of Ayavelian maids in aprons who gasped as they saw the black blood trail from his wrists. They muttered and clicked their tongues as he walked by, but he ignored them and focused on composing what he would say to the Bloods.

Demnug rounded a corner and walked through a massive set of doors into a grand throne room. Four elegant chairs were perched in front of Aislynn's three thrones. Gavin, Frine, Ithone, and Aislynn each sat in these forward chairs, waiting for him to enter.

Evelyn stood behind Aislynn, one arm on her aunt's shoulder as she glared with unmasked loathing at Braeden. The spaces behind Frine and Ithone were empty, their Heirs taken as they were in the battle. Soldiers from every kingdom lined the walls, a dozen or more bodies thick. Braeden would never have been able to fight his way out of the throne room, but he didn't intend on trying.

Though it was custom for soldiers to always stare

straight ahead, every guard in the room watched Braeden as he stopped before the members of the royal jury. Demnug bowed and walked into the crowd without looking back, his guards following him until Braeden stood alone.

Gavin groaned in disgust. "Don't insult us any further, Stelian. Show us your true form."

Braeden took a deep breath and focused on keeping his voice steady. "This is my true form, brother. This is who I have been for the last twelve years, and this is who I will be, whatever you four decide today. I kept the secret of my heritage because I knew this would happen, regardless of everything I've done to protect Hillside. I only kept my secret to protect myself, never to hurt anyone."

"Hillside is no longer your home, nor should it have been," Gavin said. The statement stung as much as the spikes, but Braeden tried not to let the pain register on his face.

Braeden turned to the other Bloods. "I want to do whatever I can to redeem myself. Blood Gavin informed me that some were taken yesterday. I will go to the Stele and free them, if you will let me."

Ithone laughed bitterly. "How is this not a trick to simply get home? Your father's reputation precedes you, after all. I doubt there is anything you could do to redeem your derelict honor."

"I have honor."

"Pray tell," Ithone said.

"I've killed a hundred or more isen to protect Hillside and its neighbors."

"No doubt with the powers you inherited from your father," Blood Frine pointed out.

"I saved Blood Gavin from my father yesterday with those same powers," Braeden countered.

Gavin tensed his jaw but didn't answer.

"Bloods, I must confess something," Aislynn said. The other three yakona on the platform turned to her.

Braeden's heart leapt.

"You recall the time I spent jailed in Carden's prisons, tortured for information on your locations. I would not speak, and when his guards failed to break me, Carden himself caused me the worst pain I have ever felt in my life."

Braeden's heart fell again. She'd lied. Except for the slivers technique, Carden hadn't tortured her; Braeden had. He looked at the queen and saw Aislynn's eyes slip out of focus.

She took a deep breath. "That night, when I lay curled in my cell and thought that I would surely break, a young woman snuck in and helped me escape. It was none other than Braeden's mother, the Lady of the Stele. She ushered me into a carriage and returned with the then-young Braeden, whom she wanted to also free from Carden's wrath.

"Braeden's mother smuggled us both out of the

Stele. Though isen ambushed her, he and I were nestled in a hidden compartment and stayed safe until Richard happened upon us. She gave her freedom to save my life, so I lied to Richard to protect Braeden. I told the boy to shift form. In doing so, he could claim to be a Hillsidian orphan I rescued from the Stele. I feel as though, in a way, we rescued each other.

"I caution you all, then, against killing a yakona who has proven himself so unlike his father. To do so would destroy the value we place on goodness in the world, as scant as it has become."

No one spoke or questioned her account. The other three Bloods stared at the floor, and a glimmer of hope sprung to life in Braeden's gut as the men fumed over this new information.

Gavin glanced up first, his brow furrowed. "Braeden, I don't doubt that somewhere in your heart is an ounce of kindness, but I also firmly believe that any good you have done was for selfish reasons. Though I appreciate Aislynn's rescue, you had nothing to do with it. Killing you would bring us one step closer to eradicating evil from our world entirely. I must consider the greater good."

"Would killing him not be an evil act?" Aislynn demanded.

"No," Gavin said, but he didn't look Braeden in the eye.

"How do you vote, then?" Frine asked.

Gavin gestured to Braeden. "I vote to kill this traitor. Blood Ithone, do you wish for the Heir to the Stele to live?"

"No. Blood Frine?"

Frine watched Braeden, dissecting him with his glare before finally whispering his reply. "No. Blood Aislynn?"

"Yes," she said with a sigh, her vote outweighed.

"Then, let's not delay this any further," Gavin said.

He signaled to Demnug, who drew his sword on command. The captain hesitated, and Gavin rolled his eyes. The conflict in Demnug's face dissolved into disgust. Braeden figured Gavin now controlled the man's mind, but he no longer had the strength to care.

Demnug flew backward as if pushed by an invisible force. He hit the wall with a groan and fell into the crowds of soldiers.

Kara stood at the open double doors and lowered her hand from where it pointed toward Demnug's crumpled body. She walked into the room, her figure shrouded in black wisps framing her like a cloak. She stopped just in front of Braeden but didn't once look at him. Judging by the swirling black wisps clinging to her body, the first Vagabond had taken over.

"You have defied me for the last time!" Gavin yelled.

He stood, but Kara raised her hand in response.

The stone of Gavin's seat sprang to life, quickly growing over his arms to lock him firmly in place.

"I am above you," she said. Her voice had two pitches: her delicate soprano, and the churning bellow of a man.

The soldiers murmured. Some aimed their weapons at her, but Kara continued after a short pause.

"I am above your rules and pettiness. I have only ever tried to unite these nations in peace, and you have only ever fought me tooth and nail. You are disgusting, all of you.

"When Kara first found the Grimoire, it gave her only a basic understanding of this world. She had to discover Ourea for herself, and in doing so, she saw the truth to which you are blind. But my book did tell her this: the power she has been given must be used to protect those who need it, not those who quarrel. She loves and respects all life. That is what it means to be a vagabond; of that, you cowards are afraid.

"You, Ithone," she continued.

Braeden's heart skipped a beat at the lack of a title before the Blood's name. The first Vagabond must have been furious.

Kara pointed to Ithone as she spoke. "Your ancestors killed my vagabonds all those centuries ago. If any in this room owes me kindness, it is you. The griffin you think I stole came to me willingly and is a friend. I did not steal him; he would simply not return to you.

"Frine"—she turned her attention to the blue yakona—"you, not your ancestors, tried to kidnap my only surviving vagabond in an effort to weigh her as leverage in your petty political duel with Kirelm. You would not be here if the drenowith had not reminded you of your debts to them. That, to me, is true shame.

"And you, Gavin," she turned to the Blood trapped in his chair, "youngest of them all, you have failed most of any. He who would kill his own brother, adopted or no, is one I refuse to protect. Braeden is the only reason you are alive, and you know this. Yet you weigh his fate as if you deserve to do so."

Gavin fought in his chair but couldn't break free. "Kill them both!"

The Blood's fury channeled into his soldiers as he controlled them. The Hillsidian guards along each wall turned with the same expression of disgust and rage as their king. Soon, the soldiers of Kirelm and Losse joined suit in the attack. Only the Ayavelian soldiers remained along the wall.

"Kara, you have to get out of here!" Braeden said.

She didn't move as the guards charged. Instead, she lifted her hands out firmly beside her. The air around her whipped to life. Soldiers flew backward into the wall, just as Demnug had minutes earlier.

As the guards regrouped, Kara twisted her palms to

the floor. The flawless tile along the room's edges tumbled into whatever lay beneath the throne room. The ground shook, and the entire castle trembled from the force. Dust fell from the roof and walls. Guards screamed and cursed. Thuds echoed from the floor dozens of feet below.

The dust settled, though bits of tile still rained from overhead. Most of the throne room survived; even in her rage, Kara had been careful with Aislynn's beautiful palace—or, at least, as careful as she could.

Kara grinned and looked at Gavin. The Blood sat in his chair, no longer struggling. He took deep and steady breaths and leaned as far from her as he could with his limited mobility.

"Compromise," she ordered.

He turned his attention to Braeden but didn't respond.

After a few moments, Ithone spoke instead. "You said you could return my daughter to me, Stelian. How would you do such a thing?"

The poison in Braeden's blood zapped more energy with every second, but he forced himself to answer. "I know the Stele by heart."

"If you rescue my daughter, I will forgive your lies. Especially after such a vote of confidence," Ithone added with a glance to Kara.

"As would I, should you return my queen and my son," Frine said, watching Kara with wide eyes.

The few yakona who hadn't fallen through the floor turned to Gavin, who twisted in his chair at their scrutiny.

"Blood Gavin?" Aislynn asked, her lips twitching in what seemed like a painful effort to hide a smile.

He gritted his teeth. "I'm warning you, Braeden. Cross us and you will not live long. You have two weeks to bring the three lost ones back, so I suggest you leave quickly."

Braeden nodded.

Kara shook her head but released the chair's hold on Gavin seconds before Demnug climbed out of the hole. With a nod from his king, the captain released the shackles from Braeden's wrists.

Braeden sighed with relief and knelt on the floor as the day-old wounds began to heal. The black blood pooled in his scars until his olive skin grafted over and all signs of the spikes were gone. Inwardly, though, he was still weak.

He looked up in time to catch Kara as she turned to each of the Bloods and locked eyes with them. Her eyes narrowed, each glare making its victim lean back in his or her seat. The Vagabond must have taken over every ounce of Kara's body to channel this much power.

"Do not make me return," she commanded.

She turned to Braeden, her hands shaking. He glanced down—her knees shook as well. It seemed as though the first Vagabond was losing his grip on Kara's mind.

"We must go," she said.

He nodded, and Demnug led them from the room without a word. Braeden toyed with what to say, but no words could articulate his gratitude. He owed Kara and the first Vagabond his life.

The three of them turned into the hall and walked a short way before Kara glanced over her shoulder, as if checking to make sure they were alone.

"Good luck," she said.

With that, her eyes snapped out of focus and rolled into the back of her head. She fell through the dissolving black wisps of the cape that had engulfed her, and Braeden caught her just before she hit the hard, stone floor. His limbs buckled, still weak from the cuffs' poison, and he fell under her.

Demnug knelt beside them. "What happened?"

Braeden shook his head. He tried to lift Kara in his arms, but with all he had suffered in the last two days, he couldn't. Demnug reached out and picked up Kara instead, so that Braeden could walk. He smiled, and Braeden managed a smile in return before his old friend headed off again down the hallway.

They turned a few corners, but every step left Braeden dragging his feet a little more. Demnug glanced back and nodded to the next door on the right. Braeden nodded and followed him into a bedroom, where the captain placed Kara on a bed.

"I'm glad to have you back, Master Braeden," Demnug said with a grin.

Braeden smiled. "I never left, and stop using that stupid title."

Demnug smirked and stepped out of the room, closing the door behind him.

A little more strength inched into Braeden's limbs with each passing moment. It would be a day before he would be fit to travel, but he had to leave now. Two weeks was not enough time to infiltrate the Stele and rescue three royals.

Despite the panic swirling in his gut as he tried to formulate a plan, he pulled a chair beside the bed and held Kara's hand. He massaged her palm with his thumbs, wishing he had something to say, even though he knew she couldn't hear.

A floorboard creaked behind him. He whirled. Adele leaned against the window, gazing out on the late morning sun.

"When did you get here?" he asked.

"I saw enough. You cannot wait much longer, Braeden."

"I can wait a few hours, right?"

"No. She will be out for quite some time. I have witnessed a powerful channeling like that before, and it is not an easy recovery. I assume that each time she has channeled the Vagabond thus far, it has been a minor act. Until today, he has not used much of her power." Adele paused. "She thinks highly of you to risk such a thing."

Braeden nodded, but he didn't know what to say. He didn't move.

Adele sat on the bed beside Kara. She leaned closer to Braeden until he had to look at her. "Greatness is not an inheritance. It is discovered fault by fault, and it is earned. You, more than anyone I have seen in a thousand years, have the potential for true greatness."

"I hope you're right," he said.

"I wish Garrett could join you, but he is distracting the council from my absence. I will stay with Kara until she awakes, and we will meet you at the village once you succeed."

Braeden toyed with the small amulet in his pocket but didn't answer.

"You will succeed," she added.

The muse stood and crossed to the window, no doubt to give Braeden a moment alone with the girl who'd saved his life. He lifted Kara's limp hand and kissed the palm, hesitating to savor the warmth of her skin as his fingers curled in hers.

It took effort, but he set her hand on the bed and forced himself to stand. He strode from the room without looking back and left her in Adele's care.

KARA

In the days following the trial, Kara dreamed only once to relive a memory. She was seven and wanted a bedtime story. Her mother tucked her in and crawled into bed with her. They lay there, reading *Where the Wild Things Are* with a flashlight.

It was only a flicker of an image, gone in an instant in Kara's unconscious state, but she smiled nonetheless.

CHAPTER EIGHTEEN
BRAEDEN

Four days had passed since Braeden's trial.

He took a deep breath and listened. In this series of caves along the outskirts of the Stele, there was nothing to do *but* listen. The dark grottoes were a labyrinth, an endless network of tunnels and hallways littered with the occasional, abandoned, dwelling carved ages ago into the rock. Guards once used these forgotten rooms as homes or defense posts, as the grottoes used to be the unofficial back entrance to the Stele, but they were abandoned when the feihl moved in.

Braeden shuddered. He'd encountered a feihl as a boy when he'd gone into the grottoes on a dare and found a wounded one curled into a small cave. Something had ripped the creature's right side open. Dark red blood pooled beneath it in what Braeden had assumed was its dying place. Even wounded and waiting to die, the thing had nearly taken off his arm. And even with his ability to heal, he couldn't grow back whole limbs.

The feihl were ancient creatures, ugly as sin and equally as mean. Their long, scaly bodies usually grew to about fifteen feet long on average, though rumor was they got bigger with each generation. Each creature had dozens of feet and poisonous venom in its saliva, but it was the thing's face Braeden most remembered: two slits in its round head served as a nose that hovered over a lipless mouth with rows of endless, razor-sharp teeth.

Little food ever roamed the old cave network, so most believed a feihl could make a meal last for days. It supposedly kept its prey alive until only the essential organs remained—dessert.

Braeden had no intention of meeting one of those monsters again. Ever.

If he remembered correctly, the creatures even made Carden nervous. Thankfully, it meant the caves would work as an undetected passage to and from the kingdom. Well, Braeden hoped so. It was still a pretty big gamble.

Because feihl had no distinct odor, he would never sense one coming. They could even crawl on the ceilings and could likely see in the dark. He was in their territory. His only warning would be the scuffle of their feet along the rock, and he wasn't even sure what he'd do when he heard it.

So, he listened.

He'd been traveling through the caves at a painfully slow pace, walking with such care that he couldn't even hear his own steps. It was a tiring game that wore on his nerves, but he had little choice in the matter. Any faster and he would probably be dead within an hour.

Braeden's hand slipped into his pocket as he checked for the Stelian talisman again. The small, black square brushed his fingers, cold as ever, but his heart slowed with relief as he touched the stone. The sharp detail from the thorns in the Stele's coat of arms scratched his skin, but it wasn't enough to break the surface.

He took slow, steady breaths that went unheard on the air, but he still expected to hear shuffling or, at the very least, dripping water somewhere far off. Instead, the silence weighed in on him—so quiet, so still he occasionally toyed with the fleeting fear he'd lost his hearing.

That quiet.

Something was wrong. Sure, stealth came naturally to him, but he wasn't perfect. He shifted his mind off the growing unease by listening to the kingdom he would someday rule.

The Stele offered all its subjects protection, but the

grounds spoke to Braeden. He knew every inch of the black forest and every dead end of the caves through which he walked. It was instinct. He and the kingdom had always shared a connection, one he guessed it had shared with every royal before him as well—even Carden.

As much as Braeden hated to admit it, the Stele was his home.

His instinct drove him now, weaving through tunnel after tunnel with a sense of direction not borne of experience. He'd never been this far into the tunnels before, and had only found their entrance by circling the Stele's perimeter until the grottoes presented themselves. His plan was one of impulse, which meant he didn't really have a plan at all.

A nagging fear in the pit of his stomach brought his feet to a halt before he could question himself. Something shuffled farther down the tunnel.

The patter of a hundred feet came from somewhere ahead. A growl rumbled through the corridor, and it was all Braeden could do to not reach for his sword. If he stood still, the creature might think of him as an extension of the wall instead of food.

The whispering shuffle of feet grew louder, and he swore his racing pulse would give him away. He took one last breath as the thing approached. His fingers itched to grab his sword.

No. Be still. Wait.

The pattering slowed until the last footstep echoed in the tunnel.

Though Braeden couldn't see in the dark caves, the hairs on his arms stood on end as if the creature hovered out of reach. His skin prickled. The creature grunted, its breath a hot whiff of air across Braeden's face.

His fingers twitched.

The beast grunted again...

...and turned away down the corridor through which Braeden had come. Its feet brushed over his as it passed, and Braeden stifled the impulse to groan with disgust. The feet continued, their claws digging into his boot as they passed. Still, he couldn't breathe. Not yet.

It wasn't until the last echoing shuffle faded from the hall that he let himself breathe again. White dots spotted his vision, despite the darkness, as air returned to his starved lungs.

He had to get out of here.

BRAEDEN

An hour later, the first blink of light appeared to Braeden around a curve in one of the tunnels. He let out a shaky sigh of relief, despite the silence, and walked a little bit faster.

It was one thing to sense the exit nearby but an altogether happier respite to see it for himself.

Light glinted off something in the shadows to the right of the exit. He pressed himself to the wall and peered around the corner, unsure what he'd expected. Down what turned out to be a side tunnel, light flashed off something in the darkness. Braeden paused at the tunnel's mouth only long enough to let his eyes adjust.

Piles of ribs and stained femurs littered the tunnel's floor. Centaur skulls and loose minotaur teeth jutted from crevices in the walls, and the tattered rags of clothing hung from splintered bones as if they'd been torn off when something dragged their owners deeper into the cave.

This was a burial ground—likely for Carden's prisoners.

Braeden gagged. He shook his head and turned to leave, but a piece of gray cloth caught his eye. He knelt to get a better look and kept his distance. The silver fabric reminded him of the uniforms Carden's men wore when they'd attacked the gala—in fact, he could make out the thorny corner of the Stelian coat of arms on it.

His stomach twisted, and he suppressed the urge to vomit. Not only did Carden feed his prisoners to the feihl, but he sentenced his own soldiers as well. No wonder the feihl hadn't tried to eat Braeden—they were full.

Focus.

He forced himself to his feet. He wasn't here to mourn those unlucky enough to cross his father.

Braeden hugged the wall and peered out into the brilliant daylight, squinting as his eyes adjusted. A small clearing separated the caves from a forest. He scanned the tree line and tensed as two guards shifted their weight not far off. They stared into the caves, scanning the entrances as if waiting for something.

He took a deep breath. These guards must have been assigned to watch the caves, no doubt to ensure no prisoners escaped after being thrown to the feihl. They must have annoyed someone important to get such a short stick in terms of guard duty.

No matter. He would have to kill them anyway.

His heart leapt. The thought breathed fresh life into him—a vigor that made him want to gag. Killing shouldn't thrill him. Only, it did.

The soldiers stared at the caves, but their eyes shifted out of focus as he watched. This would be too easy.

He lunged. The first guard snapped his head to look an instant before Braeden drew his sword and slid it through the soldier's heart. Wind pooled around Braeden's left hand as he summoned a blade from the air to finish off the second one in an identical manner.

But the other guard didn't try to protect himself. He ran. Braeden didn't even have to chase him. He squared his shoulders and aimed, the magic dancing through his fingers at the soldier's chest. Light glinted off the compressed air in his hand as it writhed, waiting for him to free it. He took one breath, narrowed his eyes, and then shot the blade into the Stelian's heart.

The guard fell to the ground. Braeden grinned without meaning to.

He grabbed the first dead soldier and dragged the corpse into a tunnel before returning for the other one. A pang of guilt rooted his feet by the second guard's legs, but he took a deep breath and finished the job. He couldn't have anyone finding the bodies. Besides, the guards were already dead. At least he wasn't feeding live subjects to the feihl. He was better than his father.

...right?

He shook his head. He needed to focus.

Braeden still wore Hillsidian clothes. Even if he changed into his Stelian shape, the uniform would give him away in an instant. He needed a disguise. Though most of the Stele knew his face, a Stelian was still harder to recognize than a Hillsidian.

As much as he hated the thought, switching back to his natural form was his best bet. Though Stelian guards had no helmets to hide his face, he would still be able to blend in.

He stole one of the guards' uniforms and changed inside the cave entrance. The fabric stretched as he pulled the loose cloth over his head, but it contoured to the shape of his body the moment it touched his skin. Such was a blessing of Stelian clothing—it was designed for their ability to change shape. It would bend and stretch as he shifted. If it didn't have the Stelian coat of arms on it, he would probably have worn the uniform everywhere.

He threw his green tunic beside one of the dead guards. When the bundle hit the soldier's hand, the corpse's finger broke off and dissolved into ash.

Braeden shivered. His instinct might always be to kill, but he hated seeing the aftermath—especially yakona. He'd never understood why his kind turned to dust so quickly, nor did he really want to.

A bird twittered in the forest, reminding him of what he'd come to do. He cleared his head. With a deep breath, he closed his eyes and reached out with his mind to further explore the grounds. The castle called to him from the kingdom's center only a mile off, pulling at his feet as if to lead him home.

He sighed and released his instinctive hold on his Hillsidian form. His skin stretched. Heat shot through his arms. Sweat pooled on his neck, staining his collar as his body swelled to its natural size. The ground pulled away as he grew taller.

The tension in his shoulders eased. His muscles popped and relaxed. Braeden looked down at his hands—gray.

He cracked his neck. He couldn't think about this.

A breeze shot through the forest canopy as he stepped once more into the sunlight. The sun's heat defrosted his skin after the still cold of the grottoes, its warmth reminding him of Kara's touch, or—

Focus, Braeden.

He sighed and slunk into the forest, leaning against a tree in case a new pair of guards came by while he got his bearings. He took a deep breath and concentrated, listening to the kingdom as he searched for a way into the Stele.

Logically, the Heirs and Queen Daowa would be in the dungeon. The problem was the halls in Carden's dungeon twisted in a labyrinth of cells and interrogation rooms. The man liked torture. It was what he did best.

If Braeden remembered correctly, Carden stored important prisoners in a string of cells beneath the throne room called the Cellar. Deep underground, these rooms had no windows and were by far the hardest to escape.

He'd forced Braeden to torture Aislynn in the

Cellar all those years ago. The royals had to be there, too.

A memory flashed across Braeden's mind too quickly for him to suppress it: Aislynn in a tattered, blue gown. Streaks of silver blood stained her forehead. Bruises littered her face. One arm hung at her side, its elbow bent the wrong way. Her eyes darted to his. She screamed.

Braeden sighed and slid down the length of the tree, remorse making him sick to his stomach. She'd screamed because he'd been commanded to use the slivers on her: a technique which turned the shadows into smoky prods that could rewire a brain. They could only destroy, and the few who survived such a technique endured lifelong shocks to the brain to slowly corrode all sense of right and wrong. Braeden hadn't been able to do it, of course—he wasn't powerful enough then. Carden had taken over eventually, leaving Braeden to run back to his room in an effort to hide from Aislynn's screaming.

The slivers technique drove its victims insane. How Aislynn had escaped such a fate was beyond him.

Escape! An idea sparked in Braeden's mind. He grinned and let the remorse slip away as he processed a new thought.

Braeden's mother snuck Aislynn out of the Cellar, so there had to be secret tunnels or a trap door somewhere in the prison. She couldn't have walked Aislynn through the halls without being questioned, Queen of the Stele or not. She'd hidden their escape carriage near the horses' grazing pens—which meant the prison's secret entrance had to be somewhere near that. Perhaps he could find a clue if he looked for something out of the ordinary by the stables.

He stood and brushed off a few dead leaves from his pants. Another breeze swept past him as he started through the trees and made his way down a hill, following his feet as he set course for the castle.

Despite the flicker of hope he might actually find the royals, Braeden's palms were slicked with sweat. Getting to the Heirs would be difficult. Getting them out would take a miracle.

CHAPTER NINETEEN

BRAEDEN

Braeden had canvassed the stables and nearly finished a full circle of the castle but still hadn't found anything out of the ordinary. He'd kept to the forest, eyeing the pens and castle walls from as far away as he could manage. He searched for mismatched stones that might signal a door or misplaced decorations indicating a hidden entryway. Anything. But so far, the only problem he had with the black stone walls was that he had to be in the Stele in the first place to look at them.

A line of Stelian guards crossed the open field beside the castle and turned toward him. He stiffened and shrank behind a bush, but they carried along a path near his hiding spot. He didn't dare move as they marched in step with each other, three in a row. Each soldier kept his hand on his sword hilt and stared straight ahead, in his own little world, when Braeden was close enough to touch.

Braeden peeked around them. The castle towered over the small clearing surrounding it, its closest wall barely twenty feet away. He scanned this section of the black walls again, just to be sure.

The sweet zing of hay wafted along a breeze from behind him. His eyes stung from staring, and he nearly moved on before an out-of-place patch of green caught his eye.

At the base of the castle near the forest line, a string of tall bushes covered an inward dip in the fortification's wall. The edge of the shrubbery led out to the trees. If Braeden stayed beneath the greenery, he would have cover from the battlement above.

He glanced back over his shoulder. Trees swayed in a growing wind, but glimpses of the stable roof broke into view every now and then through the bark and leaves. The beginnings of real hope burned in his stomach. This had to be it—the escape his mother used all those years ago. He and the royals would even be close enough to the stables to grab horses on their way out.

Braeden took a deep breath and considered his options as the guards continued marching past. The soldiers' footsteps crunched along the already-worn path, and he chanced another look around the tree as the last three guards in the line passed by.

He tensed and hovered on the balls of his feet as the soldiers' crunching footsteps faded. His fingers dug into tree bark as he examined the top of the castle, where guards blipped in and out of view. One, two—six guards made rounds within sight of him. He peered around the other edge of the tree but saw only woodland. As far as he could tell, nothing watched him from the thick, black depths of the Stelian forest.

His feet made no sound as he inched through the woods. As soon as he reached the hidden entrance, he would—

A soldier sat on a dead log near the bushes. The Stelian picked at his nails with a dagger, his eyes focused on his hands rather than the woods around him.

Braeden resisted the impulse to curse aloud. Well, a soldier only guarded what needed protection, so this had to be a way in after all.

He hid behind a tree and reached toward the ground beneath the Stelian. Tension pulled on his fingers. Dirt shifted beneath the guard at his command. Vines shot from the soil and wrapped around the man's body before he had time to scream. Braeden tightened his fist, and the vines constricted around the guard's neck, mouth, and arms. Something snapped. His eyes rolled back into his head, and his body slumped onto the dirt.

Glee coursed through Braeden at his kill, but he

shuddered to suppress it. He released the tension in his hands, and the vines retracted into the ground once more. The guard collapsed into the forest's underbrush.

He listened. A bird tweeted. The wind rushed again through the trees, as if a storm brewed somewhere in the cold sky. No guards shouted. No alarms rang. He could continue.

The bushes beneath the castle bent in the wind as he neared them. One of the guards on the battlement passed by and glanced over the edge into the courtyard. Braeden shrank deeper into the tree line, his fingers digging grooves into the tree bark again as he waited.

The guard on the battlement grimaced and continued his rounds. A second guard's head appeared at the far end of the same battlement, his eyes scanning the forest a hundred feet away.

Now.

Braeden darted into the bushes, releasing the pooling tension building in his legs. Once underneath, he ran to where the bushes met the castle wall and paused only when he could touch dark stone. He waited for the sound of an alarm or yelling.

Nothing came.

He glanced up through a hole in the bushes' leaves but could only see the black stone wall towering in the sky above. No heads peeked over. Not even the shoulder of a guard leaning on the edge of a battlement for a quick break.

Braeden sighed with relief.

Leaves scraped the tip of his head as he glanced around for a door. Thin trunks dotted the row in a line to the castle wall, creating a tunnel with their branches. He walked down the lane, hidden beneath the thick canopy. Rare gaps in the leaves let in rays of sunlight.

An old, oak door with a thick, round pull handle inched into sight from behind a particularly large trunk. Rust coated the hinges, and Braeden wondered if he'd have to yank the door off before it would open. At this point, he would do it if he had to.

He set his left hand against the stone wall and braced himself with one foot in front of the other. He pulled on the handle with his free hand—gently, at first.

It didn't budge.

His fingers tensed against the wall as he leaned into the door. He yanked on the handle again, this time with half his strength.

Creak!

Its hinges squealed. He stifled a curse and paused. A glance through the leaves confirmed his fears—a guard rushed to the edge and peered over, stretching his neck to get a better view. Braeden didn't move or breathe. Finally, after a few minutes of silence, the guard shook his head and dipped back out of sight.

Braeden let out a shaky breath. This would take ages if he had to stop each time he made a little progress.

Stupid royals.

With each pull, the door groaned a little less. The guard even stopped looking over the edge after the fourth squeak. After ten minutes, Braeden managed to open the door enough to slip into the shadows of the next room.

Voices tumbled through the darkness. He walked through a curtain of hanging shirts—probably uniforms—and into a small room. Mops and brooms covered one wall, while pails and a few boxes lined another. All in all, only a narrow walkway led through the closet to another door at the far end.

Three muffled voices floated through the door, one of them louder than the rest. Braeden sighed with relief—that voice had probably blocked the creaking hinges as he'd come in. He hadn't thought he'd have an audience inside, too.

He twisted the door handle and inched it open a crack. Light poured through and blinded him. After a moment of blinking away the spots in his vision, he saw the outlines of three guards. Two sat at a table with their backs to him, while a third paced nearby and waved his arms as he spoke. Three swords cluttered the table's surface. They mumbled and laughed at each other, talking in slang Braeden barely understood. It took a few curses from the pacing one to discover his wife had left him.

Braeden drew his sword. This time, he wouldn't kill unless he had to. Heat pulsed through him. He turned the sword slowly, so as not to catch a light on it and give himself away, and then scanned the room for any other soldiers.

The three were alone in a breakroom littered with tables and lined with a wall of ceiling-high cabinets. A wooden door in the far wall hung slightly ajar.

The pacing soldier turned away, so Braeden took his chance. He darted into the room and elbowed the closest sitting guard in the throat before any of them could react. The man fell to the floor and didn't move.

With a jolt, the pacing soldier turned. Braeden swung, twisting his sword to hit the guard with the flat part of the blade. Skin ripped on contact. The soldier crumpled, one hand over his neck. Black blood poured through his fingers. He relaxed after a few seconds and closed his eyes. His hand fell to the floor.

Braeden aimed a jab at the last guard. The man ducked and grabbed his sword off the table. He swung at Braeden's neck and missed. The blade sliced open Braeden's bicep instead. He cursed. Blood rippled down his arm, but the sting lasted only a moment as his skin stitched itself back together.

The soldier gaped at the now-healed wound. "You... you're..."

Braeden grabbed the guard's head and smacked it into the thick, wooden table. The soldier groaned and tried to stand, but Braeden followed up with three punches to the guard's face. The man fell and twitched only once before the room was still.

Braeden cracked his neck and grinned. Energy tore through him. He hadn't even needed magic to subdue them. His instinct said to finish them, to slit their throats, but he suppressed the desire with a grimace.

He grabbed the keyring around one guard's belt and paused once he had it.

Daowa, the Lossian prince, and Aurora probably hadn't been at the gala long enough to know what he was. They wouldn't follow him out if he approached them as a Stelian. And even if he changed form for a moment to prove who he was, he doubted they would follow him. They wouldn't trust any Stelians after the torture they must have already endured in the Cellar.

Braeden could use a Stelian disguise to find them, but not after. This rescue just kept getting more and more complicated.

He lifted the unconscious men and hid them in various closets or cupboards around the room, hoping he would be long gone by the time they awoke. He didn't want to kill, no matter how much he instinctively liked it.

After he set the third guard on a shelf in a linen closet, he opened the entry and looked down the empty hallways.

Think. Where would Carden take three of the most important prisoners he's ever had?

At least Braeden knew where Carden would take them to be tortured—the same place he'd been forced to torment Aislynn when he was a boy. He knew exactly how to get there, too, but only from dozens of forced marches to do Carden's bidding in the hated, cold room.

If Carden had prisoners, he would likely keep them far enough apart, so they couldn't talk, but close enough that they were within a short walk to the torture room. Braeden would start there and duck into an empty cell if he heard anyone coming. The thought alone sent a shiver of fear through him, but he didn't have a better option.

Braeden closed his eyes and took a deep breath before he began down the hall toward the torture chamber. He passed dozens of cells, each with stone doors and a bar-covered opening at the top. He peeked in and listened every time he came to a door, but every cell he passed was empty.

He thought back to the feihl, and an icy wave of fear washed over him. If Carden had fed any one of the royals to those monsters, Braeden didn't know what he would do.

After about ten minutes of walking, he heard a woman sigh from behind a cell door. He peered in. The light streaming through the hallway behind him illuminated Daowa's blue skin as she stared at the wall, her green eyes out of focus. Dirt smudged her temple. Rips in the skirts of her dress turned her once-elegant gown into nothing more than layers of rags.

She didn't look up, so she likely hadn't seen him yet. This was it. He backed away.

Heat radiated from her locked door. A silver light filled the keyhole, and the entire door buzzed. He groaned. He'd forgotten about the safety locking system.

The door would shock whoever touched it while it was locked. The curse surrounded the room from the walls to the ceiling and left only the floor to sleep on. But should someone break through the floor, the ceiling below would shock them as well. There was no escape from a locked, Stelian, prison room.

He glanced down the hallway, but not even a drop of water echoed. With a deep breath, he shifted back to his Hillsidian form. His body shrank, and his skin lightened at the same time his Stelian uniform constricted to fit his changing body.

Braeden smiled—though he would forever be Stelian, this was his natural state.

He pulled out the keys he'd taken from the guards and slipped each into the lock until one turned. Something clicked. The door cooled, and the humming faded.

Daowa turned and peered at the barred gap in the top of the entry from her place across the room, but he doubted she could see who it was with the light streaming in from behind him. Her lips pinched together, and her knees trembled even as she tightened her fists in what had to be a mask of bravery.

He opened the door, and Daowa sighed with relief. She jumped to her feet and wrapped him in a hug.

"I have never been so happy to see a Hillsidian," she said.

Braeden froze, unable to process the queen's lack of formality at first. He had no idea what she'd endured, but he didn't have time to find out. He gently grabbed her shoulders and inched her away.

"Queen Daowa, we have to hurry. Do you know where your son or Heir Aurora is?"

"My son is across the hall. He must have tried to break through the walls because he screamed earlier, and I recognized his voice." Her eyes began to water at what could only be the helplessness of a mother unable to protect her child.

"We need to hurry," Braeden repeated.

He peered into the hall and stepped out, with Daowa following right behind him.

"A—a Hillsidian? Stop!" someone yelled from the other end of the hallway.

A guard charged at them from around a bend in the stone walls. Braeden pushed the queen against a nearby wall and drew his sword seconds before the jailer attacked. He blocked the first blow and spun out of the way of a second. The guard swung wildly, as if he'd recently learned to hold a sword, and a third blow struck the wall. Sparks flew from the blade. The soldier leaned back, exposing his chest as he recovered, and Braeden speared him through the heart.

The sentry crumpled with a gurgle, but Braeden didn't hesitate. He dragged the Stelian by his feet into Daowa's cell and locked the door. The safeguard hummed to life, and heat once more radiated from the door's surface. At least now it would seem like the queen was still locked away. That might delay suspicions.

"I'm sorry for pushing you, but we need to go," Braeden said as he helped the queen to her feet.

"Just find my son."

They continued down the hall, more careful to check around corners this time.

"Here!" Daowa whispered after a while.

She pointed at a side corridor Braeden hadn't noticed. Its row of doors had no light, but he did hear the shuffling of someone pacing around in a cell.

He followed Daowa until she stopped at a door and whispered through the bars to the prisoner.

"Are you all right? Can you hear me?" she asked.

"Mother?" a man asked from within, his stern voice barely a whisper.

"Blood Gavin's brother is here. He's come to help us escape." She turned to Braeden. "Hurry!"

Braeden pulled out the keys and tried seven of them until one disarmed the prince's cell. He opened the door to see the prince waiting beyond, intense black eyes focused on him.

"How did you find us?" he asked as he walked into the hall.

"Is that something you really want to discuss right now?" Braeden countered.

"Come, boys, we must leave," Daowa said.

Braeden hesitated. "Prince, have you seen Aurora? Do you know where she is?"

The prince's skin paled until it was the color of sea foam. "I heard her screaming earlier today. It was endless. I'm sorry, but no one can survive whatever would make someone scream like that."

"Where did you hear her?"

"There's no way she's still live," the prince repeated.

Sweat trickled down Braeden's neck. He couldn't go back without one of the Heirs. His pardon depended on getting all three royals out of the Stele safely. All. Three.

"I have to try. Where did you hear her?"

"We should leave! I won't risk my mother's life while you search for a dead—"

"Tell me!" Braeden ordered.

His voice echoed through the dark hallway. He hoped no guards heard it, but he couldn't leave Aurora behind.

"She was in the torture room last I heard her," the Lossian prince finally said, apparently already familiar with the room himself.

Braeden let out a frustrated sigh. How useless. She wouldn't be there unless Carden was still torturing her, and Braeden wouldn't be going anywhere near his father—not even to save the Kirelm princess.

If Carden still had Aurora, she was on her own.

Braeden gestured to the main hallway. "Come on. I'll take you to a safe spot for now and return for you."

He locked the prince's cell door and led them down a string of hallways to the guard room by the hidden exit. The two Lossians slipped through the still-open door to wait in the bushes, but Braeden only remained long enough to make sure they were safe.

"Don't make a sound, and don't leave. Don't close this door, either," he ordered.

"You're wasting your time!" the prince said.

"If I'd found Aurora first, and she said the same about you, would you want me to leave you without even searching first?" Braeden asked, locking eyes with the prince.

The Lossian Heir didn't respond, and Braeden took the grudging silence as his answer. That he even had to ask such a question made him fear for the leader the prince would become.

Braeden walked back into the breakroom as one of the cabinet doors creaked open. He knelt to greet the newly awakened guard with a punch to the face that knocked the Stelian to the floor. Hopefully, it would buy him a little more time.

He headed back to the prince's cell, determined to find Aurora. He would have his pardon. Prison doors blurred by as he hurried through the passage. He wondered where—

Sobbing. He heard sobbing. Somewhere nearby, a woman's soft whimpers slipped through the gaps in the window above her door. Braeden looked through the row of cells in the hallway until he chanced upon her.

A tall woman lay on the floor in the center of her cell, a shaft of light from the hallway falling across her black hair. The once-braided curls covered her face. Her silver skin glistened from the sweat on it. The rest of her, from her wings to her legs, was draped in the deep shadows of her prison.

Braeden looked around to check for coming guards and, certain they were alone, reached once more for the stolen keys in his pocket. He unlocked her cell on the first try. The buzzing hum died, and he looked once more through the bars.

Aurora glared at him from the floor, her eyes

narrowed with enough hatred to stop all but Carden in his tracks. It was the scowl of a caged animal, one who had been poked and prodded and who'd had enough.

Relief pooled in Braeden's stomach that he was the rescuer, not the torturer.

The Kirelm princess stood. Light fell across her face and neck. Dirt streaked her skin like claw marks. The hallway's light illuminated one wing as she turned to face him, and then nothing but gaping shadow where her second wing should have been.

Carden had cut off one of her wings. Braeden opened the door but didn't know what to say.

"Aurora—"

"Oh, *Bloods*, it's you. Thank goodness."

She slumped forward, her glare and strength evidently a façade. Braeden wrapped an arm around her. She leaned into him without a moment's hesitation.

"I thought they were coming for the other one," she said with a whimper.

Braeden tightened his jaw and suppressed the bile in the back of his throat. "I'm here to help, princess. Let's get you home."

Her eyes trailed over his clothes. "Why are you wearing a Stelian uniform? It's not like you fit in."

"Save your questions for later, princess. I'd like to get out of here first."

She nodded, her eyes narrowing in disgust. "I can finally see why Blood Gavin hates these vile creatures so much."

Braeden flinched at her choice of words. This hatred didn't seem to fit his memory of the passive woman she'd been when he and Kara had visited Kirelm all those weeks ago.

He tried to swallow the insult. "Come on. We need to leave."

She let him lead her. Braeden couldn't be happier she had no idea of his heritage. Changing back had been the wisest move of the entire rescue.

CHAPTER TWENTY
KARA

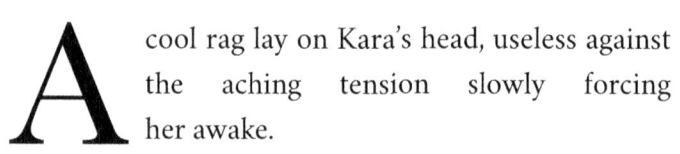

A cool rag lay on Kara's head, useless against the aching tension slowly forcing her awake.

Oh, God, when did I drink tequila? I swore after that frat party freshman year that I'd never—

Kara shot up in bed, which only made the headache worse. Memories of the trial flooded her mind: the Bloods judging Braeden as if they had the right; the fear she would lose him; a whisper in her ear; the tendrils of black smoke that crept across her fingers as the Vagabond took over.

No, the migraine had nothing to do with alcohol and everything to do with being possessed by her mentor. He'd warned her it would take all her energy.

Blinding light left her unable to open her eyes. She rubbed them as if it would help. It didn't. Mumbling drifted to her, but the fog in her mind left her a world away from everything. She strained to hear.

"Please, Kara. Lie back down."

She still couldn't see. "Who—?"

"Adele. I'm here, and you're safe for now. I need you to lie back down. You've been out for four days. You need to rest."

"Where's Braeden?"

Dang it, why couldn't she see?

"Hush, now. The Vagabond overtook you. Do you remember any of the possession at all?"

Kara resigned to cradling her head in her hands while she thought it over. No, not really. All she could remember was the fear of losing Braeden. She shrugged, hoping that would serve as an answer.

"As I thought. You need to rest," Adele said.

"You didn't answer my question. Where is Braeden?"

Silence. For a moment, Kara thought the muse had left the room.

"Adele!"

"He is in the Stele."

"Seri—are you kidding? Why would he go there, of all places?"

"If I explain, will you lie back down?"

Kara took a deep breath and returned her head to the pillow. Relief flooded through her mind as she touched the soft linen.

Adele summarized what had happened in the trial after Kara lost her memory but stopped after she described the Vagabond's possession.

"You were incredible," Adele said, breathless.

"It was the Vagabond, not me."

The beginnings of Kara's vision returned in red and blue dots. At least she could see. She rubbed her eyes again, even though she knew it wouldn't help at all. It was just nice to do something more than sit.

"No, that was you," Adele said. "The Vagabond is a ghost with no physical power. He tapped a wealth of potential within you that has previously gone unused. You could have moved mountains, Kara, and nothing alive could have stopped you. The Vagabond only released his hold when he knew his point had been made. He didn't want to use any more of your energy than he already had, most likely to protect you from others discovering what you can do. It is always safest for the powerful to go underestimated."

Kara ran her hand through her hair. Back at the gala, Deidre had said Kara was more than she knew. Apparently, she could even make stone grow. She'd scared dominant rulers into submission.

She was *powerful*.

"But how? The Grimoire?" she asked.

"No book can grant so much power, not even the Grimoire. It can only teach you to use that which you already have. No, your gift is yours alone."

"I don't understand how, though."

"Nor do I, my girl. I suppose only time will tell."

Kara sighed again. She was doing that a lot, lately. "So, they let Braeden go?"

"Yes. He has to return with the kidnapped Heirs."

"I must have been convincing if they trusted him with such a tense mission."

"The Bloods have nothing to lose at this point."

"I guess that's true, but it doesn't matter. I'm going to help him." Kara stood and teetered on her feet. Blood rushed from her head, and it was all she could do to not fall back onto the mattress.

The muse rolled her eyes. "As intimidating as you are right now, you need rest. Your body wasn't used to channeling such a strong spirit or using so much of your untapped gifts. Though you're healing quickly, you're not ready yet."

"But Braeden—"

"—is strong. You have to trust that he's capable of doing this alone."

"I know. That doesn't mean he won't need help."

"Of course, it does. You—"

"—we're going and no—"

"Child!"

"What!"

"You. Will. Sit. Down." Adele tightened her fists.

Kara sat.

The muse continued as if their little row never

happened. "Garrett is distracting the drenowith Council from my sudden absence. I need to protect you."

"Me? Seriously? No, go help Braeden. I'm sitting in a bed! I'm fine!"

"No, you are not *fine*. Gavin's face when you strode into the room terrified even me. Aislynn, Frine, and Ithone were rightfully scared, but not Gavin. He looked *greedy*. I've kept him at bay this long by moving you to a new room every hour or so. I don't know when he'll find us, but now that you're up, we can leave for the village as soon as you can move."

"No—"

Adele cut Kara off before she could protest. "You may be able to walk, but that doesn't mean you can fight Stelians. You'll just get in Braeden's way if you go to him right now. I can help you, but you have to do as I say."

"Adele, Braeden is incredibly strong. I've never met anyone more focused. But the Stele is his weakness. If he goes there, he'll be drawn to it. If Carden captures him, there's no way he'll escape again. Please understand why I have to go!"

"My girl—"

"Please, no more arguing. I'm going to the Stele."

"But you don't even know where it is!"

"Right. That's why this would be so much easier if you would just help me get there."

A voice boomed in the hallway, nothing more than a mumble until the speaker shouted a single phrase:

"FIND HER!"

"Gavin," Kara said under her breath. It was involuntary, like a gasp; there was no stopping it, however much it didn't help the situation or ease the dread.

Adele nodded. "Come, we can move into another room. The next empty one is two floors down, where they've already searched."

Kara hesitated. "If we're still going to bring peace into Ourea, I'll have to face him sooner or later. It would be better to dispel whatever half-conceived plot is running through his head than to let it simmer."

Adele opened the window and paused, her hand limp and forgotten on the latch. "You would still help them?"

"It seems like they need help now more than ever."

"They only fear you for the moment. I doubt they will help you when the need arises. You are still very much alone in this."

"I don't want them to fear me. I just want them to see reason, and even the selfish can change, Adele. I'd be a pretty useless vagabond if I gave up on them. Besides, I'm not alone. I have you and Garrett. I have Braeden. That's why I have to find him, to make sure he comes back."

"Three allies can't fight an army."

"Look, I can't run forever. None of the Bloods can control me, so—"

"Check every room!" Gavin called through the door.

The next few seconds were a blur.

The knob turned. Kara stood at the foot of the bed, leaning against the bedpost for support. Hinges creaked as the door opened. Gavin loomed in the doorframe, head turned to peer over his shoulder as he barked another command. Aislynn walked behind him, looking past Kara. The queen's furrowed brows relaxed into awe.

A whoosh of air danced through Kara's hair, sending strands into her face. A finch landed on her shoulder, and she didn't have to turn around to know that the little bird was Adele. But the muse hadn't moved fast enough. Aislynn had apparently seen her change.

"You heard m—" Gavin turned and stopped abruptly when he saw Kara.

"You are very loud," Kara said simply.

Her chest tightened, and she tried to hide the fact that breathing had become difficult. Adele wasn't a secret anymore. Sweat formed on her temple, but Gavin seemed to misinterpret the nerves.

"Kara, we were worried. I'm sorry for what I've done. You don't have to be afraid of us," he said.

"I wasn't—" She cut herself off with a deep breath.

No use letting him know about the muse on her shoulder.

Gavin arched his back. "We underestimated you, and we won't do it again. You moved stone like it was water! You proved yourself, Kara, and we couldn't be more grateful to have you as an ally if you'll still have us. It's clear you still need to learn to control it, but with power like yours, we can destroy the Stele forever! I—"

"Stop," Kara said.

Aislynn, Gavin, and even the little bird on Kara's shoulder turned to look at her. She took a deep breath as her jaw tensed on its own.

"What?" Gavin finally asked.

"You heard me. Stop! You're selfish, ignorant, and absorbed in your own little world. I've had enough!"

"How could you possibly—"

"You haven't learned a thing. You were going to kill Braeden, and you act like I've forgotten that!" she said.

Gavin narrowed his eyes. "Yes, it seems you've taken quite an interest in the traitor."

"Don't twist this into something it's not. I know an honest man when I see one, and I protected someone who needed me." Kara tasted the lie and suppressed all thought of it, choosing instead to glare at the Hillsidian king in her doorway.

Gavin took a step closer. Aislynn grabbed his arm. He shook her off but didn't continue. Instead, he leaned in with a glare that should have made Kara shiver. Before the gala, it would have worked.

But Kara possessed deep power she hadn't known about before. She apparently had more than a book to protect herself.

Gavin spoke under his breath. "I'm trying to help you. Let me."

A tickle ran up Kara's arm, and it wasn't until it stopped on her head and barked that she realized it was Flick.

"Enough, all of you!" Aislynn shouted.

"This doesn't concern you!" Gavin shouted back.

"It certainly does. This is my kingdom, and I will banish you from it if you say one more traitorous word! You have gone too far. If the Vagabond won't help you, it is because you are unworthy. When you find it in yourself to do as she says, you will be worthy of the help she gives. Until then, out!"

Gavin turned back to Kara and paused, glancing to the sparrow for the first time. He grumbled and stalked from the room, shouting orders at the guards in the hallway. He spoke so quickly that Kara couldn't even make out what he said.

Aislynn closed the door behind him. She rested her head on the wood as she took a deep breath. "Vagabond, I wish circumstances were different. It seems you and I are met with opposition at every turn."

"Thank you for standing up for Braeden. That was brave," Kara said.

"And foolish, it seems. They think of me as weaker now, though surviving the Stele's prison is no small feat. Compassion is so often punished. I simply wish—"

Aislynn studied the sparrow on Kara's shoulder and paused, as if she had forgotten what she was going to say.

The queen continued after a moment. "There's no need for me to beat around the bush. I know a muse when I see one. She doesn't need to hide from me."

When the muse didn't change form, Kara took it as a cue to play dumb.

"What do you mean?"

"I saw her shift, Kara, so there's no need for games. But it's all right. She doesn't need to shift for me. I just want the muse to know I am grateful that she saved Braeden from the Stele. He told me the true story of how he met you, Kara, and I cannot thank either of you enough for saving him."

Kara wanted to feel relieved. She wanted to think Adele's secret was safe. She wanted to laugh it off and have one more powerful ally in this dangerous world, but her gut twisted with dread. The hair on her neck stood on end, and every fiber of her being screamed, *liar!*

Aislynn nodded in the silence that settled between

them. She left, and the door clicked behind her. No lock slid into place. Kara could leave if she wanted, though she wasn't sure that was in her best interest.

Flick settled on her shoulder and purred into her ear. A gust of wind blew through her hair again as the muse shifted back to her human form.

"It seems you have yet another ally, Kara. This is good," Adele said.

"I don't think we can trust her," Kara answered.

"Why not?"

"I—I don't know. I can't put my finger on it, but something was wrong with that entire conversation."

"Don't reject kindness out of fear. You don't have many friends here, and Aislynn helped you many times over, has she not? She vouched for Braeden without knowing you would save him. No one could have expected such a thing."

"Even I didn't expect that," Kara admitted.

"Aislynn is an ally. Be careful not to push her away."

"I still don't think you should show yourself to her."

"It's a bit late. They opened the door much too quickly. I was too involved in trying to talk sense into you. I was unprepared."

"Speaking of which, we need to go—"

"Precisely."

"—to the Stele."

"No! You are infuriating."

Kara caught Adele's eye. "I'm not leaving Braeden."

Adele sighed. "Very well. But you are only to help him escape if there is an issue. Are we clear? You will not go into the Stele."

Kara nodded. It was a lie. She knew it and figured the muse had already guessed as much.

Adele shook her head and climbed out the open window. She balanced on the ledge, only her foot and fingers still inside the room, and shifted into a silver creature with a thin body and four legs. Its wings glistened in the sunlight like a dragonfly's. As Kara watched, the wings began to flutter until they were nothing but blurs. Adele let go and hovered just outside, waiting.

Kara grinned and threw her satchel over her shoulder as she marveled at the beautiful creature—whatever it was. Flick scampered into the bag, apparently guessing what would come next.

She slipped through the window and climbed onto Adele's back. Scales broke apart the light and reflected it like prisms. Their edges tickled Kara's palm as she wrapped her arms around Adele's neck.

Adele soared into the sky. Kara's gut twisted from the momentum. A fleeting worry pushed into her mind—guards might try to shoot them down. Kara had, after all, not been formally released. Aislynn had not said she could leave.

Kara shrugged and hugged the muse's neck a little tighter. It wasn't as if any yakona alive could stop a muse, anyway.

AISLYNN

Aislynn walked quickly through her castle, the skirts of her dress rustling against her legs as she did her best to contain her excitement. No one could know, no one could even *suspect* how eager she was to process what she had just seen.

This changed *everything.*

After a few minutes of a brisk pace through the vast corridors of her palace, Aislynn slowed at the old tapestry of a minotaur, one as old as the castle itself. She scanned the empty halls and, when certain she was alone, pulled back the cloth. With one hand on the bare stone, she summoned the magic in her blood, commanding the wall to let her pass.

It did.

The white stone of her palace wall shimmered, and in moments, disappeared to reveal the secret passage that would take her to a room only the Ayavelian Bloods and their Heirs knew existed. As she passed through, the wall solidified again behind her.

No longer worried about pretense, Aislynn lifted

her skirts and bolted down the hall, mind racing with possibilities. Kill. Befriend. Betray. Ignore.

What to do with little Kara and the drenowith on her shoulder. What to do...

The hallway ended in a massive room with no windows, lit only by the dozens of sconces that scaled the spiral staircase in the tallest tower of her palace. But Aislynn didn't need any of the books or scrolls on the upper floors—what she needed lay among the artifacts on this floor. Chests and tables took up most of the open space, and Aislynn rummaged through them, sifting through memory after memory as she tried to recall where she had last seen the—

"Yes!" she said softly, breathless with excitement. She lifted the small silver talisman from the velvet box in the far corner, her heart thudding in her chest as she studied it in the flickering light of the fires along the wall. Three lines of silver curved around each other, thickening as they came to the tail end of the line before it. Woven together, they looked something like a triangle.

The Broken Trinity Talisman. It was time to see if this old thing worked.

As Aislynn turned to leave, her eyes rested briefly on the small, red box filled with letters she would never share, from a man her kingdom could never know existed. Her jaw tensed impulsively, her heart aching with need as she remembered his caress on her thigh, the warm sensation of his lips on her neck, his rough hands as they slowly meandered up her skirts.

With a sharp shake of her head, she quickly shoved the memories away.

Slipping the small silver talisman into her pocket, Aislynn left without so much as a second glance at the red box. There was much the world didn't know about her—and she liked it that way.

With the small talisman in her pocket and a drenowith in her kingdom, Aislynn finally had everything she needed to fix not having an heir *and* to right an old wrong. It was a shame Kara got caught up in this, but it didn't change a thing. At this point in her long life, Aislynn was used to collateral damage.

CHAPTER TWENTY-ONE
BRAEDEN

Braeden led Aurora past the tables in the still-empty Stelian breakroom and sighed with relief when none of the cabinets creaked open. The guards still hadn't come to.

He just might make it out of this.

Aurora walked a step behind and followed him into the spare closet hiding the secret exit. Green light shone through the clothes disguising the still-open door. Braeden pushed aside a shirt and gestured for Aurora to wait. He needed to make sure it was safe.

She nodded, and he slipped out into the bushes. The tangled branches cast sunbeams on the ground. Braeden didn't see the other royals for a moment but took a calming breath when the prince of Losse walked by, pacing in the stillness beneath the low trees. The Lossian's steps crunched the leaves, and Braeden flinched when the man stepped on a twig.

His fists tightened. It was as if he wanted to get caught.

A screeching wail rang through the small grove of trees. Braeden covered his ears. As Daowa and her son followed suit, Braeden turned to see Aurora with her hand on the now-closed door.

"Oye! You heard it this time, too, yeah?" someone yelled to another soldier on the battlement.

Braeden peered through the gaps in the short trees' leaves and watched as the guard from earlier leaned over the edge of the wall. He stared at the bush to Braeden's left, but it was over.

"Get someone down there!" the guard said. He leaned back and disappeared from the edge of the roof.

"What are we going to do?" Daowa asked. She wrung her hands and looked at her son.

Braeden answered instead. "Plan B. Run like all hell is after you because soon, it will be."

He grabbed Aurora by the wrist and bolted along the tunnel of trees. He ran into the forest, pausing only long enough to glance over his shoulder and confirm the prince had likewise seized his mother and followed.

Shouts rang across the castle walls, and some even came from the woods to Braeden's right. He cursed beneath his breath and turned toward the stables.

Aurora stumbled along behind him, barely able to keep up. The prince and Daowa ran close behind. Guards yelled to each other, their voices muted as they fanned out to search the woods.

Fighting was not an option. Not against this many soldiers. Not when his only accomplices were a queen who kept tripping over her dress, a princess who had likely never held a sword in her life, and an exhausted prince. He doubted the Lossian prince would go down without a fight, but he knew they would all be captured again if it came to it.

The stable roof appeared through a gap between two trees. Braeden sighed with relief. Its back entrance faced the woods. Only a ten-foot wide stretch of grass stood between him and a barn full of horses, drowngs, and assorted other mounts. Of course, his only hope was a horse. These drowngs had been trained to only let Stelians ride them and would kill sooner than let any of the royals get close.

Braeden shot a cursory glance over the small field near the stables before he darted in and dragged Aurora with him. Horses pawed in their stalls, but no one stood in the aisle. He glanced back into the woods and waited at the door until the Lossians followed him in.

Clumps of loose hay stuck to the edges along the

empty aisle. A set of tall double doors at the other end stood open, tall enough for mounted riders to charge through. Good. It was the closest thing to a plan Braeden had left.

"Grab horses!" he ordered.

Someone gasped. Braeden turned to see a stable hand peeking from one of the adjacent stalls. A fully saddled horse peeked out with him, a comb stuck in its mane.

The groom bolted from the stall and ran out the door.

Braeden rolled his eyes. "We have to leave NOW! Do any of you need a saddled horse?"

"Hardly! The only thing I need is a boost," Daowa said from a stall. She stood by a bridled horse with a stocky build, her left hand holding the reins and a bit of the horse's mane as she waited for a lift.

"Mother! This is not the time for pride. Get on the horse!" the Lossian prince shouted.

Braeden looked at the prince, who stood in the aisle with two white mares wearing black bridles. He offered Braeden the reins to the larger of the creatures. Its shoulder came almost to Braeden's eye. He didn't know horses this large even existed.

He nodded to the fully saddled horse in the stall. "All yours, Aurora."

She nodded and pulled herself onto its back, sitting sidesaddle. She hesitated, eyeing her leg for a moment before she slipped it over to the other side. Braeden nodded, grateful she'd done so. She would have fallen off otherwise.

Daowa managed to hop onto her mount without a boost, so Braeden grabbed the reins to his and jumped onto the behemoth's back. Without hesitation, he kicked the horse's side. It flicked its tail and bolted, running through the aisle more quickly than he'd anticipated. The three royals followed suit and galloped from the stable with him, their escape violating every safety rule Braeden had ever learned.

As he burst into the sunlight, a stream of fire blazed past him, barely missing his arm. The heat seeped through his clothes. He looked over his shoulder. His stomach churned.

The ground dipped into a hill, and a horde pooled at the bottom. Most of the Stelian soldiers ran toward him on foot, but a good number of them turned toward the stables, no doubt to grab their own mounts.

Braeden tore through the forest and headed for the grottoes. It seemed like the best idea to leave the same way he'd come in, but how could his group get past the feihl if they couldn't even keep from slamming a rusted door?

He didn't really have a choice at this point. He could go to the grottoes or Carden. There was a chance they would survive the grottoes. But after an escape like this, there would never again be a way out of the Cellar.

The grottoes slid into view as he rounded a bend in the trees. He breathed a sigh of relief. A look over his shoulder confirmed Daowa and the prince of Losse still ran right behind him, but Aurora trailed slightly. The horde grew ever closer in the distance.

An arrow shot from the crowd and landed in the rump of Aurora's horse. The animal bucked, flinging her onto the ground in one motion. She rolled, the horse's front hooves missing her head by inches. The princess stumbled to find her feet.

Braeden cursed under his breath.

"Climb to the second level and wait for me once you're inside a cave!" he shouted to the Lossians. The prince nodded and kicked his horse to go faster.

Braeden turned his mount around and ran to Aurora. Once he reached her, he positioned the animal between her and the approaching mob now only a hundred feet off. Fireballs whizzed by his head as he offered the princess a hand.

"Come on!"

She took his hand as an arrow pierced his shoulder. Braeden screamed in agony. He ripped it out. His vision blurred. Steam leaked from the pores on his neck and arms. His uniform stretched without him understanding why.

He opened his eyes as the pain receded. A chorus

of Stelians yelled from behind him, but he could see only Aurora. Her eyes widened, and she pulled her hand back.

Braeden glanced down at his arms. Steam leapt from his now-gray skin.

He took a deep breath and shifted back into his Hillsidian form. His body shrank, and his skin lightened once more. He didn't have time to deal with this.

He reached his hand out to the princess. "I'll explain everything, but you need me to get out of here, and we're out of time to waste!"

She reached for his hand without answering, her eyes still wide. He pulled her on behind him and looked over his shoulder to make sure she could balance without a saddle. She wouldn't look at him. Instead, she watched the grottoes' entrance. Behind her, the horde neared.

Aurora leaned in. "After what Blood Carden did to me, I will never admit to needing a Stelian."

Braeden turned in his seat to look at her, but too late. She elbowed him in the neck, the force far stronger than he could have imagined. The blow and the surprise of an attack—from her of all living things—sent him onto the ground. She tore off on his horse, leaving him in the dirt.

"Aurora!" he yelled.

He stumbled to his feet to follow, to run, to maybe even hit her, but the horde grabbed him first.

"Welcome back!" one of the soldiers said in his ear.

Braeden punched the guard in the face. Another grabbed his arm, and a third wrapped a rope around his neck. Braeden fought, shirking them as fast as they came.

Someone yelled his name. It was a familiar voice, tense and frightened, and he turned away from the fight despite himself.

A silver creature the size of a small horse but with wings like a dragonfly landed atop the grottoes. It transformed even as he watched, becoming a great, six-legged beast with a long, clubbed tail. A muse—it had to be a muse. The Lossian prince jumped onto the muse's back and offered his mother a hand. Only then did Braeden see the person who had screamed his name.

Kara.

No, she can't be here!

A guard's head blocked his view of her. Braeden punched the Stelian in the gut until the soldier crumpled.

Aurora grabbed Kara's arm and pulled her toward the muse. Kara twisted in the princess' grip, no doubt trying to come help him, but that would have been useless. The Lossian prince finally grabbed Kara by her shoulders and pulled her onto the creature.

Wings beat on the air, and the muse took off. A rush of wind scattered Kara's hair into her face as she struggled against Aurora, who held on even when the prince let go.

At least she'll be safe, Braeden thought.

A sharp pain burst through his neck and ran down his spine. He fell to the ground, and all went dark.

CHAPTER TWENTY-TWO

KARA

"Braeden!"

Kara threw her leg over Adele's back and tried to jump off when Braeden fell. Aurora grabbed Kara's arm and held fast. Kara twisted in the grip but couldn't slip free. She couldn't believe the princess' strength.

"Braeden said to go on, Vagabond! Don't waste his sacrifice!" Aurora yelled.

The horde neared. The creature beneath Kara—whatever it was Adele had changed into—took to the sky, lifting them higher. Kara couldn't use Flick to teleport down if the princess didn't let go, so she had only one option left.

"I'm sorry, Aurora," Kara said.

She punched the princess in the stomach. The hold

on Kara's arm slipped just enough that she wiggled free. She aimed for a ledge in one of the grottoes and slid off, landing with a light *thud*.

A *crack* sounded somewhere above. In the same second, a furry tail brushed Kara's chin. Flick sat on her shoulder with wide eyes.

Adele hovered and sighed, the breath a huffing gust of hot air that rolled over Kara.

"I'll grab Braeden and teleport out. We'll be fine. Please, go!" Kara yelled.

The muse growled but nodded and flapped her wings. Wind tore through Kara's hair as Adele unleashed the full strength of her new form and darted into the sky. Kara even had to hold on to Flick to keep him from being swept away in the small gale. Adele grew quickly smaller as she headed for the horizon with Aurora and the Lossian royals safely onboard.

A ball of flame shot through the air, pulling Kara back into the moment. The fire's heat warmed her face as it passed. A chorus of yells and curses she couldn't understand wafted from below, some growing closer with each second.

The horde had seen her fall, then.

Kara summoned the Grimoire and stepped back into one of the caves. Flick couldn't teleport without first knowing where to go, and she didn't know where they were taking Braeden. She couldn't even teleport into the forest below because the cracking noise Flick always made would give her away. She needed another way to follow the now-unconscious Braeden.

When the book solidified in her hands, Kara opened the cover and paused as she tried to come up with something. She looked out over the dark forest, her thoughts racing. She needed an idea before she burnt to a crisp or was taken herself.

The Grimoire's black dragon! It had saved her from Losse. It could help her again. She summoned the dragon with a few words, speaking so quickly she barely understood her own voice.

Black dust pooled from the Grimoire in a flurry, blocking Kara's view of the forest beyond. The stream of powder glittered and twirled too slowly. Voices clamored below.

The trail of dust from the Grimoire solidified into the familiar black dragon moments before a hand reached over the edge of the cliff. The dragon snapped at it and bit into the skin. The Stelian's black blood splattered along the rock. Someone screamed, and the hand slipped away. Moments later, something heavy hit the ground.

The dragon turned its lipless head toward Kara. Its teeth glistened, coated in the soldier's blood, and she suppressed a shudder. She would never get used to the way it always seemed to be grinning.

She patted its neck and jumped onto its back. Flick dug his claws into her shoulder, but she didn't blame him. She held on tight and tapped her heels against the dragon's sides.

The beast tore off the cliff and toward the forest, wings ripping through the air. It hung close to the canopy. The dark leaves swished below like a black ocean.

Once Kara got her bearings, she directed the dragon closer to the path where she'd last seen the horde of Stelian soldiers. She heard them before she saw them; the sneering laughter of the small band sent a shiver up her spine.

"Hey, slow down," she said to the dragon.

It obeyed. They stayed above the canopy, thus far unseen as they followed the road through holes in the trees. Kara intended to keep it that way. She strained to hear what the guards said, but she still couldn't understand them.

The castle neared, and the looming edge of the forest meant she would soon lose her cover. She tapped the dragon's neck, and when it tilted its head to look at her, she pointed downward.

It nodded and slipped through the canopy, a sleek bullet that barely broke any twigs on its way through. The dragon was stealthier than she'd given it credit for. She could use this.

The forest line neared.

"Stop," she said under her breath.

The dragon reared and landed just within the forest. Flick purred in Kara's ear from his perch on her shoulder, but she resisted the impulse to pet him. She needed to pay attention. One false move would get her caught.

The treeline ended on a small cliff. A dozen feet below, the path curved along the rock wall and toward the castle gates. Stelian soldiers trickled by, and Kara held her breath as she saw the two biggest guards holding Braeden. His feet left behind a trail of blood as they dragged him along the dirt, unconscious but somehow still in his Hillsidian form.

Kara's fist tightened, but she resisted the impulse to jump out at them now. Even with the dragon, she couldn't take on all of them.

The clump of soldiers turned down the path and walked through the gates, clearly headed for the castle. She scanned the fortress' windows, but she was too far away to see anything. There were really only two places they would take him: to a cell or to Carden. Maybe both at once. Kara shuddered. She had to find him before Carden got to him.

Movement along the castle wall caught her eye. Six guards ran onto a massive balcony jutting from one of the central towers. The opulent red drapes contrasted with the black stone walls, even from her distance.

Why would Carden move soldiers onto a balcony?

Unless—she grinned. That had to be Carden's study or bedroom. It was a risky assumption, but now she had a pretty good idea as to where the guards were taking Braeden.

The hard part would be getting up there unseen.

CHAPTER TWENTY-THREE
BRAEDEN

Braeden woke to the sharp kick of someone's boot in his gut. Pain splintered across his side. He sputtered, but healed, and the pain receded almost as quickly as it had come. A cold stone floor sent shivers through him. The last thing he remembered was watching Aurora drag Kara onto the muse, and—

His attacker kicked him a second time, square in the stomach. Braeden curled around the pain. After a moment, he pushed himself to his feet. He staggered and tried to get his bearings, though his head still reeled from the blow that knocked him out in the forest.

The world blurred. Wind blew against his back. The heat of a fire warmed his right side. Streaks of brown and black furniture clotted his vision as the room came into focus. But the first thing he saw, much to his dismay, was his father standing beside him.

"Oh, good. You're awake," Carden said with a sneer.

Braeden glanced around, taking in bookshelves and a desk while still doing his best to keep his gaze trained on his father.

The study was as Braeden remembered: dark. Even the light streaming through from the open balcony wasn't enough to illuminate the room. Soldiers stood on the terrace, no doubt standing guard in case Braeden changed into his Kirelm form and tried to fly off.

A blur of gray skin moved in his peripheral vision, but Braeden didn't react quickly enough. His father punched him in the gut. He doubled over. White spots flashed across his vision.

Carden laughed. "Always keep your eye on your enemy, boy! Didn't I teach you that much before you left? You do think of me as the enemy, don't you?"

"You have no idea," Braeden said as his body healed.

A flicker of white among the Blood's gray skin caught Braeden's eye. When he looked closer, he gritted his teeth to suppress the bile.

Boils and scars littered the withered stump of Carden's left hand. The longest scar ran from his thumb to the crease in his elbow. A white bone peered through a tear in the skin on his knuckles.

"Ah, yes," Carden said, his sneer fading away.

"Why did you take the queen's Sartori?"

Carden examined his scarred hand. "She cut me with it. I needed to make the antidote, and you can only do that with the blade that cut you. Surely, you know that."

Braeden shook his head. Of course, he did, but he'd expected some ulterior motive. "Let's not waste time. What do you want? How am I not—"

"Chained? Dead? I thought about it. But I want to give you the chance to be sensible. You carry my bloodline, after all. You can't escape that. You're a royal, and royal men don't lead quiet lives. We don't have freedom and choices, only power. I may be cruel in some ways, but I do what I must to protect my people. It's more than you have ever done."

"I don't want your people. I don't want any of this."

"You have no choice in the matter. Someday, you will be king, and a king only survives if his people do as well. We don't belong in the snow, Braeden, banished like criminals. Our time has finally come, thanks to me. We will finally be free."

"There are other ways. A war is hardly necessary."

Carden grimaced. "You're pathetic. What legacy will you leave? Cowardice? I will be remembered for greatness, and I'll do what it takes to ensure you are as well."

Braeden arched his back. "What are you going to do to me, then? Kill me before I get the chance to run again?"

"Tempting, but there isn't time for me to sire and train another Heir before the war begins. No, I intend to break you. You're valuable, Braeden. You're trained to kill, and you love doing it. I can see it. Everyone can. Why do you think the others fear you? They were fine when they thought your hatred could be contained by killing isen. But now that they see you as a threat, they will end you."

Braeden wished he could laugh and deny everything, but Carden had a point. Killing the guards back at the grottoes had sent a rush of joy through him. Hurting the guards on his way to save the Heirs had been thrilling. A rush of power and excitement flooded through him every time he watched the life fade from an opponent's eyes.

He was a murderer and liked it, even if he hated himself for it.

Carden continued. "Boy, you are a killer. A survivor. A threat. You have battle experience that cannot be taught. I need that. You've lived with the enemy. You may even know where all the kingdoms are. You're my final puzzle piece, Braeden."

"You can't make me care about the Stele. I would gladly kill everything in it."

"That won't happen. Breaking you will be easy. I don't have to do anything but make you realize how deeply you deny yourself your own freedom."

"What?"

"You are what you were born to be. You cannot change that, not ever. Whatever you do, you cannot deny that you feel pleasure when you kill. Others' pain gives you strength. I've seen it. You murdered your own subjects at the gala—and you liked it."

"Don't be vulgar."

Carden laughed. "But that's what we are. I wish you could have seen Kara's face at the gala when you took on your daru. Even your little human doesn't want you. She's scared of you, of what you can do to others... and to her."

"Don't start. Let's get this over with, you and me."

"Ah, but she is your weakness. It's so obvious it almost hurts to see. All I'd have to do to break you is torture a girl."

Braeden's jaw clenched, but he didn't respond. He had to change the subject and take his father's mind off her. The king had to think something else could get to him, but a wave of panic swam through Braeden as he tried to think.

He didn't care about the Bloods or the countless lives no doubt to be lost in this coming war. He didn't even care about his own freedom, not if he was tied to his bloodline and could never escape it.

Nothing but hurting Kara could get to him.

Carden laughed again. "She won't last long, of course. I would probably start with a few shocks through the body to get her blood moving."

"Stop," Braeden interrupted.

But Carden continued as if Braeden hadn't spoken. "Eventually, I'd burn her alive, bit by bit. She doesn't heal, so it'll have to be short bursts, just enough to leave a scar. The pain would last for days, of course, maybe longer. Then—"

"Stop!"

"—we'd move on to the slivers. After that, there would be nothing left of her but an empty shell. Well, that would be a fate worse than death, don't you think? And all because you wouldn't make a small sacrifice and obey—"

"Enough!" Braeden yelled.

Carden slapped his hand on a nearby table, shattering the wood. Splinters fell to the rug. "She makes you weak! She will be the end of you, if only because she will eventually lead you right to me."

Braeden ignited a gray fire in his hand. There was no use lying anymore. "Some things are worth it."

"A woman is never worth it."

"I'm not keen on taking advice from you after what you did to Mother."

Carden eyed the fire in Braeden's hand. "Your mother was the one thing I ever loved, and she betrayed me."

"No, Mother saved me from you. She saw what you really are—what I will never be."

"Never? You're already so close! Ostentatious, determined, a brilliant fighter—all you're missing is an enemy. Not me, of course, but a real one. If torturing the girl is what it takes—"

"I will kill you if you lay a hand on her!"

"You would let that happen? If you truly care about her, you'll trade with me."

Braeden paused. The fire in his hand flickered.

"What do you mean?" he asked.

"I have Deidre, who can find anyone, anywhere. If you fight me, I'll break you anyway and order Deidre to bring Kara here. She won't last long. But if you willingly return, it will make life much easier for me. Thus, I will spare your woman. I rarely bargain, boy, and this offer won't last."

Braeden tightened his fist as he considered this new option. "I don't trust you to keep your end of it."

Carden smiled. "If you obey me, I'll never have a reason to hurt her."

Braeden frowned, but he had few options. It wasn't like he would be able to escape again. Since Carden now had him cornered, there wouldn't be a waking moment when he wasn't watched. Hell, his father could simply order him never to leave the kingdom, and Braeden would have to obey.

The only reason Braeden hadn't been killed was because Carden needed him. If there wasn't a way out, he might as well bargain for Kara's safety.

"I…" Braeden paused, not quite able to say the words.

"Yes?" Carden asked.

The king grinned, and Braeden knew why—after twelve years of running, Braeden had finally lost.

The guards yelled on the balcony. Something screeched in a pitch so high Braeden had to cover his ears. Carden did, too, and Braeden used it as a chance to inch closer to the terrace and possible escape.

A great, black creature landed on the balcony, knocking several Stelians over the edge and pushing the rest off with its long tail. They screamed on their way down. The creature arched its neck, and Braeden caught a flash of lipless teeth frozen in a grin. It took him only a moment to recognize the blonde sitting on the creature's back.

The dragon pushed into the room and screamed at Carden, the noise shrill enough to knock the king back into his desk. As Carden toppled over his chair, Braeden saw a familiar hilt sticking from a leather sheath mounted on the wall behind it.

The Hillsidian Sartori.

He leaned forward, ready to lunge for it. If he

grabbed the sheath, it wouldn't burn him. But as he started forward, Carden stood. The king glared at the dragon, a red tint to his eyes. Energy drained from Braeden's feet as his father donned his daru.

There were only a few seconds left to escape, and Braeden wasn't about to waste them on trying to grab a Sartori. Gavin's Sartori, at that.

He ran to the dragon and jumped on, wrapping his arms around Kara's waist as the beast backed through the door to the terrace. Fire rained after them as Carden ran to catch them.

The fleeting worry that the king would follow them made Braeden turn and pull a blade from the air. He aimed at his father's chest and loosed it.

The blade landed right over Carden's heart, and the king stumbled backward for a few steps before he fell to the floor.

It was a risk. If he'd killed his father, Braeden would have to face being the Blood. For all his talk of wanting freedom from Carden's control, he'd never meant to take his father's place. The thought terrified him, but if Kara still wouldn't make him a vagabond, it was the only option left.

He wrapped his arms tighter around her as they flew over the Stele and its forests, burying his chin in her neck. He didn't care about propriety, or even the possible rejection.

She'd come back. When anyone else in the world

would have left him to a lifetime with Carden, Kara came back.

She looked over her shoulder. "I have Flick. Where should we go, Braeden?"

He watched the forests speed by beneath them. Even if they flew for an hour, they wouldn't be a safe distance from the kingdom. The sun inched into the horizon, and it wouldn't be long before it was dark. One of his limited options stood out above the others.

"You don't need Flick. Fly low and head that way," he said, pointing off to the left.

She glanced back at him in question but nodded. Her eyes narrowed, so serious he couldn't help but smile. He tried to remember the scared girl she'd been—the one who stumbled into his life without a clue of what to do—but that girl was long gone.

"What am I looking for?" she asked with a glance to the setting sun.

"A series of caves dug into the side of the mountain."

"You mean where we found you?"

"Yes."

"But that's almost doubling back to the castle!"

"Exactly. They won't expect it. Besides, Stelians are afraid of those caves. Even Carden doesn't go in there. We need shelter because we don't want to be outside when it gets dark."

"But I can take us back to Ayavel. Or we could teleport to the village."

"I don't want to go back to Ayavel yet. Have you mastered teleporting?"

"Well, no, not completely. But—"

"When will you learn not to try new things in the heat of the moment?" he asked.

"Okay, okay. Scary caves it is," she said with a laugh.

They skimmed the canopy, the leaves whistling as they passed. It took about ten minutes before the grottoes came into sight. For the second time that day, hope flashed in Braeden's gut as he saw the caves. He prayed things turned out differently this time.

The dragon landed on the ledge outside of a cave. A dip in the rock led to a cave entrance on this second level. No guards remained in the clearing below, probably because Braeden had escaped.

Kara patted the dragon's neck, and the creature dissolved into dust.

Braeden grabbed her hand and led her into the cave, pausing as he passed the threshold. He strained his ears. Footsteps echoed down one of the other tunnels. He tensed and nudged Kara against the wall. He leaned into her to block her with his body and hide her from view.

Well, it was one reason, at least.

A woman with curly brown hair walked into the

clearing from a first-level cave and sighed, staring off toward the castle. He could hear the rustle of something heavy being dragged across the grass, but the edge of the cliff blocked whatever she pulled behind her. She dropped it and examined the grottoes.

Braeden's grip on Kara tightened when he recognized Deidre. The isen turned back to the castle, apparently without seeing him, and smoothed her hair. Her voice carried along the rock. "I can't wait to be done with these idiots."

She carried on down the trail toward the castle. Once she disappeared into the forest, he looked over the edge to see what she'd dragged into the clearing.

The carcass of a feihl lay in the field, the last half of its body still in the cave. Any question as to how she had survived the grottoes disappeared. Braeden shuddered. There was more to that isen than met the eye, and he hoped they never again crossed paths.

"What the hell is that?" Kara asked, peering over the edge beside him.

"You don't want to know. Come on," he said.

He led her through the cave but didn't dare light a fire when it became too dark to see very well. Instead, he tightened his hold around her fingers and maneuvered the tunnels, using his connection with his kingdom to find an abandoned guard tower.

When an old, stone door came into view, he let Kara go in first. The feihl couldn't fit through the entry, so they wouldn't have visitors. He closed the door behind him and set a trap on its handle. Whoever tried to open it would lose an arm.

Still without a word, he led her up a short flight of steps to an old room with a small window overlooking the forest. A stone table sat beneath the window, but it proved to be the only décor. He closed this door, too, and set a trap against it as well.

When he finished, Kara stood in the middle of the chamber, her eyebrows furrowed as she looked him over. Flick jumped off her shoulder and onto the windowsill, where the little creature studied the trees.

Kara inched closer. "Braeden, are you okay? You're all fidgety. I'm worried about you."

"This is the other reason I wanted to stop," he said without really answering her. He cupped her face in his hands. Without a second thought, he kissed her.

Her cheeks flushed under his touch. He grinned through the kiss. The panic and fear melted away, and all he could do was continue. He inched her toward the wall until she had nowhere else to go. He never let her move away for more than a breath, but she didn't resist. She didn't fight it.

She leaned in with a sigh that tied his stomach in knots. Her fingers traced his back, moving slowly upward until they found the base of his head. She pulled him closer.

He slipped his hand just under the hem of her shirt

and ran his fingertips along her waist. She gasped. He grinned.

Braeden couldn't contain himself. He couldn't stop, nor did he want to. In fact, he wasn't going to break away until she begged for air.

CHAPTER TWENTY-FOUR

KARA

A crevice in the wall pushed into Kara's back, but she didn't care. Braeden's hands slipped to her waist and pulled her closer. Bolts of heat raced through every inch of her he touched. She couldn't get enough of him. Her fingers traced circles on his arms until her fingertips went numb.

Stop, Kara.

That was most certainly not her consciousness. No sane woman's mind would tell her to stop a kiss like this.

Push him away.

She huffed but didn't let her lips stray from Braeden's for very long. She closed her eyes and grinned.

Leave me alone, Vagabond.

Push him away, Kara!

Is there a way to turn you off?

An image of Helen, bloody and lifeless, flashed before her. The vision consumed even Braeden's beautiful face.

Kara gasped and shoved away from him until her head curved against the stone wall. Her pulse thudded in her ears.

Oh, that wasn't fair. The Vagabond had shown the same image he'd forced her to relive in an effort to stop her last kiss with Braeden. Her only other kiss with him, for that matter.

But Braeden pressed his lips against hers, apparently oblivious to her reaction. He brushed his thumb across her cheek and reached a hand up her back. Energy danced through her like jolts of lightning. She sighed and leaned into him again.

The first Vagabond could go to hell.

A new scene flashed before her eyes. The Vagabond fabricated one, this time of Braeden. He lay on the floor, not breathing, and stared at her with glazed-over eyes. Black blood spilled from his mouth. She gagged.

You will do this to him, the first Vagabond said in her mind.

Kara choked on a sob and pushed Braeden away.

"Stop," she said, her voice cracking.

Braeden cupped her face in his hands and kissed her nose. He teased her by brushing his lips against hers. She longed to lean forward but resisted.

He looked her over and spoke in a voice that came out like a growl. "Why?"

"You know why," she whispered.

He shook his head. "Don't pretend you don't want this."

"I obviously..." Kara sighed. She had to keep him at an arm's length, but she had no idea how to do that. All she wanted was another kiss.

He shook his head. "Never mind. I don't want to upset you. I'm sorry I grabbed you like that. I thought," he rubbed his face, "never mind."

If she kept him talking, it would reduce the urge to pull him closer. "No, you can tell me. We should get this out in the open."

He leaned against the wall next to her. "I thought I was never going to see you again, Kara. When anyone else would have left me, you came back. Words aren't enough to thank you."

"I'd do anything for you," she said without thinking. She instantly regretted the confession.

He grinned. Her breath quickened, and he resumed his position in front of her. He wrapped his hands around her waist and pressed her back against the wall.

"Then, kiss me again," he said.

Nope, she wasn't strong enough to resist that.

Change the subject!

"You're," she cleared her throat, "you're making this

difficult, Braeden, just like back when you rescued the royals. What were you thinking? You didn't need to sacrifice yourself to let us escape!"

It wasn't her best topic change, but it would have to do. As long as he touched her, she wouldn't be able to think right, and her heart wouldn't beat at a steady pace.

Flick chirped and curled up against the wall nearby. With a pang of guilt, Kara realized she had forgotten her pet was even there.

Braeden took a step back. "I didn't sacrifice myself during the escape, Kara. I knew we could have gotten out of there."

"But Aurora said—"

"Aurora knocked me off the horse. My form slipped when I went back to save her. She saw the real me."

The breath left Kara's lungs for a moment. "She knocked you off the horse? Why?"

Braeden sat on the floor and leaned against the wall. Kara followed suit, careful not to sit too close. She still didn't trust herself around him, especially not after a kiss that could make her knees buckle.

"You know why," he said.

"Because you're Stelian? But you saved her life! Twice!"

"She obviously didn't care."

They sat in silence. Braeden stared at the opposite

wall while Kara watched him. The angry lines in his brow deepened with each passing second—his glower frightened her.

When he finally spoke, he rubbed his temples and seemed to look everywhere but at her. "I'm not good, Kara. I'm not. I never will be. I like killing. I like pain. I like being feared. I've been ashamed of it my whole life but no more."

"Those might not exactly be your best traits, but that doesn't mean you're evil. You protected me when you didn't have to."

"It was selfish. I only kept you safe because I thought you could turn me."

"What about that night on the way to Losse? I told you I couldn't turn you into a vagabond, but you stayed anyway."

Kara lingered on the memory. He'd left for a while. She'd sat on a rock for hours before the raw fear crept through her that he might not come back. Until then, it hadn't even dawned on her as a possibility.

"When I walked off into the woods, my first instinct was to leave you," he said.

She leaned away. "What?"

"It was instinct. Only, I couldn't do it. For the longest time, I didn't understand why, either. I walked around for hours trying to understand. I tried to tell myself how all I'd wanted from you was freedom, but I realized it wasn't true.

"All my life, I've kept people at an arm's length. I lied to everyone. I've never loved anyone. But around you, I can be myself. It's a new freedom. You accept me. And I wanted to repay you by keeping you safe. You needed someone to trust as much as I did."

Kara took a deep breath, but she didn't have a response.

"I don't kiss just anyone, Kara. You mean more to me than anyone alive," he said with a sigh.

He reached for her hand and massaged her fingers with his. Though she couldn't force herself to pull away, she did manage to keep herself from tightening her grip.

She couldn't let this go any further. She didn't want Braeden to end up like Helen or to be used as leverage again. But before she could muster the courage to speak, Braeden continued.

"I can't deny this anymore, Kara. I would do anything to keep you safe, and even admitting the truth out loud terrifies me."

"Braeden," her voice was so much quieter than she'd intended, "I know what you want, and I can never give it to you."

He held her gaze, but his expression hardened into something unreadable.

She plowed on. "Vagabonds can't love anything more than our purpose. The first Vagabond made that clear enough. And when I wouldn't listen, when I thought—"

When I thought I was going to lose you, she wanted to finish, but her voice broke as she remembered that agonizing fear. Her gut twisted at the thought of his pain in the dungeon and the way he'd hung his head, too weak to fight and resigned to fate. That fear still made her heart race. The first Vagabond had used that against her.

She took a deep breath. "He manipulated me. He made me swear to make more vagabonds in exchange for saving your life. You were leverage, Braeden, and he'll do it again and again to prove his point. Gavin, Ithone, Frine—all the others will do the same."

"So, you were referring to this pact you made with him when you said you'd do anything for me?"

Kara nodded.

He pulled her into a hug. She let him hold her, but she couldn't hug him back. She just wasn't strong enough. If she even reached for him, she would cave. He cradled her head in his palm, and she leaned into his neck. The world melted away when he touched her. He was her one safe place.

"I'm not exactly helpless," he said in her ear.

She caught his eye and paused before she spoke. She had to make him understand. "You were helpless in that throne room, and that helplessness is the reason I compromised what I believed in to save you."

His jaw tightened, but he didn't respond.

"You're incredible, Braeden, on so many levels. You're strong, powerful, clever, smart. But some people will do anything and kill anyone to control the Grimoire. Carden can likewise control you if you have a weakness. We can't do that to each other."

"Caring about someone doesn't make you weak."

"The Vagabond threatened to let you die to get what he wanted. I sure wasn't strong."

Braeden let her go. Cold seeped into her skin now that he'd left. He pushed himself to his feet and leaned against the window without looking at her. For a long while, neither of them spoke.

Kara wanted to say something, but she needed a new topic. They might as well talk about the rescue.

"How did you get the Heirs out of the Stele?" she finally asked.

"I killed my own subjects."

Kara sighed and leaned against the wall. He was angry now. She kept quiet.

He looked down at the floor. "Killing is the one thing I'm good at doing. The way Aurora looked at me, you'd think it was the only thing I knew. I should have seen it coming. I didn't think she would do such a thing to someone who had just saved her life. And she's only the start. Gavin would have had me killed. Richard never came to speak to me when I was in the dungeons of Ayavel and will probably never speak to me again. Aurora I can understand, I suppose, but not them. A family isn't supposed to care about what you are, only what you've done. I can't care about what they think of me anymore."

"Don't give up, Braeden. That will make Gavin right. It makes all of the Bloods right. It makes Carden right. You can't want that."

"Giving up doesn't mean I'm going to kill everyone or succumb to Carden. It means I stop lying. I get to do whatever I want—and I know exactly what I want."

"What's that?"

"You safe and Carden dead."

She let out an exasperated sigh. "Braeden—"

"We don't ever have to be together, Kara, if it's not what you want. But I will always make certain you're safe."

She rubbed her eyes, and the bubbling frustration with the Vagabond and his stupid meddling manifested in a statement she would forever regret. "Braeden, people already know about us! Aislynn, Gavin—the whole flipping world, probably. If you want to keep me safe, you should give me space!"

Wind howled past the window, rattling the glass. He didn't respond, and a chill crept through the room. Kara shivered as goosebumps raced up her arms. Braeden leaned closer at the motion, like he wanted to hold her, but he looked away when she caught his eye.

Way to go, idiot, she thought. And she was an idiot.

Guilt churned in her gut. But if getting him angry would push him away and keep him alive, then so be it.

"Should we leave?" she finally asked.

He shook his head. "Not at night. Besides, I don't know where I want to go yet."

Kara wanted to bridge the gap, to reach out to him before the trip back, but she had very little to go on. Braeden lay down beneath the window and stared at the ceiling, but it wasn't long before he closed his eyes. Kara resigned herself to a chilly night curled up against the far wall.

"Gavin changed when he became Blood," Braeden said, his voice steady.

Kara looked back over to him, but his eyes didn't open. She got the feeling she wasn't supposed to answer, so she let him continue.

"I don't even recognize him anymore. If you don't make me a vagabond—if you don't free me from this—there's no telling what I'll do with my people when they're mine."

"I can't make you a vagabond. It would kill millions."

"But you would trust me to be Blood?"

"Of course, I trust you, Braeden."

"No, you don't. If you did, you'd let me in. You wouldn't push me away to protect me. Me, of all people! Caring about someone isn't a weakness. If you truly believe it is, then you aren't as strong as I thought."

Kara turned again to the wall, unable to answer from the ball stuck in her throat. If he had to hate her, fine. She wouldn't let the Vagabond's prediction come true.

CHAPTER TWENTY-FIVE
KARA

The night dragged on, and Kara couldn't sleep. She waited until Braeden's breathing evened and then turned over to look at him.

He kept his Hillsidian form even as he slept. Amazing. He had more control of his power than she'd thought if he could keep his shape in his sleep.

But he was giving up. Focusing on the darkness within him—the love of pain, as he'd called it—would destroy him. She just knew it. It would make the Bloods fear him. They'd get rid of him.

Kara rubbed her face and sighed. This was such a mess.

The cold pendant slid across her neck, and she debated whether or not the Grimoire could help. If a way for Braeden to control his darker side existed, she doubted even her book would know.

She summoned the old text anyway. Blue dust twisted from the pendant's stone and illuminated the room with its inner light. It settled into her lap and congealed into the Grimoire's leather cover. She slipped a finger under the binding and opened it to the crinkle of paper.

"How can I help Braeden?" she asked in a whisper.

The pages didn't turn.

Kara bit her cheek. Did that mean the Grimoire didn't have an answer? It had always answered her before.

She opened her mouth to reword the question, but her voice froze in her throat. The air died, and a slow realization crept along her neck. Nothing moved. The trees outside hung in the air, framed by clouds that didn't move on what had once been a vicious wind. Even Braeden didn't breathe.

The blue moonlight faded from her world, taking with it the colors in her shirt until only tints of gray remained. Eventually, all light faded from the room.

Her breathing slowed. The darkness pulled against her chest and lifted her to her feet. She floated in the void.

A fire sparked to life in her peripheral vision. Someone walked toward it in a familiar cloak, his hood down. The flames lit the depths of a small fireplace and reflected light onto the figure. He leaned on the hearth, staring into the fire. His shoulders hunched as if he didn't have the strength to arch his back anymore.

The first Vagabond.

Kara wanted to throw something at him. Did he have to be so theatrical all the time? If he wanted to pull her into the Grimoire, just do it. It didn't have to be a show.

He turned around, the same young Vagabond who had shown her his memory from the night he died. The same Vagabond who would not let her try to love anyone because he, himself, had lost.

The people Kara loved always died, but she had been willing to try again. To feel alive again, to feel love—was that worth the risk of Braeden dying? It was so much easier to blame the Vagabond.

Anger, rage, and an unknown fury flared to life in her stomach. She tried to name the emotion, but she couldn't at first—she wasn't just upset, or frustrated, or cornered. The negativity burned within as she tried to figure out this new feeling.

It dawned on her, finally—hatred.

"Vagabond, Braeden needs help. He's giving up and—"

"That's enough."

Kara paused. "What?"

"You promised to make more vagabonds, and I intend to hold you to it."

"Well, yeah, but first—"

"I will not help you, nor will the Grimoire answer you, until you create your army."

"That's ridiculous!"

"I warned you. You can't escape a promise made to me."

"But Braeden needs help!" She stifled the urge to add, *and I don't want to lose him!*

"You can't hide your thoughts from me, Kara," the Vagabond reminded her.

A knot caught in her throat, and she fought back the tears that wanted so badly to be freed. This wasn't leverage. This was about the Vagabond having absolute control.

"I'm starting to hate you, Vagabond."

"I sensed it. Hate is quite a strong emotion."

She bit her lip and glared at the floor. She couldn't even look at him.

The Vagabond's voice lacked emotion. "It's all right for you to hate me, at least for the moment. You must learn these lessons somehow."

"No, it's not! You're supposed to teach me what to do, not police my every thought!"

"I am doing all I can, Kara, but you need to remain focused! You are here to end a war, not to be courted!"

"I didn't sign up to end anything! I never even got a choice!"

"You opened—"

"I opened a book, Vagabond. How was I supposed to know what that would mean? I was dragged down a dirt hole by roots and stumbled into a locked library with no way out! There were no hints, no signs to the effect of 'hey, opening this book is going to screw you over.' Nothing!

"And I've gone along with it. Despite this crazy, gorgeous, backward world, I've learned. I've listened. Hell, maybe it's only because I have nothing to go back to. Dad's soul was stolen because I dragged Ourea into my old life with me. But every time I try to enjoy my life here or find some beauty in it, you take it away!"

The first Vagabond paused, as if waiting for something. "Are you done?"

Kara's fist tightened. Any second now, she would lose it and attack him. She just knew it.

He crossed his arms. "Losing Helen taught me the meaning of true sacrifice. It's a lesson you should have learned by now!"

His voice boomed so loudly that Kara's heart skipped a beat. Her voice died in her throat.

He continued. "Love destroyed everything I ever accomplished. I thought Helen was my savior. She taught me happiness, but happiness made me soft. Vulnerable. And as Braeden was leveraged against you, she was leveraged against me. No leader should have to choose between his lover and his followers. I couldn't choose, and you will never have to face such a cruel choice if you listen to me."

Kara tightened her fist. "But you did choose! You stayed behind as a ghost when she said she would wait for you in the next life. You chose duty. All I want is to be happy."

"You're a hero, Kara. You don't get to be happy."

"Why the hell not?"

"Your idea of happiness is to love and be loved. You'd hold the lives of your family and your lover as more important than those of the masses. Their needs and desires would mean more to you than the greater good. That love is a distraction from your purpose. It becomes leverage, which means it is weakness. If you let yourself love only a few, you will fail."

"How can you be so calculating? This is life and purpose and love!"

His shoulders slouched. "With all the death and betrayal you've already seen, how can you not?"

"Because I've seen the other side of it, Vagabond, a side I thought you'd already seen with Helen. Love is a blessing. It's what makes life beautiful and gives us purpose. You were hurt. I'm sorry about what happened to Helen, but you can't be afraid of life because it screwed you over in the past."

"You don't understand."

"I do! You sacrificed everything for your cause but come on. That wasn't purely out of selflessness. Somewhere in there was love, love for the greater good maybe, but part of what gives us purpose is what we love. Who we love. Without it, without them, there is no reason for trudging through. I refuse to be afraid to love someone because you are."

He rubbed his temples. "You are hardheaded, frustrating, and right to a degree. But you must understand that our kind is lonely. We must be self-reliant and distrusting. It is the only way to survive.

"Yes, I was hurt. Everything I loved was taken from me, and I failed. I failed Helen. I failed my vagabonds. I failed my teachers, my friends, and my people. I failed myself. History has twisted my memory and warped me into a convenient myth. The world has forgotten what I set out to do. But with you, I can reignite my old purpose. I can redeem myself. Kara, you are my last chance!

"If Carden wins this brewing war, there is no hope for Ourea. You cannot fail. You won't get a second chance at anything. You cannot be lost to either the evils or the beauties of the world. Can you understand why I push you so hard? You are my last chance to do this right. With you, I can fix everything I broke in life."

Kara looked at the floor. Her body ached from exhaustion. "I'm trying, Vagabond."

He smiled. "You are. You're doing so well. It's one more reason why it's so crucial you succeed. You can't be distracted. Bring about peace, and then you can have your happiness."

"I'm beginning to doubt that's even possible," Kara said under her breath.

"If you don't believe in peace, then it will never be. You of all people must know anything is possible as long as you keep an open mind."

"Look, we won't get there if I make more vagabonds. It's just going to make the Bloods angry. It will make them fear me and make them doubt everything we've done to pull them together."

"The Bloods aren't dependent upon you, and that's where the danger lies. If you become uncontrollable or simply unnecessary, they will revolt against you. Everything is still volatile, and so much is uncertain. A vagabond army of your own will protect you. Protect the village's location and protect your vagabonds. That is the only way to survive this war."

Kara shook her head. "You make it sound like the yakona aren't worth saving."

"They are, but that doesn't mean you must trust or like their leaders. Our purpose is to unite them for the good of Ourea and of the world. We're trying to make the Bloods see reason against eternal war."

"By starting one?"

"Don't give yourself so much credit," he said with a

soft chuckle. "This war began well before my time. We're here to finish it."

She sighed. "So, what do I do?"

"Build your army, which is not something you should orchestrate alone. Find a second-in-command and charge him or her with starting the army while you distract the Bloods. Hopefully, the Bloods will never need to know you have an army, and hopefully, your vagabonds can live forever in the village, safe. But these vagabonds must be ready should you need them. Your second must be someone you could trust with your life."

"Braeden."

"Like I've already said, he's not an option."

"Twin, then."

"Change her, and I will guide you to the next step."

"So how do I change her?" Kara grimaced, still hating this plan, but her hands were tied.

"Give her one of the unopened Grimoires. If she is worthy, it will do the rest."

"But there has to be another way to make vagabonds. I mean, you didn't always have those Grimoires, but you made vagabonds nonetheless."

He caught her gaze. She resisted the impulse to squirm.

"I don't trust you with such information. Not yet," he said.

"What? Why not?"

"When you stop secretly hoping you can free Braeden from what he is, I will tell you. He must face what he is and discover his own purpose. You cannot save him from his fate."

She looked away.

The Vagabond continued as if they'd never discussed Braeden at all. "When you turn Twin, she will be free. All your vagabonds will be without a Blood, and they will relish their freedom. So, remember, they will never be forced to follow you. You must earn their respect to remain their leader. Be kind, be honest, and be firm."

The Vagabond looked her over and sighed. He waved his hand. Blurred wisps of white light spun from the void in front of Kara. They twirled around each other and made the outline of a couch. With a flash, they congealed together, and a leather sofa floated in the darkness.

The first Vagabond gestured toward the chair. "Would you like a seat? You look exhausted, Kara."

She was, though she didn't want to admit it. As sleepless as her night had been, it wasn't for lack of trying. Her body shook with fatigue, but her thoughts raced too quickly to let her mind rest for even a moment.

Kara nodded and settled into the couch. It bent beneath her, soft enough to put her to sleep, but she stared into the darkness above her in an attempt to stay awake. The endless black reminded her of the lichgate back at the village.

The Vagabond walked to the fire. "It's a special lichgate, in case you hadn't guessed."

"Huh?" Kara hadn't said anything.

Oh, right. He could read her mind. He'd referred to the lichgate back at the village.

He nodded. "Lichgates are imperfect things and easy to corrupt. In my travels, I discovered how to change the destination of a portal. I think that's how Carden lured the Queen of Hillside away from her home, to be honest. I didn't want anyone to do that to my village, so I created an unbreakable lichgate. That one will always take you back to the temple."

Kara nodded. Sleep pulled at her eyes. Good to know.

"Kara? Are you paying attention?"

She leaned forward and forced her eyes open. "Yes, yeah. I'm awake."

"As much as I don't want you to know him, you should visit Stone."

"Who is that?" she asked.

The name seemed familiar, but her tired mind failed her. Her eyes drooped.

The Vagabond continued. "Stone was my mentor. He taught me much about Ourea, and I never learned as much from anyone as I did from him. He is a powerful isen, but always seeks to understand the science behind magic and the world. He's been around long enough to have found hidden entrances into the kingdoms, so Twin can go unseen."

Sleep tugged on Kara's eyelids, but she forced them back open. "Wait, I thought the muses were your mentors. Adele and Garrett said they taught you."

"They taught me much, yes, but muses have a habit of taking more credit than they deserve. A muse named Bailey introduced me to them and taught me more than even they did. Still, no one has ever taught me more than Stone."

"Who's Bailey? You never mentioned him before."

"He asked me not to name him in the Grimoire to protect him. He was not permitted to help me."

"Did something happen to him?"

"Yes, but I will not be the one to tell you. I'm biased. If Adele and Garrett haven't told you, neither should I. Muses are slow to heal."

"Look, if this concerns me, I need to know."

"I don't believe it does. Therefore, the muses will tell you when they are ready. Do not ask Stone."

"Did he have something to do with it?"

"You ask an annoying number of questions about matters that do not involve you. Do not ask me again."

"That was a yes, right?"

He rubbed his temples and chuckled. "You're infuriating."

"You find me amusing."

"Confusing is more like it. Slow to change your mind."

"Speaking of that—" She leaned forward, shoulders hunched, but she had to make one more argument. "Please just stay out of my feelings for Braeden. Let me do this. I promise you, it will make me happy. It will give me strength when I need it most to know what I'm fighting for."

"Listen, Kara. What if it doesn't work out between you and Braeden? You could never be impartial. He's the Heir to the Stele, after all. He'll distract you both during your time together and when your relationship ends. He—"

"When? Don't you mean if? Unless I'm mistaken, you can't tell the future."

"No, I can only make predictions. And based on his father, his heritage, his upbringing—"

"Stop."

The Vagabond paused, his mouth open to continue.

Kara pushed herself to her feet. "You, who preach equality, peace, and freedom, would dare imply that Braeden's using me solely because it's what any other man in his lineage would do?"

"It's a factor, yes."

"You hypocrite! You won't let me free him, but you won't trust him because of the lineage he's bound to?"

The Vagabond rubbed his neck. "I never said this was fair."

"Has it ever occurred to you that you might be wrong about something? About anything? Ever? Does that thought ever come to you before it's too late and things can't be fixed?"

The Vagabond flinched as if she'd slapped him. "Kara, that was cruel."

"No, it was a wakeup call. You have to see yourself as I see you right now. Yes, you're wise. You're brilliant and powerful and amazing. But you aren't perfect. You make mistakes, and no amount of time locked away in a book simmering on your thoughts can make you omniscient. You're mortal! You're still—"

"I'm what? Human?"

Kara tightened her jaw and stepped back. She needed to remain calm.

But the first Vagabond's shoulders tensed, and it was clear she had pushed him off an emotional ledge. "If you're willing to risk millions of lives for puppy love, Kara, be my guest," he seethed. "You seem to know far more than me!"

"Look, I think we both need to calm down. I'm sor—"

"If you waver, you will fail. I will not let you fail, even if it means getting rid of him myself!"

"And what does that mean?" Kara's eyes narrowed, and she gritted her teeth at the threat. She squared her shoulders. "Are you saying you'd kill Braeden? You've already used him against me, Vagabond, and I don't like where this is going. Because I swear to God, if you so much as *touch* him, I will sabotage everything you've built!"

"Get out!" the Vagabond screamed.

Before Kara could say a word, before she could so much as blink, a sharp pull on her stomach wrenched her over the chair and into the darkness.

CHAPTER TWENTY-SIX
KARA

Kara sat quickly upright, the sun blinding her as it streamed through the window. It took her a moment to get her bearings. A second ago, she had been about to placate the Vagabond. She'd been about to apologize in an effort to calm him.

He'd kicked her out. Just like that. Oh, he was definitely imperfect. So was she, but at least she knew it.

The Grimoire still lay open beside her. She wished it away before she noticed Braeden standing by the door.

"We need to go," he said without looking at her.

Kara nodded, but all she could think about was grabbing his shirt and pulling him closer. Should she do it? Kiss him again? Did he want that anymore? Maybe sleeping on it had changed his mind. Maybe he was already over her. The prince had likely broken plenty of hearts in his time.

She would always care for him. He'd done so much to help her. But the Vagabond's face haunted her. He'd been angry. Violent. What would he do if she gave in? He'd already threatened to let Braeden die if she disobeyed him. Would he outright kill him? Could he even do that?

Braeden wouldn't survive a fight with the Vagabond. The first Vagabond didn't have a physical form, sure, but he could possess Kara. He'd done it twice already. If he did it again, Braeden might not defend himself if it meant hurting her. The Vagabond had to know that, too.

However much she hated it, Braeden would only be safe if she remained distant. She sighed, cursing under her breath, and couldn't look at him.

"What are you going to do once we get out of the Stele?" she asked.

He stretched. "I'm going back to Ayavel. The Bloods and I want the same thing, and I get a say in the war now. I'll make sure of that much. Are you going to the village?"

Kara almost missed the pause before he asked the question. She almost didn't catch the slight tremor in his voice. He'd obviously been trying to be casual about asking. The hesitation, the fear—it was hope she would go, not a real question. He wanted her at the village and out of harm's way.

A sliver of happiness twisted in her gut without her wanting it to. Maybe his apathy was just an act to appease her. Maybe nothing had changed, except that he would pretend not to care.

Kara sighed. Maybe, when this war was over, she really would find happiness. Flick stretched as he woke up from where he'd curled along the wall.

She looked up at Braeden and couldn't help smiling. "No, I'm not going to the village. I have—um—an errand to run in Ayavel. But first, I need to visit an isen named Stone. He was the first Vagabond's mentor, and I'm supposed to ask him something."

The prince cringed. "An isen? I'm coming with you."

Kara should have refused. She should have told Braeden to go to Ayavel and kept him at a distance. But she wanted his company, and she couldn't tell him no.

KARA

Five hours later, Kara and Braeden tore through the forests on Ryn's back, following a map from the Grimoire to Stone's last known home somewhere in a distant mountain.

"I think that's it up there," Kara said, pointing through the trees as Flick squirmed in her satchel.

A path, now worn and beaten with age, cut through the mountain. It led to a low cave almost completely hidden by a row of trees. If Kara hadn't been looking for it, she would have never known it was there.

"Let's go, then," Braeden said, his voice still flat.

Kara patted Ryn's neck, and the giant wolf dissolved into dust. With a sigh, she wished she and Braeden could go back to the way things were. She missed seeing him smile.

"I think I should go. Stay here," she said. "Um, please," she added when she saw him glare at her out of the corner of his eye.

"It's an isen, Kara. I can't have him stealing the Vagabond's soul and controlling the Grimoire."

Kara nodded. Valid point. The first Vagabond trusted Stone, but even an isen could change in a thousand years.

They started up the trail and crunched their way along the loose rocks and dust. When she neared the cave entrance, Kara looked around the corner and resisted the impulse to gasp.

A man sat cross-legged on the floor. He'd already

been looking at her as she rounded the corner, as if he'd known exactly where her head would appear.

He wore a simple set of brown linen pants and a white tunic. A thin shower of gray dotted his otherwise black hair, and a thin beard lined his mouth.

"The bloody hell do you want?" he asked.

His British accent and beard reminded Kara of Shakespeare. Needless to say, Stone had lived far longer than the dead poet. His brusque tone, though, told her he wasn't one for pleasantries or small talk.

"I'm Kara, the Vagabond."

"Oh, you," he said with a shrug. He closed his eyes and took a deep breath.

Kara waited, but Stone didn't move. Was she supposed to say something? She turned to Braeden, but the prince shrugged. He hadn't even been acknowledged yet.

"Why are you traveling with an Heir?" Stone asked without looking up.

Braeden crossed his arms. "How do you know who I am?"

"Who doesn't? Your little stunt back at the gala is legend already."

The prince huffed but didn't say anything more.

The isen shifted in his seat. "I take it you both know who I am, as well?"

"Stone," Kara answered.

"Very good. And you know what I am?"

"An isen," Braeden said with a hint of disgust.

Stone chuckled and mocked Braeden's tone. "Yes. So, have you made more vagabonds yet, child? This boy hasn't asked, has he?"

Kara balked. "How do you know about that?"

"Child, I made those grimoires for your master. You're asking all the wrong questions."

Kara shook her head. "Look, that's why we're here. Do you know of a way to get into the kingdoms without being seen? The first Vagabond said you might."

"You refer to him by his title?"

Kara paused. "Well, yeah. He hasn't told me his name."

"Have you asked?"

"Did you teach him to love annoying questions?" she asked without a pause.

"I suppose he wouldn't tell you anyway. He rather hated his name," Stone said with a sigh.

"What is it?" Kara asked, interest piqued.

"Why ask me? Ah, wait. I know. You two are not on the best of terms at the moment?"

"No, not really."

Braeden raised his eyebrows, but Kara didn't acknowledge it. There was no hiding anything from Stone. It sucked.

"Cedric," Stone said.

"Oh." She thought it would be harder to get that

from him. So, the first Vagabond was named Cedric? It made him sound so... normal.

Stone glanced at Kara. "You smell strange. It's not terrible, but there's the barest hint of something... off."

"So, entrances to the kingdoms," Kara muttered, resisting the urge to roll her eyes. This guy was too much.

"Right, right," Stone muttered, lost in thought. He stared at her.

"Do you know of any?" Kara asked.

"Yes. It has been four hundred and seven years since I last used one of them, but they might still be open. Stay here."

Stone disappeared into the shadows of the cave, leaving Kara and Braeden standing in the sunlight.

"Do I smell bad?" Kara asked without looking at her friend.

Braeden shrugged. "You smell fine. I mean, for sleeping in a cave."

She laughed and pushed him, reverting for a moment to their old ways. He grinned and batted her hand away. They caught each other's eye, though, and their smiles faded. Braeden looked back into the cave, even though Kara couldn't see through the shadows.

"He is the strangest isen I have ever met," he said.

"Yeah, I believe that," Kara answered.

Stone reappeared a moment later with a few sheets

of paper in his hand. Symbols and landmarks Kara didn't recognize littered the maps.

"Sew these into your grimoire. Adding an entry to one of the books will automatically update the others. If you don't do it yourself, your second should do it," the isen said.

Kara's gut twisted in annoyance. There wasn't hiding anything from this guy.

"Your second?" Braeden asked.

"Oh, you don't tell the boy everything. No bother. Have you picked one?" Stone asked.

Kara glared at him, but Stone arched his eyebrows as if he still waited for an answer.

She grabbed the pages and turned to leave. "Thanks."

Braeden followed her down the path, but Kara looked over her other shoulder to glare at the isen standing at the top of the trail. He'd been helpful, yes, but annoying. It seemed as though he didn't even have emotions.

"So, what's a second?" Braeden asked when they got to the foot of the path.

Flick ran out of Kara's satchel and sat on her shoulder. She scratched the little guy's ears as she debated whether or not she should answer Braeden's question. It would just be another chance for him to be involved. She took a deep breath and nearly told him anyway, but Braeden didn't give her the chance.

He glared into the forest. "Never mind. I forgot how badly you want your space."

Kara's stomach tightened. "Let's just get going. I figure it'll be easiest to use Flick."

Braeden nodded, but he wouldn't look at her. She reached for his arm. He flinched.

She sighed. "It means you have to touch me, remember?"

He nodded and didn't move as she reached for him this time. She remembered the clearing in front of Ayavel, the one through which they'd entered when Braeden was a prisoner. He might want to see the cherry blossom trees, and—

Stop it.

She shook the thought from her head and touched Flick's forehead. They had to go.

She shot one last look back up to the cave. Stone leaned against the rock, watching them with the barest traces of a grin.

A loud *crack* whisked Kara and Braeden out of the field.

CHAPTER TWENTY-SEVEN
BRAEDEN

The cracking noise of Flick teleporting left a ringing in Braeden's ear long after the little creature scampered back into Kara's satchel, apparently proud of its work. The plummeting roar of water joined in with the ringing.

Braeden studied the surrounding forest as mist rolled off the waterfall. Braeden's hair stuck to his face. Kara's frizzed, but he couldn't help thinking she still looked beautiful.

Trees bordered a lake at the base of the waterfall, which broke away into a river on its left. The chorusing roar of rapids wove through the trees. A wide cobblestone trail led from the woods and ended at the lake, perfectly centered with the waterfall.

For what he assumed was the secret entrance to Ayavel, it wasn't very subtle. He didn't remember this from his first trip to Ayavel, but he'd slipped in and out of consciousness and didn't recall much of the journey in.

Kara cleared her throat. "Rather than going right to the Ayavelian lichgate, I thought you might want to see the way in. It's beautiful, and you weren't exactly coherent last time."

He caught her eye and smiled. Words pooled on the tip of his tongue, hitting each other as they fought free. He wanted to say ridiculous things like *I still want you* and *let's run away* and *why are we even here? They hate us.* Each word stumbled, halting the others, until he almost—

A twig snapped. He whirled, eyes darting through the trees. He caught glimpses—a boot here, a tunic there. The trees teemed with soldiers, each waiting for... what, exactly? Were he and Kara even welcome?

He turned back to Kara. She stared at the waterfall with a smile on her face, lost in thought.

She clearly had no idea of the soldiers in the trees. Braeden wanted to sigh, to just grab her and teleport to the village. Maybe lock her somewhere she couldn't get hurt. As much as she'd learned, she still wasn't ready to face the Bloods. Yakona politics became more treacherous with each generation, and she couldn't possibly understand that yet. She had a good heart. She trusted. All of them would use her. All of them would hurt her, and Gavin would probably show his hand first.

Braeden had to face facts, though—even if Kara mastered magic and learned to tread through Ourean politics, he would still want to protect her. He needed to step back. She would have to find her way on her own. He could only hope her plans involved him.

Kara gave him direction. A sense of purpose. He didn't understand it, but he thought it might become something like love over time. It was the closest he'd ever come to it, at least. She cared at least a little—hell, after a kiss like theirs, she had to feel something. But she pushed him away, time and time again. She was hiding something from him, and he didn't have the slightest idea what it could be.

"Braeden, did you hear me?"

He blinked his eyes back into focus before he realized he'd been staring off into space. Great protector he was.

"What? No, sorry. What did you say?"

"Are you ready? I don't know how they'll react to you coming back."

"They'd have attacked by now if they wanted to."

"Huh?"

"There are dozens of soldiers hidden in these trees. You really didn't see them?"

She looked around with a jolt. Apparently, she hadn't. He resisted the impulse to pull her close.

"Shall we get going?" he asked.

"If you're ready, sure."

She stepped onto the cobblestone path facing the waterfall and cleared her throat. After a deep breath, she whispered something he couldn't make out—a password, perhaps. The ground shook.

A flash of blue light caught his eye, and he turned in time to see an Ayavelian guard's silver hand set a painfully bright orb into the trunk of a nearby tree. Clever bastards. They tricked visitors into thinking a password would open the Ayavelian lichgate when, in fact, they had simply hidden the keyhole along the bank.

Braeden studied Kara. What else had the Bloods done to let her think her role in their world was an easy one?

A low groan echoed through the trees. Water pulled away from Kara and made walls in the lake until a path appeared. Stone stairs covered in moss led to the lake's bottom as the water became a fifty-foot wall on either side. A golden temple waited at the bottom of the lake, beneath the waterfall. Mist pooled over it and the now-accessible path through the lake water.

Excellent. He rolled his eyes. If he and Kara took the path, the guards in the trees could close the lichgate and drown them at any time.

"Are you coming?" Kara asked.

She looked at him with those gray eyes, and his heart melted. Though every fiber of his being said it would be a mistake to go, he nodded and followed her. Should the path close on them, he might be able to change form into a Lossian or Kirelm and get them out of there in time.

Maybe.

Braeden set a hand on Kara's back and followed her. He pushed ever so slightly, urging her forward without a word through the makeshift tunnel at a faster pace than she would have taken on her own.

He walked up the steps to the temple. He caught shimmering gold, but he couldn't take in its splendor. Tension pulled at his shoulders.

The crash of waves set his heart racing. The wall of water began to cave behind him. It splashed to the ground. His body hummed, ready to change and fly off with Kara in his arms.

"Braeden."

He turned to Kara, who he had apparently pulled tight to his body. She watched him with a grin.

"Everything okay?" she asked.

He turned back to the water, which he had thought would pour into the tunnel. It crashed against an invisible blockade at the temple entrance. The unseen barrier sealed them inside, dry and safe.

No treachery. No death. Nothing but a hidden temple beneath a lake.

"I'm fine," he said, letting her go.

She ducked her head, but she couldn't hide her smile as she led him deeper into the temple. Golden sunlight streamed from somewhere above. The gleam highlighted her cheekbones and gave her blond hair a red tint. His fingers twitched as he suppressed the impulse to touch her.

The temple arched hundreds of feet above him, nearly as tall as it was wide. Eight, closed, wooden doors lined the hall on either side of him, and one giant doorframe covered most of the wall at the far end. Through this larger opening, a paved road lined with cherry blossom trees curved over a hill. The world through the doorframe danced in a breeze, its color diluted. It had to be another lichgate.

Two guards stood by each door, watching him as he passed. Braeden kept up with Kara and remained behind her, ready and waiting for the tension in his gut to break loose. Any second now, something would go wrong. It always did.

They crossed through the largest doorway. A shudder raced up Braeden's back. The cherry blossoms came into full color as he crossed the threshold, their rows of pink petals bending in a gentle breeze that also whipped through Kara's hair. The sun rose in the distance from behind a forest and shed its rays across the spires and roofs peeking over the tall, white wall that surrounded Ayavel.

"It's beautiful," Braeden said.

Kara smiled. "I thought you'd like it. You're not a criminal, Braeden, and you should never have been brought to such a gorgeous place without being able to see it for yourself."

He wanted to reach down and kiss her again but hesitated. The hair on his neck stood on end. His ear twitched. The whistle of a hundred swords leaving their sheaths filled the air. Feet marched along the grass.

Braeden pushed Kara behind him and turned. Over a hundred soldiers with iridescent skin quickly marched toward them in white tunics with a gold trim. They'd been hiding along the edge of the temple wall, out of sight to any who walked through the doorway. Someone yelled commands he didn't understand. They rushed forward and surrounded him in a matter of seconds.

A tall Ayavelian barked an order at a younger soldier, who tore off toward the castle as fast as he could. The man crossed his arms, his sword still in its sheath, and looked down at Braeden.

"I am General Krik. If you both would kindly follow me," the Ayavelian said with a nod to the palace.

Braeden frowned. "Don't waste time with courtesy after such a rude welcome."

"We are merely being cautious. We don't yet know

you. The Bloods are gathered, so your timing is convenient. Shall we?"

Kara laughed. "Don't lie. You just sent that boy off to assemble them."

Krik smirked. "I did. I didn't know you understood our language."

"Why were you waiting for us?" she asked.

"To lead you to the Bloods, as I feel was rather evident. Shall we?"

"Don't you think this is all a bit excessive?"

"Kara, let's get this over with," Braeden said under his breath.

She sighed and nodded. "Lead the way, General."

Krik walked down the path without looking back, but the army remained. Kara stepped along after the general, and Braeden followed suit. Only then did the group of Ayavelian soldiers sheathe their swords and march behind them.

Cherry blossoms littered the cobblestone road as the palace neared. Braeden walked beside Kara. He wanted to put his hand on her back, to let her know he was there, but he couldn't push his luck. She wanted space. She would get it.

The white gates opened as they neared to reveal a familiar road. The street led past homes and storefronts with closed doors and drawn curtains. After about a mile, it ended at the golden doors of the palace. Roofs from the various homes below it hid the far ends of the palace walls, but the great domes and golden spires touched the sky.

A set of stairs rose from the cobblestone to the main doors, and General Krik hurried up them without hesitation. The small army behind Braeden inched closer, leaving him with little choice but to follow.

The doors opened onto a towering hall lined with columns. The hallway went on for ages, its white walls interrupted only here and there with the occasional golden door. The general stopped at the first entry on the right and opened it without looking in. Light poured into the hallway.

"They're waiting," Krik said.

Braeden entered first. Columns lined the hall. Four thrones covered a platform to his right—he cringed. The general had led them back to the throne room where he'd been sentenced to death.

A royal sat in each throne. Everyone had come to see him return—even the Heirs. Though Gavin sat alone, the other Heirs stood behind their Bloods. The Lossian prince grinned as Braeden entered and nodded once to him. Braeden returned the gesture. Evelyn grimaced when he caught her eye, but he'd expected as much.

But he hadn't expected Aurora to be there. The princess stood with one hand on her father's chair, her good wing curled in tightly to her left side. General

Gurien stood to her right and arched his back as if trying to hide the stump where her other wing used to be.

Aurora's eye twitched, and her lips curved into a frown.

Uh-oh. Braeden tensed to prepare himself. This wouldn't be good.

CHAPTER TWENTY-EIGHT
BRAEDEN

As Braeden stood in the vast throne room, Aurora shoved past Gurien and stormed down the steps in front of the Bloods. She teetered ever so slightly without her other wing, but she pointed to Braeden and glared with the full force of her hatred.

"He is a Stelian!" she screamed.

Her voice echoed through the silent hall. When it settled, Aurora pinched her eyebrows and looked over her shoulder. "Did you not hear me? He is a liar!"

"We know," Ithone said. He raised his eyebrows and peered down the brim of his nose at his daughter as if patiently scolding an infant.

"When did you learn that, Father?" she demanded.

"He was discovered at the gala and used his gift to save your life. You should be thanking him."

Braeden grinned. "Twice, actually. I saved your life twice."

Aurora snapped her head around with such force that her bun pulled loose. Curls trailed over her shoulder. "I would never waste my breath on a Stelian."

Braeden grimaced.

"Leave," Ithone said with a strained tension in his voice.

"Why, of course, Father. I always do your bidding!" she screamed.

Braeden's mouth fell open. Everyone turned to Ithone.

The Kirelm stood. "How dare you speak to your Blood—"

"I don't speak to my Blood. I'm talking to my father! The man who taught me to be ashamed of the power I was given. I've hated myself all these years, but no more! I lost a wing to your ignorance, old man. I will never—"

"Hold your tongue!"

"—I will never fly again because you would not prepare me for the life of an Heir! Waiting for rescue was a crueler fate than learning to defend myself!"

"This is your last chance—"

"To hell with you! I will never bow to your whim again!"

Aurora turned and ran past Braeden, nearly barreling over Kara in the process. The princess ran out the nearest door, her one wing barely making it through as it closed behind her.

Braeden glanced back to the platform. Ithone stood with his mouth open, apparently unable to process whatever had happened. Gurien, however, leaned forward with one hand on the throne. He looked about ready to run after the princess. He tensed his jaw. His eyebrows turned upward in a way similar to how Braeden imagined he looked at Kara. It seemed like all Gurien wanted was to pull Aurora close and tell her everything would be okay.

Gurien caught Braeden's eye. The general's face relaxed into the familiar mask of indifference, but his attention returned to the door.

Braeden couldn't believe it. Gurien loved Aurora, even though the princess barely seemed to notice him.

Ithone sat again on his throne and rubbed his face. "I apologize for my daughter."

Kara tensed, and an indent appeared in her cheek. Braeden clenched his fist, hoping she wouldn't play with fire by commenting. She and Ithone couldn't seem to find a common ground.

Instead of speaking, Kara folded her arms and took a deep breath as if swallowing whatever comment she'd nearly let loose. Braeden nearly sighed with relief.

Aislynn stood and lifted the hem of her gown as

she walked down the steps. She smiled when Braeden caught her eye.

"Braeden, we owe you a great debt. Thank you for forgiving us," she said.

He nodded, but he had nothing to say.

"You both must be tired. Kara, I heard that you and the Hillsidian named Twin are close. I asked her to take you to your room. Braeden, Richard wanted to show you to yours."

Her words got Braeden's attention. He thought Richard didn't want anything to do with him.

"Both are waiting in the hall. Please, make yourself at home."

He nodded and caught Aislynn's eye again. Though she smiled, a shudder ran up his spine. Something was wrong. She—no, she couldn't be hiding something from him. Not after everything they'd endured.

He followed Kara from the throne room but couldn't shake the lingering worry. He glanced over his shoulder and surveyed the faces watching him leave. All but Aislynn eyed him with a calculating glare, as if reserving their next move for the opportune moment.

It didn't matter. He had earned his place in their war.

Braeden pushed open the door and held it as Kara slipped through. She smiled at him when she passed, and his heart fluttered. How could one person have such an effect on him?

It wasn't fair.

Richard and Twin whispered together in the hallway as he and Kara left the throne room. Both turned when the door closed. Twin ran to Kara and wrapped her in a hug. She laughed, and Kara joined in with a big smile. Twin pulled Braeden in as well. He ended up behind Kara, somehow crushing her in the middle of this strange group hug. He had to force himself to back away when Twin released them.

Richard shook his head and laughed. "I think it's fairly evident I missed the both of you as well. I hope a hug is not required of me."

Braeden laughed. Twin pulled Kara down a hallway lined with rooms toward a grand staircase at the far end. The girls spoke in whispers, but Kara never turned to look back.

"You should at least try to hide your longing, boy," Richard said.

Braeden groaned. "Was I obvious?"

"Painfully so. You're lucky none of the Bloods saw you."

He shrugged. "They likely already have. I think I lose a little more control every time I'm near her."

"Don't say it aloud." Richard shot a glance back to the closed throne room door.

"Is everything all right?" Braeden asked.

"Let's take a walk."

Richard spun on his heel and passed through a smaller door nearby. Braeden followed, but sunlight poured through from outside. Richard disappeared into the light, and Braeden had to pause for a moment as his eyes adjusted.

They'd walked into a garden. Silver walls covered in dark green ivy hid a portion of the orchards ahead. Tall apple trees peeked from above the walls. A thin, silver gate stood on their right, open to any who wanted to peruse the Ayavelian gardens.

Richard gestured to the gate. "Shall we?"

Braeden nodded. The silver walls continued down the lane and split farther down into two paths in what appeared to be a labyrinth. Braeden followed Richard, who turned through the garden as if he'd walked it one hundred times already.

"My boy, I am so sorry," Richard said after a while. Tears pooled in Richard's eyes, but the old man wiped them away. He grabbed Braeden and pulled him into a hug, one even tighter than any Twin had ever forced him to endure.

Braeden didn't know what to do. He hugged back.

"After you were discovered, Braeden, I broke down. It was all too much, too fast. The boy I'd raised to be my son actually belonged to the man who killed the woman I loved? I couldn't think. I was still so weak from Lorraine's death, and—" His voice broke in a sob.

"I thought you didn't want me," Braeden admitted in a hushed voice.

Richard took a step back. His cheeks flushed, but he broke through Braeden's doubt with a single, proud smile. "You are and always will be my son. That you ever doubted me is my failure and mine alone. I may be old, my boy, but it doesn't mean I can't make a mistake now and again."

Braeden laughed through the knot in his throat as he tried to grapple with what exactly was happening. "Rarely, old man. You make mistakes rarely."

Richard laughed, too, and continued down the row. Braeden didn't keep track of the path they took. He suddenly didn't care.

"When Gavin chained you like a criminal, I refused to even look at him. I still haven't," Richard said.

"You haven't seen him since the gala?"

Richard shook his head. "I told him Lorraine would have been merciful, and reminded him to do the same. So, he banished me from the trial."

A wave of regret shot through Braeden. Now he knew why Richard hadn't been at the trial. "And he's allowing you to speak to me now?"

"Avoiding him has its privileges, including avoiding new mandates for a short while longer," Richard said.

"What happened to the brother I grew up with? He was arrogant, sure, but never this controlling."

Richard rubbed his beard. "Power corrupts, and I

fear he is nearly gone. Much longer, and no one will be able to save him. What sort of son calls his father by name? I'm not his father. He doesn't see me as his superior or even as an adviser. I try to be his conscience, but he sees me only as an annoyance."

"Why does he do it?"

"What?"

"Call you Richard. What happened?"

"Oh. You."

"Me?"

"Until I found you in your mother's carriage, I had only Gavin—a little boy with selfish ambition. I could never shake it from him, no matter what I tried. Humility was lost on him. Compassion, a mystery. All he knew was war and pride. He led a campaign against the squirrels once for moving into an abandoned attic when he was six. In his mind, they invaded his home."

Braeden laughed, but Richard shuddered. He frowned and shook his head as if still disgusted with whatever it was Gavin had done in his campaign. "No, Braeden. It isn't funny. For weeks, he killed any squirrel he found, even if it wasn't in the attic. He butchered them. I tried everything to make him stop—disappointment, pleading, disgust. It wasn't until I asked Lorraine to step in did he leave the animals alone."

"He was only a boy, and a prince with privilege to make things worse. He made a mistake, but he's grown up. I'm sure he can see reason if we say the right thing."

Richard stared into the sky, shaking his head as he paused in thought. Finally, he sighed. "Has he grown up, though?"

Braeden continued walking. He didn't have an answer.

Richard smiled. "But then I found you. You were such a sweet, little child and so scared those first few weeks. You did everything we asked ten times faster than we thought possible. You listened when I told stories. Your eyes," Richard laughed, "oh, your eyes always went wide with wonder. When you began training, you devoted all your soul to learning. I had never seen such a warrior, especially in such a small package.

"You were afraid of the word 'father,' though, and I never pressed the matter. I knew it had to be from some horror you endured in the Stele. I figured, maybe Carden murdered your father, maybe even in front of you. I had no idea, but I wanted you to know I was here for you, and I would protect you. You protected the Hillsidian people from isen on your own accord."

Braeden smiled. He'd forgotten it all.

Richard grinned. "One of the best days of my life was our first isen hunt. It was the first time I truly felt as though I had a son. Even if I have lost Gavin, at least I still have you."

Braeden didn't know what to say. His throat stung, and the corners of his eyes were wet. Tears? Not possible. Braeden didn't cry.

But Richard did. The retired king who had killed hundreds of isen and an untold number of yakona in battle now stood before Braeden in a foreign kingdom, crying. The tears were rare—even now—and slid down the sides of his face in one or two, thin streams. There was no sobbing. No sounds. Merely a warm smile and happy tears.

"Come here, my boy," Richard said, beckoning with one hand.

Braeden leaned down and hugged him again. When the shock faded, and he still couldn't bring himself to cry, he simply hugged his father tighter.

This man was his father, not Carden.

Richard took a deep breath. "Gavin might be beyond my ability to help, but you can still save him from the madness. Remind him what it means to be a king."

"I'll try, Father."

Richard laughed and patted his shoulder. "Please, always call me Father."

"I will."

Movement caught Braeden's attention. At the far edge of their row, Gavin leaned against the garden wall with his arms crossed. His brows furrowed when he met Braeden's eye, his face a mask of cold hatred.

Braeden loosened his grip. Had Gavin been controlling Richard all this time? Had this been a ploy to make Braeden weaker?

Considering the strength of a yakona's blood loyalty, how did Kara trust anyone in this world? How could she trust Braeden, even? He didn't know how she did it.

"May I have a word, Heir?" Gavin asked.

Richard sucked in a small gasp at Gavin's voice, and Braeden all but sighed with relief at the retired king's legitimate surprise. His reaction meant he hadn't known Gavin was near. He'd spoken the truth. The look of hatred on Gavin's face, though, implied he'd heard the confession. It was a potentially deadly problem.

Braeden whispered in Richard's ear. It was so quiet, he knew Gavin couldn't have heard it. "Find Twin. Kara will be with her, and she will watch out for you."

Braeden turned to Gavin and spoke in a normal tone. "What would you like to talk about, Blood Gavin?"

He led Gavin away from Richard and out of the labyrinth. He had to get the king far enough from Richard to give their father a chance to leave.

"What would you like to talk about, brother?"

Braeden prodded. He used the term intentionally and got the grimace he'd expected. Hopefully, it would redirect the Blood's anger.

"I believe I made it clear you're never to use that term with me," Gavin said.

Gavin stalked out of the garden when they neared the exit, letting the gate swing shut behind him even as Braeden passed through it. Braeden caught the door and brushed it off, following the Hillsidian Blood into a small side door in the palace.

Five minutes of silent walking and unrecognizable hallways ended in an open door. Gavin stopped in front of it and gestured inside.

"Ah, no. After you, Blood Gavin," Braeden said with a grin.

Gavin shook his head and walked inside. He stood in the center of the room and raised his arms as if to say, *are you happy now?*

Braeden followed. The door slammed on its own behind him, but Braeden resisted the instinct to flinch at the sound.

"What do you want, Gavin?" he asked as calmly as he could muster.

"I wanted to discuss the rescue. I want to know how you did it."

"And why would I tell you?"

Gavin sneered. "Aren't we all friends here?"

"You don't care about the rescue. You would have

left them if the Vagabond hadn't interfered. So why am I really here?"

Braeden had been careful to avoid using Kara's name. He didn't want to imply intimacy. If he could make them think he didn't care about her, he would. He didn't think it would do any good, of course, especially if his expressions were so out of control that Richard had picked up on the longing in an instant. No, it wouldn't do any good, but he would try anyway. For Kara.

Gavin laughed. "Yes, you are so perceptive. A lifetime of lying to those who treated you like family—"

"Get on with it!"

Gavin arched his back but didn't respond. He stared at Braeden as if internally debating with himself as to whether or not to continue. "You are here, Braeden, because I have a plan to kill Carden. I need your help."

Braeden wanted to grin but resisted. It had to hurt for Gavin to admit he needed assistance of any kind.

"What's your plan?"

Gavin began pacing. "I want to draw Carden out of the Stele. So far, everything has been on his terms. We have been exposed when we thought we were safe, even in our own homes..." he paused, eyes slipping out of focus for a second before he continued. "But I want to trick him. I discovered a valley not far from where we believe the Stele to be located. I want to lure him to a camp and ambush him."

"Where I come in, I suppose?"

"We need someone he trusts. Someone who will take him there. All we need to do is kill him, and the war is over."

Braeden tensed his jaw. Somehow, he doubted the war would end with Carden. There was the whole matter of Braeden following in Carden's footsteps, of becoming the next—no. He didn't want to think about it. He couldn't.

"Carden does not trust me," he said.

"Make him. Tell him whatever it takes to make him think we did wrong by you."

"It won't take too much convincing, Gavin."

"Blood Gavin," he corrected.

"When you begin acting like a king, I'll address you like one. All you've done since—"

"Don't. I heard Richard's tirade. I don't need to be saved."

Braeden relaxed his shoulders. "If you don't need to be saved, then where is the Gavin I knew before you took the throne? You—"

Gavin held up his hand. "Please stop."

The "please" made Braeden falter. He'd been prepared for yelling, cursing, or even a fight, but not courtesy.

The Blood leaned against a wall. "The weight of a

kingdom will change you. I always dreamed of greatness without knowing the consequences. I was a child before. I'm a man now. If you can escape your fate, Braeden, you should."

Braeden took a step back.

Gavin continued as if their tangent never happened. "As I said, I need you. I can't make this plan work without you. Can you do this?"

"Say, I do. Say, you kill Carden on the battlefield. What then?"

"What do you mean? The war would end."

"I would become Blood. Are you telling me the rest of you would simply let me be? Let me go back to my mountain and rule my cold, little, pocket of Ourea?"

Gavin looked at the floor and didn't respond.

Braeden slammed his fist on the door. It rattled and sent shivers into the walls. "Answer me!"

"You hate what you are as much as we do, Braeden," Gavin said.

Braeden could barely breathe. They meant to kill him before he even got the chance to rule.

But wouldn't Ourea be better off without Stelians? He'd already said as much himself. All his people knew was pain, murder, and torture. They were vicious. Evil, even.

He looked at the rug. Was Kara better off without him, too? He'd nearly killed her once already. She'd gone into the Stele to save him and nearly been killed a second time as they escaped. He'd gotten her into more trouble than she'd managed on her own, and that was saying something.

He wanted her. For a while, he'd thought he wanted her more than anything. But even more powerful than his desire was his wish to protect her: the one thing in his life giving him peace.

Kara was safest without him. The whole world was safer. The first Vagabond had told him once about how Braeden's part in the war would be more important even than Kara's. Is this what he'd meant?

"I need an answer. We don't have much time," Gavin said.

Braeden nodded. "I'll do it."

"Thank you. Come. We have to meet with the Bloods. I need to show you the maps and discuss the full plan."

Braeden nodded again and waited for Gavin to lead the way. He didn't have much time, true, but he would use what time he had left wisely. When he finished speaking with the Bloods, he would find Kara, tell her to protect Richard, and kiss her once more. Afterward, he would be out of her life forever.

CHAPTER TWENTY-NINE
KARA

Kara took a deep breath of the brilliant, late summer air. Instead of taking her to her room, Twin had surprised Kara with a picnic by one of Ayavel's many waterfalls. Flick nuzzled against Twin's leg, purring as the girl stroked him.

Beams of light broke through gaps in the trees. The lake shimmered. Ripples broke the water whenever a fish swam too close to the surface. In the quiet of this isolated bit of the forest, Kara almost forgot about how much she wanted Braeden or how the first Vagabond—Cedric—had threatened to kill him if she gave in.

"I missed you," Twin said with a grin.

Kara smiled. "I missed you, too."

"How was the rescue? I was so scared when you

and Braeden didn't come back. I thought—we all thought—"

"I know. It's a miracle we escaped at all."

Twin winked. "Did you enjoy the time alone?"

Kara's smile disappeared. She cleared her throat and looked into the lake without responding.

Twin sighed, apparently gathering all she needed from the lack of an answer. "Do you want to discuss it?"

"Not really."

"Well, what do you want to talk about?"

The tiara. Before Twin became her second in command, Kara had to know exactly what happened the day Twin had brought her Gavin's cursed tiara. Twin had snatched it from Kara's fingers seconds before she put it on. If she hadn't, the tiara would have pricked Kara with some of Gavin's blood—he'd have been able to control her until his bloodline worked its way out of her system. But he could always add more. If she'd been infected, Gavin would have had unlimited control over her. Yet Twin had somehow defied her king to save Kara.

Something didn't add up. Yakona couldn't disobey.

"I need to ask you about the tiara," Kara said.

Twin sighed. "I already apologized a million times, Kara. I never wanted to hurt you."

"I know. But how did you defy a direct order from Gavin?"

"It wasn't a direct order."

"Wait, but I thought... what was it, then?"

Twin shrugged. "I'm not sure. I feel so guilty about it that I keep playing that day over and over in my head, just trying to figure it out. He handed me the tiara and told me to give it to you. That was it. He didn't tell me not to say anything—I just assumed I wasn't supposed to. I think he knew I'd been eavesdropping and that I knew what it could do to you."

"Then, why would he give it to you?"

"I think he tricked me. It's the only thing that makes sense. He scared the life out of me—I still can't look him in the eye—and I think he wants me to go with you to the village. He wants to know where it is."

Kara nodded. Now *that* made sense.

"You should leave me behind, Kara. I can't let Gavin trick you again."

"He wouldn't be powerful enough to do that if you became a vagabond."

Twin caught her breath, the hope in her eyes almost too painful to bear. "Really?"

"You'll even have a grimoire of your own."

"Yes! I'll come!" Twin lunged and wrapped Kara in a hug that sent them rolling onto the grass.

Kara laughed and brushed loose dirt from her pants. "Great. I need to find Braeden, so I'll meet you somewhere. Your room, maybe? Where is it?"

Twin pointed at the palace. "See that door? It leads

to a stairwell. Take it to the third floor and turn right. I'm the first door on the left."

"Got it. I'll meet you there. Pack lightly—only what you need, okay?"

"I will! Thank you for trusting me, Kara."

"You're one of the kindest people I've met in Ourea, Twin. I'm just lucky to have you on my side."

Flick nuzzled closer to Twin, so Kara left her pet with her friend for the moment and turned toward the castle.

BRAEDEN

Braeden settled into a chair in an office behind the Ayavelian throne room. The Bloods trickled in, sitting in the plethora of chairs littering the room, silent while they waited for everyone to join them.

Icy apathy seeped into his core. He didn't let himself feel or worry or think, afraid doing so would change his mind.

Ithone said something involving the word "Stelian" as he walked into the room, but Braeden hadn't been listening. It had no doubt been a taunt, anyway.

The insult didn't matter. Nothing did.

KARA

Kara marveled at how easy it was to find Braeden. She had only to ask the first maid she saw and watch which way the girl's eyes darted. But such was the curse of being feared: everyone kept tabs on him.

She traced her way back to the throne room and waited on the steps beneath the vacant thrones. One of the guards had told her Braeden was speaking with the Bloods and would be out soon, so all she could do was wait.

A hidden door behind the thrones slid open, and the Bloods walked out. Only Aislynn acknowledged her with a smile; the rest, except for Braeden, didn't even look at her. Braeden, though, wouldn't stop frowning as he approached.

"What is it, Kara?" he asked as though he had better things to do.

This distance between them hurt, but she'd brought it on herself. The hair on her neck stood on end as Gavin turned to watch them. She needed to find a place where she could talk to Braeden alone.

"I was going to take a walk through the gardens. Care to join me?"

He shook his head and stalked off, gesturing for Kara to follow. She frowned, but obliged. They walked in silence until he turned into a small office just beyond the main hall. Books lined the dark shelves, and the drawn curtains shut out the light.

He shut the door. "I have an errand to run."

"Um, all right. After that?"

He sighed. "No, Kara. I'm occupied."

"Since when are you so cryptic? We can still work together—"

"Look, I'm doing what you asked!"

Kara wanted to believe he was still just hurt, but the way he narrowed his eyes made her step back. For several seconds, she couldn't form words.

His eyes softened as he watched her expression, which seemed to weaken his resolve. He held her shoulders, but his fingers inched up to her face.

Before she knew it, he kissed her.

This kiss—number three, wow—was different from the others. The first was timid, uncertain as to what either wanted. The second was raw passion. But this one was fearful. His fingers barely brushed her skin, holding her as if she would break into dust at the slightest touch. Her mind numbed, and neither confusion nor happiness coursed through her.

This kiss was full of a new emotion: loss.

He broke away.

"What—?" she asked.

He brushed a thumb along her cheek. His touch spread sparks along her skin.

"I have to go, Kara. It's all I can say. I tried ignoring

you, tried pushing you away like you did to me, but I can't do it. I could never hurt you. But do me one last favor, okay? Take Richard with you. Make him a vagabond. He's not safe here anymore, and you're the last chance for him to have a home. I told him to find Twin, so he's likely with her now. Will you do it for me?"

"Of course, but—"

"Thank you."

He kissed her again, and the loss seeped into her once more. Her thoughts trailed out of her grasp, and she wound a finger into his hair. He stopped at her touch, let out a sigh, and rubbed his nose against hers.

"Goodbye," he said.

"Braeden, what is going on?"

He smiled, took one last look at her, and let go. "Stay out of trouble, at least."

He opened the door and left, just like that.

Air wouldn't stay in Kara's throat long enough for her to respond. She didn't know what to think or say. The kiss made her question the hope she'd felt back before they'd left that hidden room in the Stelian grottoes. A kiss like that left her without any hope at all.

He'd said goodbye and meant it. Whatever happened in that meeting with the Bloods ruined everything.

She took a deep breath before she noticed the stares coming through the open door. A few ladies in trailing gowns, and even a half dozen guards, watched her. At least the Bloods were gone.

"Are you all lost? Move it!" Kara shouted.

Most of them flinched, but they all hustled back to their lives. The guards looked away from her and twitched back into position.

She turned down the hall and walked toward Twin's room. Whatever Braeden had gotten himself into, it was bad. Guilt churned in her stomach. She'd wanted to keep him at an arm's length, not lose him forever.

Kara's feet stopped on their own in front of Twin's door, but she didn't look up until it opened.

Twin looked her over. "Why are you staring at my doorknob?"

Kara glanced through the doorway without answering. Flick jumped over a packed bag on the bed, chasing something she couldn't see.

The hair on Kara's neck stood up, so she looked over her shoulder. A figure moved back behind the corner in the hallway, out of sight, as if someone had been watching her and not wanted to be spotted.

Great, now she had a tail. She slipped into the room and closed the door behind her.

BRAEDEN

B raeden ducked back behind the wall in time for Kara to only see a lingering shadow. She would know she was being followed without knowing who it was.

Good. Hopefully, it would make her leave.

Braeden's head still reeled from the kiss. It had been painful. It was a real goodbye, a terrifying one that left him sick to his stomach. He'd hidden to watch her as she left and seen the way she had lashed out at those who stared at her in the hall. She was angry, confused, and had every right to both emotions.

He had wanted to tell her everything would be okay, but it would have been a lie.

The sooner Kara left Ayavel, the better. She needed to be in the village, out of harm's way. He could only hope they would keep her distracted long enough for him to kill Carden. Once the man died, she wouldn't need to be in the middle of this mess anymore.

At least, it's what Braeden kept telling himself. He had no idea if it was really true.

He took a deep breath and returned down the hall, pausing only to kick a soldier's foot back into a broom cupboard. He closed the door with more force this time to lock the dead spy inside.

Braeden had also let Kara think the Bloods were following her because, in truth, they were. This spy had been Ayavelian, too.

He headed to the drowng Gavin had waiting for him outside, but took one, last look at the closed bedroom door. He hoped he'd made the right choice.

KARA

Kara took a deep breath and sat on the bed. She needed to get it together. If she had been crying, it was no wonder everyone stared at her after Braeden left.

"Is everything okay?" Twin asked.

"No, but we have a job to do. Is Richard here?"

"Yeah, he just needed to wash his face."

Richard came out of the bathroom at the mention of his name. He still held a towel to his chin, and droplets of water clung to his beard. He paused when he saw Kara.

"Vagabond," he said with a nod.

"What's wrong with Braeden?" she asked.

Inwardly, she cringed. Jumping into a conversation without returning a welcome was rude. She meant to apologize, but Richard answered as if she hadn't done anything offensive.

"I have no idea. After he and I spoke, he walked off with Gavin and told me to find you."

"Why?"

Richard sighed. "Gavin heard me confess something I have kept from him his whole life. I cannot remain here."

Kara nodded. "And you're like a father to Braeden. A real one. So, he wants you safe."

"Yes."

No one spoke as she processed that. If Braeden wanted her to protect Richard, she would do everything in her power to make it happen.

Richard cleared his throat. "Last time we talked, Vagabond, I was not kind to you. I didn't realize my son would stoop so low as to try to control you, nor did I believe you were telling the truth. I was wrong."

Kara smiled and held up her hand. "Please, Richard. It's all right. I'm sorry if I came off as harsh. Everything is happening so quickly that I tend to forget my manners. I promised Braeden I would protect you, and I'll do that. But I need you to become a vagabond if you're going to come to the village. Can you do that?"

Richard's beaming grin lit his face. "My dear, I would be honored."

"Then, it's settled. Are you two ready to go? We have to move."

Twin paused as she reached for a trinket on the top shelf of a nearby dresser. "Why so soon?"

"I think I'm being followed."

"But how are we going to leave without being seen?" Richard asked.

"We're using Flick," Kara answered.

Flick barked and jumped onto Kara's shoulder. She ran her finger along his head. He purred.

Twin's face brightened. "Really? He can—"

"Shh!"

Twin tried again, this time in a whisper. "He can teleport? I'd always heard some could do that, but I never thought I'd meet one who could!"

"Well, Flick is pretty awesome."

Twin wrinkled her nose at the word "awesome," and Kara wondered if the girl even knew what the term meant. She shrugged it off. They had to leave.

Twin picked up her bag, but Richard quickly grabbed it from her and slung it over his shoulder.

"Aren't you bringing anything?" Kara asked him.

"I didn't want to risk being seen carrying a bag. It would be too obvious."

"Maybe we could teleport to your room, or—"

"They're only possessions," he said with a shrug.

Kara sat on the bed. "All right, then. We can't teleport through a lichgate, unfortunately, so we need to find a way out. We can't use the main exit, since that's too public. However, I have a map of the kingdom. Maybe we can find a hidden lichgate few know about."

She summoned the Grimoire. Blue dust spiraled out of her pendant and into her hands, forming the shape of a book. Richard smiled. Twin even clapped her hands.

Kara opened the Grimoire to the back cover, where she'd stored the folded maps Stone had given her. She paged through them, suddenly grateful for listening to the Vagabond. If only he didn't force her to do things his way, they might actually be friends.

She thumbed through the sheets and peeked at their titles, stopping only when she saw the word "Ayavel" scribbled at the top of one of the maps. She pulled it from the book and unfolded it onto the bed.

A series of circles clung together in the middle of the page, marked by the word "castle." Forests covered most of the map, and she even found a small temple hidden in a corner. But Kara skimmed over the page, only looking for a way out. She paused when she noticed four blue stars marked with the word "lichgate" that glowed and glimmered like tiny suns in the four corners of the paper.

Twin pointed at a drawing of a small pond not far from the castle. "That lichgate is by the waterfall where we had our picnic!"

Next to Twin's finger, a group of rocks with water flowing over them represented the waterfall. The blue star for the lichgate hovered just behind the falls.

"Was it busy while you girls were there?" Richard asked.

Kara shrugged. "Not an hour ago, but that could have changed."

Twin shook her head. "No, it's suppertime. I haven't been here long, but I can tell you Ayavelians are strict with their schedules and always eat together. I doubt anyone would be out there. The only non-Ayavelians here are the various kingdoms' guards, and they don't seem like the type to picnic."

Kara rubbed her neck. It still posed a risk. If they appeared, and someone was there, she would make it known that Flick could teleport. Considering the consequences she would face if she was found stealing two of Gavin's subjects to make them vagabonds, though, it was a risk she should take. They could always try to go to another lichgate if they ran into trouble.

She wished away the book and stood. "All right. Let's go. Will both of you please touch my shoulder?"

Richard and Twin each set a hand on her sleeve. Kara visualized the waterfall from earlier and touched Flick's forehead.

"So what do we—?" Twin began to ask.

A sharp *crack* cut her off.

In the blink of an eye, Kara stood by the waterfall. Mist swirled over her arms and clung to the back of her neck. She took a deep breath to savor the water's chill as it churned around her.

The rest of the group didn't enjoy the trip as much.

Twin cursed and put her hand on a tree to get her balance. Richard doubled over, hands on his knees, and heaved. Kara set a hand on his back, but he muttered something about her needing to make sure they were alone.

Kara glanced around. The sun's evening rays burned through the trees, casting dappled shadows along broken twigs and spots of grass on the ground. A squirrel knocked an acorn against a tree root sticking up from the dirt but couldn't quite crack the thing. Nothing else seemed to have seen them.

Twin laughed and pushed Kara's shoulder. "What's wrong with you? Warn me before you do that!"

"I'm sorry, but I had to get us out of there. We still need to hurry." Kara forced a smile. They were wasting time.

Twin just shook her head and walked toward the waterfall. The girl knelt and peered behind the tumbling water, her body blocking the small passage. After a moment, she wiggled inside. Her feet disappeared. Ragged breaths and muffled curses drifted back as she pushed her way through.

"I see it!" she said, her voice muffled by the small space.

Richard bowed to Kara. "Ladies first."

Kara knelt. The perfectly round hole only gave her about three or four feet through which to move, and she couldn't see the other side. She couldn't see Twin for that matter.

"Twin!" she called.

If Twin responded, the water's rush drowned the reply. Kara hesitated. This didn't look like a lichgate—only darkness, dirt, and a little bit of mold filled the tunnel.

"Something wrong?" Richard asked.

Kara shook her head and sighed. "Here goes nothing."

She slid into the small space and crawled on her forearms and knees. Dirt clung to her skin. Twigs pinched her elbows. The waterfall's echo doubled in here, the noise overtaking even the sound of her own breath. She wanted to call for Twin again but didn't see the point.

Light flashed ahead. Shapes formed a short way off. As though through a screen door, the gray outline of a fallen log sat in the twitching grasses of a meadow. Kara grinned.

What a relief.

Blue light split through her peripheral vision, and her stomach twisted as she passed through the still-unseen lichgate. As if on cue, the meadow came into sharp color. The murky greens of moonlit grasses blinked back at her.

She stuck her head out of the tunnel and took a breath of air. The sweet tang of honeysuckle blooms floated on a breeze that flew down her collar. Sweat dried on her neck. She wiped her face and sucked in another deep breath.

A hand grabbed her arm. Thanks to Braeden's training, Kara's first instinct told her to counter, grab the attacker's wrist, and twist until it broke. She grabbed the hand but paused long enough to look before breaking anything.

Twin smiled, apparently oblivious to the fact she'd almost gotten a broken arm. Kara took a deep breath and smiled back.

Richard grunted from the tunnel. "A little help, ladies?"

His head poked free, sandwiched between his arms as he groped for the leverage he needed to pull himself out. Twin giggled and grabbed one arm while Kara grabbed the other. Together, they pulled the retired king from the tiniest lichgate Kara had ever seen.

"Where to next, Vagabond?" Richard asked with a grin.

Kara smiled and wiped the dirt off her hands. "Next, the village. Are you two ready for this?"

Twin grinned. "You have no idea."

Richard and Twin set their hands on her shoulder as if on cue. Kara scratched Flick's head and closed her eyes. She envisioned the Amber Temple, with its four towers and cobblestone road—

Crack!

"It's beautiful!" Twin said before Kara could even open her eyes.

Kara peeked through an eyelid and sighed with relief when she saw the Amber Temple's main entrance. Leaves tumbled over the cobblestone and fell from the low-hanging branches above, but the lyth was nowhere in sight.

"All right, guys. Let me show you to your new home," she said.

Kara would have to introduce them to the lyth later. Some guardian he was. Right now, she had to hurry. She wanted to stop Braeden from whatever mistake he was about to make, but she had to make some vagabonds first.

CHAPTER THIRTY

KARA

Kara opened both doors to the Vagabond's study.

She grumbled under her breath. She really needed to call it her study. A ghost hardly needed a desk.

She had given the barest of tours, showing them the war room, treasury, kitchen, and a few bedrooms—just the basics. They could explore the rest on their own. She had to get out of here.

"Are you two ready?" she asked.

Richard leaned against the door to catch his breath. "You took the stairs three at a time, Kara. Why are you rushed?"

"I need to get back, but I can't leave you here without changing you. I need to turn you both now."

"You evaded my question. What happened to get you so upset?" he asked.

Kara sighed and walked to the bookshelf holding the grimoires without answering. She stared at the books without looking at them. To distract herself, she thrummed her fingers along the top of the shelf.

"Did something happen between you and Braeden?" Twin asked.

Kara sighed. "No. I mean, sort of. Something's wrong with him. I can feel it. He's going to do something stupid, and I need to get back before he does it. I don't mean to rush you two, and I'm sorry. I'm just worried."

Twin nodded. "Well, let's do this, then."

"Before we start, I need you to know why I'm turning you. I didn't want to talk about why in Ayavel, but I need you both to create a vagabond for every Grimoire on this shelf. I have maps to get you into the kingdoms, just like the one in Ayavel. Do you think you can do that?"

"How will we travel?" Richard asked.

Kara paused. Flick purred on her shoulder, his eyes closed. She didn't want to do it, but it made the most sense.

"You need to travel fast," she said.

"Yes," Richard agreed.

"You'll have to be stealthy. Unseen."

"Right," Twin added.

"So, I think you should take Flick," Kara finished.

Breep!

Flick made his angry noise as if he'd understood her. Most of the time, she was pretty sure he could.

"Don't you need him?" Twin asked.

"Not as much as you do. I need to distract the Bloods while you two turn vagabonds, but even that won't buy you much time. You need to move quickly and stay under the radar. Flick is the fastest way to go. If you want to split your efforts, I can also call a flaer."

Richard laughed. "A flaer! A real flaer! How do you do it?"

Kara chuckled. "I guess we know which one Richard wants to take."

Flick nudged Kara's neck, which pulled her away from the plotting. She scratched his tiny head. He whimpered.

"It'll be okay, boy. Twin will take good care of you, and I'm not leaving yet. I still have to show her how to teleport with you, silly." She turned to the Hillsidians with her. "Twin, Richard, do you both understand what I'm asking?"

"I do," Richard said with a nod.

Twin smiled. "Me, too. How does this work?"

"Both of you pick a grimoire. The first Vagabond said they're similar to mine. Mine has an attitude, so I can only imagine that each book has its own personality, as well."

Twin stepped to the shelves first. She lifted her finger over the spines of each book, her hand hovering without touching any of them as she scanned her way across them. After a few moments, she pulled a tome from the shelf.

Her fingers brushed a string of silver wrapped around the leather cover. She yelped and dropped the book. It landed on the floor with a *thump*.

Kara cringed. "I'm sorry, I forgot about the silver. It'll sear your skin."

"I figured that one out, thank you." Twin picked the book up with the edges of her dress and carried it to the desk. The unclaimed grimoire made a *thud* again as she set it on top. A chain dangled from a pendant set into the lock.

Richard followed suit. He grabbed a book and set it on the desk, careful to avoid the silver chain wrapped around his grimoire. Both he and Twin eyed the pendants.

"This is going to hurt," Kara said.

Twin looked up with wide eyes. "How much?"

"A lot."

Twin groaned.

"Hey, I'm here. And you don't have to do this if you don't want to. It's your choice. Being a vagabond... it's lonely, but at least we'll have each other. This is a hard life, and I want you to know that before you get into it. I didn't have that warning."

Twin took a deep breath, nodded, and grabbed the pendant from the lock without hesitating.

A gale ripped through the room. Both Kara and Richard watched in horror as Twin seemed to stifle a scream. Their hair whipped about them, Kara's stinging her skin as she held onto the desk for support. Twin writhed in agony. Her skin glowed blue.

A mist blew from Twin's mouth like a ghost. The pale green haze spun from her mouth and dissolved into the air. When the last of it disappeared, the gale stalled. Twin fell into the office chair, panting.

Kara knelt and grabbed her hand. Richard appeared on the other side. Twin couldn't speak. Kara didn't expect her to.

"Ow," Twin finally said.

Kara laughed, and soon the others joined in.

"So, this is mine?" Twin asked, rubbing her finger along her grimoire's spine.

"Forever," Kara said.

Twin laughed again, and strength seemed to seep slowly back into her. "So, we have to find owners for the rest?"

"As many as you can. Choose the best of the best—soldiers, scholars, healers, you name it. I brought you here because I trust you. I only brought Richard because Braeden trusts him. No offense, Richard."

"None taken."

Kara stood. "I don't think either of you should bring anyone else here until they're turned. The first Vagabond isn't big on trusting those with the blood loyalty."

Twin laughed. "He must love your little trysts with Braeden, then."

Kara looked down at the floor. "How obvious is it?"

"I just know you," Twin said.

Richard rubbed his eyes. "Kara, you're tough to read. I only knew about the two of you because Braeden cannot help himself around you."

"What do you mean?" she asked.

"He watches when you leave, waiting for you to turn around and catch his eye. He dove in front of you at the gala, protecting you when Carden had you at his mercy. My girl, I'm fairly certain Braeden would die for you."

"I don't want that!"

"Love is a strange thing and not often wanted," Richard said.

"I never—"

Richard shrugged. "Some things need not be said."

Kara sighed. "Well, neither of you can tell anyone. As far as I know, that's over anyway."

"What?" Richard asked.

"Oh, Kara, I'm sorry," Twin said.

"Don't be. Just please don't mention it."

"What do you mean, over?" Richard insisted.

"He found me after his meeting with the Bloods and..." Kara trailed off. She couldn't explain what had happened.

"And what?" Twin prompted.

"He said goodbye," Kara softly said.

"You need to find him and stop him from doing whatever he's about to do," Richard said.

"I will. But first, I need to show you both something. I'm not sure what help they'll be, but there are keys to Losse and Kirelm in that drawer," Kara said, nodding toward the desk.

"How—?" he asked.

"Drenowith."

"My life just got a lot more interesting," Twin said.

"That is one hell of an understatement," Kara said with a laugh.

Richard rubbed his hands together and reached for his grimoire.

"All right. My turn," he said with a grin.

The grin faded, though, as soon as he pulled his pendant from the lock. Kara watched his face distort in pain, and the pang of fear that she'd made a mistake shot through her chest. But Braeden trusted Richard, and so should she. She would show him and Twin how to teleport. Only then would she let herself go back to Braeden.

Trust. She had to trust that this was a good idea.

KARA

"Are you sure?" Twin asked.

Kara nodded and looked around the moonlit meadow near the lichgate that would take her back to Ayavel. Twin had teleported her here as practice while Richard sewed the maps she'd given them into his grimoire.

Kara couldn't bring herself to look at Flick. He sat like a lump on Twin's shoulder, staring at Kara as if she were leaving him at the pound. She reached to pat his head, but he pinned his ears back and grumbled.

"Take care of him," Kara said.

Twin pulled her into a hug. "I will. You take care of yourself."

Kara laughed. "I'll try. Now get out of here before I cave to that little tyrant and take him from you."

Twin smiled and brushed her finger over Flick's forehead. She closed her eyes, but Flick glanced back to Kara.

Crack!

Kara flinched at the booming echo. Twin and Flick disappeared in another blink of an eye, too quick to see.

She turned back to the small tunnel that hid the lichgate. She groaned. In five minutes, she would be on her way back to the Ayavelian castle, drumming up some excuse about how she'd gotten lost on a hike and desperately wanted food. Or something.

After she found Braeden and knocked some sense into him, she would have to distract the Bloods from the fact that their subjects were disappearing. The question was how.

Kara took a deep breath and shimmied into the hole. The stink of mold and wet dirt burned her nose, but she kept going. A kick in her gut and the telltale flash of blue light told her she'd crossed through the lichgate. The sudden roar of the waterfall on the other side confirmed it. After the silence of the forest, the water seemed to thunder.

She pulled herself from the hole and stood, trying and failing to brush all the dirt from her clothes. She stretched and looked around, but she was alone. She headed toward the castle and kept her eyes on the forest floor as she tried to come up with a good lie. The longer she toyed with the words, the faker they sounded.

She groaned and ran her hand through her hair. She would wing it.

KARA

Kara didn't have any trouble getting back to her room once she found the castle. A maid showed her through the labyrinth of hallways, a huge smile on the young woman's face. Kara asked about Braeden, but was told he'd left. The woman didn't know where and said the Bloods wouldn't be available until the next day. After the maid left, Kara punched her pillows in lieu of screaming in frustration, but there was nothing she could do but wait.

And wait, she did. The Bloods wouldn't see her. She spent the entire next day trying to meet them or catch one or two in the hall, even going so far as to simply sit in the throne room until they showed up. They never did. They definitely hadn't left for their homes because none of their soldiers left the kingdom.

The Bloods were avoiding her.

Entire, agonizing days passed this way. As the sun set on day four, Kara paced her room in an effort to drum up a plan when the door opened without a knock.

She groaned. "Knocking isn't hard to—"

She stopped when she looked over to see Aislynn in her doorway.

The Ayavelian queen smiled and bowed her head in the briefest of welcomes. "How has your stay been so far, Kara? I've missed speaking to you."

"I—what? I've been trying to find you for days."

Aislynn's brow furrowed. "You have?"

"Yes! I needed to ask you about—"

Aislynn interrupted. "I must apologize. I thought you were avoiding me! But I have something exciting to show you. I can promise you will not want to wait, and it might answer your questions. Even Braeden was too excited to wait until tomorrow morning."

"He was? I thought he left."

"Who said so?"

"One of the maids. She—"

Aislynn laughed. "The maids gossip like a swarm of bees. They're usually wrong. He'll be there if you want to see him."

Kara suppressed a sigh of relief. "What exactly is this thing you want to show me?"

"My scholars found an ancient artifact, one they believe was created by the Vagabond. We have no idea what it is, but I cannot escape the feeling it will turn the tides in this war. It might finally be the answer to stopping this incessant fighting altogether."

Kara waited for her intuition to flare, like it had the moment the queen saw Adele change form. While the twinge of worry sat at the bottom of her gut, it didn't shoot through her like it had the first time. Aislynn might be telling the truth.

"Where is it?" Kara finally asked.

"In Ethos. Braeden is trying his best to dislodge it. The other royals all tried and failed. It's embedded deep into a cave wall, and we cannot remove it. We were hoping you and the Grimoire might have better luck. Will you try?"

She nodded.

Aislynn relaxed her shoulders. "Thank you, Vagabond. My griffin is saddled and waiting. I've heard you can summon mounts with that book of yours. Do any of them happen to fly?"

Kara couldn't help it. She grinned.Blank page.

CHAPTER THIRTY-ONE
KARA

Kara flew for hours, Aislynn always slightly ahead and leading the way on a beige griffin. To keep from scaring Aislynn's mount senseless, Kara had chosen to summon the Grimoire's griffin as well. The black dragon would have probably made the creature jump out of its skin.

They soared through a small valley between two mountains. These low peaks didn't have snow on them, but the chilly night still ate into Kara's body. She hoped they would land soon.

Finally, Aislynn slowed until they flew side by side. "See that cave below with the light? It's where we're going."

Kara glanced down, and sure enough, light emanated from one of the mountain's caves. Guards stood on the ledge in front of it. A figure with dark hair, clad in Hillsidian clothes, walked up one of the paths, too far away to distinguish. That had to be Braeden.

"We're in Ethos already?" Kara asked.

"Yes and no. The gala was held far from here, but Ethos is a massive place with many lost caverns. Shall we?"

Kara nodded. They slowed and headed for the cave, but Aislynn pulled back to let Kara land first on a narrow ledge by the entrance. Kara braced herself as the griffin's feet clattered on the rock. She dismounted and peeked into the tunnel.

Narrow walls and a low-hanging ceiling meant she wouldn't have much space to move. She patted the griffin on his shoulder and wished him away. He disappeared in a puff of blue dust.

She walked in as Aislynn's griffin landed outside, its claws clattering on the rock. Kara headed for a large bowl against the far wall. A fire crackled within it. Its flames cast sparse flickers across the cave, the light barely enough to illuminate the only item in the room: a stone table.

The table legs jutted from the stone, as if the rock had melted to swallow them. Its surface, however, caught her eye. Thin crevices wove across its face like a tiny maze, or a network of tiny veins. She ran her fingers over them, tracing the indents.

Only two chairs sat in the cave, one on each end of the table. They, too, had been carved from the stone and melted to the floor. A small, granite square lay on the surface in front of each seat like a thick placemat. She walked closer to one to get a better view. The raised stone on the table was about as wide as her shoulders, with two, curved indents in each one. Kara didn't have a guess as to what the indents were for, though.

She hadn't seen the Grimoire symbol anywhere on this table, and she definitely had no idea what it was.

"Aislynn—"

Kara turned, but the Blood hovered only inches from her face. She stifled a gasp and stepped out of Aislynn's reach. The queen stumbled, eyes widening and perhaps caught off guard that Kara had ducked out of the way.

Kara reached for her sword. No. This wasn't happening. Aislynn had just tried to—well, Kara didn't know what exactly had just happened. She couldn't process the idea of Aislynn attacking her.

But Aislynn shot a beam of light at Kara. She ducked on reflex. Sparks danced along her skin as it brushed her neck. Her muscles tensed and twisted. Numbness seeped into whatever bit of her the sparks touched.

A trap. This was a trap.

The queen reached her hand out again and aimed

for Kara's chest. Kara dropped her sword and summoned the air into her palms. Her neck wouldn't relax. Her eyes began closing as the numbness spread. She would probably lose control over the rest of her body soon.

Kara drew the air into a shield. Tension pulled on her fingers as the air bent around her hands and blurred her view of the queen. She pushed against the tension and threw the shield at Aislynn, hoping to knock her over.

All Kara needed was a second to summon the Grimoire, and the griffin would fly her to safety. She just had to hold on.

Aislynn leaned into the blast of air and broke through it. Kara summoned the blue sword into her palm, but Aislynn moved faster. She shot another beam of light at Kara's chest. Kara pulled another handful of air to block it, but the light tore through her shield and hit her square in the stomach.

A bolt of electricity burned through Kara's body. Her arms and legs tensed like her neck. Numbness seeped into every muscle. Her throat closed. She slumped against a wall. Her vision blurred until she could see only shapes.

Currents of crippling pain tore through her wrists and up her arms. She screamed. Someone grabbed her collar. They dragged her along the floor and threw her against something solid. She blacked out.

KARA

Dry panic scratched against Kara's throat with each breath as her mind cleared. She looked around. The same bowl flickered nearby, its fire illuminating the stone table as it had before. She sat against a wall, no clue whether seconds or hours had passed.

Aislynn sat in one of the chairs, Kara's sword lying on the table beside her. The queen stared at the hilt, her eyes out of focus. "At least you fought back, Vagabond. I wasn't expecting it."

Kara bit back the urge to spit at the queen. "Traitor."

"Do be quiet."

Kara shifted her weight to ease the numbness in her thigh. Pain shot up her arms. She looked down. A pair of shackles wrapped around her wrists, inward-facing spikes dotting her skin with a dozen bleeding wounds. Red streams wound down her hands and into the crevices of her palms.

Kara gritted her teeth through the pain. "Braeden is right outside! What are you doing? He'll kill you!"

Aislynn laughed. "You saw one of my guards dressed in his clothes."

Kara flinched at the realization. The spikes in her

wrists dug deeper into her skin, tearing it open. She stifled a scream. Tears blurred her eyes.

Aislynn shook her head. "Stop whimpering. When I was in the Stele, I spent four days in those chains. Four days straight. You can't even take ten minutes."

"I don't heal instantly."

Aislynn leaned back in the chair. "It doesn't matter. You won't be in those cuffs for much longer."

Kara tensed. "Just tell me what this is about, Aislynn."

"You can't deduce for yourself? This is about power, child. You were the most powerful thing in Ourea until I realized the muses who rescued you were still helping you. I discovered a way to take their power. You are nothing but bait."

A tall soldier walked in—the same general who had given Kara and Braeden such a rude welcome when they'd returned to Ayavel. Kara took a longer look at him now. The beginnings of wrinkles covered the edges of his eyes, and his long, silver hair was paler even than Aislynn's. He wore an ornate tunic with gold trim. Medals lined his chest pockets.

"What is it, General Krik?" Aislynn asked.

"Still no sign, Your Highness."

"The muse should be here by now."

The Ayavelian Blood pulled a dagger from a sheath hidden in the forearm of her gown. She walked to where Kara sat against the wall and knelt, pressing the dagger to Kara's arm.

"Aislynn, don't!"

The blade cut her skin anyway. More pain shot through Kara's arm and up into her neck. The muscles around her throat tightened. She couldn't breathe. Another stream of red blood pooled and dribbled across the freckles on Kara's arm.

"You are the bait, child." Aislynn's voice softened. "I wish there had been another way."

Kara gritted her teeth. "There is another way."

"No, there isn't."

"But they were already helping us!"

"It was not enough. What a muse is willing to give is never enough."

"What are you going to do, Aislynn? What could capturing one of them possibly do for you?"

Aislynn crossed to the table without answering. She ran her fingers along the veins in the table's stone, her eyes downcast as she spoke. "Do you know what this is?"

"Answer my question!"

"It's the reason Ethos fell," the queen continued. "That nameless Stelian Blood created it, all those thousands of years ago, with the help of an isen. Together, they discovered how to transfer powerful blood from one being to another.

"He killed the isen as soon as it was finished. A short legend is all we have of him. We don't know how the other Bloods discovered it, but when they did, they wanted it destroyed. Only, he'd hidden it. They couldn't destroy it. Out of fear for themselves, they disbanded. That's why Ethos fell, Kara. They couldn't trust each other.

"But in our era, the other Bloods know of this machine. They know I found it. They think it's brilliant. Barely a week ago, I used it to give Evelyn my bloodline. This machine saved the Ayavelian race. And now, thanks to more research from my seers, I can use it again—this time, to take power from an immortal. Only, I'll take it all.

"It's risky, but I have an Heir now and nothing to lose. None of the other Bloods would dare try it. They fear the power, thinking it will be too much. But I can handle absolutely anything."

"You've lost your mind, Aislynn."

"Perhaps." Aislynn sat again in her chair. For several minutes, neither of them spoke.

"Does it hurt?" Kara finally asked.

"What?"

"The table. If you catch them, will the muse feel it?"

Aislynn's voice softened again. "It's agonizing. Evelyn almost couldn't bear it. She begged for us to stop, but I refused. I thought it wasn't the pain of the machine, but the thought of losing Gavin that made her beg us to stop. I would not allow such weakness."

Despite the pain of the shackles, Kara laughed. "Wait, Evelyn and Gavin are together?"

"For years," Aislynn said with a hint of disgust.

"It's not like they're obvious about it."

"They were. You simply didn't know what to look for, I suppose. She still loves him, but no lover should interfere with the right to rule. Evelyn has a responsibility to her people, one I ensured she would fulfill. No one was meant for the throne but her."

"If she were meant for the throne, she would have been born with the Bloodline." Kara hadn't even tried to stop herself. She was right.

Aislynn glared through the corner of her eye in a look that sent a shiver up Kara's spine. Regret flared for a moment in Kara's gut, but she refused to show it. She straightened her back and met the queen's eye. Aislynn stood in a movement too fast to see and smacked Kara across the face.

The sting crept up her neck. Her cheek ached where Aislynn hit her, but she bit her lip to keep from showing how much it hurt.

Aislynn paced the cave. "No wonder none of the Bloods respect you! I tried. I tried to make them see you as an asset, but you're a tool. You don't understand politics. You don't understand what it takes to rule. If my niece had chosen Gavin, she would have lived a lie, exactly as Braeden did for so long. No matter how accepting Hillsidians may seem, they would never accept a queen of a different race. No Blood is powerful enough to change the will of every subject, and there is no denying Gavin would urge her to live in her Hillsidian form. She is so much more! Evelyn sees the truth, now. She knows in her heart what is right."

"I bet Gavin was devastated when he found out."

"Yes, and he needs to hate her for it. It's the only way he can get over this... this infatuation."

"I had no idea you were so completely heartless, Aislynn."

"You can't bait me, child. I'm not heartless. I have loved. I am in love. And he would never dream of distracting me from my people."

"Why does no one know he exists?"

Aislynn turned the full force of her glare on Kara. The look made breathing difficult.

Kara didn't care. This information could be useful. She prodded further. "He isn't Ayavelian, is he?"

Aislynn lunged with stunning speed and lifted Kara by her shirt until she stood. "You will never mention this again."

Pain tore through Kara as the spikes ripped open her wrists. She reached for Aislynn's arms out of instinct, but that made the agony worse. The careful control the Vagabond had taught her in her week at the village disappeared. Instinct returned, and Kara's magic pulled from Aislynn the queen's most influential memory.

Light dissolved from the cave. Aislynn disappeared. Wisps of white and gold light blipped into being around Kara. They twisted around each other and created the glowing outline of a forest. A path of broken grasses wound through a meadow, and Kara—seeing through a younger Aislynn's eyes—watched the dark sky above.

A horse unlike any Kara had ever seen walked over the hill ahead. A thick beard covered its chin, and a long mane hid its neck. A silver horn protruded from its forehead.

Information sped through Kara in an instant, the stream of thought unlike any other memory she had ever experienced. Knowledge flooded into her brain bit by bit and pooled there until she didn't know what to do with it.

Aislynn had only recently begun hunting for a way to pass along her bloodline. She was barren. That shamed her, but she was also in love with an isen—Niccoli. She could never bring herself to marry another Ayavelian, especially when a barren queen would do no good.

Her seers brought her rumors, useless bits of information with no truth, until one found ancient scrolls with everything she needed. To pass her bloodline on to another, she had three possibilities: steal the blood of a drenowith; steal the horn of a unicorn; or find the lost table of Ethos. These were her only leads.

Drenowith were nearly impossible to find. She'd hunted everywhere for them without any luck, but she'd always thought she had better odds of finding a drenowith than a lost table or an extinct animal.

But unicorns weren't extinct. One stood before her now!

Aislynn walked slowly to the creature, but it shied away at the same pace. She followed it through the field, into the forest, into a glen—

Pain. Pain shook the foundations of Kara's mind, nearly kicking her from the memory. This part of the memory fragmented. The wisps broke apart into shards. They sped by, each showing a fleeting image with no meaning.

The unicorn shifted into a snake and slithered away—a drenowith. Aislynn cursed, the sound booming in the darkness.

Carden's laughter echoed around her. His face appeared in a shard of glass, wrinkles smoothed into a younger image of himself. A young boy with Braeden's dark eyes whispered an apology to her. A woman screamed. A dark line creased across Kara's vision, blotting out all light and all hope. Something wriggled into her mouth and shocked her from within.

Kara screamed and pushed away. Rocks dug into her back as she fell, no longer held against the wall by Aislynn's hand.

The mountain cave and the table reappeared in blurry streaks. Men's hands grabbed her, pulling her away. Aislynn screamed again. A guard's grip on Kara tightened. She looked up.

General Krik narrowed his eyes in a glare that told her she'd done something wrong, something out of line. His fingers pinched her skin, cutting off her circulation. Kara's fingertips bleached from the lack of blood.

Aislynn slapped Kara across the face. "You should never have seen my memories! You had no right!"

Even as her cheek stung, hatred pooled in Kara's gut. Aislynn was a coward. She had hunted drenowith and learned nothing from her experience. Hunting drenowith the first time had cost her days in Carden's dungeons, and even that had been for a nobler cause than stealing power for a war.

Kara glared back. "The drenowith tricked you because you deserved it! You were hunting them!"

General Krik shook her. "Be silent, child!"

The spikes struck a bone in Kara's arm, and she buckled under the pain.

Aislynn pushed the guards aside. "Do not slander me! I never hunted drenowith!"

"Your memory said otherwise, you liar!" Kara screamed.

"My lady, the muse is coming! It is close!" a soldier called from outside.

Aislynn balled her hand into a fist. "Then, let us welcome her."

The Blood's skin rippled, sending waves of red and purple light flashing across the ceiling. She grew. Her hair curled, the ringlets getting tight as her hair shortened and glowed like the moon. She turned to Kara and grinned, eyes pink.

"Is that—?" Kara pushed herself against the wall. This had to be Aislynn's daru, her soul. If Aislynn's daru was anything like Braeden's, even the muses might not stand a chance.

This wasn't the Aislynn she had come to know—this was the true ruler of Ayavel. Aislynn was insane. Whatever Carden had done to her all those years ago had broken her completely.

Men screamed outside. Kara willed the muse—she assumed it was Adele—to go away. Her brow wrinkled as she wished fervently to alert her friend of the trap waiting in the cave. No luck. Their connection was one-way.

Adele broke through a line of men. She dove into the cave, a fury of feathers and talons. But Aislynn braced herself as if she had nothing to lose. She caught the charging muse with both hands. They flew backward into a wall. Guards closed in at the entrance, too many of them to count. The tiny room became suddenly smaller, and Kara feared Adele would pay for her kindness with her life.

CHAPTER THIRTY-TWO
AISLYNN

Aislynn ducked a jab from the muse, inwardly wishing she hadn't let the Magari girl distract her. She was supposed to take the muse off-guard and surprise the wicked thing. This drenowith spun and attacked almost too quickly to see. Aislynn had to be faster.

Two of her guards' bodies flew past and slammed into the wall. Their silver blood splattered onto her gown, but she couldn't falter. She couldn't pause. This was her one and only chance to steal a muse's blood and thereby steal its magic.

It was finally Aislynn's time to be truly powerful.

She dodged the muse yet again. Her daru was a gift, certainly, but it was not enough. Every Blood's daru was different. She'd heard tales of the dead Queen of Hillside—rest Lorraine's soul. That woman's daru was a vicious thing that could barely discern friend from foe. It sacrificed control for power. Gavin's daru was nothing but focused rage; whatever the object of his desire, it was either taken or destroyed. Carden—that vile man seemed to have focused control and increased power. She had no idea why he didn't walk around in his daru all the time.

No—Aislynn's was different. Weak. It had very little physical power, only enhanced senses. She could predict movement, hear a branch snap a mile away, taste a change in the weather—she could even smell emotion. But each of those gifts was useless if she couldn't be strong enough to stop an attack.

So today, finally, she would have the power of a god and her revenge, all at once.

The muse's movements blurred across the cave, always a streak of brown and gold. Limbs flew as it tore through the room, clawing and decapitating Aislynn's men. There was no telling what it was the drenowith had changed to, but Aislynn didn't care. All she needed were its wrists and neck.

It. Muses were creatures—monsters that had lived too long and deserved to die.

A black shadow snaked across Aislynn's vision. Her heart skipped beats. She faltered as the sliver of darkness passed. No other eyes acknowledged the streak; none stopped to gape nor to wonder why their Blood had all but frozen in place.

The slivers from Carden's torture never left her.

She waited for the telltale shock, the tremor that always rattled her brain when the slivers made an appearance. It came. The agony burned in her neck and raced up to her temples. She closed her eyes, fighting the bile in the back of her throat. Her mind tensed. The veins in her neck bulged. Her breathing stopped. One, two—three seconds, and it was over. Barely enough to even notice.

"MY LADY!" a guard screamed.

Aislynn opened her eyes.

Time slowed as her senses felt around the world, discerning and predicting movement before it happened. The muse, in its human form, stood over a fallen guard. Its copper hair fell over the guard's face. Its hand blurred, changing shape into a claw. It raised its arm to strike. The soldier screamed.

Aislynn aimed her hand at the muse, focusing her energy into an attack. White light shot from her fingers, arching in shattered lines to the muse. It traced the creature's body, engulfing it in jagged traces of broken light. The muse opened its mouth to scream, but the sound was a cacophony of heartbreak: splintering wood, snapping bones, sizzling flesh. It was not a scream, but a wail.

A call.

"It's summoning its mate!" Aislynn yelled.

Aislynn doubled her effort and focused all her

energy into slowing time. With her weak daru, it was the only way to get the upper hand. Her body tensed. She called on every ounce of energy from her guards —she needed it all to make this work.

Everything knelt to her: her guards, even the tension in the room bent before her, yielding as she gave forth every ounce of her magic into suspending time. It wouldn't last long, but she only needed a few seconds.

The muse's claw hovered in the air, the guard's face wrinkled in frozen fear. Aislynn walked to the drenowith.

With her free hand, Aislynn pulled a symbol from her pocket. It was the Broken Trinity—supposedly the one bit of magic that could subdue a drenowith. Three lines of silver curved around each other, thickening as they came to the tail end of the line before it. Woven together, they looked something like a triangle.

The Broken Trinity's silver glowed at Aislynn's touch and parted in her hand. The three curves of the symbol now rested in her free palm, ready to break the monster before her. General Krik had found this thing, and if it didn't work, Aislynn would kill him herself.

She shoved one of the curves against the muse's throat. It burned the skin, fusing itself to the creature. The beast's lips parted in a slow arc as if to scream, but Aislynn slapped it hard across the face with the remaining symbols to silence it. Two gashes marred the drenowith's cheek.

Two symbols remained. Aislynn placed one on each of the creature's wrists. With a sigh of relief, she saw that they, too, burrowed their way into the muse's skin. If this worked, the muse would not be able to move on its own until Aislynn removed the symbols.

Time resumed with a *hiss*. The muse knelt, dropping its weight to its knees with the fury it had just directed toward the guard. It hung its head such that Aislynn couldn't see its face.

"What have you done?" it asked. Its voice trembled.

"I have put you in your place."

With that, Aislynn nodded to whatever guards survived. Two rushed forward and lifted the muse into a vacant seat at the table—the giving seat. Aislynn moved the muse's hands until the wrists settled into the raised platform before the table. With a shove, she pushed the muse's wrists into seven short spikes in the indents.

It screamed again. When the shriek faded away, the muse spoke in a whisper Aislynn didn't hear.

"What now?" she asked.

"Let Kara go."

Aislynn laughed. She hadn't been expecting that at all. She turned to face the Vagabond, who leaned against the wall. The girl's eyes flittered open and closed again. Her chest rose and fell in an irregular pattern. Weak as she was from the cuffs, she would survive another few hours at least. Aislynn didn't need to hurry.

"The Vagabond lured you here, and you would have me release her?" she finally asked.

The muse nodded. "I vowed to protect her. Though faith means little to your kind, I will not break my promise."

"My kind? You ridiculous thing. Your people have done nothing but torment and destroy for eons! Every natural disaster has been your doing! The lot of you practice magic you could never hope to understand and unleash the fury of nature on the innocents who happen to get in your way when you make a mistake!"

"A few of us are so foolish, yes, but not all!"

Aislynn grimaced. "I've heard enough."

She waved her hand, and the muse's mouth shut in response. Aislynn resisted the impulse to smile in surprise at yet another ability of the symbols. She had done that quite by mistake.

Aislynn walked to the other end of the table and sat at the opposite seat. She set her wrists on the platform and took a deep breath. This would hurt.

She pressed her hands into the spikes on the platform. Her blood trickled over the table's surface, but she closed her eyes to keep from being distracted. She spread her fingers, calling to the magic in the table.

Humming filled the cave. Warmth spread over her shoulders and spilt down her back.

The ritual had begun. Only Aislynn could stop it now, and she wouldn't stop until the muse died.

§⚬

GARRETT

Crickets chirped in the forest below, singing to Garrett as he stalked his prey through the night.

Drenowith rarely received orders to kill. These tasks came from Verum himself, the master of their drenowith Council, and were only levied against those who would harm the drenowith race.

It was an honor to be chosen to hunt, but Garrett could only think of Adele. They were weak when apart. He and Adele were the only muses to love—the rest thought only of themselves. But Adele was Garrett's world. When they were together, no force alive could touch them. When they were apart, they were susceptible. They could die.

But Verum made himself clear. Garrett was to do this—alone. Adele could not join him, likely because they suspected she was still helping Kara. Garrett had no need to make things worse by questioning authority.

No, he would run this errand and be done with it.

A twig cracked a quarter mile off. He stifled a chuckle. Every drenowith possessed incredible senses. Like the others, he could even taste water in the air or hear breathing two miles away. Luckily, only the muses themselves knew of these traits. Such was the benefit of keeping their existence mostly secret.

His prey thought it was the hunter. He finally allowed himself a grin. This would be too easy.

An isen made its way up the path, creeping along the trail at a pace to rival a turtle. Garrett could smell the lilac scent pooling on the sporadic breezes, and it set his hair on end. Even drenowith hated the isen—soul stealers could take any soul they pleased, even an immortal one.

Garrett lost himself to thought as the isen approached. He would know when Niccoli came too close.

Niccoli—it made sense that the Council would want him dead. The man was a terror. He had survived fifteen hundred years and built the strongest guild known to Ourea. He openly hunted drenowith—and that was where he went wrong.

None hunted drenowith and survived.

A boot crunched the earth beneath it in a footstep too slow for human ears to recognize. Niccoli stood perhaps fifteen feet away now.

About time.

Garrett leaned forward and used the movement to loosen up his hand. Centuries ago, Adele had taught him how to summon a sword from the air without using his own energy at all. He had never again carried a weapon. There had been no point.

A leaf scraped against the linen of a shirt. Weight shifted to another leg as Niccoli prepared to lunge. Garrett didn't move, preferring to let the isen think he'd truly snuck close to a muse.

Niccoli dove forward. Garrett rolled away from the cliff edge, half-hoping the isen would simply run himself off the cliff.

He didn't.

Garrett summoned the sword and dove for the isen's heart.

One thrust should have been enough. Garrett rarely missed. He rarely made a mistake. But tonight, he was without Adele. He could be easily distracted.

The sword plunged into the isen's side. Niccoli doubled over and fell to the ground with a *thump*. Garrett sighed. Niccoli fought to push himself up, to recover, but even an isen couldn't ignore a wound so deep. His arm shook and gave out each time he tried to stand, always sending him face-first into the dirt.

Garrett needed to put him out of his misery. He lifted the sword to the isen's neck, to sever it and be done with the whole affair. He applied pressure, aimed, and—

A wail flew by on the wind. The sound broke his heart, made it flutter. Panic raced through him, though Niccoli continued in his fruitless endeavor to stand.

It was the call. Adele was in danger.

Garrett ran to the cliff edge and jumped off, shifting as he fell. Leathery wings broke from his back. Hair sprouted on his hands and face. He had only envisioned the wings; he had no idea what he'd become. Only finding Adele mattered.

AISLYNN

Aislynn dared open her eyes only when the first sting of pain burned in her wrist.

The muse's clear blood filled each crevice in the table's surface as it made its way closer. Very soon, Aislynn would have magic known only to the most powerful creatures in Ourea.

The muse's head drooped over its hands. Its hair hid its face. It leaned forward, most of its blood already in the tiny chasms composing the table's surface.

Pain splintered up Aislynn's arms. Her chest rose and fell faster and faster, but no air reached her lungs. Her wrists stung as the muse's blood crept into her body, and the pain grew each second. Her veins tightened. Her arms shook, and every fiber of her being told her to pull away. But she would fail if she stopped the transfusion. She would lose the power. The glory. She would never be able to use her new magic to forever end the bickering in Ourea.

Even if this failed, she didn't fear death. She had an Heir; though Evelyn still had much to learn, at least the bloodline wouldn't die out. Aislynn had nothing to lose but Niccoli.

She faltered. Niccoli: her one light in life.

Memories flittered by in glimpses: the moon framing his silhouette; the brush of his hand on her face; his breath on her neck; his first words to her. She had been only sixteen when he found her gazing into a pond on the edge of Ayavel.

"It would be torture to never again see that face of yours, and that alone saved you tonight," he'd said.

She took a deep breath, expelling his rough voice from her mind. He was immortal. He would live forever; she would die. To him, she was a toy. As much as she loved him, he would forget her when she died.

Unless—unless a muse's blood made her immortal, too. She could be with him forever.

Aislynn grinned. She wouldn't stop the transfer. This would either work or kill her.

CHAPTER THIRTY-THREE
GARRETT

Garrett flew too quickly to be seen. In a matter of minutes, he'd covered hundreds of miles. It was unsafe, unwise even, but he might already be too late.

If Adele had called to him in such agony, it was life or death.

His panic pulled him toward a mountain that first appeared as a blip on the horizon. He could sense her in a cave, likely dying. He would kill everything in there until he found her. Not even the spiders were safe.

He reached a row of guards long before they realized there was danger. A sentry scratched his head, the arm blocking Garrett's path at the wrong moment. Garrett took the limb with him into the cave. The owner screamed in agony outside.

He only caught glimpses of the room: a table, the chained Vagabond girl, the Ayavelian queen, blood—Adele.

He landed first on the Ayavelian queen's neck. His momentum pushed her against the cave wall before she could scream. Something popped. He ran his claws across the queen's neck, spilling her iridescent blood down her dress. Guards rushed forward, but he tore off their heads and limbs until nothing remained. Blood pooled on his hands.

Garrett stopped only when Adele came into view once more. He knelt beside her and lifted her into his arms. She slumped, unable to even hold up her own head.

He paused. His senses numbed until he couldn't smell or hear or feel anything. The world returned to its normal pace, as he could only stare at his love. His life. He lifted her head to his and brushed his nose on her cheek, but her eyelids didn't even flutter.

Someone sobbed. The Ayavelian queen lay crumpled against the wall. She reached out blindly with her hands, as if she couldn't see.

Not far off, Kara watched him with wide eyes, but she didn't speak. She didn't plead, and it seemed as if she didn't hope, either. She did not ask for forgiveness, which was for the best—he assumed this was somehow her doing.

He ran to the edge of the cave, past the still-assembling guards, and flew off into the night before they could tell him to stop.

The Vagabond was on her own. She had caused this by trusting the wrong people, and she would have to find a solution. The drenowith would no longer solve her problems for her.

He raced as fast as he could for the cave he and Adele had long called home. It had dozens of entrances and even more exits, but he needed only one at this moment.

He fell into a dive when he found it—the cave they had used only once before. He flew through the twists and turns and stumbled to his feet once he found the cavern hidden deep within the mountain.

A crystal coffin lay in its midst, illuminated by the pale, blue glow of crystals embedded in the cavern's walls. They jutted from the rock; sharp lanterns that glowed with all the brilliance of the moon.

The coffin lid rested on the floor, clear as glass. A pillow lay at one end of the coffin to make the hard walls a little more comfortable for its guest.

He laid Adele inside and shut the lid before he could question himself. This had not saved Bailey. The coffin used ancient magic that was unreliable at best, but it was the only option Garrett had left. He had to hope.

He retreated until his back touched a wall. He slid against the mountainside and crouched on the floor.

Unable to look away from the coffin, he covered his mouth and cried. He could not lose Adele. He could not lose the one muse who had survived the world's beginning with him. She was meant to stay with him until the world's end.

His fists tightened. The young Vagabond did this. He would kill her. He would—

No.

He couldn't think such thoughts. For some reason, Adele loved the girl like the daughter she could never have.

Adele would not die. She couldn't. He couldn't bear it.

He pushed himself into the wall and watched Adele's frozen body. She hovered in the coffin, suspended and hopefully healing. A pang of regret tore into him because he'd left Kara chained and at the whims of the Ayavelian queen, but Adele would always be more important. Love was more important.

Something glinted on Adele's neck. The silver light caught his eye. He walked closer. A thin line, coiled at one end, stuck from Adele's skin. He opened the coffin only long enough to wrestle the silver free. She didn't move.

Is this the Broken Trinity?

He glanced at her wrists, hoping he was wrong—but he wasn't. There, clear as day, were the other two pieces.

His neck burned as he fumed. Somehow, the yakona had found the Broken Trinity. Not only that, she'd known how to use it.

He pulled the last two pieces from Adele's wrists and once more closed the coffin's lid. He set the symbols back together. They fused, resuming their original shape.

He threw the artifact against the wall. It bounded off the rock and bounced along the floor with a *tink, tink* each time it hit the mountainside. He had no idea where it landed.

The Broken Trinity—none knew of it. It was the drenowith's best kept secret. Seven Broken Trinities existed in the world, all of them kept in a vault with the drenowith Council.

All but one.

This had to be a message from Verum. The Council must have known Garrett and Adele had defied a direct order by helping Kara. They would probably kill him, too, should he continue to disobey.

Oh, he would disobey.

If Kara survived, he would help her. He would kill Aislynn himself and rid the world of the vile woman's hatred, but he would otherwise do as Kara needed of him. She had few allies, and at least now she understood what it meant to trust the wrong people.

And once the war was over—once he had proven the Council wrong—he would kill them all as well.

AISLYNN

Aislynn opened her eyes to the golden and white tile of her bedroom ceiling. That is, until her vision blurred again.

Her head ached. The sores on her wrists continued to drip blood. Her body wouldn't heal. Her senses spiked, washing her with the same scents from the cave: sweat, bark, honey, blood, perfume, musk.

"Krik!" she screamed.

"Yes, Your Highness?" he asked in her ear.

"You are an idiot!"

He didn't respond. Aislynn wished she could see more than colors. She wanted to see remorse on his face, but he would have apologized by now if the emotion had even registered within him.

She grated her teeth together. "This was your plan! You brought me the Broken Trinity! You told me this would work!"

"It should have worked, Your Majesty. In theory, it was flawless. It—"

"I read the manuscripts! I know the theory! You—"

A woman spoke from far away. "I think she needs rest, Krik. You may leave."

"Thank you," he said, voice tense.

Aislynn wanted to scream after him, to blame, to yell, but a cool hand touched her face.

She lay back and sighed. "Is that you, Evelyn?"

"Yes. You need to stay calm, Aunt Aislynn. You need to rest."

"Where is the muse? The Vagabond?"

"The muse escaped, but we do have the Vagabond. It seems they abandoned her."

"I'm not surprised."

Evelyn didn't say anything for a while. That could only mean the girl was trying to word a controversial question.

Aislynn groaned. "Just ask, Evelyn."

"What happened to make you hate the drenowith so much?"

Aislynn tensed and closed her eyes, embracing the darkness instead of the blurry white of her ceiling.

"If I survive this, I will tell you."

The hand brushed her face again. "I'm sorry I asked. You should be sleeping."

Aislynn grabbed the hand without opening her eyes. "Evelyn, has anyone seen the Vagabond? Do they know I failed?"

"No. I'm keeping her in the other room for now. She's unconscious. I have not let anyone know you returned."

"Good. Keep her there for as long as you can, and

keep her sedated. How long until the other Bloods become suspicious?"

"I—I don't know. A day or two? Three at most?"

"Keep her here as long as you can. Tell them whatever you have to, but delay returning her until you must. I need to get well before they decide what to do with her, and I need time. Take the grimoire pendant from her before you deliver her to them. We have lost our leverage against the other Bloods, and we need to get it back."

"What leverage?" Evelyn asked. Her voice trembled.

"Do not question me. Do you understand?"

The silence scared Aislynn more than a refusal.

"Evelyn!"

"I understand what you want me to do but not why."

"You will soon."

"Then, tell me now! Why must you—"

"Leave, Evelyn. I am too tired for this. Just—please, child. Please, do as you are told. It will make sense to you soon."

There was a sigh and the sound of chair legs scraping against the marble floor. The door closed. Aislynn suppressed a smile as relief washed through her.

But the relief dissolved into fear. The Vagabond's touch had reminded Aislynn of memories she wished could have remained forgotten. Aislynn had hunted the drenowith, as much as she'd tried to tell herself otherwise. How Kara had known—it wasn't something Aislynn wanted to think about.

Evelyn couldn't know too much of the world she was to inherit, not while Aislynn was alive. Too much shame and loss remained for Aislynn to ever admit her part in it all.

🌶

GAVIN

Gavin couldn't believe it.

As the other Bloods left the meeting room, Gavin merely sat in his chair, astonished, blown away by how quickly everything had just unraveled. He stared at the table, barely able to breathe, barely able to even *think*.

The door shut, the sharp click of the latch echoing in the war room, and that finally snapped him out of his daze. He stood, hands resting on the table as his mind raced, trying desperately to come up with an idea, something, *anything* at all to fix this.

For the first time, he didn't have a backup plan.

What had begun as an intricate, finely woven plot to make the Grimoire his had unraveled. Everything he had done, every command, every lie had backfired, and now, he had failed not just his people, but the Vagabond herself.

Gavin had completely lost control.

With a cold pang of dread, he wondered if there's a way out of this—or if, in his attempt to make Kara his, he had just doomed her to a slow and painful death.

CHAPTER THIRTY-FOUR
BRAEDEN

Braeden kicked a loose piece of asphalt deeper into the gutter outside Kara's old rental home. No light shone from the windows. A crooked *FOR RENT* sign teetered in the middle of the lawn.

He leaned against the lamppost across the street, not wanting to go in yet. He needed to find Carden, but he couldn't waltz into the Stele unannounced. If Braeden wasn't careful, Carden might want to make an example of him in front of the subjects.

Braeden needed to be subtle. He needed Carden to find him.

A sheet of paper stapled to the lamp caused a double take. Kara's picture covered the page, her face printed in black and white beneath the word "Missing." She grinned at the camera as if caught off guard, but her eyes pinched with happiness. A block of text covered half the page beneath it.

Kara Magari has been missing since May. She was last seen on Salish Mountain at the visitor center. She is a kind girl who wouldn't swat a fly, so please approach her if you see her. Tell her that her grandparents miss her and love her dearly, no matter what. We just want her to come home. Please, if you know anything at all, call us at the number below.

Braeden stopped reading. It wasn't like he could call them and explain what their granddaughter had been up to all this time.

People were looking for her. People cared. He paused, wondering if he should find a way to tell her. It would probably make matters worse to have a tie to the human world. She couldn't come back, so he wouldn't torture her by letting her know how much she was missed.

Besides, she had changed. Kara might not swat a fly, but he had seen her kill shadow demons without a flicker of regret. The granddaughter they knew was growing up in an entirely different world. She didn't belong to them anymore.

Braeden pulled down the flyer and stared at her picture, memorizing how the skin creased around her eyes when she smiled. He didn't put it back. If he went to the Stele for what was likely the last few days of his life, he wanted Kara there with him in some small way.

He folded the paper and tucked it away in a small pocket on his shirt.

He walked without discretion, since there were no other streetlights on the road to advertise his presence to any nosy neighbors. Not as if it mattered. He wouldn't be here long.

The door was locked, and unlocked itself at his command. He ducked his head as he entered, remembering how he'd whacked himself pretty hard against the frame on his last attempt. He chuckled, but the smile didn't last long.

He didn't want to do this.

The hallway hadn't changed, except the photo cabinet was gone, and there were no longer holes in the walls.

A small piece of paper sticking from the baseboard caught his eye. He reached down and pulled it out. It was a small, wallet-sized picture of Kara sitting on a riverbank. Her father sat behind her with another woman, who Braeden assumed was Kara's mother from what he could remember of seeing their family photos. Kara was laughing, as if whoever had taken the picture said something funny, and her eyes wrinkled with the joy of simply being happy. He smiled and slipped the photograph into the same hidden pocket as the missing poster.

The air cracked behind him, much like it did whenever Flick teleported somewhere. Braeden spun in time to catch Carden cross his arms and lean against the doorway into the dining room. It was all Braeden could do not to stare at his father's scarred hand again.

A gray version of Flick sat on Carden's shoulder, its large eyes glossed over as it stared at the wall. It seemed to enjoy Carden's company as much as Braeden did.

"Ah, isn't he handy?" Carden asked with a nod to the creature. "He was especially useful in killing the Hillsidian queen. I doubt I would have made it back to the Stele in time to make the antidote without him."

Braeden silently wished it had happened.

Carden frowned. "Well, aren't you quiet? I assume you wanted to see me or you wouldn't be here."

"I want to return to the Stele."

Carden quirked an eyebrow. "Is that so?"

"They won't accept me, even after everything I've done," Braeden said.

"You're surprised?"

"I've done everything right, Carden. Everything. I even saved their Heirs."

"Yes, that was annoying."

"But even after all my loyalty, they ostracize me. I've had enough. They hold meetings without me, make decisions without me, and think I don't hear."

"What have you heard?"

"Enough for revenge."

"Why should I give you another chance, boy? You've only ever defied me."

"If we can agree on a few terms, I won't disobey you anymore."

"What terms?"

"You're hunting Bloods. I don't know why and frankly, I don't care. Do what you want. Dominate Ourea. I'll be your general."

"And your price?"

"Kara is never to be touched or harmed in any way."

Carden laughed. The gray creature on his shoulder sighed deeply as he brushed up against the doorframe.

His father nodded. "I'll agree to your condition. As long as you do as I say, I won't allow any harm to come to her."

"Then I think we are finally on the same page, Carden."

"Ah, none of that. Your new life starts now. You will address me properly, as either your Blood or your father."

Braeden steadied himself and suppressed a deep breath. Richard would always be his father.

"Yes, my Blood," he said.

"Much better."

Carden lifted his scarred hand to Braeden expectantly. Braeden stifled the urge to shudder and reached to shake it.

Crack!

Weight settled into Braeden's gut, disorienting him. His head reeled. The world spun around him. It took several moments to even realize what had happened, much less realize where he was.

The small gray creature had transported them.

A cold, stone hallway stretched around a corner in the distance. Jail doors lined the hall every ten feet or so. Whimpers and muffled crying came from a few of the closest cells, while moans drifted from down the hall. Carden's boots echoed when he began walking, the sound silencing the noises of his prisoners.

Braeden turned in time to see Carden's gray version of Flick—he could never remember what that thing was called—turn around and stare at him. The creature crouched on the edge of Carden's shoulder, watching him as if seeing him for the first time.

"I thought those creatures couldn't teleport through lichgates," Braeden said absently.

"Kara's can't?" the king asked. "Each has different powers, so this is useful information."

Braeden cursed under his breath. He shouldn't have said anything.

"Come on, boy, we haven't got all day," Carden said. The king turned so his head hid the creature on his shoulder. He sneered.

"What?" Braeden demanded.

"Look at yourself. I didn't even have to ask."

Braeden looked down, confused, only to see his gray hands. He'd changed form. Well, he couldn't change back now.

Carden began down the hall, and the small, gray creature watched Braeden the entire way. Its massive eyes simply stared, as if waiting for a magic trick.

It was unnerving.

"Your return was inevitable, you know," Carden said. "You belong here. This is your home. Your duty is to your people. You will be forever remembered, Braeden. But first, you must prove yourself."

They stopped at a door in the center of the Cellar. Braeden knew the door too well. A flight of steps behind it would lead to the torture room where he'd mutilated Aislynn as a boy.

Braeden would have to prove himself by torturing someone.

Carden opened the door and started down a stone staircase with no railing. Walls closed in on either side. The gray creature on his shoulder stared at Braeden the whole way down. Its eyes glowed in the growing darkness until the two massive beads bobbed in the shadows as if on their own.

There would be light farther down. Only the stairs were this dark, but they were dark for a reason: to terrify prisoners before the torture even began. Thin light pooled at the bottom of the steps, illuminating a sharp turn in the stairway. There, the wall on the left would open into a low ceiling. A row of windows would illuminate the lines of stone tables, where thousands of yakona and other creatures had died over the years. One wall would be lined with knives and saws. The other wall hosted a row of mirrors designed to allow the prisoners to watch their torturer's handiwork.

Braeden hesitated. He couldn't.

But he forced himself to take the first, shaky step. He pressed on down the stairs, foot by foot, hoping all the way that his irregular steps wouldn't give him away. He'd come so far.

There was no going back. There wasn't room for error. There wasn't room for hesitation. If he had to kill someone to prove himself to Carden, to lead the terrible man to the ambush waiting for him, then it was exactly what Braeden would do.

Carden turned into the light below and disappeared into the chamber. Not good. Braeden had let his greatest enemy walk first into a room filled with tools designed to inflict pain.

He hurried and rounded the corner. The sudden light blinded him, but he blinked away the glare. He had to be ready to face whoever waited on the tables for him.

Twelve tables lined the room, each six feet apart and all of them empty.

Carden stood by the first table, arms crossed. He

watched Braeden with a complicated expression of furrowed brows and a half-sneer. Braeden couldn't make out whether he was disappointed or trying not to laugh.

This had to be part of the hazing. Carden wanted to drag this out, to see his reaction as the prisoner walked down the stairs. He wanted to make Braeden nervous as he waited.

Well, it wouldn't work.

He crossed to the table and ran his hand over it. The stone glided under his fingers, smooth from the weight of the countless bodies strapped to it in its years.

The world tossed around him—no, he'd been flipped. His back hit the stone table and knocked the wind out of him. The ceiling—oh, *Bloods*. He faced the ceiling.

Cold metal whipped over his body. Chains, slithering on their own accord, tightened around his legs and torso. He wanted to laugh. Chains couldn't do any—

Barbs dug into his skin anywhere a chain touched him, springing to life as if they'd been coiled and simply waiting. Poison dripped from their ends and coursed through his blood. He screamed, unable to suppress the agony.

Carden patted him on the head. "I'm not as stupid as you seem to think, son."

Braeden leaned back into the table. Panic set his heart racing.

His father paced around the table. "Your friends sent you here. You would never come back without an agenda. You've already run at every chance you've had. You've always ran, Braeden! Like a coward! You've hidden when any other Heir would have fought. So why would you come back unless you were trying to help those other Bloods? You're pathetic!

"I know a loyal man when I see one. I also know how to break a loyal man so that all he remembers is what I tell him to believe. It's a lesson I was trying to teach you with Aislynn all those years ago. You could have been truly great, Braeden. But now I must start again. Now, I will burn the defiance out of you forever."

Carden stood at the foot of the table, blocking Braeden's view of the mirrors. The king's hands changed color from dark, charcoal gray to a hot, fiery orange. Steam radiated from his fingers, which lost their defined outline. They simmered and shook as if they were melting, as if the slightest touch would send them spilling to the floor like molten rock out of a kiln.

"Carden, don't—"

But Carden grinned and set his steaming hands on Braeden's feet.

Searing pain roared up Braeden's body. He

screamed. The spiked chains tore into his skin as he thrashed, trying to escape. His boots melted, bits of the liquid leather sticking to him as it cooled. He couldn't see his feet but knew they would burn to a crisp from Carden's molten touch.

He would never escape this.

"Come now, boy. You're stronger than that," Carden said with a laugh.

The Stelian Blood let go. Aches ripped through Braeden's feet. His legs twitched, and a sting raced up his side each time.

Carden paced around the side of the table and stopped at Braeden's torso.

"Please, no—"

"You coward. Don't worry. I'll burn that out of you as well."

Carden set his molten hands on Braeden's chest but didn't stop there. He traced one finger up Braeden's neck and along his cheek. Braeden screamed again. Carden allowed it.

Burnt skin and singed fabric clogged Braeden's nose until he thought he would either vomit or pass out from the overwhelming stench.

In the mirror, he saw a trail from his stomach to his left eye, a steaming, black line that marked Carden's path. His shirt's fibers melted to his skin. Red embers simmered in the scarred tissue.

"Do hold still," Carden said from behind him.

The two molten hands grabbed each side of Braeden's head. The splintering pain was too much. Agony tore apart his mind, snapping and stripping his resolve. Everything burned away—his hair, his skin, his hope.

Braeden didn't even know if he was screaming anymore. He couldn't hear. The world fell perfectly silent, marred only by the intense pain coursing through his skull. It bubbled on his face.

He closed his eyes. He didn't want to see the rest.

CHAPTER THIRTY-FIVE
BRAEDEN

At some point, Carden left. Braeden knew as much only because the pain receded long enough to hear again. His ears rang, the sound a deafening roar after the incessant, painful silence.

His sight returned next, though he wished he couldn't see once he looked at himself in the mirror. Black blood dripped from his fingers into pools on the floor or fell from the half-tattered clothes hanging from his body. Black handprints and trails from Carden's burning hands covered everything.

Carden hadn't stopped with the molten hands. They had been the warm-up. The scorched patches on Braeden's shoulder, stomach, and legs meant that, somewhere along the way, Carden had switched to using controlled bursts of lightning. Jagged lines had been carved into Braeden's arms. Little remained of his boots, though the soles had melted into the skin on the soles of his feet.

And this was only the beginning.

He groaned and shifted his weight. The chains ripped new holes in him, so he tried to lie still. So far, he hadn't revealed anything—at least, he didn't think so. There were moments he couldn't remember, wounds appearing from nowhere. Carden might have left to release a herd of troops to take care of the Bloods while he finished—

"Oh, good, you're awake."

The voice came from the stairs, but Braeden didn't have to turn his head to know Carden was back.

"You're a good deal stronger than I gave you credit for, boy. I admire tenacity. But my patience is running low, as I have things to do."

Carden stepped into view. Braeden looked up from half-raised eyelids—oh, *Bloods*. He had two swollen eyes as well.

Braeden forced a raspy laugh. "Show me what you got."

"There's my boy," Carden answered.

The room darkened as if the sun had gone behind a cloud. The darkness continued, fast and sudden, until the only light came from Carden's palm. The Blood stared into his hand, apparently focusing his energy.

The darkness shattered. Each of the black shards

pulsed, shivering and rippling as they snaked their way into Carden's palm. White sparks broke in waves across each one as it floated. The room's light returned more with each shadow lying in Carden's palm or wrapped around his arm.

Braeden choked on a gasp. He tensed.

No.

Carden smiled. "Ah, you do remember the slivers. It's my favorite technique. I tried to teach it to you with Aislynn. Do you remember? She must have endured them for, what, two days? Three? You never quite got it right. Usually, a yakona doesn't survive so much exposure to the slivers, though I can't imagine she was ever the same afterward. The slivers never leave a yakona the same as he was before."

Braeden tried to push away, but the chains held him tight. His strength was gone. His resilience was gone. If he had to endure the slivers, there was no telling what he would be when Carden finished. Aislynn had likely only survived because Braeden hadn't ever been able to go through with torturing her himself.

"Welcome home, boy." Carden sneered.

The slivers dove from the Blood's palm onto Braeden's stomach. One pushed under his shirt and forced its way into his belly button. Braeden yelled, twisting as he flexed his stomach in an effort to fight it off. The rest slunk into the wounds on his body or wriggled toward his face, burning whatever skin they touched.

One pushed into his mouth. He gagged. It scratched his tongue, as if the thing had one million, clawed legs propelling it forward. He tried to scream, but another forced its way in after the first.

White light broke across the back of his eyelids. It was only a flash but with it came relief. Peace.

The brilliance faded as quickly as it had come. He reached for it with his mind. Instead, different images spun past: the queen, Gavin, Richard, Mother.

He grabbed the first memory he could. Mother's face came into view, smiling as she kissed his nose. She said something, her voice echoing incoherently in his mind. Ice crackled across his nose. He shivered.

The slivers raced into the memory, wrapping themselves around her. She didn't react, apparently oblivious to the smoky things slithering into her ears and mouth. Her eyes turned red, and her sweet voice became Carden's booming laugh.

Braeden pushed away. Carden was taking everything—even his memories. He couldn't. Braeden wouldn't let him.

He reached for the queen, for Gavin, for Richard—but each had the same effect. Their faces became distorted ghosts, their voices the resounding boom of Carden's laughter.

Braeden pushed away again, with nothing to grasp for anymore. This was it. He had truly lost.

A hand reached around his waist. The flash of white broke across his vision again, and with it came that same wave of peace. But this wasn't a mere flicker; it remained. As long as the hand touched him, Braeden would be safe.

He looked down to see small, pale hands wrapped around him as if someone hugged him from behind. He turned to see a blond head smiling up at him.

"Kara," he said. Relief flooded through him.

But—this was all in his head. None of this was real.

"Don't question it," she said, as if she'd read his thoughts.

She pulled him away from the darkness and slivers. The two of them floated in the vacant white relief from the pain.

"What's going on?" he asked.

"Let go," she answered.

"Let go of what? I'm not letting go of you."

She smiled. "Let go of the pain. Leave that behind."

"I don't know how to."

"Try."

He nodded. "Distract me."

She grinned and kissed his neck. "I think I can do that."

His skin flushed, and he gripped her tighter. He ran a hand through her hair.

She leaned into his chest and sighed. "That's better. Don't think about anything but being here with me."

"Where are we?"

"In the deepest part of your mind, where Carden can never find you. It's the goodness you've developed despite everything, the kindness and love you're capable of, even though you were born to kill. Hide here with me, and he'll never find us."

Braeden pulled her closer. The relief grew stronger.

"I won't let you go, Braeden. You're safe here."

This wasn't real. He knew as much. This was a safeguard. He had retreated, unable to stomach the pain or the fear anymore. But he wanted to believe in it anyway, this alternate world where Kara would always be with him because it was all he had left to hold on to.

"When this is over, let's run away. Let's escape," he said.

She laughed. The sound rang in the void. "Where to?"

"Someplace far away from everything. I don't know. Russia? Australia? Europe?"

"I've always wanted to go to Europe."

"Okay, Europe it is," he said.

"Where in Europe?"

"Scotland, maybe? I love Scotland. It's full of tiny villages where everyone knows everyone else, and we can hide from the rest of the world. There's this one town called Dailly—I found it on an isen hunt years back. It's beautiful."

"Then, we'll go to Dailly," she said with a laugh.

The flash of white faded away, and Kara's face disappeared along with it. She faded into nothing, reaching for him as she disappeared.

"What the—? Kara!" he called.

"Come back!" she said.

Braeden's eyes snapped open. Darkness filled the torture chamber, and the only light came from the silver moon barely visible through the windows on the far wall. The mirrors tempted him to examine his wounds, but Braeden didn't want to know how much worse it had gotten.

Pain broke along the side of his body, but he didn't stay long enough to find out what it was. He closed his eyes and slipped back into his mind, hunting for the flash of white that meant safety.

"That was close," Kara said in his ear.

He opened his eyes. The white void returned. His head lay in Kara's lap, and she smiled as she ran her fingers through his hair.

"Don't let me leave again," he said.

She shushed him and caressed his face. The touch sent shivers of joy up his spine. He could barely move, but he would allow himself to enjoy her touch. In a world full of pain, it was a blessing to have her.

"You can't stay long," she said.

"Why not?"

"You're almost awake again." She laid a protective arm across his chest.

"I don't ever want to wake up. I don't want to go back."

"If you don't, the real me will die. She needs you, Braeden. I'm just your imagination."

"But Carden—"

"All tyrants fall," she interrupted.

"Not if I'm his slave. It would be impossible to fight him."

She grinned. "Sometimes, 'impossible' just means you have to try harder."

Her words rang a distant bell. They were familiar, but he couldn't remember why.

"Bye, Braeden. Stay good."

"I don't want—"

He coughed and sputtered. The white void faded away. He opened his eyes once more to sunlight streaming through the windows. He avoided looking in the mirror. The slivers receded.

"Say it again," a dark voice commanded in his ear.

Carden stood beside him. He had choice words for his father, but he could only remember wanting to tell Kara not to let him leave.

Instead, his mouth spoke for him. "I was supposed to lure you into an ambush in Lutirena Gorge with the false story that Blood Gavin is camping with a small army and can be easily taken. The Bloods will be waiting there with their armies. They'll kill you. I believe they will also try to kill me, but I was prepared for it so long as I killed you first."

Braeden tensed. He had revealed everything, and in an emotionless monotone. His mind and body had acted as separate entities.

Carden grinned. "Good boy. That is a clever trick on their part. I guess we'll just have to bring a bigger army."

Braeden wanted to scream at him, to curse and yell and fight, but his body wouldn't allow it.

Carden cracked his neck. "In the meantime, you and I can actually begin now that you're finally cooperating."

The Blood's hands heated once more until they steamed like molten rock. Braeden pressed his head back into the table and closed his eyes. This wouldn't end well, but at least he could retreat into his mind. As long as he had Kara, he might still come out of this with his free thought intact.

CHAPTER THIRTY-SIX
KARA

Kara woke with a throbbing headache. Bile stung the back of her throat. Her tongue ached and stuck to the roof of her mouth. All she wanted was water. How long had she been out?

A convoluted mess of memories spun through her skull. Aislynn had chained her. Adele had been captured. There was screaming—Adele's screaming. The sound rang again in Kara's head, deafening and painful. But Garrett had come—and in his glare, blamed Kara for everything.

He could have saved Kara, too, but he left her shackled on the floor.

Something bumped against her foot. She opened her eyes—they hadn't been open before? The world blurred by, like she was moving. Her mind raced.

What was I thinking about?

Two guards dragged her through a stone hallway. The heavy shackles no longer hung around her wrists, but the cuffs' poison still racked her body. Scars from the spikes dotted her skin. Her veins tightened with each movement.

A flickering, lucid thought revolved around how she wouldn't be able to think straight until the poison worked its way out of her system. Magic, at this point, would be too much to manage.

A swish of fabric caught Kara's attention. A tall Ayavelian woman walked just ahead. Her arched back came to a regal head adorned with a thin tiara.

Evelyn.

"How—" Kara meant to ask how long she'd been unconscious or ask for the date, but her voice came out as barely more than a whisper. She wanted to vomit but knew she would be too weak to even manage that.

How pathetic.

"Stop," Evelyn said to the guards.

They obeyed. Kara hung between them, unable to stand. Evelyn spread her thin fingers toward Kara, and the grimoire pendant unclasped itself from around her neck as if on command. It floated into the princess' pocket.

Since Evelyn hadn't touched it, the necklaces defenses didn't shock her. Inwardly, Kara cursed at her rotten luck. Outwardly, she barely had the strength to muster a single word.

"You have been unconscious for three days. You had an allergic reaction to the cuffs' poison."

Evelyn's eye twitched. Kara squinted. Had the princess just lied? Three days didn't just disappear like that, allergic reaction or no.

Evelyn cleared her throat. "Do yourself a favor and be silent. That mouth of yours is one of your worst vices."

Kara forced herself to speak louder, which made her voice crack. "This is a mistake. Aislynn made a mistake! Don't become as heartless as her."

"I am focused, not heartless."

"You had me fooled."

The princess narrowed her eyes and, for a second, looked as if she would hit Kara. Instead, she smirked. "Apparently, fooling you is not difficult."

Kara cringed. Yep. That stung more than any slap could.

Evelyn turned to a set of doors nearby and then pushed them open. The guards followed her inside, dragging the otherwise immobile Kara with them.

The doors led to a large room with vaulted ceilings. Fire burned in a few sconces along the wall, illuminating the shadows. Windows covered a wall to the right. Outside, a silver moon hung above a still forest.

The doors slammed shut behind her, and the

sconces burned brighter at the sound. A large table consumed most of the room, its chairs filled either by a Blood or his Heir. In Ithone's case, however, Gurien took Aurora's place.

Each of the yakona leaders stared at the table or out of the window, eyes unfocused. Some covered their mouths with their hands, while others leaned back in their chairs and rubbed their temples. Apparently, it had been a long and anxious night for them as well.

Gavin caught Kara's eye—the only one to do so. She shook her head in disgust. He swallowed hard and turned away.

She suppressed the second urge to vomit as she realized the truth.

"You all knew," she said, her voice hoarse from the pain and queasiness.

"We did," Gavin admitted. He wouldn't look at her this time.

Evelyn tapped her fingers on the table. "Everything was going as planned until the muse's companion interrupted. Aislynn was unable to complete the ritual and is currently ill because it was ended early, but it looks like she will heal in just a few days. We knew that was a risk. The Vagabond didn't take well to the poisoned shackles and has only just awoken."

Frine leaned his elbows on the table. "It looks more

like you didn't take the shackles off her. Look at her. Has she even eaten since the incident?"

Evelyn arched her back. "She'd be dead if she hadn't."

But the princess' eye twitched again. She was lying! Someone must have kept Kara unconscious all this time, probably to keep her quiet. If Kara ever got her energy back, she would punch the princess first thing. In the face.

Ithone sighed. "Focus, everyone. Aislynn failed, and we lost the willing aid of the Vagabond. I simply wish there had been a way to trap the muses without her."

Evelyn nodded. "We must decide what to do with her. The poisons in her blood are still strong enough to subdue her for at least another day. She will need the cuffs again soon if we wish to subdue her."

Kara looked again to Gavin, though she doubted he would actually help her. He refused to catch her gaze. He leaned back in the chair, rubbing his temple as if lost in thought. Dark circles lined the space beneath his eyes. "What will happen to Kara when the poison wears off?"

Evelyn turned to Ithone, as if the Kirelm had asked the question instead of her ex-lover. "We must decide… and soon. She cannot be controlled by the spikes for much longer without permanently damaging her body and mind. However, Aislynn has asked to be present for that discussion. I believe we should keep the Vagabond subdued with the spikes' poisons until Aislynn is well enough again to join the debate."

Gavin smacked the table. "Let's not kid ourselves! You're saying you want Aislynn around when we decide who should control the Vagabond."

"That was implied, yes."

Kara pulled every ounce of her energy into her next words. She had to make them count. "I only wanted peace, but none of you deserve it!"

Everyone turned to her. Her neck ached as she forced herself to stare at them one at a time. Her ears rang. Most of the leaders turned away or looked out the window when she caught their eye.

Only Ithone maintained eye contact. "I think we've heard enough for one night. I vote to wait for Aislynn."

Frine nodded in agreement. "And I. She has proven how far she will go for our cause."

"I agree," Gavin added. Kara couldn't help but wonder if there was a dual meaning to his words.

The guards dragged her from the room. As she left, she tried one last time to catch Gavin's attention. He watched her leave, but a wave of nausea swept over her as he did.

More gray walls blurred by, until her eyes closed of their own accord. The world stopped moving, eventually, but her head continued to spin. A door latched. Crickets chirped somewhere far away, their orchestra conjuring a memory of her dad once telling her that crickets were nature's thermometer.

She shivered. Her cheeks flushed, and she wanted to vomit.

Kara had failed, just like the first Vagabond. Those she had tried to protect had turned on her. According to Aislynn, they hadn't ever respected her to begin with. And not only that, but they had turned on those who'd protected her as well.

She didn't know where Braeden had gone. Richard and Twin had no way of knowing what had happened. Garrett would likely never speak to her again. Adele might be dead.

Kara was most definitely on her own. She didn't know what was worse, though: that she was alone, or that she had absolutely no idea what to do about it.

DEIDRE

Deidre hid in the shadows of Ayavel, in a secret passage few knew existed, staring through a peephole as she waited for her prey. This was a special soul, someone she needed, someone without whom her plan would fail.

The clatter of footsteps echoed down the hall, twenty by the sound of it, and she shrank back into the darkness, her nerves on fire as she waited. Every moment she spent here, she risked a very painful death.

Gritting her teeth, she stood still as a stone as the cluster of guards marched past her hiding spot, blissfully unaware that merely two feet and a wall separated her from them.

When they had passed, Deidre resumed her sentry, determined not to let this man slip through her grasp again. She had seen him enter the meeting room across the hall, and though he didn't know it yet, the last thing he would ever do was sit in a painfully dull meeting about perimeter checks.

On edge, but determined to wait, Deidre settled in, patiently biding her time. Her revenge was quickly falling into place after hundreds of years of waiting. If it meant she could finally slit Niccoli's throat, she would happily wait another hour.

CHAPTER THIRTY-SEVEN
BRAEDEN

Braeden awoke to the relief of the chains sliding off his arms.

He opened his eyes. The sunlight blurred the dungeon into smeared streaks of gray. He lay still to let his body heal around the poison.

His feet pushed the burnt boot soles out of his skin. Each landed on the floor with a *thump*. Joints popped into place. Broken bones creaked as they fused back together. Burnt patches of skin dissolved into the unmarred, charcoal, gray he so hated.

He stared at the ceiling. He'd be here a while.

Hair pushed through his head, growing back wherever it had been burnt off. Bits of his ears had melted in the torture but now grew back. His fingers twitched as feeling returned. He shuddered as tremors shook his body, no doubt healing internal bleeding.

Braeden did not sit up until his body recovered. He wouldn't look at himself until he was whole again. He never wanted to know how bad it had truly been.

When he did finally push himself into a sitting position, his arms shook under the minimal weight he applied to them. The room wobbled. He took a deep breath and sat still until he regained his balance.

His vision returned, but he barely recognized the man staring back at him in the mirror. It was him, but he didn't show an ounce of emotion. His eyes were dead, and even though he was terrified at seeing the cold creature he'd become, nothing registered on his face.

The cold floor stung his bare feet. He looked around. Clothes and a new pair of boots sat on the first stair, so he grabbed them and changed.

As he threw his now-tattered clothes on the floor, a piece of paper slipped out of a pocket and slid across the tiles. A small square of photo paper followed shortly after.

Braeden knelt and picked them up—the pictures. A rip or two marred the singed corners; otherwise, the people in the photographs all smiled up at him without a scratch.

His thumb brushed across Kara's face. If he ever found her again, if he ever escaped this, they would run away to Scotland like he'd promised.

He slipped on his pants and stuffed the images in a pocket. The shirt stretched as he pulled it on.

Footsteps echoed down the stairs. Though Braeden's heart fluttered with panic at the sound, his expression did not change. He simply turned to see who it was.

Feet appeared first, and Carden's head appeared above them not long after. He grinned and crossed his arms. "You are now fully broken-in, boy. You can go wherever you please, so long as you do not leave the Stele. Also, we have a visitor, an isen you've met before and seem to dislike. Therefore, you are forbidden from harming Deidre in any way. Those are my rules. You are free to do whatever else you like. This is your home, after all."

The mandates twisted in Braeden's gut. He couldn't disobey.

"Thank you, Father." Braeden's mouth moved on its own again. He wanted to cringe at calling Carden his father but couldn't force his muscles to obey.

"I will show you your room. We leave for the ambush in three days, so rest until then. I need you refreshed for the battle."

Braeden nodded and followed Carden up the stairway and into the hall. They ascended more winding staircases and crossed more hallways but never again spoke. Braeden followed, keeping his distance.

He had failed. Even with his free thought, he'd failed. He had no control over his body, yet consciously understood everything he did. Maybe Carden wanted this. Maybe he'd done it on purpose and left Braeden's free thought to make the punishment worse.

No, that couldn't be it. Carden wanted obedience, to "burn the defiance" out of him, after all. He'd probably meant to reset Braeden's morality or simply destroy all his memories of the world and people he'd grown to love.

Kara alone had saved him from forgetting who he was. Thanks to her—well, Braeden's affection for her—he'd defeated Carden, at least partially. But now Braeden was left in a disconnect between his thoughts and his actions. He didn't own his body anymore. Even with his free thought, he'd never be able to disobey.

Braeden blinked himself from his thoughts as Carden stopped at a door isolated at the far end of a hallway. Braeden bowed and let Carden walk away before he opened the door to what had to be his bedroom.

The ceiling towered overhead, at least twenty feet high with a chandelier in its center. Couches circled a giant fireplace off to the left with a coffee table in between. A plate of jerky and a bowl of fruit lay on the table. Braeden's stomach growled. He picked a few pieces of dried meat from the plate and chewed on a slice as he continued through the room.

Two other doors stood open on either side of the fireplace. One led to a king-sized four-post bed, while the other room held a desk and walls filled with bookshelves.

Windows covered the wall opposite the fireplace, and a giant set of double doors led onto a balcony. Braeden walked out then leaned against the railing. The Stelian forests covered most of the landscape, while the mountains blocked most of the sky in the distance.

Braeden's room also had a good view of the Stele—most notably, Carden's study. The doors to his father's balcony were closed today, the curtains drawn.

He had this room for a reason. Carden meant to keep a close eye on him. An ember of hope burned in his gut. For him to get this room, it meant Carden had the slightest worry he would lose control. Braeden might overcome this after all.

"Indifference is a good look on you," someone said from inside.

Braeden stuffed the jerky in his pocket and turned to see Deidre lounging on a couch. She snapped her fingers, and flames roared to life in the fireplace. Her skin glowed in the warm flicker, but he recoiled from the lilac-pine perfume of the isen race.

"Get out," he said.

"I see Carden has also improved your manners. This has been a lucrative trip for you."

"I won't repeat myself, isen."

She grinned and batted her eyes, running her hand along her neck. "You don't really want me to leave, do you?"

"I do."

"Too bad. We could've had a lot of fun."

Braeden grimaced. "Not interested."

Deidre shrugged. "You just don't want me because you're hung up on that girlfriend of yours. Such a travesty, that one. Wish her story had ended better."

The isen was baiting him. Braeden knew it, but he still couldn't stop himself from prodding her for information. "What do you mean?"

"While you and your daddy were bonding, little Miss Kara got into a spot of trouble. Let's just say she doesn't have the sway over the Bloods that she used to."

Deidre stretched farther back onto the couch and smiled up at him through narrowed eyes. He figured she wanted him to ask more questions, but he was on thin ice already. He didn't know how much free will Carden had intended to leave intact; he doubted he should still care about anything.

But Braeden had a compromise.

He summoned a blade of air and threw it into the couch arm, barely missing Deidre's head. He'd missed on purpose. He may not be able to hurt her, but she didn't need to know.

"Out with it or leave," he said.

The isen laughed. "I love it when you're angry!"

Braeden waved his hand at the door, pulling at it with his mind. It swung open and hit the wall with a *bang*. The sound echoed through the room.

Deidre rolled her eyes. "Kara was used as bait, Prince. Aislynn somehow got it into her head that she could steal a drenowith's blood and take its power. She's such a stupid fool. Power hungry, too. And now, little Kara is in a dungeon somewhere. She'll be auctioned off soon, controlled by the highest bidder. When Aislynn's little plan fell through—honestly, I don't know how that woman is still alive—they locked the Vagabond away. But is there enough of you left to care?"

He glanced at the isen but caught his reflection in the mirror mounted over the fireplace. His features didn't shift.

Inwardly, his stomach twisted. Panic raced through him. He wanted to run out the door and grab a horse, but his body suppressed the impulse.

"Interesting." Deidre stood, grinning, and left the room.

When the door clicked shut behind her, Braeden sank onto the couch. If a Blood ended up controlling

Kara, she would definitely be at the ambush. They had witnessed her power at his trial, and they would want it for themselves—Gavin most of all. But if she posed a threat, Carden would kill her. In all likelihood, the king would order Braeden to kill her. He figured Carden's agreeing to protect Kara was a ploy to get Braeden to the Stele. Kara wasn't safe from the Stelian Blood.

Braeden couldn't leave the Stele, not after the mandate from Carden. Yet, he didn't dare send someone else to help Kara, either. He couldn't get in touch with anyone he trusted.

He had to find her. He had to save her.

But how?

He looked out the window. The sun beamed its heat onto the balcony. He couldn't think in here. He had to get away and walk around.

Braeden pushed himself to his feet and strode from the room at a much slower pace than intended. He let his thoughts run wild and headed for the forest. A long walk might clear his head.

It didn't make sense. Deidre had no reason to tell him about Kara unless the isen merely wanted to brag. Well, that made sense. Somehow, Deidre had tricked a few of the most powerful leaders in Ourea into ostracizing the one person who wanted to help them create sustainable peace. She no doubt wanted to hurt Braeden, too, to make him feel powerless. As he was locked away in the Stele, it would be impossible for him to help Kara.

Impossible: the word struck a chord somewhere in the recesses of his mind. When he'd retreated during the torture, Kara had said something about it. He racked his brain, trying to remember.

"Sometimes, 'impossible' just means you have to try harder."

That was it. She'd said it months back when they had realized the only way to the village was to get a Stelian amulet to show them where to go. He'd been unwilling to go out of fear of running into Carden.

At the time, she had questioned his lifetime of slavery to his father. She made it sound trivial, childish even, that he couldn't fight his blood loyalty. He'd been disgusted by her blatant dismissal of something that had ruled his life. After all, he had always fought it.

He stopped in his tracks, realizing for the first time he stood on a dirt path in the forest. Sunlight poured through gaps in the gray leaves and illuminated his trail.

Braeden had never fought. He'd always run away.

His mother had smuggled him out of the Stele all those years ago. She had given her life so he could run away from the Stele and never have to face what he was.

He hid in Hillside, skittish of any assignment taking him too close to the Stele. He'd even let some isen go when they travelled beyond his range of comfort. He'd lied, telling Richard he'd lost the trail.

When the drenowith rescued him and Kara from Carden, he'd pushed them to run. As soon as the small army had passed by their little cave, he'd said it was time to go. Time to run.

When Carden cornered them in the chamber with the Stelian amulet and forced Braeden to strangle Kara, he'd been offered a way out: obey Carden, or watch everything he cared about die. He had considered the latter as the better of his limited options.

Braeden had always ran. Every time he and Carden crossed paths, he'd done everything in his power to get away. His duel with Carden at the gala was the only time Braeden had ever fought his father, and he'd nearly disobeyed the mandate to change form.

A pang of hope made Braeden dizzy. He sat down on a log, deep in the Stelian forest.

If he'd resisted a mandate at the gala, maybe he could resist the one tying him to the Stele. And when he did, he would save Kara. They would escape.

He shook his head. The hope died in his gut. He couldn't escape this life. Running away had always failed him. It was time he embraced what he was—an Heir. He didn't want the crown. He had only ever wanted freedom, but to be free, he would have to become king.

He knew so little about his people. He had always

assumed they were as cruel as his father, but the bones in the feihl caves proved Carden could kill his own kind. Some obviously dissented. How many did as their Blood commanded to survive?

Carden posed the real threat, not the Stelian people. Braeden couldn't punish the Stelian race for the acts of his father. He couldn't let them die; he would simply kill their king. With Carden gone, he could show the Stelians what a real life was. A good life.

A renewed vigor rushed through him. He needed to uncover how to disobey Carden's command, but he didn't have the slightest idea where to start. In a way, he hoped an idea would present itself. After all, it seemed like he messed everything up whenever he tried to be proactive.

Braeden sat in the woods, staring at the ground until he lost track of the hours he spent waiting for something to make sense. He finally sighed. So far, he'd only managed to waste time. He needed a plan. Sitting on a log wasn't helping.

He glanced up and froze when he caught sight of an animal standing a dozen feet off in the trees.

The creature blotted out a chunk of the woods with its massive frame, its shoulder easily six feet tall. It crouched on its four feet, glaring at Braeden with green eyes glimmering in the low forest light. Scales covered its jet-black skin.

Its pupils focused on him, and it snorted. Its tail flicked behind it, dragging on the ground and kicking up dust.

He'd stumbled across a vyrn—one of the most vicious and least understood creatures in Ourea. It was stealthy, fast, and smart. It could even run faster than the giant wolves.

It crouched, watching him, and Braeden kicked himself for letting his guard down. He hadn't heard anything or even sensed he was being watched, but he knew very little about vyrns. Maybe their stealth was better than the legends claimed.

He sat up straight on the log and kept eye contact with the creature. He swallowed to suppress the fear. No matter what it did, he would be able to heal.

It dug its claws into the ground. Smoke rose from its nose as if the thing would breathe fire any minute, which really wouldn't have surprised Braeden in the least.

His first instinct told him to subdue the creature enough to ride it. He suppressed the thought. His rash choices had gotten him into this mess in the first place, and the last thing he needed was another enemy.

He shifted his weight on the log. Something pressed against his leg. He reached for it without looking, and his fingers brushed the outline of the jerky in his pocket. An idea sparked in the back of his mind.

Instead of attacking, Braeden withdrew the jerky as slowly as he could. He stretched out his hand and set the meat flat on the log, offering it to the creature.

The vyrn's shoulders relaxed. Its eyes softened, and its tail came to a stop. It still watched him, but now it inched closer.

Braeden tensed and dug his fingers into the tree bark on his fallen log but made himself sit still.

A twig cracked beneath the vyrn's foot, sliced in half by one of its silver claws, but the creature didn't flinch. It only stopped when it stood directly in front of Braeden. It sniffed the meat and snapped, snatching the jerky from the dead tree in a move that ripped bark loose with it. Braeden tightened his hand into a fist and slowly pulled away.

The vyrn lowered its head until it was eye level with him. Braeden had no idea what he was supposed to do. He'd always heard of vyrns killing yakona and everything else they came across. This one—well, it looked like it wanted him to pet it. Maybe it was rabid.

He shook the thought from his head. His fingers twitched as he stretched his fingers toward the beast's nose. It grunted and flinched before he could touch it.

Part of Braeden expected the thing to snap at him or to try to take off his hand. Another part expected the creature to run off, scared of him like almost every other animal he'd met in his life. Yet another part—the smallest part—hoped it would let down its guard.

The vyrn sighed, shooting hot air over Braeden's knuckles. It relaxed and lowered its nose into his hand.

I'm Iyra. And no, I am not rabid.

Braeden resisted the impulse to pull back in surprise. At her touch, a female voice had crept into his mind.

The creature—Iyra—snorted a few times in quick succession, which Braeden could only guess was a laugh. She never pulled away from his touch.

You're a funny Heir. Nicest of them yet. Strange.

"Yes, I'm pretty strange," Braeden agreed with a laugh. He rubbed her muzzle.

She hummed. *Why are you sitting out here alone?*

"I need to find a way out of the Stele."

She laughed again. *You are royalty. Can you not leave your own kingdom?*

Too many thoughts crashed through Braeden's mind to articulate only one. Iyra tensed as he thought of Carden's torture, of receding to Kara in his mind, of his mother's face distorting into the slivers. His history with Carden passed in the matter of a few seconds, all broken images strung together with grief and regret.

I am sorry for your pain, Braeden.

"What—?" he asked.

The vyrn nuzzled his chest. *I share your thoughts when we communicate.*

"I didn't know a vyrn had telepathy."

Most yakona never try to learn about my kind. So many attempt to tame us, and they die trying. But not you. I've been watching you today, and you don't move like the rest. You're different, somehow. Kinder, maybe. I prefer to help those who deserve it. It's clear you need to find this young woman of yours, so I will do what I can. I can get you to her faster.

He sighed with relief. "Thank you."

Now, how should we leave?

Braeden hesitated. There was a thin trail, hardly used, winding through the mountains. It was the closest to Ayavel, if Braeden remembered the way properly.

"Can you give me a boost?" he asked, nodding to Iyra's back.

She knelt instead. Braeden jumped behind the vyrn's shoulders and set his hands along her short neck. Iyra leapt to her feet and bolted toward the path, apparently having read his thoughts as to where to go.

He hoped this would work.

CHAPTER THIRTY-EIGHT
BRAEDEN

Balancing on Iyra was one of the easiest things Braeden had ever done in his life. Her back dipped into a seat, as if built to carry riders. Steering, too, was simple. As long as he touched her, he could hear her thoughts—and apparently, she heard his. He tried to keep his mind from wandering to Kara but barely managed. Thankfully, Iyra didn't mind. She had seen his memories; she understood what Kara meant to him.

Iyra charged into a tunnel through the mountain when she neared it. They were close to a lichgate at the edge of the Stele, though Braeden had no idea what he'd do when he got there. He was trying not to think about it.

The tunnel was easily hundreds of feet long, but Iyra crossed it entirely too soon. Sunlight flared into view at the other end. As they grew closer, a figure blocked the light.

Someone yelled. Iyra roared, the rumble thundering through the cave in echoes. She lunged at the figure, throwing Braeden off her back. He rolled, landing with a hard *thud* against the cave wall.

When Braeden recovered, Iyra had her teeth around a Stelian's neck. The guard twitched one last time before he fell limp in her mouth. She spat him out and walked to Braeden, nudging him with her head.

He would have warned others. I had no choice.

"You did the right thing," Braeden said, patting her neck.

She hummed again. *This is the border, my friend. I cannot force you past it if Blood Carden has forbidden you from leaving. You must send us across.*

He eyed the forest beyond the tunnel. Snow lined the treetops and covered a small clearing beyond the exit. A branch, bent beneath the weight of the snow on it, finally bent too far, releasing its burden to the ground with a *thump*. Otherwise, nothing moved in the icy meadow.

Braeden walked forward, Iyra's footsteps following him as he moved. His feet slowed as he neared the lichgate at the end of the tunnel, his body obeying the mandate to remain in the kingdom. Finally, his feet stopped altogether. He urged himself forward, but his body did not move.

Iyra nudged him.

A flash of white broke across his vision, brighter even than the reflection of the sun off the snow through the lichgate. Peace engulfed him in that second, and he saw Kara's face. He smiled.

The peace disappeared as quickly as it had come, but Kara remained. She stood at the far edge of the clearing, her face so pale he couldn't even see her freckles. Frost lined her eyelashes. Her breath came in quick bursts, leaving thin pools of steam on the air.

"You're better than him," she said.

Frustration churned in his chest. The shame of a life spent running made his heart race. His fingers itched with anger and rage and the desire to kill something, but his feet wouldn't move.

"Braeden."

He closed his eyes to shut her out. He needed to focus. Hatred burned in his gut. He shouldn't have to fight. He should be able to live a peaceful, quiet life if he wanted.

"Braeden."

He snapped his eyes open. "What!"

She stood a foot from him. His jaw tensed. She smiled, and the anger in his gut melted away. The tension in his shoulders dissolved.

She reached for him, and he took her hand. Her

cold fingers sent a shiver through him. She wasn't real, so how could she be solid?

He closed his eyes and shut the thought away, focusing all his energy into his feet instead. All he had to do was walk forward. That wasn't impossible. That, he could do.

He pulled the air to push him forward. He borrowed energy from the ground to nudge him on. He called on the fiery hatred within him to grant him this one ounce of freedom, to let him do something good for once, to—

A ripple of ice shot through his veins. He shuddered. Kara's frigid hand disappeared from his. Weight lifted from his shoulders. Strength tore through him from nowhere. Blue light flared through his closed eyelids. His gut twisted.

How odd.

He opened his eyes. He stood at the edge of the clearing, where he'd seen Kara. She was gone, undeniably an apparition he'd created, but it didn't matter. Hopefully, the hallucinations would fade with time as he healed from his onslaught with the slivers.

He turned back to the tunnel. Iyra's green eyes widened. She leaned on her front paws, head to the ground as if she couldn't believe this any more than he did.

Braeden had done the impossible: he'd defied Carden's order.

He had no idea if he had broken the blood loyalty or if he had merely learned how to disobey, but it didn't matter. He wanted to jump and flip and scream in happiness, only he didn't have time.

"Hide that guard in the bushes over there, Iyra," he said.

She nodded, snapping out of her daze, and obeyed. She bit the guard's arm. Black dust blew from his skin as she dragged him to the edge of the forest and dumped him in the dense brush. He'd be hidden there. As far as Carden knew, Braeden couldn't disobey an order and was still in the Stele. They had no reason to believe he had anything to do with the guard unless they realized he was gone.

Braeden was coming back. He would help Kara first and hide her away, but this was the best chance he'd ever had to destroy Carden. He didn't quite understand what defying a mandate meant, but he'd done it once and could probably do it again. He would wait until the opportune moment to turn on his father and end the tyranny.

He had reasons to live now—not only Kara but his people, too. And when he became the Stelian Blood, he would do everything in his power to never be like his father.

CHAPTER THIRTY-NINE
KARA

Kara curled into a ball on the bed in her cell, the ache in her head growing stronger with each heartbeat. She wanted desperately to sleep, but anxiety twisted within her. Her convoluted thoughts kept her awake—as did the fear of what would happen in the morning.

The door creaked open. Kara peeked out of the corner of her eye. Gavin closed the door, locking them both inside.

She tensed.

He held up his hands. "I only want to talk."

Too many rebuttals raced through her mind to pick just one—oh, now he wanted to talk, when she could barely move; why hadn't he stood up for her; how could he let this happen; what was wrong with all of them?

The Hillsidian Blood walked over to her and sat on the edge of the bed with a sigh.

"I haven't slept through the night since Mother died," he confessed.

Kara eased away, but each movement made her skull throb more violently. She finally stopped when her head rested against a pillow and closed her eyes. It wasn't like she was a match for him in her condition, but she might as well preserve her energy in case the need to use it arose.

Whatever he had in mind for her, she wouldn't go down without a fight.

Gavin cracked his neck and continued. "I thought I was ready to be the Blood, for a short while at least, but I'm not. I never fully understood how distrusting the Bloods are or how manipulative they can be. I'm sorry you were brought into this, Kara. I tried to tell them that this plot with the muses wouldn't work, but Aislynn said her source was certain. It seems I don't know my mother's friend as well as I originally thought."

"I wasn't exactly expecting it, either," Kara said with a dry laugh, eyes still closed. Her head throbbed more with each word she spoke.

Warm hands touched the sides of her face. She tensed again and opened her eyes, but she could only see patches of color. Gavin's face came into focus above her, floating as if without a neck. She pushed the hands away.

Gavin frowned. "I'm trying to help, Kara. Please, relax."

He set his fingers on her head again. The ache unraveled in her forehead and neck at his touch. Warmth and a deep calm swam through her body, clearing her thoughts.

When she opened her eyes again, she could see clearly. The throbbing and tension disappeared. She sat up, marveling at the sudden clarity. Her body still moved a second slower than she meant it to, but at least the pain no longer consumed her.

"What was that?" she asked.

"An interrogation technique. It clears the prisoner's mind so he can better articulate whatever he's trying to tell me."

Oh.

"That was... honest," she said.

He sighed. "I've tried manipulating you, seducing you, tricking you, controlling you. Honesty is the only thing I haven't tried at this point. So yes, I was honest. I will try my best not to lie to you again."

Kara shook her head. "I don't trust you, Gavin. I haven't since you tricked Twin with the tiara."

"Again, I apologize. I know you turned her, though, and I'm not angry. She deserves to be free for what I nearly made her do to you, especially since it ended up being unnecessary."

"What do you mean?"

The Blood took a deep breath and stared at the floor. "At the gala, I let you believe Richard berated me after you told me off about the tiara and left me in the hall with him. I let you believe I was sorry."

"And that's not the case?"

"No. I ordered him to be silent when he did try to scold me. I then had my best trackers follow you to the village. I and three of my best soldiers know where it is."

Kara's heart skipped beats. She stopped breathing. "You WHAT?"

"It was a gamble. You are unaccustomed to our methods of stealth, so you didn't sense the trackers, but they almost lost you several times—your wolf is fast."

Kara gagged. He'd had trackers follow her back when she'd first found the village. He'd known all this time.

Gavin rubbed his face. "I had to know where you were going. Following you to the entrance of your legendary village was sheer luck. I know the temple has to be the way in—it was clever, putting the village there—but my men were forced to retreat when they saw you speak to the lyth. There were only a few of them, and they were no match for such a creature. It's brutal, fast, and always hungry. We would need an army to kill it, which is the only way to pass without its master's—your—approval.

"I had a few choices, none of which I liked. The most obvious was to declare war against you by openly attacking the village. We would have overtaken it, but it would have made the other Bloods furious. I'd have made a move of war without speaking to them first, and it would have violated the treaty I had talked them into signing later at the gala. I would also have a powerful new weapon—you. They would have singled me out as a traitor, and even while controlling you, I would have lost to them if they attacked.

"The other option was to confess what I knew to the Bloods and work together to overtake your village. The treasures and resources rumored to exist there were likely enough leverage for me to bargain to keep you. All I wanted was your power against Carden. They could keep the gold. I couldn't care less about material things."

"No, all you want is revenge," Kara spat.

He chewed on his lip and nodded. "But telling the Bloods risked exposing my upper hand, and I therefore didn't like the alternative, either."

"Do you always think like that? With cold calculation?"

Gavin caught her eye. She wanted to look away, to

show her disgust or grimace, but his cold gaze snared her. She couldn't look away. She shuddered.

He stared again at the floor, and Kara resisted the impulse to sigh with relief.

"I chose instead to confide in someone I could trust," he continued. "I couldn't tell Richard. All he cared about was protecting the Vagabond, even when leveraging you could avenge Mother."

"You have to be kidding—"

"And none of Mother's generals had ever dealt with such delicate matters. I didn't feel I could trust them." Gavin carried on as if she hadn't spoken, pushing through her words without pausing to let her in.

Apparently, he hadn't come for conversation. It was a confession. It seemed like he needed to get this off his chest. His life must have been a lonely one if he hadn't confessed any of this sooner. He must not have had anyone to talk to.

Kara sat back and listened. She could grant him that much. Besides, it would likely be helpful. In Ourea, information was more valuable than money.

Gavin ran a hand through his hair. "In the end, I turned to Aislynn and told her everything the night after Braeden's trial. I needed someone to trust, and Mother always seemed to believe in Aislynn. Of the Bloods, she had the most experience with diplomatic negotiation. She always spoke of peace and unity. I knew we had similar goals, she and I, and she had a compassion which would point me in the right direction."

He took a deep breath. "Or so I thought. I'll never forget the look on her face when I told her I knew your village's location. It was glee. Unadulterated joy, like she'd uncovered the winning move in a game. I had no idea she'd already been planning to lure you as bait to catch the muses, but it was as if the village made the final piece to her puzzle.

"She called a meeting right then and told the rest of the Bloods everything, without even telling me what she was about to do.

"I was horrified. A guard of mine overheard her invite you to Ayavel during the gala—and I suddenly understood why she'd offered. She'd wanted to lure you there under the pretense of safety. She revealed her plan to use you as bait, since by then, Braeden had left to find the Heirs. You were unconscious and exposed after his trial, though we didn't know then you'd disappeared from the room Braeden had taken you to. We all know he cares for you. It's been evident for a while now. He would have interfered to protect you from what Aislynn was planning, so he needed to be out of the picture.

"They also acknowledged that we would lose your trust after using you, so bargaining began before I could stop it. Aislynn was given the power of the muse she stole, and Ithone, Frine, and I would duel for the right to control you after the process was complete. The losing pair would be left splitting the spoils from your village, and all kingdoms would be evenly rewarded for their contributions.

"I lost the upper hand, even though I knew better than to interfere with the drenowith. The other Bloods were nearly salivating at the prospect of controlling such power. I never realized how excellent a speaker Aislynn is, either. She spun the story, making it seem as though it was all my idea. Her ruse kept the suspicion off me and made me seem like the good little boy, reporting back to his superiors. I lost all say in the matter.

"The truth came out, then, about how Frine and Ithone watched you in your time with them. They feared the legend of the first Vagabond. They had no idea of your power, so they gave you free rein. They wanted to observe you to see how much you truly knew. The first Vagabond was a legend, and here he was—reincarnated, they believed—in the form of a young human girl. It baffled them. It baffled all of us, though I know you aren't a reincarnated soul. The Vagabond never really died, did he?"

Gavin turned to Kara for confirmation, but she didn't answer. He might be confessing, but he wouldn't get anything from her.

He shrugged and continued. "I was merely curious. It doesn't matter. Frine watched you while you were in

Losse, fascinated as you tore through his gardens on the first day. A spy of his saw what you found—that little blue square—but he didn't know what to make of it.

"Aurora apparently told Ithone that your pack was heavier when you left the garden and hung lower on your shoulder. He was furious because she hadn't discovered what you took, but he didn't dare challenge you for it when he was still uncertain of your abilities. He let it go."

Kara's gut twisted. And here, she'd thought she'd been clever in finding the map pieces. There was still so much she didn't know.

"Aislynn just gave me the Ayavelian piece," Kara finally said.

"She said she didn't know what it was, back then. Richard did, though."

"What do you mean?"

"The Hillsidian bit of the map appeared for you, didn't it? Without explanation?"

Kara bit her cheek to suppress a gasp. "That was Richard?"

Gavin nodded. "There's an old rumor from around the time the Vagabond went into hiding. It claimed a blue map would lead his true successor back to the village if he ever died. I always thought it was ridiculous and gave fools false hope, but Richard believed it. He believed you were the true successor. He confessed later to leaving you the map piece, which had long been in the Hillsidian vaults. Richard has always believed in you, even more than he believes in me."

Gavin looked at the floor again. He hunched his shoulders in defeat, but Kara didn't set a comforting hand on his shoulder. She couldn't bond with him, not with Gavin. She just couldn't trust him. This could be yet another of his ploys, though it admittedly wasn't likely. He slouched too much. His head hung with a weight that didn't come without authenticity.

No. She couldn't trust him. Not after everything he'd done. She could pity him, though.

"Did you tell anyone the village's actual location?" she asked, forcing herself to be still, even though she wanted to shake him and slap him all at once for knowing.

"Not yet, but it's just a matter of time before I can't tactfully avoid answering them."

Kara buried her head in her hands and pulled her knees to her chest. She didn't know what else to do.

He sighed, sounding far older than he looked. "I brought the Bloods together, and I have since lost all control."

Kara shook her head and laughed.

"Why are you laughing?" Gavin asked, watching her with a suspicious glint out of the corner of his eye.

"All I wanted was to unite you all. And I did. I just didn't expect to become the thing you united against."

"I'm sorry," he said.

He set his head in his hands. Despite everything he had done to prove the contrary, she believed his new remorse. Kara didn't respond, though. Sure, she believed him, but she wouldn't forgive him yet.

He rested one hand on his cheek and stared at the stones on the floor. "This has all gotten out of hand."

"No kidding," Kara said.

"We sent Braeden to the Stele," Gavin confessed without warning.

She cursed, and Gavin flinched. When she finally processed the full weight of what he'd said, she cursed again, louder this time. Braeden's goodbye, the sense of loss, that painfully terrifying kiss—it suddenly all made sense.

"You're all insane! Why would you do that?" she snapped.

"You disappeared from the room where Braeden left you after his trial. We reasoned you would be weak immediately after your possession, and it would be easier to use you as bait, but we couldn't find you anywhere. I was desperately trying to get to you first to get you away from them. I knew if they went through with this plan, that I'd lose my last chance of getting your help in this war. But Aislynn knew what I was doing. She wouldn't leave me alone. And when we found you, I tried to tell you—"

Kara rubbed her face. Of course, hindsight was

twenty-twenty. "She told me you all thought less of her because she stood up for Braeden. She made you out to be the villain. She's clever."

"Aislynn was happy to have found you, though admittedly disappointed you were awake. I think she ordered me out because she suspected what I was trying to do. She wanted to lull you into a sense of security while she decided what to do next.

"But then you left. Gone with no warning. The Bloods didn't know what to do. I was relieved. I thought maybe you'd guessed what we had planned and went back to the village. But no. No, you'd gone to help Braeden." Gavin said the name with disdain.

They both sighed before Gavin continued.

"Aislynn insisted we have a backup plan in case you returned. At her recommendation, of course, we agreed to give Braeden false information should he return from rescuing the Heirs. And imagine our surprise—my frustration—when you returned with him.

"We reconvened as soon as you and Braeden left the throne room, only us Bloods. Aislynn claimed Braeden couldn't be trusted, especially not after returning from the Stele. So, I told him to lead Carden's forces to a camp, where I claimed we'd be waiting to surprise them. We will ambush them much sooner in a ravine serving as the only entrance to the camp. The location will leave them virtually defenseless. I don't expect Braeden or Carden to survive."

Kara's heart skipped a beat, and it was all she could do not to punch Gavin in the face and run for the door. Since it was locked, that would be useless. Punching him would feel pretty good, though.

"You all are disgusting," she said instead.

"Let me finish."

Kara leaned against the wall but wouldn't look at him. How there could be more was beyond her. She motioned for him to continue.

"What I didn't realize was Aislynn slyly tricked me into getting Braeden away from you. She knows he loves you. I think all the Bloods do at this point, though we still aren't sure of how you feel about him. Frine thinks you're using him."

"I would never—" She stopped, but too late.

Gavin watched her with a sideways glance, and she sighed. She had walked into a trap. So much for him not manipulating her.

He leaned back. "I know what you must be thinking, and even though you have every right to believe I'm tricking you, I'm not. You genuinely care for him. You can admit it now. There's no use in hiding it any longer."

"You're mistaken," she softly said. She had to at least try to cover her tracks.

Gavin shrugged and continued without pressing

the subject. "Everything Aislynn told me about the ambush was a lie to make you vulnerable. Braeden trusted her to protect you from the rest of us, but in the end, Aislynn is the one to be feared."

He took a deep breath and rubbed his eyes before he continued. "In the morning, Kara, they will spike you again, so the poisons prevent you from resisting. They will do it daily until Aislynn is well, unless..."

"Unless what?"

"Unless you escape or align yourself with one of the kingdoms."

"I don't suppose you'd just let me walk out?"

"I will, but I want you to consider my proposition first. Will you?"

Kara caught his eye. "You would really let me leave? Just like that?"

"Yes, as long as you consider what I have to say before you go."

"I'm listening."

"If you leave, Kara, you will be hunted down like an escaped animal. When they find you—because they will—you will be chained and caged. Whoever catches you will have the most say in who controls you once Aislynn heals, which means there will be a full-on hunt once the Bloods realize you're missing. It will become sport."

"And you'll join them?"

He looked at the wall but eventually nodded. "Kara,

it will mean declaring war on you. Any other vagabonds you've turned will be killed. Twin will be killed. But if you stay in this tower to wait it out, I have no doubt Losse or Kirelm will ultimately win the duel to control you. Ithone and Frine are stronger than me. I don't stand a chance against them.

"The only way for you to avoid such a fate is to align yourself with one of the kingdoms and become a Blood's or Heir's wife." He paused. "My wife."

"You can't be serious."

"You would be royalty, and they would be forced to treat you with respect. They would have no right or ability to control you."

"And you would?"

"No. Instead, I'll make a bargain with you. Your village will be safe and your vagabonds safe, all if you help me avenge Mother."

Kara pushed herself to her feet and ran her hand through her hair.

"This has to be the worst marriage proposal ever," she finally said.

"Braeden's not coming back, Kara. Not from the Stele. We sent him there knowing his fate. I knew it, but I did it anyway because it's only a matter of time before he accepts what he is. As good as he tries to be, he was born to destroy. It's in his blood!"

"And you don't destroy?"

"This is different."

"It isn't different at all! Braeden is one of the only people I trust, Gavin. Especially after this."

Gavin grimaced. "He will break your heart. He can't fight what he is, and no one's going to save you from this. You have three choices: slavery, running, or me. Is this really a contest?"

Kara walked to the fireplace, stretching her stiff arms as she did. The poison still swam through her blood, but thankfully it didn't hurt anymore. She waved her hand over the cold logs, and a lavender fire danced to life beneath her fingers. The rush of magic and heat further cleared her head.

The mattress squeaked as Gavin shifted his weight on the bed. "All I want is justice for my mother, Kara. You can help me find it."

Revenge—Kara could appreciate that. Deidre still had her dad's soul locked away within her, keeping him from resting in peace. But Kara had exposed him. It was her fault he'd been in harm's way at all. Hating Deidre—killing her—wasn't going to make that guilt go away.

It wasn't any different for Gavin. Not really.

She stared into the fire, the flames leaving twisted imprints on her vision. "Peace is something you have to find for yourself, Gavin. No amount of revenge will ever give you that."

He stood and walked slowly closer. "Please, Kara. I will forever protect you if you will only help me kill

Carden. You can even turn Braeden into a vagabond if you like, if he's not too far gone. I can bring him back from the battle if you want. This is no small favor I'm asking of you, but it's one I will forever reward."

She sighed. He hadn't listened to a thing she'd just said. It wouldn't be any different if she agreed to this crazy little scheme of his. He would never listen.

"And what happens after the war? You and I go our separate ways?" she asked.

"No, Kara. Yakona bond for life."

"This is ridiculous, Gavin. I can't even give you an Heir."

"You probably could, actually, but Evelyn's new bloodline has proven it to be a moot point. I've thought this through. I don't offer it lightly."

"Do you still love her?"

His jaw tensed, and he didn't breathe for a moment. Eventually, he nodded.

Kara leaned against the wall. "So, you're giving up on ever loving someone else because she broke your heart?"

"Hardly. I'm sacrificing a marriage based on love so you and I can destroy the Stelian race and mend an evil which has plagued Ourea for too long. I'm not saying you have to be faithful to me. You don't have to hate me for it."

"That isn't going to work, Gavin."

"Kara, listen!"

Hot anger flashed across Gavin's face, and he reached a hand to either side of Kara's head. She flinched, unprepared for the outburst, but he seemed to contain his temper just as quickly as it flared. His fingers rested lightly on her cheeks instead of grabbing them.

Gavin leaned in close. "I cannot kill Carden on my own, Kara, especially not with Braeden at his side. Even though draining the muse failed, the Bloods are still going to go ahead with the plan to kill Carden's forces when Braeden leads them into our trap. When I face Carden, I'll need extra power on my side to actually defeat him. If you aren't there, I can't win. The Grimoire is incredibly powerful, Kara, and the Vagabond is a serious enemy. I need you to win this."

"I don't even have the Grimoire. Evelyn stole it."

"She will be forced to return it when you become my wife."

Kara's heart skipped a beat at that word—wife. It terrified her. Heart hammering in her chest, Gavin unnervingly close, Kara wracked her brain, trying to figure out what to do. The world had unraveled before her eyes—Braeden was gone, the Bloods were after her village, and she was faced with impossible odds.

But marrying Gavin, giving up her power to the man who had tried so hard to control her from the very beginning—there simply had to be another way.

CHAPTER FORTY

KARA

With Gavin's palms resting lightly on her face, his body close—too close—Kara set her hands on his chest. His heartbeat quickened under her fingertips. His hands slipped lower, cradling her head with a more tender caress than she'd imagined him capable of achieving.

But that wasn't what she'd meant when she touched him. She pushed him away.

"I can't give up that easily," she said.

"Marrying me isn't giving up. It's fighting!"

"No, it's giving up. I would rather take my chances than be your pawn."

"But I can't protect you when you're caught, and you will be caught if you leave. This is your one chance to have a voice in the yakona court—your one and only chance."

"Since when are the royal spouses at the war room tables, Gavin? I wouldn't have a say. I'd be playing along, useless and unhappy. Compliance isn't going to change anything. That's exactly what marrying you would do—nothing.

"Ourea is broken, Gavin, and whenever I play by your rules, it gets worse. Uniting the four kingdoms was meant to eradicate Carden because he's murderous and cruel, but all it did was give you a common enemy to hate. Two enemies, if you count what you all did to me. That was my fault, really, for not seeing it sooner. But what happens when you kill Carden? If you kill Braeden?"

Her lip trembled ever so slightly at the thought of someone running Braeden through with a sword. She took a deep breath, hoping Gavin hadn't noticed. According to what he said earlier, though, it didn't matter if she showed how much she cared.

She stepped closer to the door. "Even if the Stelians all die, the yakona kingdoms will be down to four, and you all will just continue bickering. Maybe they'll turn on you, Gavin. Maybe Hillside will become the next 'threat.' It won't get better. It won't stop."

Gavin ran his hand through his hair and let out an exasperated sigh. "So, what are you going to do, Kara? Run around Ourea picking fights? Will you make more vagabonds? At least you have a direct line to the Bloods if you stand beside me!"

"I'd stand behind you, Gavin, not beside you."

He groaned but didn't correct her. He didn't have to. She was right.

She continued. "They won't listen to me just because you make me go through the motions of a wedding or whatever it is you all do here. They don't respect me. Ithone thinks I'm obstinate because I won't wear a dress. Frine thinks I'm a weak tool, and no amount of training will ever change his mind. Aislynn has already made it clear what she's willing to do to further her own agenda. And you..."

Gavin arched his back and crossed his arms. "Yes?"

"You want me to kill the man who killed your mother. I'm just a weapon to you. You're no better than them, Gavin. You're just a little nicer about it."

Gavin didn't respond for a while. He didn't even breathe. It wasn't until he rubbed his face and sat again on the bed that he moved at all. He waved a hand toward the door, which swung open on its hinges at his command. A stairwell disappeared into the shadows of a dark hall.

Kara knelt until she was eye level with him. Gavin looked up at her.

"Thank you," she said.

"You should really go before I change my mind," he answered.

She couldn't. Not yet. She needed her grimoire

pendant back. "Can you tell me where Evelyn's room is? I assume you must know by now."

His shoulders sank lower, and he nodded. He pulled out a small piece of paper covered in elegant script.

"What's this?" she asked.

"Evelyn slipped a note to me at dinner. It has the directions to her room from the dining hall, which will be on your right as you walk out of this stairwell. She's expecting me, not you, so you'll have the element of surprise on your side when you see her."

"Thanks again," Kara said.

She grabbed Gavin's shoulder and smiled, but he shook his head. That was likely her cue to leave.

The only guiding light in the stairwell came in a cold, blue stream from a few, small slits in the wall below. She hurried down the steps. The outline of a door appeared as her eyes adjusted to the darkness. She set her hands against the wall and peeked through the slits in the stone.

The room beyond her hidden cell was none other than the grand hall. Though she couldn't see it, Kara knew the throne room was to her left and the dining hall, as Gavin had said, was to the right. No one stood in the massive hall, so Kara pushed the door open.

The stone grated against the floor. She cringed, but she had no other way out. The door scraped against the tiled floor, and she only stopped when she could slip through into the hallway. She had to hurry in case anyone heard the noise. Kara looked again at the paper Gavin had given her, but she didn't have time to read it.

"You!"

Kara looked up to see Evelyn standing opposite, blocking the only way out of the hall that Kara knew.

"Guards! G—!"

A blinding light rushed past Kara, knocking her to the stonework as Evelyn's voice cut off mid-sentence.

Kara hit her head against the wall. Her vision blurred again. The world came slowly back, first as black and white dots, then as gray blurs. When Kara could fully see, Gavin sat across the hall, kneeling by Evelyn's unconscious form.

"What—?" Kara asked.

"I don't think anyone heard her, but I'm sure guards will be by soon," he said without looking up.

Gavin examined something in his hand. Its silver chain slipped from his fingers as he rubbed his thumb over the sparkling metal. His skin blistered from whatever it was he touched, but if he felt any pain, he didn't flinch.

That had to be her pendant.

"Gavin," Kara said softly.

It took him a moment to catch her eye, and it almost hurt to see the desire on his face. Between the pendant and the unconscious princess, he held the two things he so craved but couldn't have. Kara took a cautious step closer. The bags under his eyes made her wonder if he'd gone without sleep for days.

"May I have that back, please?" she asked, reaching for the pendant.

"Without this, you're nothing but an ordinary girl," he said.

She ignored the jibe. "Maybe. But without me, it's just a necklace that burns you when you hold it."

His jaw tightened, and he rubbed his thumb over the clover symbol in his hand.

In a motion so quick she barely registered it, Gavin tossed the pendant to her. She caught it in reflex. Relief flooded through her body.

"I would carry it everywhere, too, if I'd taken it," Gavin admitted.

"Thanks for giving it to me, then."

He shrugged. "I almost didn't."

Kara didn't know how to respond, so she put the necklace on and headed for the hall. Gavin stood, though, and stopped her by putting one arm around her waist. His touch made her skin crawl, but she resisted the impulse to push him away. He'd helped her, after all.

He glanced over his shoulder. "Take the first left and keep running. It will take you to the forest line, and from there, you can get a head start. Look for a path. Once you find it, it will take you to a lichgate leading out of Ayavel. Once they call the Bloods together, I won't stop or slow them. Try not to get caught."

"Thank you, Gavin."

"Don't thank me. I'll be hunting with them."

She grimaced, and his eyes locked on the pendant around her neck. Her skin itched under his scrutiny. With no time to waste, she slipped out of his reach and didn't look back as she ran toward the exit. Of course, Gavin would know where to go if she followed the path he'd told her about, but she didn't have any better ideas. Running willy-nilly through the forest would be stupid. At least Gavin's instructions gave her direction.

Just as Gavin had said, the hall ended in a door that opened onto a field. A forest began about a dozen feet away. Kara bolted toward it, her throat already stinging from the exhaustion, adrenaline, and panic. Tendrils of the spikes' poison still lurked in her body, slowing her movement and thought.

Once a few feet into the forest, Kara summoned the Grimoire. Its weight materialized in her hands, and she sighed with relief as it opened on its own. She had worried the Vagabond was still too angry to let her use the Grimoire to even escape.

"Get me out of here, Ryn," she said under her breath.

BRAEDEN

Braeden charged through the forest on Iyra's back, urging her to run faster than he imagined she'd ever had to in her life.

Kara was worth it.

He stopped within the treeline on the outskirts of Ayavel. The waterfall loomed nearby, but he didn't need it. An army waited in the field by the lake. Some poured into the forest, even.

Troops from every kingdom pooled together in close ranks, restless and yelling at each other. Some prodded those from the other kingdoms, pushing as they passed or taunting each other with sidelong glances and sneers.

Braeden's shoulders tensed. Everything had gotten far worse.

One Ayavelian soldier nearest to the trees ran by, still tucking in his uniform as he hurried to another soldier nearby. "What are we waiting for? The Vagabond attacked Heir Evelyn! We should be chasing her!"

Braeden smirked.

One of the other soldiers in the group answered. "We're waiting for the Bloods. They want to lead the chase themselves."

Blinding, silver light appeared at the base of the

waterfall. The roaring water parted as the stone path and carved stairs once more appeared.

Gavin, Ithone, Frine, and Krik the Ayavelian general charged along the path from the temple. They all rode griffins and tore through the pass as if racing.

Braeden cursed under his breath and turned Iyra back into the forest. Spurred by his panic, she bolted through the thick woods he'd once thought were safe. He had never been so wrong.

If he didn't get to Kara first, there was no telling what would happen.

CHAPTER FORTY-ONE
KARA

With no time to spare, Kara raced through the lichgate Gavin had mentioned. Ryn ran to the thrum of her heartbeat which, thanks to the still-pumping adrenaline, was pretty fast.

Kara directed Ryn toward the village. If anyone caught up with her, she would switch gears and find Stone instead.

She toyed with the idea of going to her haven no matter what. Gavin already knew where it was, and she had to warn Twin and Richard. But if he truly hadn't told the other Bloods about its location, she might buy her vagabonds some time by leading the Bloods in a different direction. Kara just needed a moment of peace to search the Grimoire for a way to contact them.

Trees blurred by as Ryn sped to the village, his steps the quietest thing in the forest. Even though a deep hush had settled between the dark branches and underbrush of the woods, Ryn's feet barely touched the fallen leaves as he ran over them. The occasional crunch under his feet or swish of his tail mingled with the cold breezes that rustled through the trees.

A branch snapped far off to the left.

Ryn stopped, and Kara held on too tightly for the sudden halt to throw her off. The giant wolf's ears perked. He turned toward the noise and tensed. His shoulder trembled under Kara's hand.

"To Stone's cave, boy," she whispered with a sigh.

So much for going home. Ryn tore away in a different direction than they had originally travelled.

Another twig cracked, closer this time. A growl rumbled through the trees.

The trees ended, giving way to a mountain. It rose into the sky like a cliff without so much as a deer path winding up it. Kara pushed Ryn around it, but the huffing breaths of whatever chased them grew ever closer. She looked over her shoulder, but nothing passed between the trees.

Even on Ryn, Kara couldn't outrun this creature. Its growling came closer with every second. She didn't have time to summon the griffin and change mounts, either—not if it was so close she could hear it breathing. She needed a plan. She needed to trick it.

Kara rounded a curve in the mountain, leaning in so that Ryn hugged the rock face. A path appeared not far off, cut into the mountain. She tugged on Ryn's fur to signal him up the narrow trail.

The mountain closed in on both sides of her. At first, Kara thought she had made a mistake. But, thankfully, the rock broke away after a minute. Boulders littered the sides of the narrow road.

Kara leaned back, and Ryn slid to a stop. She hopped off and jumped behind a boulder. Her giant wolf tried to follow.

"No, over there, silly. There's no room for both of us," she said, pointing to a rock his size across the way.

He whined but nudged her shoulder and obeyed.

Kara slid behind her boulder and waited, her ears straining as she listened. Sure enough, the scrape of claws on rock echoed down the pass. The mysterious creature's breath came closer with each pounding footfall. Panic raced through her; this thing sounded huge. She debated letting it pass, instead of trying to trap and kill it.

The breaths grew louder, the rasping and grating noises enough to make Kara breathless, too. She peeked around the rock, just enough to get the slightest look at the monster when it passed.

But the creature didn't pass. It stopped by her boulder. She stifled a gasp. Its skin was as black as the Stelian forests, covered in scales. Its silver claws dug into the rock, splitting the stone without effort. But its head—it looked like a giant panther with silver teeth.

Someone sat on its back. From her limited angle, all Kara could see of him was that he wore the silver tunic of the Stele.

Great. Carden was looking for her now, too.

Kara focused her energy into her palm, where a pearl blue blade erupted from the air around her and clung to her fingers. She stood as quietly as she could and climbed onto the boulder.

The man began to turn toward her, so she jumped at him while she still had the element of surprise. Ryn growled, and the scaly monster the man rode let out a piercing scream.

Kara landed against the man, his body warm and hard as she slammed into him. He grabbed her arm and tried to speak, but his mount twisted and reared. Kara fell with him to the ground. The world tumbled. Kara couldn't get a look at the Stelian's face until she had him pinned to the rock with her blade at his neck.

He shrank, his body changing form until the gray skin became olive. His gorgeous eyes tied her stomach in knots.

"Braeden?"

"Iyra, stop!" he called over Kara's shoulder.

The dark creature growled. Kara twisted in time to see the black monster twitch at Braeden's voice. Iyra relaxed, but kept her gaze fixed on Ryn. The wolf took a step back, his body tensed to spring. He bared his teeth, his shoulders hunched and his hair on end.

"Kara, are you all right?" Braeden asked.

He pulled her into a hug. She held him close, letting her magical blade splinter and fall away as she did. She burrowed her nose into his neck without thinking or second-guessing herself. Relief made her shake. His arms tightened around her.

For the first time since she'd left Twin and Richard at the village, Kara felt safe.

"Kara, are—"

"I'm fine, but what about you?" she countered.

"Fine," he said. But his voice wavered, and his whole body tensed. She could tell it had been a lie.

She set a hand on his cheek. "Gavin said you were gone. He tried to get me to marry him, Braeden, can you believe—"

"He did what?"

She laughed. "It doesn't even matter. I knew he was wrong. I knew you'd come back."

"He's wrong a lot lately." Braeden smiled and brushed away the hair in her eyes.

She hugged him again. She wanted to say that she missed his touch, his voice, having someone to trust. But all she could manage was, "I missed you."

He tensed again and sighed. "I missed you, too,

Kara. I wish we could stay like this, but we have to get you out of here. I only found you first because Iyra is faster."

"We can't go to the village. Gavin knows where it is."

Braeden cursed under his breath. "Well, they're coming for you. You should wish Ryn away. He can't outrun them, but Iyra can."

"Okay," she said.

She hurried to Ryn and patted his muzzle. He looked up at her with hurt eyes and whined, but she shook her head and kissed the giant wolf's forehead. "It'll be okay, boy. You're still my favorite."

He nudged her shoulder and dissolved into floating dust with a *poof*. Kara turned, now alone with Braeden and his monster mount, Iyra.

Braeden jumped to his feet and climbed onto his giant mount with ease. He turned to Kara and reached for her.

"Come on. I'll help you up," he said.

She slipped her hand in his. He pulled her in front of him, wrapping his arms around her as he leaned forward. Kara had to suppress a smile at his touch. She had missed him entirely too much. She wanted to reach back and show him exactly how much.

No. She clenched her fists and took a deep breath. The first Vagabond still wouldn't talk to her. She couldn't forget his threat to kill Braeden. She couldn't risk his anger.

"Kara," Braeden said in her ear.

She wanted to lean into him, to feel safe again, but she took a deep breath instead. "Yes?"

"When I said I have to get you out of here, I meant out of Ourea."

She looked over her shoulder. His face hovered inches from hers. He held her gaze, his eyebrow turned in the slightest hint of remorse.

"I'm not leaving," she said.

"I'm not asking."

"Braeden, you can't make me leave Ourea because things got a little dangerous—"

"A little dangerous? Are you joking? I know what happened, Kara. Don't downplay what the Bloods did. They're out of control."

"No, you don't want me to be at..." She trailed off, remembering what Gavin had told her about the false information he'd given Braeden.

"I want you to be safe, Kara."

"Forget about me. Gavin is playing you. They plan to kill you at the battle with Carden."

"I figured."

"You—you did?"

Voices echoed from the pass' entrance.

"We have to go," he said.

Iyra sprinted up the path, so fast the wind stung Kara's eyes. She closed them and leaned her head against Braeden's shoulder. He tensed and tightened his hold around her waist.

He leaned his chin into the nape of her neck as they ran. The world bled away at his touch. "To answer you, Kara—yes, I know what they're planning. At least, I probably know most of it. I said my goodbye to you. Getting to see you again beforehand is a blessing."

"You can't give up like that!"

He laughed. "Come on, you know me. I'm not giving up. But if it's the four of them against me, I'll lose. I wanted to make sure you knew I didn't abandon you. I care."

He burrowed his cheek into her neck again. Her frustration melted at his touch. He took a deep breath and kissed her temple. Heat rushed down her neck, and she resisted the urge to shiver with delight.

"Braeden, I can help. Tell me where this battle is," she said.

"I'm not going to, Kara. I hope you forgive me for doing this instead."

"What?" she asked.

But her suddenly drooping eyelids were answer enough. She managed to look up at him before whatever magic he'd used lulled her to sleep. He looked down with a rueful smile, and she fought the impulse to slap him.

"I'm sorry," he said.

Kara's world went dark before she could answer.

CHAPTER FORTY-TWO
BRAEDEN

Braeden sat on a footstool beside a very pink bed in the human world. He had never asked Kara her favorite color, but he was pretty sure it wasn't pink.

Still, she looked peaceful. She lay in the bed, her hair spread over the pillows. Dirt smudged her cheeks, and the sheets wrinkled whenever she tossed in her sleep. She probably hadn't had much time to herself since he'd left for the Stele.

Braeden gritted his teeth. He couldn't decide who he wanted to kill more: Gavin or Aislynn.

He rubbed his eyes, still not wanting to leave. It hadn't taken him very long to get to a bed and breakfast in Scotland thanks to Iyra's speed. He'd made up some lie about jet lag to get the caretakers—Lori and Andrew—to let him carry Kara inside. He'd insisted they'd lost his reservation. It wasn't the kindest thing to do to these nice people, but he was short on time and better ideas. They'd let him in, as they happened to have an extra room, and he'd silently counted his lucky stars as they led him up the stairs.

He'd asked Lori for a pen and paper, which she had pulled from an overstuffed desk downstairs before going back to bed. He'd used it to write Kara a letter, which he now held in his hands. He had even put some money in the desk drawer for her, since he often stored human currency and clothes near the lichgates when he travelled.

He needed to go; he simply couldn't bring himself to set the letter down and leave. He wanted to lay next to her and sleep, but it would be running away again. Peace at such a price wouldn't last. Carden would find him and maybe kill him if it became evident that he could now defy orders. Braeden laughed. How he'd managed to do it, he might never know.

He kissed Kara's forehead and reached behind her head. With a pang of remorse, he unclasped the grimoire pendant from around her neck. He set the necklace in his palm to examine it, but it burned his skin. He winced and gritted his teeth through the pain long enough to shove it in his pocket. The burns disappeared as his skin healed itself.

She would probably beat him senseless if he were here when she woke up. He should definitely leave.

He needed to take the pendant, though. She couldn't stay out of trouble for two minutes. She would find the battle if she had the Grimoire. Braeden didn't quite know how she would do it, but she would manage. She was the Vagabond. She could do anything.

He set the letter on the desk as he left. Iyra waited for him on the other side of a nearby lichgate, and he was running out of time. He still had one more stop to make before he went back to the Stele, and he had to do it quickly.

BRAEDEN

Braeden hated the thought of trusting Stone, but he really had no better options.

He'd shared with Iyra as many of the memories of his and Kara's trip to Stone's cave as he could recall. Apparently, it had been enough. She tore off the moment he showed her the isen's home. She insisted it would take no more than an hour to reach him, but after that, he only had another few hours before daybreak at the Stele. He had to be back before anyone realized he'd left. It might already be too late.

He pushed away the thought. He had to get the Grimoire someplace safe, and Stone was the closest thing. The village was too far away; besides, according to Kara, Gavin already knew its location. Taking it there wouldn't help. He wished he could warn Twin and Richard, but he didn't have time. He barely had time to go to Stone.

Braeden shuddered. How the first Vagabond could trust such a powerful isen was beyond him, but they seemed to have history. If Stone helped create the grimoires, he obviously didn't need their magic. He wouldn't be interested in the book, and therefore it was safe to give it to him—or so Braeden hoped.

Iyra slowed to a gentle stop. Braeden blinked himself out of his thoughts.

Wow, that was fast.

Iyra laughed. *Thank you.*

Braeden slid off and began up the trail to Stone's cave. Iyra made to follow him, but he waved her back and smiled. He wanted a trump card if this went awry. Who knew—maybe Stone had a fear of vyrn.

He inched his way to the entrance and took a deep breath. He turned the corner only to see Stone leaning against the same wall, already staring at him.

Braeden's heart skipped a beat. He took a step back.

"Well, out with it, boy. Come to kill me already?" Stone asked.

Braeden shook his head. "Kara needs a favor."

The isen looked around, eyebrows quirked as he mockingly searched for her. "Does she, now?"

"Look, she needs you to hold onto the grimoire pendant for a day or two. I'll be back for it soon."

"I imagine you will be. And where might the young Miss Magari be at this hour that she needs you to do her errands?"

"Can you do it or not?" Braeden snapped.

"Of course, I can, but that's the wrong way to ask," Stone said with a smirk.

"Well? Will you?"

"You need to say please."

"For the love of—" Braeden wanted to run his sword through this isen. He was so annoying.

"I'll give you a choice. It's kind of like truth or dare, except my version is truth or say please."

"Truth about what?"

Stone laughed. "What, are you averse to manners? 'Please' is a completely reasonable request."

Braeden sighed. He wondered where else he could put the pendant. Perhaps he could bury it somewhere. That might be the better option. He should've thought of that sooner—

"Are you in love with Kara?" Stone asked.

Braeden caught the isen's eye. For a while, the crickets in the woods made the only sound.

"Please, hold the pendant for a few days," Braeden finally said.

"That's what I thought," Stone said with another smirk.

Braeden lifted the pendant out of his pocket by its chain—careful to avoid the pendant itself—and handed it to Stone.

"I'll be back for it soon, so don't even think about leaving this cave," Braeden said.

"Uh huh, of course. You can go now," Stone said. He turned and walked into his cavern, his figure receding into the darkness.

Braeden hesitated. He had quite possibly made a huge mistake, but he needed to leave. He was out of time.

He ran down the path and used the momentum to jump onto Iyra's back. They tore off into the forest.

STONE

If Braeden had stepped a few feet into Stone's cave, he would have seen the isen grab his coat and set the grimoire pendant on a small coffee table by a marble sofa covered in red cushions. He would have also heard the isen humming before muttering something about hurrying if he was to make it to Scotland in time.

BRAEDEN

Braeden slipped into his room at the Stele one hour before sunrise. He barely made it, and only because Iyra ran faster than any vyrn he'd read about.

Iyra promised to wait out of sight along the forest's edge in case he needed her. He planned to take her up on that, actually, when Carden assembled everyone to leave for the ambush. Carden would think it a sign of vanity to have a vyrn for a mount, but Braeden wanted Iyra with him in case Carden survived the battle. After this, Braeden had no intention of returning to the Stele until it belonged to him.

He needed a bath but was too tired. Instead, he found a pair of clean pants and slipped into bed. He stared at the ceiling, slowly dropping off to sleep. He hoped Kara would forgive him. He wasn't sure what life would be like if she refused to ever speak to him again, but he took solace in knowing it would be a better world as long as she was in it.

His memories of Kara had saved him from mindless slavery to Carden. Without her, he would have succumbed. Without her, he never could have disobeyed Carden. He would never have freed himself.

Braeden owed Kara his life, and he would forever protect her with it.

CHAPTER FORTY-THREE

KARA

It was more the headache that woke Kara, rather than the actual desire to wake up. The throbbing pain made it hard to open her eyes, but she forced them open anyway. The last thing she remembered was Braeden apologizing, and—

She sat upright. Pink paint covered every wall, and a white bay window to her left let in daylight. A desk and dresser filled most of the wall across from her, and the long mirror on the back of the closed white door reflected a few framed photos on the wall behind her. The door's golden handle glittered in the sunlight. Pastel roses covered the bedspread on top of her.

Where the hell was she?

A whir sounded from somewhere in the walls. Kara flinched. A warm breeze flowed through a ceiling vent and played with something on the desk, pushing it farther against the wall.

She held her breath.

Is that an air vent?

The heating vent in the ceiling was real. It most definitely blew air onto what appeared to be a note.

Kara jumped out of bed and snatched the paper. She unfolded it, and something fell from it onto the desk. She didn't care. The moment she recognized Braeden's handwriting, she couldn't tear her eyes from the letter.

Kara—

Yes, you're in the human world. Dailly, Scotland, to be exact.

I brought you here because there's going to be a battle in Ourea which will hopefully end this war. If it doesn't, it will turn the tides. I hoped you would be in the village while it went on, hidden without even knowing what was happening, but Aislynn's betrayal changed everything. You've become a weapon they're fighting to control.

Here, you're isolated. Here, you're safe.

I know you too well to think you'd stay in the village or here. Because I know you would never stay out of trouble willingly, I took the Grimoire. I'm sorry. It's safe and away from Carden. Away from me.

I can only imagine how angry you are, and I never expect to be forgiven. I still mean what I said after we escaped the Stele—well, the second time. The only cares I have in the world are killing Carden and keeping you safe. You're a strong woman, Kara, but the Bloods' hatred is stronger. They would have controlled you if you'd remained in Ourea.

I will come back for you the moment this battle ends. I promise. Please, lie low. Use a false name. Stay away from people.

Lori and Andrew, the humans who own this bed and breakfast, think your name is Anne. I told them I'm Mark. Please don't contradict me.

These people are very kind, and they will take care of you. Feel free to help yourself to anything you want. There are clothes in the closet. I told them the airline lost our luggage, so they found some things their daughter-in-law left behind on her last visit. Apparently, she forgets things a lot.

I told them you had terrible jet lag and I had business in Glasgow, but that I would be back soon to start our vacation. Feel free to degrade me in front of them as much as you please. I left some money in the top drawer of this desk in case you need it.

Though I don't expect you'll ever talk to me

again, I do hope you'll forgive me some day. You taught me that there can be goodness in life, instead of just evil. I cannot lose that.

I can't lose you.

—Braeden

In a small way, Kara wanted to be flattered. She wanted to be grateful. But she crumpled the paper into a ball. Her palms burned with her anger, and she expected the note to turn to ash in her hands.

It didn't.

She opened her palms and stared at the wad. It hadn't even charred.

Her breath caught in her throat, and panic made her heart race. Her fingers tightened around the ball again. Heat sped through her hands as she tried to turn the note to ash, but no amount of focus could heat the paper.

Kara took a deep breath to relax the growing tension in her neck. The air cleared her mind.

A cloud passed by outside, and a beam of sunlight fell onto her shoulder, warming her skin. She borrowed its heat and tried again. Seconds later, ash dropped from the space between her fingers until nothing was left of Braeden's note.

Relief flooded her body. She still had her magic,

but it was weaker. How could that be possible? Unless—

She smacked the desk in frustration. The Grimoire had to be the source of her magic. Of course, she was weaker when she didn't have it. She cursed Braeden under her breath.

He had taken the Grimoire. He'd taken her choice in the matter. He'd made the decision, as if he had the right.

He most certainly did not have the right to lock her out of the only life she had left. This wasn't his call. Not only that, but he wanted her to hole up in Scotland and not speak to anyone. To hide.

To hell with that.

The air vent came to life again, though she couldn't remember when it had shut off. A small square of paper slid off the desk and fluttered to the floor.

Kara bent to pick it up without thinking. She examined it, and her breath caught in her throat.

It was a photo of her parents.

Her mom and dad grinned up at her, posing behind a younger version of her on a riverbank. It was from one of the summers they'd gone to Yellowstone. They'd found a small river by a waterfall and dared each other to climb over the slippery rocks before begging a stranger to take their camera and snap a photo as proof they'd all made it.

She turned it over to see Braeden's handwriting on the back:

They're gone, not forgotten.

She laughed. Tears welled in her eyes. Oh, now this wasn't fair. The photo made it harder for her to be mad at Braeden.

Harder. Not impossible.

She still wanted to burn down the house and throw the desk through the bay window, but she took a deep breath instead. She closed her eyes and let the anger sizzle until it subsided. It wasn't gone; it wouldn't disappear until she forgave him. But a strange calm covered her frustration and hid it deep within.

When she could breathe normally again, she opened her eyes. Braeden would still have to answer for what he'd done. She would thank him for the photo first, of course, and then yell herself hoarse. Until then, she couldn't punish innocent people by ruining their home and business.

Most likely, Braeden had chosen this place because it was as far away from a lichgate as he could manage. Looking for one anyway probably wouldn't turn up anything, but she had to try.

Fear sparked in the back of Kara's mind. She hesitated. If by some chance she found a lichgate, it wouldn't do her any good. What would she do—wander around in Ourea and hope she bumped into someone she knew? That was stupid. A Scottish lichgate could lead anywhere, including the Stele. Without the Grimoire, there was no way of knowing where to go.

She leaned into the desk and stifled a sob. She wanted to scream, but she cursed under her breath instead.

Braeden had trapped her in the human world.

Kara pushed herself to her feet. She didn't want to think about it. She had to get outside and get some air before she really did lose it.

She reached for the door handle and caught a look at herself in the mirror. Her tangled hair clung to her face like a deflated tennis ball, and red lines still dug into her cheek from the wrinkles in the sheets.

No use scaring the townsfolk. She needed a bath, but she might be able to get away with just some clean clothes for now. She sighed and opened the closet.

Inside were a few changes of clothes—human clothes. Graphic tees, sneakers, jeans. She chuckled, remembering how Captain Demnug called denim a "terrible fashion." She certainly hadn't missed jeans as much as she thought she would. In Ourea, she had pants, boots—everything she needed. It worked.

Her grip tightened on the closet door. Braeden had no right to lock her here! He—

She took a deep breath as the anger threatened to resurface. If it did, she would lose control. She would hurt people. So, she swallowed hard, grabbed one of everything in the closet, and yanked it on.

She opened the door and glanced around. Three other doors lined the hallway, all open. One led to a bathroom, and another revealed a second bedroom. The last door sat slightly ajar, revealing piles of towels stacked on shelves. A railing separated the hallway from a flight of wooden stairs covered in blue carpet. Spaces between the railings revealed glimpses of an ornate glass door at the bottom.

Kara began down the steps and toward the front door. She skipped the final step and landed with a *thud* on the hardwood. A voice came from the kitchen as she twisted the handle and pushed open the door, but she didn't stop. The voice probably belonged to one of the owners, and she didn't feel like dealing with small talk or questions.

KARA

Kara walked for about an hour, just following her feet. It hadn't taken long to realize she'd been dumped in one of the tiniest towns she'd ever seen. Judging by the vast expanses of grassland surrounding the village, Braeden had left her somewhere between a field of sheep and a field of cows.

Any other time, Kara would have been excited to discover Dailly. Its white brick buildings and ancient stone bridges would have charmed her. She would have wanted to go in every shop and talk to the locals who smiled when she passed them on the sidewalk.

But Kara just wanted to go home. She wanted to stumble across a lichgate like she had all those months ago while in the Rockies, but she figured that sort of luck was a one-time deal.

She had rounded back to the house after a while with every intention of going back inside, but a walking trail caught her eye. It wandered into a forest across the street from the bed and breakfast, and Kara figured she might as well continue her walk. If she couldn't do anything useful, she might as well go for a hike.

The forest canopy cast a shadow on the path, but more than enough sunlight flittered through gaps in the leaves. She ambled for about twenty minutes, not really paying attention to anything but the dirt beneath her shoes.

The trail dissolved into grass. Kara looked up and sucked in a breath.

Before her lay the ruins of a small castle, spread across a clearing on the top of a hill. Trees surrounded it on all sides, and streaks of white clouds hung low in the sky.

The structure had probably been something more

like a manor, really. Only its stone frame remained: a half-decayed rectangle about three stories high. A rounded keep in the back corner was the only fully surviving structure. Blocks of gray stone littered the ground.

Kara walked in. Her eyes wandered over the ruins but kept returning to the keep. Curiosity made the skin on the back of her neck prickle. Shadow hid the keep's depth from view. Slits in the rock let in the occasional rays of sunlight, but very little light managed to find its way inside at all. She walked closer, hoping for a better look. Something glimmered inside.

"What are you doing without a hard hat?" someone asked.

Kara jumped and turned. A young woman about her age stood at the edge of the forest, a leashed black lab waiting next to her. The dog's ears perked, and it took a step closer.

"Why would I need a hard hat?" Kara asked.

"In case the stones fall, of course. Now come out of there before I watch you get a brick in the head! I don't want it on my conscience," the girl said.

Kara nodded and obeyed. She didn't want a stranger to see her try to perform magic anyway.

"I'm—uh, I'm Anne," Kara lied.

"Bonnie. You're not from around here, are you?"

Kara shook her head. "My accent gave it away, huh?"

"Actually, it was the look of awe on your face. Castles are a dime a dozen around here, so the locals don't look at them like foreigners do."

Kara laughed.

Bonnie smiled. "What brings you to Dailly?"

"Oh," Kara hesitated, "it was a surprise vacation."

"You don't sound too thrilled."

"It's the way my—uh—boyfriend planned the trip." Kara fumed inwardly at waking up alone in a strange place. She closed her eyes to suppress the anger again.

Bonnie laughed, though. "Not the best trip planner, huh? Is he sleeping on the couch?"

"Something like that."

"Well, no one should fight while on vacation, and we're pretty friendly here. There's a local pub I can show you. We can all drink until you forget why you're mad at him."

Words failed Kara as she tried to remember what lie Braeden had told the innkeepers when he'd left. This was ridiculous—she couldn't even carry on a conversation without lying. She had to lie about why she was here. She had to lie about where Braeden had gone and about what she'd been doing for the last few months. She couldn't tell the truth about her family or her past in case someone knew about how her father had died—which had probably raised more than a few eyebrows.

Kara didn't belong in the human world anymore. And since the Bloods had used her as bait, it was pretty clear she didn't have a place in Ourea, either.

Bonnie set a hand on Kara's shoulder. Kara flinched, and her eyes snapped back into focus.

"Is everything all right?" the girl asked.

Kara bit her lip. She had nothing, and no one, left. The closest thing she had to a friend now was a stranger she'd met on a random hiking trail.

She caved. "He left me here alone and went to Glasgow on business. I don't even know anyone here."

Bonnie's jaw dropped. "Forget the pub. You need a good meal and someone to listen. Follow me."

KARA

Kara hadn't thought she would want to talk at all—especially since she'd have to tell mostly lies—but she couldn't turn it off once she started.

Bonnie took her back to the bed and breakfast. Lori, one of the owners, sat them at a wooden table in the kitchen and whipped up some toast, eggs, and tea. Lori's short, brown hair framed her oval face, and she bustled through the kitchen with practiced ease.

While Lori worked, Bonnie asked questions. Kara told them an altered version of how Braeden had pulled her away from everything she had with no notice, only to leave her alone. She wanted to tell them more, but—considering her magical abilities and why Braeden had whisked her away in the first place—she refrained. Still, it helped to have someone listen.

The two Scottish women sat across the table from her and just let her talk. On more than one occasion, Bonnie frowned as if she noticed something off about Kara's story. Thankfully, though, she didn't push the matter. She kept quiet and simply listened.

When Kara finished, no one spoke. The teapot whistled, but Lori didn't get up.

"We need to get you pished," Bonnie said after a while.

"Huh?"

Lori sipped her tea. "She means drunk, dear."

"Oh."

Kara thought about it. She hadn't been drunk since the semester before her mother died. Drinking would never solve her problems, but maybe one night of partying would help her relax. The only problem was she didn't have any sort of identification to offer if they carded her.

"Do I need to bring my passport as ID?" she hedged.

Bonnie shrugged. "If you want. I'd like to take you

to a club I frequent, and they never check. I'm not letting you say no, by the way. It sounds like you need this."

Kara resisted the impulse to sigh with relief. Finally, some luck. She didn't have a clue how she could explain getting to a foreign country without a passport.

CHAPTER FORTY-FOUR

BRAEDEN

Braeden awoke to a distant order from Carden. The command told him to eat the breakfast that would be delivered in a few minutes. In an hour, he was to head to the king's study.

He grinned and sat up. Even though he had an instinctive urge to obey, he could resist the command. He would have to test it further. He still didn't know exactly what had happened, or how much he could resist. Had anyone before him ever disobeyed a Blood's mandate?

He stood and looked in the mirror. He had to practice his expression from before—what was it? Indifference.

He relaxed his face and stared at the mirror. No, his eyes were too sharp. His expression wasn't right.

He had to look as if he had no internal thought. His eyes had to stay calm no matter what. Bored, even.

Bored! It worked. He could do bored.

Someone knocked on the door. Braeden waved his hand, and the entry swung open at his command.

Deidre stood in the hall, leaning on the doorframe. She balanced a tray on her hip.

Braeden reeled inwardly in surprise but practiced maintaining his bored expression. He had to be better prepared for such surprises; they would give him away if he wasn't careful.

She smirked. "Miss me?"

"If you've touched the food, I want nothing to do with it."

"Now that isn't nice." She walked in and set the tray on the coffee table before lifting the lid and helping herself to a grape.

His stomach growled. The tray's selection impressed him. He could choose from a half-dozen plates. Apples, grapes, and pears sat next to a tray of ham and what he guessed from the sweet aroma was honeyed turkey. A few loaves of sliced wheat breads and a white cheese block of some sort completed the feast.

"They didn't make a spread this big for one person," he said.

"The chefs knew you'd be hungry after the beating

your daddy served you yesterday. I know better, though."

"What do you mean?"

She picked up a knife from the tray and cut a few slices of cheese. "It means I saw you go into the forest last night, even though you were expressly forbidden to leave."

Braeden laughed. "The forest is part of the Stele. Did you have a point?"

"I know you left."

"Stop wasting my time. Disobeying an order is impossible," he lied.

Deidre set down her half-eaten cheese then stood. She inched closer, taking slow steps until she stood only a foot or so away. "In over two-hundred years of living, I've learned that nothing is impossible, dear, little prince. But, all right. I'll bite. If you happened to resist your blood loyalty and leave the kingdom, I would be very much impressed."

"If I did happen to defy the command, it would mean I could also kill you now despite Carden's order not to harm you."

She grinned. "You're adorable. You can't hurt me. However, I know you wouldn't try. You don't want Carden knowing about you. Not yet."

Braeden's jaw tensed. "And you plan to share your little theory with him?"

"No," she said with a shrug. She sat back down and continued eating her cheese.

"No?"

"I don't see a point. You would likely still pass any test he gave you. He might put you back into torture, or he might kill you. I don't see a personal benefit in any scenario. Thus, your secret is safe with me. For now, anyway."

"I don't have a secret," he said. She couldn't trick him into admitting anything.

"Of course not."

"I thought you were Carden's servant. You do what he tells you."

She laughed. "Is that what he said? Hardly. Your father and I simply have an agreement. We—how do I put this—we help each other."

"I don't believe you for a minute."

"It's probably wise to not trust me. However, it just means I can tell you the truth and you won't believe me."

Braeden gritted his teeth. *Bloods*, how he hated this woman.

Deidre stood and then headed for the door. "I have an errand to run. Do enjoy your little war, though. Ah! And I'll tell Kara hello for you when I see her."

The isen shut the door behind her. Braeden wanted to rip the door off its hinges, but he forced himself to stay still. He didn't believe she knew where to find Kara. She couldn't. Nothing alive could follow a vyrn.

Kara was safe. She was in a tiny village in Scotland, out of harm's way. She would never find the closest lichgate to her. She wouldn't find her way back until he went for her. He had to believe in his plan. Deidre wouldn't find her so long as he didn't show her where to go.

Carden's orders to eat pulled again on his gut, even after he'd ignored them once already. They were easier to defy the second time.

He walked toward his bathroom for a bath, passing on the food. Orders or not, he refused to eat anything the vile woman touched.

❧

BRAEDEN

Twenty minutes later, Braeden knocked on the door to Carden's study. After a shower and a clean change of clothes, he'd still managed to arrive early.

The door opened to Carden sitting in a chair in front of a blazing fire. The heat warmed the room until it was hotter than the summer day outside.

"A fire? Aren't you overheated?" Braeden asked as he entered. He focused on maintaining a bored tone.

"I haven't been warm in years," the Blood absently said.

"Why?"

"Greatness has its costs."

The little gray Xlijnughl jumped onto Carden's leg from where it had been sitting by the fire and curled up on his lap. The king scratched its back without looking down.

Braeden shrugged when Carden didn't elaborate. He would probably find out what the king meant soon enough.

"I've heard that the Vagabond will be attending this little ambush," Carden said.

Braeden didn't move or answer. He didn't know how to react. This was supposed to be a new Braeden, an obedient one. "She won't be a problem."

"If you see her, you are to kill her. Do I make myself clear?" Carden asked.

The order pulled on Braeden's gut. For a moment, it consumed him. An image of Kara flashed in his mind, and he longed to wrap his hands around her neck.

But he pushed against the command. He suppressed the desire with a memory of their kiss in the Stelian grottoes. Heat rushed down his neck. His pulse slowed. The need to kill crumbled away. The urge to obey disappeared, and relief flooded his body.

Outwardly, he nodded as if agreeing to his father's

order. Inwardly, he suppressed a grin. Braeden was his own man. He would never again blindly obey.

Carden sneered. "Good boy. I like this new you."

"As do I," Braeden said with a smirk.

"Look on my desk."

Braeden walked to the table where six swords lay on the polished wood. Each was unique: some broad and thick, others thin but sharp.

"Pick one," Carden said. "It's time you had a real blade."

Braeden looked up in time to see the king draw Braeden's old Hillsidian sword from its sheath. The Blood weighed it in his hands, and it was all Braeden could do to not grab it. Richard had given him the sword before Braeden could even hold it properly. He'd killed hundreds of isen with it. The steel had been a part of him for years.

Carden gripped the blade. White light splintered through his fingers. Metal split. In seconds, the sword lay in pieces on the floor. The hilt dropped to the carpet with a *thud*.

Braeden kept still. He never let the boredom leave his eyes, even though he wanted to scream.

He looked down to the swords again. No emotion. He couldn't show his hatred or his anger. He had to simply look bored. He already despised the expression. Hopefully, he wouldn't have to wear it much longer.

He picked up the sharpest sword, which had an even longer blade than his old one. The Stelian crest glittered on the tip. Its hilt twisted around his hand, protecting him as he held it.

He would kill Carden with this sword. Sure, it wasn't a Sartori, but even Bloods could die by decapitation. And for Carden, it was only a matter of time.

DEIDRE

In the waning light of another dying day, Deidre surveyed the empty bedroom. The crumpled sheets, the lingering scent—she was certain the Kara girl had been here.

I missed her by an hour, tops. Deidre frowned, disappointed in herself. As focused as she had become on her budding vengeance, perhaps she was losing her touch.

The isen sat on the edge of the bed, wrestling with her thoughts as she tried to decide what she should do next. Clearly, Braeden had left the girl here—only one towel hung over the chair, only one side of the bed used, no clothes or effects of any kind. He had abandoned her here, likely in some foolish attempt to keep her safe.

Deidre smirked. Silly boy.

"Did they make it safely?" a woman asked from downstairs, her voice carrying up the hall as footsteps ascended. Something scraped against the wall, likely a basket of laundry, and Deidre drew her knife. This wasn't a soul worth stealing—though it didn't serve her to do so, Deidre would simply kill the woman if she entered the small bedroom. Witnesses complicated plans; corpses, not so much.

"Oh good, good," the woman said, nearing the top of the stairs as Deidre pressed her back against the wall, ready to slice the throat to minimize screams. "That American girl needs a break."

Deidre leaned in, tense, certain now that this woman was talking about Kara—and, more importantly, where the girl had gone.

"No, I agree." The woman huffed and set the basket down, the wooden boards creaking just feet away as she shifted her weight in the hallway. "Bonnie and I both say her story didn't add up, but I think she and her boyfriend are running away from something bad." The woman paused, no doubt listening to whoever was on the line. "No, no, Kit, that's not what I meant. I think they're harmless. Did Bonnie tell you where they ended up going?"

Deidre's grip tightened around the knife handle as she waited, breathless, straining her ear to hear the answer. Through the door, the voice on the other end of the line was too muffled, and she wondered if she would need to torture the info out of the woman later.

"Oh, I know that club." The woman laughed. "It's the one at Bridgegate and Clyde Street, yeah?" She paused as someone chatted on the other side of the line. "Thought so. They'll have fun. Your boy is keeping an eye on them?"

Deidre quirked an eyebrow. Good, at least she wouldn't have to torture the woman after all. It would delay *everything.*

"Aye, well, call me when you hear something." The creak of footsteps retreated down the hallway, her voice getting more distant by the second. "I'm just at home today, doing chores."

Deidre slipped her knife back into the hidden sheath at her waist, satisfied. Even though she would return to Niccoli without the girl, she had the next best thing—Kara's location. And this time, the girl wouldn't slip through her fingers.

Quickly, she scribbled a note on a loose piece of paper—a fun little way to tease her favorite prince. She chuckled darkly and, for effect, stuffed it in an envelope she found in the night stand. She set it on the pillow, wishing she could see his face when he read it.

Too bad she had more pressing matters to attend— including killing his darling little love.

CHAPTER FORTY-FIVE
BRAEDEN

Braeden was expressly forbidden to train in the two days leading up to the ambush. He still didn't know why, either. Carden claimed his son needed to be rested, but there had to be more to it. Braeden merely hadn't discovered it yet.

He hiked around the kingdom in his spare time. He hated the rising tension, the calm before the storm, but he had no choice. He had to keep up pretenses, and as much as he hated the bored expression, it was the only one he wore.

He spent most of his idle hours crafting theories as to how he had defied Carden's mandate to not leave the kingdom. He didn't know if he'd somehow become stronger than his father, or if being far away from the king at the time had something to do with it. Either way, the commands became easier to resist every time he tried.

The throne room had been fixed since his—he took a moment to count—since his second escape from the Stele in his life. It was when he'd met Kara, when the drenowith had grabbed them and torn through the stained-glass ceiling. It had since been repaired, and no evidence of the two dragons remained.

Braeden frowned. He wished the muses had killed Carden right then. They probably could have done it, too, but he supposed the drenowith Council would have been angry at them for killing a Blood.

At some point, Deidre left. A guard in the throne room said he'd seen her heading for the grottoes the day before. Braeden had known she wouldn't stay, though. He simply hated to think about where she'd gone. He despised her company but still preferred to keep an eye on her.

In his free time, Braeden practiced defying orders, which never came in short supply. It was as if the king survived on royal decrees and commands. If Carden told him from afar to eat, Braeden would throw the food away or eat only when hungry. If Carden was near, Braeden waited until he suppressed the desire to obey before he obliged. These practices went unnoticed, but he needed more proof with each passing day that he was really his own man.

Carden had prisoners in the dungeon. Braeden

could hear their screams. Some were women, and he could have sworn he even heard a child. It took all his will to not run down the stairs to stop the torture but doing so would have given him away.

Braeden often debated ending his father before they even left. It would be the better option if he could only do it. If Braeden killed his father during the ambush, he would become Blood in the middle of a battle. He would be vulnerable, and he would have four enemies—the other four Bloods—trying to kill him in his weakened state. If he killed Carden at the Stele instead, he would be able to rest as he adjusted to the new power of being king, but only if the kingdom didn't revolt after hearing their Heir had killed his father to take the throne. Revolution was always possible. At least during a battle, he could make it seem like the enemy killed Carden instead of their Heir.

With so many factors, Braeden couldn't make even one mistake.

"Heir Drakonin, your father wishes for you to join him."

Braeden looked up at the voice and blinked himself out of his thoughts. He'd been sitting on a bench in one of the Stele's many courtyards, elbows on his knees.

The voice belonged to a young Stelian girl, maybe sixteen. She wore the armor of a guard, even though the sword at her waist made her lean slightly off balance.

"Are you a soldier?" he asked.

"Yes, my lord."

"But you're a child."

She looked at the ground and clenched her teeth, as if biting back a scathing remark.

Braeden laughed. "Go on, tell me off. This should be interesting."

"I would rather not, my lord."

He could probably guess what she was going to say anyway: something about being plenty grown up and ready for war. Honor. Nobility. The like.

"Where is Blood Carden?" he asked.

"His study, my lord."

Braeden stood and then left. He wanted to thank her, but decided it wasn't something a cold, bored prince was supposed to do. He hated playing this part, but he was so close. Tomorrow, they would leave for the ambush. Tomorrow, he would rid the world of Carden.

No one walked the halls as Braeden neared the study, which didn't make any sense. They were preparing for war; the hallways should be filled with soldiers packing bags and tying up loose ends. His intuition flared, ready for a surprise attack. Carden may have discovered him. If so, he had no idea what he would do. Fight? Run?

Fight.

He reached Carden's study sooner than he would have liked. He rapped on the closed doors and waited. Many feet shuffled inside—six pairs. Not exactly an army.

"Come in, boy," Carden's voice called through the door.

Braeden entered to find the Blood and five other Stelians standing around a table littered with maps.

Carden waved his hand at the other men. "Meet your fellow generals. They answer to you. Now tell us more about the planned ambush. Where, when, who."

Braeden nodded and stepped up to the table. The largest map depicted the gorge Gavin had chosen for the ambush. There was no use lying; Carden had already heard the truth during the torture. Braeden had to hope Gavin had another plan up his sleeve. And knowing the conniving son of a—

Braeden cleared his throat. He needed to focus. "They claimed they would be camping here," he pointed to a small valley, "but they will actually be farther along, likely here," he pointed again a bit up the gorge.

One of the generals laughed. "How stupid do they think we are? No leader would walk blindly into a gorge without a way to escape."

Braeden could only nod. "The original claim was that Gavin got into a fight with the Bloods and broke off on his own to come find us. However, every Blood will be there."

Another general bent forward. "Including the Blood of Hillside? But he has no Heir."

"I assume so," Braeden admitted.

Carden leaned against the table, an arm stretched on either side of it. "It doesn't matter. Kill what Bloods are there but spare him. Wound him only. He must survive."

Braeden studied his Blood and allowed a quirked eyebrow through his mask of boredom.

"You'll see," the king said with a smirk.

"As you wish, Blood Carden," Braeden answered. He wanted to prod but couldn't do so without sounding insubordinate.

He had been given a clue, though. Carden wanted the Bloods dead—but hadn't mentioned the Heirs. Gavin was to survive, likely because he had no Heir. The Queen of Hillside had been the first Blood to die, leaving her inexperienced son to take the kingdom's reins.

What is Carden planning?

"It seems there are trails along the edges of the gorge. This will give us an advantage," one of the generals said.

The shortest general nodded. "We should split up at the mouth and each take a side."

"Braeden, you are to remain with me," Carden

ordered.

The command pulled on Braeden's gut, but this one he was only too happy to obey. "Yes, sir."

"Half of the army will remain here, in case this is a trick to capture the Stele. Generals, prepare the other soldiers to leave at sunup. Braeden, be rested for tomorrow," Carden said with a nod to the door.

The unspoken command was, *"leave."* The generals bowed. Braeden followed suit.

As they left, one of the generals kept pace beside him. The man kept his eyes forward and didn't speak. The others dispersed into the hall, but this one remained until the rest disappeared.

"Two days ago, I saw you leave for the forest, Heir," the general said.

Not this again.

"Congratulations," Braeden answered.

"You are under express orders not to depart."

"The forests are part of the Stele, idiot."

"I would hate for your secret to—"

Braeden grabbed the general and spun him against a wall. He lifted the man by his neck until he was eye level and his short legs kicked beneath him.

Braeden sneered. "I don't like you. Keep it in mind because someday, I'll be the Blood. You would be better off dying before that day comes."

The general's eyes popped wider, and he nodded.

Braeden dropped him to his feet, and the man scurried away.

Braeden grinned. He didn't like parts of himself—namely, the desire to inflict pain and fear. Since he wasn't running from what he was, though, he might as well inflict pain on those who deserved it.

CHAPTER FORTY-SIX

BRAEDEN

Braeden could barely sleep the night before the ambush. He ended up on a couch by his fireplace and watched the sun rise through his open balcony doors.

The morning went by in a blur—a command called him to the study; he walked to the throne room with Carden; the entire army listened to a speech from their king; Braeden called Iyra and met the army at the front gates.

Carden grinned and made a comment about his audacity to tame such a feral creature, but Braeden merely forced a nod in response. Iyra couldn't be tamed.

Their journey to the gorge would take four hours. Braeden rode beside his father for most of the trip, lost in thought as the army rode in silence.

The day sped by until the tingling sensation of being watched rippled down Braeden's back. He tensed. The entrance to the gorge blipped into view on the horizon. Time slowed once more, and he didn't know if he was ready.

"Exciting, isn't it?" Carden asked.

Braeden nodded, but kept silent to avoid saying anything stupid. He gripped his sword hilt, but left it sheathed.

The army split at a wordless command from Carden. The other generals led half the soldiers up a path along the far edge, while Braeden followed the Stelian Blood up the left side.

Braeden could only guess at how many corpses would line these trails in less than an hour.

The silence continued after they reached the top of the gorge's cliff. Even the trees kept still. No birds sang. No animals ran through the branches. The only sounds came from the clip-clop of a few mounts' feet as they caught stones in the dirt.

Braeden drew his sword, unable to take the tension any longer. The movement saved his life.

A blade swung for his head. Iyra reared in time for him to duck. He blocked the attack with his sword and shot a bolt of gray flame into the brush. It caught fire. Someone screamed. A Hillsidian guard rolled onto the path, smoke drifting from his green uniform.

All hell broke loose.

Hillsidians dropped from the trees. Kirelms dove from above and shot arrows into the Stelian troops. Water soaked the dirt as Lossians appeared and disappeared, popping in and out of the ground exactly as they had in their performance at the gala. But instead of graceful dancing, they swung their deadly blades and disappeared into the mud before anyone could trample them.

Carden bolted ahead, and Braeden followed. He would not let the man out of his sight for even a moment.

"You're mine!" Carden shouted at someone. He shot a bolt of lightning into the sky.

A second later, a Kirelm fell to the ground with a thud. Braeden sucked in a breath. Carden dismounted but frowned as Braeden caught up.

"Not the one I was aiming for," the Blood said. He hopped back on his mount and took off.

Braeden threw one glance at the Kirelm, who glared up at him through half-closed eyes. Braeden bowed his head and whispered a silent prayer for the soldier before tearing off after his father.

He rounded a corner as Carden shot a ball of fire into the sky. A Kirelm leaned back to avoid the attack and hovered out of reach—General Gurien. The general stretched his wings and dove at the Stelian king, sword first. He yelled, as if giving the attack everything he had.

Carden blocked it with his Sartori. A clang reverberated through the forest. He countered, and Gurien only ducked out of the way. They inched apart, each eyeing the other as they waited for the other to attack.

Movement along the edge of the clearing caught Braeden's attention. Gavin crept toward the duel, spinning his sword in his hand. The Hillsidian glared at Carden, never shifting his gaze even as he stalked over logs and tree roots.

That idiot would get himself killed. In the heat of battle, Carden might disobey his own order not to kill Gavin if the Hillsidian got in the way.

Braeden dismounted and set a hand on Iyra's neck, so he could speak to her privately. *Find a safe place nearby, Iyra. If anyone attacks you, don't kill unless you have to. When I kill Carden, I'll be weak. Becoming the Blood is painful. I'll need you to grab me and run for Stone's cave as fast as you can. Can you do it?*

Yes, my friend. She ran into the brush and disappeared.

Braeden raced to the duel, but only paid mind to Gavin's movements. The Hillsidian watched Carden, now only a dozen feet away from the fight. He leaned his weight onto the balls of his feet, and Braeden could already guess what would happen next. Gavin would feint for Carden's side and aim for his head—since Gavin didn't have a Sartori, only something drastic like decapitation would work. Carden would expect as much.

Gavin leaned forward, ready to lunge.

Braeden dove at the last second, blocking Gavin's blow with a kick that sent them both into the forest. It was a doubly important move—he'd saved Gavin's life, and Carden would think he was loyal for a few minutes longer.

Gavin stood and spat into the brush. "I knew you couldn't resist what you are. Kara should have listened to me."

Braeden's grip on his sword tightened. "You never gave me much of a chance, did you? What are you even doing here? You have no Heir! If you die, your kingdom dies!"

"He killed Mother and—"

"You're an idiot!"

Gavin swung at the insult. Braeden ducked the slice to his face. Sweat dripped down his temple. He pooled the air around him and focused it into an arrow. He shot it into Gavin's arm. The blow would be good enough to make Carden think it had been a real attempt if the man was watching.

Braeden looked over his shoulder. Gurien dipped in the sky, his left wing smoldering. He couldn't quite hold his sword anymore. Three of his left fingers were bent the wrong way.

Gurien fell to his knees. Carden laughed and set the tip of his blade on Gurien's neck.

A sword sliced the air by Braeden's ear. He ducked out of instinct, and the blow missed him by inches. He backed away and ran toward Gurien. He couldn't let the man die. The Bloods with Heirs should fight Carden, not their generals.

Carden grinned, no doubt pleased with the promise of killing an important player in the war. He said something to the general. The Kirelm looked up and narrowed his eyes, as if ready to die.

Braeden leaped onto a rock and jumped off to give himself added momentum as he dove for Carden's neck. The added force would be enough to make it happen with one blow. As long as Carden didn't look up, he'd—

Gurien's eyes darted to Braeden's sword.

No.

Carden pivoted, eyes wide. He rolled out of the way. Braeden's sword hit the ground at Gurien's feet. A boot landed hard in Braeden's gut, shooting him backward into the forest.

"I command you to kill yourself, traitor!" Carden shouted.

The order pulled on Braeden's gut. It shot through him with all the force of Carden's anger, but Braeden suppressed the urge to slit his own throat. He forced a laugh. "I'm not yours to command, Father."

Braeden summoned a horde of arrows from the air. They pulled on his tired mind as he aimed and loosed them all at once. They flew toward Carden one after another, forcing the king to inch away even as they sliced through his arms and tore holes into his clothes. A few dug into his torso and neck, ripping open the skin with their force. He cursed and swatted them away, but Braeden drove him even farther backward.

Commands and mandates interrupted Braeden's instinct. His father's silent orders told him to run into trees, to throw himself off the cliff, or to simply turn the blades on himself. In the instant they popped into his head, the ideas seemed brilliant. It took a second each time to remind himself they weren't even his thoughts.

The orders flew through him so quickly his attacks missed their mark out of sheer distraction. He would hit trees or even other soldiers. His aim slipped. He grunted and refocused, trying all the while to push away the conflicting thoughts.

A blade of air ripped through Carden's arm. The Blood's eyes burned red as the skin healed. Braeden cursed under his breath—Carden had given up. He would tap into his daru any second now.

Black fire burst across the king's skin. His body cracked and popped as he grew taller, and Braeden had no choice.

Carden's daru would destroy Braeden unless he tapped into his daru as well. He might lose even then. He didn't know if he could control himself once he let his daru take over. The only time Kara had ever seen it, he'd nearly killed her with its power.

He gritted his teeth. He had to try.

He released his hold on the layer of control that kept the daru at bay. The air hissed. Fire rushed through his body, feeding his muscles as they grew. Black flames erupted across his arms, too, the color uncomfortably similar to Carden's. Smoke coiled around him, some of it from the now-burning hems on his shirt.

But with his control went his self-loathing. His disgust for the black flames dissolved. Steam whistled by his ear. An untapped stream of magic fizzled in his palm. His fingers itched to strangle something. His pulse beat in his ear, a slow *thump, thud, thump* as he savored what he was born to be: powerful.

The commands, once distorting his instinct, faded until they buzzed in the back of his mind like a gnat. Murderous glee ripped through him. Carden would die.

Carden narrowed his eyes and conjured lightning from the air. Yellow bolts zapped between his fingers as he held it back, no doubt to aim. His arm shook, as if he couldn't quite contain the pooling energy.

He wouldn't get a chance to fire.

Braeden pulled the wind toward him and funneled it into his left hand. The air compressed on itself, glimmering in the light as he aimed. In one, swift movement, he shot the energy at Carden's neck. A whirlwind of leaves ducked out of the way, and the sword-sharp blade of air spiraled toward the king.

Carden tried to duck, but the spear hit him in the shoulder and went clean through. The force threw him back into a tree trunk. Its branches shook from the blow, releasing a wave of green leaves onto the king as he slid to the ground. The sparks in Carden's hand sputtered out completely.

The Stelian Blood pushed himself to his feet. His breath raced, and he gritted his teeth. Good. He should feel pain.

Gavin joined the fight. Braeden barely acknowledged the man, but he did catch a glimpse of thorns pushing through the Hillsidian's pores as he took on his own daru. Vines ripped from the trees and shot for Carden.

No. Gavin needed to stay out of this.

Carden dodged the vines and ran. Braeden followed, and light breaths not far behind meant Gavin had come as well.

A cliff edge flickered into view from between the trees, darting in and out of focus as the trunks came closer. Carden ran for it, as if he intended to jump off.

Maybe Braeden could wound him and send the king hurtling a hundred feet to the rocky ground below—

Pain blistered through Braeden's stomach. He tripped. Blood dripped down his side from a hole in his stomach not there a second ago. Carden sneered over his shoulder. Gavin ran ahead without looking back.

Braeden hadn't been paying attention. He'd been so wrapped up in killing he'd let down his defenses. Whatever technique Carden had used to wound him hadn't even made a sound. The injury was slow to heal, too.

The forest blurred as Braeden tried to get back up. Ahead, Carden stopped at the cliff edge and looked over. Gavin ran toward him. Someone shouted. Gavin didn't see the Stelian Blood duck out of the way at the last minute.

Gavin teetered on the edge of the hundred-foot gorge. Carden kicked him into the void.

"NO!" Braeden yelled.

"Him or me, son," Carden said.

The Stelian Blood's skin stretched and popped as the charcoal gray bled away into silver. Black wings tore from his back in a fury. He soared off into the sky, now in his Kirelm form. A wordless command pulled on Braeden's mind as Carden ordered all Stelians to retreat. It took nothing for Braeden to suppress the order.

Panic rippled through him. He pushed himself to his feet and looked over the edge. Gavin had already fallen almost halfway down. Stelians pooled at the bottom of the gorge, eyes on the Hillsidian king. If Gavin survived the fall, those soldiers could easily kill him.

Braeden hesitated. He could either follow Carden or save a man he disliked.

He cursed and dove off the cliff, changing form as he fell. Wings ripped from his back, and the Stelian uniform stretched to accommodate them. His wound hadn't healed yet. It tore open even farther as he shifted. He stifled a yell.

Despite the pain from his injury, he reached Gavin in a matter of seconds. Braeden wrapped his arms around the Hillsidian Blood and pulled him back toward the cliff. Gavin didn't resist.

They reached the forest edge and landed on the precipice. Gavin slumped in a heap. Braeden doubled over. He couldn't catch his breath. Fresh blood pumped from his wound.

Gavin pushed himself to his feet and looked out over the gorge. "You're letting him get away, Braeden!"

"You're welcome for saving you!" he spat back.

General Gurien limped forward and froze in place. "Wait. You?"

Braeden caught the general's eye but couldn't hold it. He retreated to his Hillsidian form which, he noted with a twinge of relief, made his wound slightly smaller as it healed.

"I fought the Heir to the Stele in the sparring ring?" Gurien asked.

Braeden hung his head and nodded, too exhausted to lie. "You weren't supposed to know."

"Why is no one following Carden?" Gavin interjected.

Braeden leaned against a tree. "He's gone. You can't catch him at this point. He called the army into retreat. I blew my one chance!"

He punched the trunk beside him. The force ripped open his still-healing wound for a second time. He cursed again.

Gavin glared at him. "This was a trick! You—"

"Blood Gavin! Heir Braeden saved your life, and you should thank him!" Gurien shouted.

Braeden and Gavin both stared at the general: Gavin most likely because a general of another kingdom had given him an order; Braeden, because he had never expected anyone to stand up for him.

"We need to regroup," Gavin said after a while. He stalked off into the woods.

"Thank you." Braeden nodded to the Kirelm general.

"We should be thanking you, Prince. You disobeyed your Blood. I have never seen anything like that in my life. You truly are one of the greatest fighters I have ever met."

Braeden grinned. "Likewise, my friend. And call me Braeden."

Gurien smiled. "Whatever you prefer. I owe you my life."

"Then buy me a beer or something." Braeden laughed, but pain splintered up his side. He groaned.

"You need to rest," Gurien said.

"I'm fine. You, however, need a healer. Did Aislynn send any of hers?"

"Yes, but I have no idea where they are. It was chaos, Braeden. Everyone split up. I have no idea where Blood Ithone is, or Blood Frine. My guess is they got into a sparring match between themselves."

Braeden laughed. "They do seem to hate each other."

"Not hate. They compete. Everything with those two is a sport. If they didn't duel each other, they likely made an event of seeing how many Stelians each could kill."

Braeden shook his head. "But this is serious. Why didn't all of the Bloods attack Carden at once? Didn't they have a plan?"

"They can barely sit in the same room for ten minutes, much less fight together."

Braeden laughed again. "Your honesty is refreshing, Gurien. I wish I could steal you from Ithone."

Gurien laughed with him. "I'd never be allowed to marry Aurora if you did that."

Their laughter died. Gurien cleared his throat and shook his head, as if he had said something stupid. Braeden remembered the general's look of longing when Aurora stormed from the Ayavelian throne room not long ago. It reminded him of Kara, who would probably never forgive him for holing her away in Scotland.

"Does Aurora know you love her?" Braeden asked.

Gurien stared at the ground. He didn't answer.

Braeden ran a hand through his hair. "I'm sorry. I shouldn't have—"

"At least yours loves you back," Gurien interrupted.

Braeden sighed. He didn't have a response. Kara might not ever find it in her heart to love him after what he'd done.

His skin cooled as the wound finally finished healing. Too bad the weight of Gurien's words made Braeden's stomach sink lower.

"We really do need to regroup," he finally said.

"I agree."

Braeden stood and then helped Gurien to his feet. He wrapped the general's arm around his shoulder, so the hobbling soldier could lead the way toward a reassembly point.

They'd lost the battle, yes. But Braeden had made a valuable ally in this never-ending war.

CHAPTER FORTY-SEVEN
KARA

After an afternoon of testing hairstyles, a makeover, and an hour's drive, Kara followed Bonnie into a club in Glasgow. She wore a borrowed outfit and—in her opinion, at least—too much makeup, but there was no stopping Bonnie once the girl unzipped her cosmetics bag.

A massive dance floor consumed most of the club. Black tile covered the floors and walls. A short way off, a DJ plugged in a microphone on a stage. Music blared through the speakers, though Kara didn't recognize any of the songs.

Bonnie slipped her arm through Kara's and led the way toward the bar. "Let's start off with shots!"

Kara laughed. "If you insist."

A twenty-something, young man with spiky, blond hair stood behind the bar and nodded toward Bonnie as they came closer. He flashed a smile that probably got him anything he wanted in life and leaned on the counter. Bonnie sat on one of the stools in front of him.

"The tyrant returns!" the bartender said.

Bonnie laughed. "It's good to see you, too, Kent."

"Shots?" he asked.

"Yeah, the usual."

He turned and grabbed three shot glasses and filled each with Patrón. He poured in one, seamless line across all of the glasses without spilling a single drop.

"How did you do that?" Kara asked.

He laughed. "Magic."

She grinned. "Magic, huh?"

"Oh, yes. I'm a wizard."

Bonnie nabbed one of the shots and threw it back. "I'm going to stop this joke before it goes any further. In about two more lines, he'll tell you he's a wizard in bed and that you should see how he uses his—"

"Bonnie!"

"What, Kent? It's exactly what you were going to say."

He laughed. "True. I suppose I test out too many of my pickup lines on you."

Bonnie nodded. "Well, little Miss America over here is taken, so hands off."

Kent took one of the shots and glanced at Kara's empty ring finger as he handed her the last drink.

"Yeah? Where is he?" he asked.

Instead of answering, Kara examined her shot. She'd come this far, but drinking it would mean letting her guard down. She would be vulnerable. Could she handle that, even for one night?

She hesitated and thent picked up the shot glass without another thought and downed it all in one swallow.

Gah, that burns. She shivered.

Bonnie leaned on the bar. "They're having a lovers' quarrel. Can I get a tequila sunrise?"

"Sure, love," he turned to Kara, "and don't forget to enjoy yourself. Just because your man isn't here doesn't mean you can't have fun."

"And by fun, he means with him. In bed," Bonnie said with a grin.

Kent smiled again and grabbed some bottles from behind him. After a few minutes of shaking and stirring, he poured two bright orange drinks then indicated a free table along the wall.

The dance floor was empty, so Kara followed Bonnie to the table. They slipped into the booth and just… talked. They laughed and poked fun at each other. As people trickled in, Bonnie pointed out a few boys she knew. And for once, nothing else in the world mattered to Kara but relaxing.

They took turns getting another round when the time came for it, and hours passed like minutes. A gentle buzz resonated in the back of Kara's mind. Her defenses dissolved, and all thoughts of Ourea slipped away.

She felt amazing.

Bonnie poked her shoulder. "Let's get one more round and then go dance it out of our systems!"

"I'll get them this time," Kara offered.

She slipped from their booth just as the lights lowered. Strangers pushed by her as she fought her way toward the bar. She hadn't even noticed half of these people come in.

She managed to edge in close to where they'd been earlier, but Kent kept his eyes trained on a group of ladies in tight dresses down the line. Kara found an empty barstool and waited for him to look her way. For entertainment, she played with a mini plastic sword someone had left behind, laughing as she tried to stab a peanut. When did little, plastic garnishes become so entertaining?

The hair on the back of her neck prickled. She shivered and looked over her shoulder. Bodies pressed by, but no one eyed her. Still, the feeling wouldn't go away.

She scanned the rows of people in the low lighting until she saw him. A man stood along the far wall, staring at her. Her heart skipped a beat. He had olive skin, dark hair, black eyes...

...and was not Braeden.

She took a deep breath.

Relax, Kara. He's not here. That's not him. Why should you feel guilty? He left you! You don't have to twiddle your thumbs, waiting for him to swoop in and—

"We have to go," someone said nearby.

The Braeden lookalike inched in beside her, frowning. His eyes darted about without landing on her, and his fingers tapped on the bar as if he couldn't get out fast enough.

Wait, is he talking to me?

"Excuse me?" she asked.

He grabbed her elbow with a grip so tight it stung. "Come on. We need to leave."

"Ow! No way! Who are you?"

"There's no time for this, girl. Let's go. We—"

Another voice, this one with an English accent, broke into the conversation. "He isn't bothering you, is he?"

Kara looked over her shoulder to see a young man with rich, blond hair and sharp green eyes. He had a thick build that was mostly muscle and glared at the lookalike who still had a firm hold on her elbow.

She twisted in the first man's grip. "He is, actually."

The lookalike let go.

"Good thing he's leaving, then," the blond man said.

The Braeden lookalike tensed his jaw and hesitated, but ultimately slipped into the crowd without another word.

"Well, aren't you my knight in shining armor?" Kara asked.

"Nah, I'm the villain," he said with a chuckle.

Kara grinned. "Clever."

He offered his hand for her to shake. "My name is Theodore. What's yours?"

"Of course, your name is Theodore."

"You can laugh all you like, but you should tell me yours, too."

"Kara."

She cringed. Oops. She'd meant to lie and say Anne. What should she—

Ah, screw it.

The little, plastic sword shot out of her hand and landed somewhere in the throbbing pulse of dancing bodies that had materialized in her hours spent at the table with Bonnie. She was pretty sure magic had not been involved in her losing her little toy. Oh, well.

"Can I call you Teddy?" she asked.

"Good lord, no. What are you drinking?"

She laughed. "The only thing I know to order is a tequila sunrise."

"It does the job. Might I get you away from your alcoholism for a dance, though?"

She hesitated. Her smile faded as she thought of Braeden.

Theodore reached for her hand and smiled. "No harm in a dance."

"Okay then, Theodore, but I need to let my friend know first," she said.

He slipped a hand around her waist. "Lead the way."

Kara headed back for the table with Theodore in tow, only to find that Bonnie had company of her own. The Scottish girl winked when she saw Kara and pointed toward the dance floor.

Have at him! Bonnie mouthed.

Theodore laughed. "It looks like we have her blessing."

Kara grinned. Theodore took her hand and led her to the middle of the crowded floor. Bodies twisted to the music. The thundering bass lines reverberated through Kara's body. Her ears hurt from being close to a speaker. The recorded vocalist told everyone to dance, mentioned a few sexual innuendos, and then—yep, chorus. Not altogether imaginative, but fun nonetheless.

And thanks to Kara's ever-waning attention span, fun was all she cared about.

Theodore reached around her waist and pulled her close. His hands pushed and swayed with the music, moving her body in time to the beat, even if she missed the cue. She could smell his cologne: an earthy combination of spices and musk and bark and sweat and just the slightest hint of something floral, too.

He smelled good, but Braeden smelled better.

But he abandoned me!

Her grip on Theodore's arms tightened as the veiled anger deep within her flared. The lights flickered. For a moment, the club-goers danced in complete darkness.

Theodore brushed back the hair covering Kara's ear and leaned in. Her skin prickled. His breath rolled over her neck.

"Is something wrong?" he asked.

Kara's stomach lurched. The edges of her vision darkened. Blue and purple spotlights spinning around the deejay veered in and out of her peripheral vision. Her knees shook and gave out, but Theodore caught her.

She didn't know what had just happened. Kara pushed herself upright, but Theodore's grip on her arms sent pins and needles into her fingertips. She had to stand, to get back to the table.

"I'm fine," she said.

Theodore caught her as she teetered again. "No, you clearly aren't. You look like you could use a break. I actually have that VIP room up there."

He pointed, and Kara forced herself to follow the direction of his finger. A wall of windows above the bar overlooked the dance floor. Stairs wound up to it from the right. The windows reflected the scene below, no doubt tinted to keep anyone from peering in.

Theodore leaned down to speak in her ear again, but he held the back of her neck this time. Warmth rushed through her at his touch, quelling the nausea. A treacherous thought flickered in her mind, and she wanted him to just hold her like that forever.

"Come sit for a while. I promise to be a perfect gentleman. I'll ask the bouncers to bring up your friend if that would make you more comfortable."

Buzzing swirled in the back of her mind. Queasiness pitched in her stomach. Her cheeks flushed, and she nodded.

"Thank goodness. You look ill," he said with a sigh.

Theodore tightened his hold on Kara's hand and wrapped his other around her waist. He led her through the crowd and gestured to a bouncer. They shared a few words Kara didn't hear before the bouncer jogged off. She glanced at Theodore, and he smiled.

"He recognized you. He'll be back in a few with your friend."

She smiled. If he lied and tried anything once they were alone, she would just beat the tar out of him, drunk or no.

He led her up the stairs, guiding her the whole way. Kara looked out over the dance floor, hoping to see Bonnie, but the hundreds of bodies pulsed together in a constant rhythm to the music. She could barely tell the girls from the guys, they were all so close.

Theodore opened the door and let it swing inward before guiding her inside. A row of black couches covered the wall to their left. To the right, the wall of windows revealed the dance floor and a perfect view of the deejay on his stage.

Theodore led Kara to a couch and shut the door. As soon as he let her go, the nausea abated. Her head cleared a bit, and the room brightened. She saw new details, now. A woman stood at a mini-bar on the far wall, her back turned. Fake plants added a splash of green to each of the room's corners.

The woman by the mini-bar turned and grinned.

Deidre.

Kara gagged and pushed herself to her feet. Panic raced through her body, paralyzing her for a moment. Cold dread ate away at the buzz in her mind.

Theodore shoved her back into the couch. "Sit, Kara Magari."

Kara obeyed in that she sat on the edge of her seat. She eyed him, pulse racing. Her fingertips danced along the edge of the cushion, waiting for the right moment to push off and race for the door.

Only an arrogant drunk would try to fight Deidre. Kara had to get out.

Theodore crossed his arms. His skin began to peel away, cracking and dripping like wax until the blond Englishman faded and a taller man glared down at her. He had a slender build and short, dark hair. A well-trimmed beard accented his perfect features.

Kara stifled a curse—she'd managed to run across yet another isen. And if he'd come with Deidre, he was probably evil, too.

"Who are you?" she asked.

"Take a guess, my dear," he said, his voice thick with a Russian accent.

"Niccoli?"

He nodded.

"I thought you didn't run your own errands," Kara said, glaring at Deidre.

He grinned. "I do run the important ones."

So, the floral note of his cologne had been lilac, and the woody smell had been pine. Kara kicked herself for letting her guard down, but the drinks had dulled her senses. That's what she'd wanted them to do. She had allowed herself one night of genuine fun because she'd never dreamed that someone would find her. Not in Scotland. Not on such short notice.

Lavender fire erupted around her hands, but the flames barely reached her wrists. Her strength and power were too far away to reach.

Niccoli frowned. "Is that the best you have? I'm disappointed."

Kara glanced to the exit, trying to figure out how she was going to get away from this mess, but Deidre clicked her tongue and laughed.

"You really shouldn't try," she said.

Niccoli took a step closer. "It wasn't easy to find you. Don't you want to know why I'm here?"

"You want the Grimoire. I've heard this a million times. You're nothing new."

"I couldn't care less about your little book. It's useless to me. No, I want you."

A wave of confusion crashed over her, and the fire in her hands dulled. "Why?"

"Because you, Kara, are an isen. I couldn't steal your soul if I tried."

The flames in her hands went out. Her brow wrinkled. She looked to Deidre, who frowned in disappointment.

No. That was impossible.

Kara's pulse raced as she tried to process what Niccoli had told her. She wasn't an isen. She couldn't be. It was a trick or just a blatant lie.

Niccoli inched closer. The flames reignited in Kara's palms. He shook his head and stopped moving.

"I am not an isen," she said.

"I do not care if you don't believe. I do not waste my time. Is the water ready, Deidre?"

"Yes." She turned off the faucet. A few lingering drops fell from the tap, spreading ripples across the full sink.

"What's that for?" Kara asked. She needed to get out of here.

Niccoli paused, as if unsure whether or not he should answer. "Being awakened is a painful process, Kara. To turn, you must meet Death. To meet Death, you must die."

Kara's throat went dry. These crazy people were going to drown her.

A fresh wave of panic stabbed through her. She raced for the door without another thought or even a plan.

Niccoli grabbed her wrist and spun her away from the exit. Pain shot through her arm at his grip. He pinned her against the wall with her hands over her head. His force kicked the air from her lungs. The flames dancing over her fingers went out with a *hiss*.

Deidre sauntered forward with a small, wooden box in her hands—the wooden box Kara's dad had told her to find, all those months ago. Deidre must have filched it. Of course, she'd known about it; she'd stolen his soul and with it, his memories.

Kara shot her knee into Niccoli's gut. He grunted, but the blow hadn't been enough. His grip tightened. He pressed his thumb against her forehead. A chill began at his touch and coursed through her body, freezing her in place. Her finger twitched, but otherwise, she couldn't move.

Deidre smashed the box against the wall and picked up the small, leather item that fell out of it. It was a wrist guard, but with one tweak: a row of small barbs pointed inward, where its wearer's skin would be, in a strange pattern Kara couldn't recognize.

Deidre wrapped the guard around Kara's wrist and pressed on the leather until its spikes dug into her skin. Kara yelled from the pain.

Niccoli covered her mouth with his hand, and the scream died.

He leaned in. "When you're first awakened, the power will be almost too much to handle. This wrist guard is a training tool to help you control yourself."

Kara tried to speak, but pain still coursed through her arm. It brought back memories of the spikes Aislynn had used to subdue her. The pain throbbed with every heartbeat.

"Look at me," Niccoli said.

She glared at him. The edges of his hands covered some of her vision.

He sneered. "You have nothing. Your master is gone. Your book is gone. Your lover, your friends, everything you know—all gone. I am all you have left. Without me, you are utterly alone."

In response, Kara bit his hand with everything she had.

He flinched and pulled away, cursing in a language she didn't know. She kicked him hard in his stomach. He curled over, pressing against her as he recovered from the blow.

She leaned in. "I can save myself."

Heat charged through her body. Purple flames erupted over everything: her hair, her cheeks, her clothes. Niccoli screamed and pulled away, letting her hands go as the flames clung to him. It was enough.

The sprinkler above her roared to life, dousing her with indoor rain. The fire on Kara fizzled out as she bolted for the door. Her magic blipped through her like a pulse, and she reached with her panic to the rest of the sprinklers. With a sharp tug of her mind, the rest of the sprinklers sprang to life as well. A torrent of water fell from the ceiling.

Deidre lunged, but Kara shot a fist into the isen's throat without a second thought. Deidre gagged. Kara threw open the door and jumped over the stairwell to the floor. She landed with a *thud*. A sharp pain shot up her calf.

A small part of Kara nagged her about how easy it had been to escape Deidre. The isen couldn't be taken out by a quick punch, not after everything Kara had seen the terrifying woman do. Yet she'd barely fought. Kara wanted to analyze it, to guess at what Deidre had up her sleeve, but she didn't have time. If it meant not being drowned, she would have to run with it.

People raced by, yelling as the sprinklers over the dance floor soaked them. Puddles formed in the dips on the floor. The deejay pulled plugs and threw tarps over his equipment, cursing loud enough for Kara to hear from the other side of the room.

An exit sign blared from under the stairs, so she limped toward it. That was, at least, until a hand grabbed her arm and pulled her into the shadows beneath the stairwell.

She cursed.

"Quiet, Kara! I'm trying to help," a man said.

In the dim shadows beneath the stairs, she saw the boy from earlier—the one she had mistaken for a moment as Braeden.

She twisted in his grip. "Get away from me! How do you know my name?"

The boy's skin cracked and peeled, just like Niccoli's. She cocked her arm to punch him—not another isen—but he grabbed her wrist. She wrestled with him, but it took only a moment longer before she recognized Stone.

She groaned. He let go of her wrist.

"Find her!" Niccoli yelled over the screams from drunken girls getting soaked by the still-pouring sprinklers.

Stone pushed open the door beneath the stairs and gestured through it with a bow. "Unless you'd like to die or be enslaved for eternity, we should probably go."

Kara nodded. At least she knew this isen. He'd helped her once already. Of her limited options, he was her best bet.

She ran through the exit as fast as her limping leg

would carry her, but Stone followed at a stroll. His long legs carried him faster than her down the sidewalk, even at his leisurely pace. Kara huffed, half-wishing he would offer her a hand, but she knew better.

They turned a corner, and a sudden realization hit Kara hard enough to make her stop in her tracks.

"Wait! Stone, I need to find my friend."

"The human you came with? She'll be fine."

"But Niccoli—"

"—is after you," Stone interrupted. "The girl will be safe as long as you stay away from her."

Kara's shoulders slumped, but he had a point. Stone began again down the sidewalk, and she forced herself to continue after him.

"How did you find me?" she asked.

He smirked. "By chance, really. I monitor those I don't trust. Niccoli mentioned a trip to Scotland not long after your stupid boyfriend showed up with the Grimoire and not you. I put two and two together. The rest was luck."

"The rest? There's more?"

"I have a hotel room across the street, so we can hide there until Niccoli takes his search back to Ourea," Stone said.

"You didn't answer—"

"Would you like a monologue or a place to hide? It's one or the other at the moment."

She bit back a retort. "Where's this hotel of yours?"

"There." He pointed to a double door entrance with a red carpet out front. A teenager in a red polo shirt sorted through what looked like valet tags while a man in a slim-cut suit tapped his foot, waiting.

Stone walked into the hotel without changing his stride and ushered Kara forward by pressing his hand against the small of her back. A clerk behind the black, marble welcome desk glanced up and did a double take when he saw them, though Kara had the nagging feeling he was looking at her frizzy hair, smeared makeup, and flushed cheeks. She must have looked like hell.

When they made it to the elevator, Stone pushed the button for the top floor. The elevator chimed, and the motor began to pull them up.

Kara looked over to the isen standing beside her, who slid his hands into his pockets as the elevator climbed. Not even a week ago, she'd walked up to his cave in a freaking mountain in a hidden world that wasn't supposed to exist. They had talked about magic and books and immortal beings. And now, they were on their way to the penthouse after she'd destroyed a nightclub by setting off the sprinklers.

"This is surreal," she said under her breath.

"Magic has that effect on the young," he answered.

"I—yeah, I guess."

"That did not require an answer."

The doors chimed again. Kara shook her head and followed Stone into an ornate hall. He led the way to a door on the far end and swiped his keycard in the lock.

"I prefer real keys, but no, humans enjoy fixing things which aren't broken," he mumbled under his breath.

He opened the door and walked in. Kara followed. A full kitchen stood off to her left, a living room filled the space in front of her, and a hallway to the right led to a few doors that must have been bedrooms or bathrooms.

"Thank you," she said.

Stone nodded and closed the door.

Kara wanted to add more, to explain that she didn't know what she would have done without his help, but her head ached. She just wanted sleep.

Stone lifted her chin and examined her eyes, as if looking for something. "How do you feel?"

"Tired."

Every inch of her body ached. She scratched her wrist. Her fingernails scraped leather. She looked down to see the wrist guard with a trail of blood coming from it.

"I guess I can take this off, huh?" she asked.

She reached for the guard, but Stone grabbed her hand. In a move so fast she barely saw it, he gripped the back of her neck. Something slid into her skin at the base of her head. She gasped, but it came out as more of a choking gurgle. Numbness spread down to her fingers, her stomach, her toes. Spots dotted her vision.

He had just pricked her spine with the barb in his palm. If she were human, he would have stolen her soul. Niccoli had said an isen couldn't steal another isen's soul if he tried, so—she gagged.

Kara really was an isen.

"Wh—?" she asked, but it was all she could manage. Her throat closed.

Stone didn't answer. He picked her up so that her head rested on his shoulder and carried her through the hall. White paint whizzed by. He kicked open a door. Her eyes flitted around and caught only glimpses of a bathroom. Porcelain toilet. Roll of toilet paper with the little fold marking it as unused since housekeeping last visited. Black towels with the hotel insignia.

A bathtub filled with water.

Stone paused at the entry. "I'm going to awaken your isen nature, Kara. It's a painful process. First, I had to prick your spine—it will rouse the isen instinct within you and give you the strength to fight if you want. But it will also make me your master if you come back. Second, you must be killed, typically by suffocation or drowning. I've found drowning to be less—impactful."

No. No, his voice was too calm, as if this were routine and not murder. But she couldn't speak. Her body wouldn't move.

He continued. "Third, you will face Death. You must have a reason to return. If you do come back, I will tell you the truth about what you are. You will have unimaginable power. You can save millions. You don't have to be evil. You can be good, if you want."

He offered the choice as if it were the same as choosing chocolate over vanilla.

Stone placed her in the tub. Cold water lapped over her ears. She forced her chin up so that she could stay above the water, and a happy pang raced through her when her body obeyed.

But it wasn't enough. Stone set his hands on her shoulders, face as blank as if he were reading an encyclopedia.

"Ah, one more thing," he added. "This hurts less if you don't hold your breath."

Weight pressed against Kara's chest as he forced her under. Fear tore through her. She would never avenge her dad. She would never see Twin's army. She would never hear Flick purr in her ear or make that odd gurgling noise that meant he was happy.

But above all else, she wouldn't see Braeden again. She'd never get to tell him—

Water rushed into her lungs as she released the breath she didn't know she was holding. Oh, God, it burned. The movies, books, television that describe drowning—they were all wrong. They were too gentle. Drowning was the ultimate death, the most painful of them. Her blood pulsed in irregular beats, thrumming as her heart lost oxygen.

But the panic—that was worst of all.

Her body convulsed, twitching until she lost all feeling. She lost touch with her fingers. Her toes went next. Her lungs stopped trying. Her heartbeat slowed.

Light splintered through the ripples in the water. Stone reached for her pulse, looked at his watch, and stood.

The room blurred. Something pressed against her cheek. Her stomach lifted, like when she used to float in the pool during summer break.

There, the pain hadn't lasted all that long. At least it was gone now.

CHAPTER FORTY-EIGHT
KARA

When Kara opened her eyes, she stood on top of a circle of jet-black cliff about a hundred feet in diameter. Fog hugged its sides in all directions. The pillar hovered in the sky like an island surrounded by clouds. A red sun burned the horizon, distorting the world around her into shades of orange and amber.

A tall man with dark, red skin stood near the edge, his back to her. She couldn't tell if the strange light tinted his body or if he was actually red. He wore only black pants. Layers of muscle seemed to push against the skin on his shoulders and back in an attempt to find space on his body.

The man cracked his neck and turned. His eyes made her stomach lurch—they were all white, with no irises. He watched her. For several minutes, neither spoke.

"Am I dead?" Kara finally asked.

"It is your choice." His voice echoed in her ear.

"Then, I want to go back. What do I have to do? Stone said—"

The man held up his hand. She stopped talking.

"You must first answer to me," he said.

She hesitated. "Who are you?"

"I am Death."

"I thought you would have less," she paused, "skin."

"A mortal's imagination is often quite impressive."

"I'm imagining you?"

"No. You are in the middle ground between your old life and the next world."

"But I can go back, right?"

"Why would you want to return?"

"What kind of a question is that?"

"One you must consider. You may easily move to the next world, but you will not as easily return to the last. You must prove yourself. Answer me. Why should I let you go back?"

Her back straightened involuntarily at his blunt tone. When she did finally speak, her voice came out far softer than she'd intended.

"I'm not done yet," she said.

"You aren't done with what, exactly? Your mentor

abandoned you. The Grimoire will not answer you. Those you protected betrayed you for the thinnest hope of greater power. And as an isen, you will be thought of as a monster for the rest of your life."

"How do you know all of that?"

"I am Death. I know all."

"That must make your job simple."

"Focus!"

The cliff shook, as if trembling at Death's voice. Kara lost her balance and fell to her knees. The terrifying sound of splitting rock rumbled beneath them. She braced herself with her hands, but Death didn't move until the trembling stopped.

He continued. "You forbid yourself from loving Braeden in an attempt to protect him, which is foolish at best. But worst of all, he left you, defenseless, in a world you no longer understand when you had no one else to trust. He did not think you were capable of protecting yourself or others, and in his misguided effort to save you, he made you vulnerable to Niccoli —the one creature in all of Ourea who wanted you most. You are here with me because of Braeden's decision. What do you have left? Who in that world will want you when they learn what you are?"

A lump formed in Kara's throat.

Wow. Death was a jerk.

Her forbidden anger pulsed beneath the layer of

calm that kept it in check. It threatened to rip free and force her to say what she couldn't even admit to herself. She bit her cheek.

Death eyed her. "More often than you might think, it takes getting to your lowest point before you realize you need to make a change. This moment is your lowest point. The world you knew tried to break you, child, but nothing can take away a person's will to fight. Tenacity is something you have to forsake. Still, you don't have much to gain by staying. You're not a fighter."

Kara arched her back but couldn't speak. Not a fighter?

An orb of blue light floated by, distracting Kara with its movement. It slipped past, much like the healing lights the Ayavelian seers had performed with at the gala. It dove into the ground next to Death. Spindles of light grew from the rock. They spun and splintered until they formed the outline of a person. Details emerged: eyes, a nose, a mouth. Shadows and depth developed along the body, creating everything from a neck to bare feet sticking out from beneath a hospital gown. Hair sprouted from the glowing light, curling over the figure's shoulders.

Recognition set in. Kara gasped. Her throat tightened. "Mom?"

The woman made of blue light opened her arms and curled her fingers, beckoning Kara to come closer.

Kara stepped forward, more than willing to obey, but a hand grabbed her shoulder. She looked up to see Death's white eyes staring down at her. She shuddered. A second ago, he had been on the other side of the rocky tower. She hadn't even seen him move.

"If you touch your mother, you will die and go to the next world with her," Death said.

Kara's voice failed her, and her words came out as a whisper. "That's not fair."

"No, it isn't."

"Can I at least talk to her?"

"No. She is dead, and you are not. Not yet, at least. If you go with her now, she will explain everything—why Niccoli wants you so badly, why she never told you the truth of what you are, why you never met your maternal grandparents. Of course, none of it would matter anymore. But if you return to your old body, you will have to live a full life and learn those things for yourself."

Kara bit her lip. "Do you like what you do? This is just cruel."

"This isn't cruel, child. Dying isn't good or evil. It simply is. Your mother is waiting for you, restless to find peace with her mistakes. You owe her as much."

Kara brushed Death's hand off her shoulder. "Don't tell me what I owe her."

"Then, you tell me."

She tightened her hand into a fist. "You want to

talk about what I owe people? Fine. I owe it to Mom to bring Dad back to her. I owe it to Dad to free his soul from Deidre. I have to help Braeden find peace with himself."

Death shrugged. "You have all the time in the world to wait here for those things to unfold naturally. Deidre will die in due time and release your father's soul. Braeden is guaranteed to find peace when he dies, which will likely be soon. You can simply wait for both deaths. Tell Braeden how you feel when he crosses over. I can ensure you appear when I see him, if you wish. So why should you go through the pain of being Stone's slave only to expedite your parents' reunion or Braeden's peace? What if you fail?"

Kara paused. Her gut twisted. "I won't fail. And what about Twin? She and all the vagabonds she created are waiting for me to come back. I can't just leave them."

"Why not? They are intelligent enough to survive."

"I'd be abandoning them like the first Vagabond abandoned me! I refuse to be remembered as a coward!"

Death didn't react or respond to her outburst. He simply waited. Kara took deep breaths, but it wasn't enough to slow her racing pulse. Death just got under her skin.

She paced. "Whether I like it or not, history will

remember me. That's the consequence of being the Vagabond. But I control what's written. I won't let Ourea remember me as the pathetic girl chained in a cell because the Bloods beat me. To hell with that! If I go down, it'll be with a fight!"

"Why is pride so important to you?" he asked.

She paused. "It's not pride. It's more than that. Yes, I have eternity to wait for my loved ones. But I only have a limited time to make a difference in life. To enjoy life. I can change the world. The powerful cause so much pain simply because they have never known what it means to be weak. If they have, they've forgotten. I can remind them."

"So, this isn't about peace. It's a vendetta."

Kara suppressed a groan. "No. This is my chance to show the yakona how strong they could be if they'd only unite with each other."

"Why you? You're hardly qualified."

"I'm beginning to think that doesn't matter. For whatever reason, yakona believe in the Vagabond. They believe in the Grimoire. I might be an isen now, but I was the Vagabond first. I don't know how to lead. I have no idea why people should follow me. But I can't run away from that anymore."

"But you can run away. You can run to your mother and never have to think about it again."

Kara glanced at the woman made of blue light and

swallowed hard. "I misspoke. I don't want to run away. There's so much left of my life in Ourea. For once, I want to be great. I want to do something that changes lives for the better."

"Whose lives, exactly? Those you meant to save betrayed you."

"So, you're saying I shouldn't forgive them?"

Death was silent.

Kara crossed her arms. "What they did was wrong. I won't deny that. Maybe I should hate them. Maybe I should make them figure things out on their own, but that won't fix anything. They won't change. They'll keep fighting until they kill each other off."

Death shook his head. "Nothing is left for you in your old life but a war, and I will meet most of your friends before it ends. They will not have the option to return. So, tell me, what do you have to live for in a world full of loss?"

"Everything," Kara said without thinking.

The anger within her dissolved at the word. Peace surged through her in a way magic never had; it rippled and pulsed with its own life force, strengthening everything it touched with an unimaginable power.

Kara smiled. "There are good people who make life worth living. There's beauty. Have you ever sat beneath a waterfall and just watched the mist? I have. I sat next to Mom on a trail, and we just listened to the forest. We didn't say anything, and it's one of my favorite memories. She and I used to watch sunsets after hiking trails most people don't even know about. Mom taught me that I can find peace from the world if I just walk out into it.

"Ourea is beautiful. My life there is complicated, but it's mine. I don't know what comes after death. I don't want to. Whether it's terrifying or breathtaking, I'm going to enjoy as much of this life as I can while I still have the option."

The corner of Death's mouth rose in the barest hint of a grin. "So, you wish to return despite all the yakona have done to prove themselves unworthy of your help?"

"Yes."

"Are you certain?"

Kara studied her mother's ghost. The woman wrapped her arms around herself, which left wrinkles in the hospital gown. They watched each other for a moment, guilt churning in Kara's stomach. But she had to free her dad. She had to help Twin. She had to find Braeden. But most of all, she wanted to live.

"I'm sure," she finally said.

Death eyed her, and Kara resisted the urge to squirm under his glare. He nodded. The cliff shook yet again as he moved.

Kara's mother blew her a kiss and smiled. With a *hiss*, the blue light dissolved into the windless sky.

"Do you remember asking the Grimoire if you could bring back the dead?" Death asked.

Kara's jaw tightened. This was a trap. She didn't answer.

He continued. "You must know by now that you cannot do such a thing. I will come again for you someday, exactly as I have come for every living creature since the dawn of time. Today is not your day to die. You may return, but use your second chance at life well. Few ever have this opportunity."

Death offered her a giant, red hand. Kara reached for it but hesitated, examining the crevices in his palm. There were folds, wrinkles, even fingerprints. Death looked so... mortal.

Kara drew her hand back. "Can I ask you a question first?"

"If you wish."

"Deidre and Niccoli are crazy. Evil, even. Why did you let them go back when they turned?"

"I judged only on how much they valued being alive. Goodness has nothing to do with it."

He offered his hand again, and she took it. White light consumed everything. The cliff disappeared from beneath her. She floated, unable to see even herself in the brilliance of Death's touch.

A sharp kick in her chest knocked the air from her lungs, and she awoke to the sound of crickets chirping. Darkness clouded her vision, even when she opened her eyes. A soft breeze rolled over her face, tickling her skin with the loose curls on her neck.

Kara took a deep breath, and it was the sweetest feeling she had ever known:

Life.

CHAPTER FORTY-NINE
BRAEDEN

No one spoke as Braeden stared at each of the Bloods in turn. They watched him, wary but quiet, as if no one wanted to go first and explain.

Bloods, afraid to speak? The world had gone mad after all. Braeden leaned back in his chair and sighed.

"At least it wasn't a complete loss," Gavin finally said.

"Carden lost a good deal of his army," Ithone agreed.

"A fifth of what he brought," Braeden corrected.

The room went silent again.

"A fifth, and we have you back," Gavin said with a small nod.

"Much to your disgust, I'm sure. Kara told me

about all of you. Especially you," he added with a glare at Gavin.

The Hillsidian looked out the window.

Aislynn leaned forward, eyes wide. "You saw her? Where?"

Braeden didn't even look at her. "You are never to speak to me again, Aislynn, unless it involves diplomacy. And you are never to ask anyone of Kara."

In his peripheral vision, the queen's eyes narrowed. She didn't respond.

He tapped a finger on the table. "You all fed me false information. You expected me to succumb. It's obvious none of you expected me to escape the Stele with my free will intact. Are you disappointed?"

"I think the word is 'surprised,'" Frine admitted.

"No, we did not expect to see you again," Aislynn said evenly.

Braeden wanted to fling a chair at her. All these years, he'd thought of her as a friend. He should never have told her they'd found drenowith at all. He had exposed this side of her. This ugly, evil side of the woman his mother had sacrificed herself to save. Aislynn was unworthy of such an honor.

He glanced out the window, unable to look at her anymore.

Ithone grumbled. "I'll say this if no one else will. You have a dark nature, child, and an evil family. You cannot judge us for fearing you will not overcome it forever."

"Don't call me a child, old man, and don't chastise me for judging you when you have done nothing but judge me."

Ithone glared over the bridge of his nose.

Braeden grinned. "And I hardly deny what I am. I spent years lying about it and being ashamed, but no more. I embrace it. I am a Stelian."

Ithone stood. The Bloods reached for weapons. Voices bubbled over each other, creating a wall of noise. Braeden laughed and debated changing into his Stelian form, but ultimately decided against it. Looking like the enemy would only hurt his cause. Still, they needed to learn not to trifle with him.

Braeden was no longer the politically inept brother of a future king. Braeden was an Heir, a royal himself, and their equal.

He cleared his throat. They hushed.

"I won't turn on you all, however much each of you deserve it. You all showed me it does no good to lie. Sooner or later, the truth comes out. The longer you wait, the worse the consequences become."

The skin on the back of Braeden's neck itched. He could sense Gavin watching him.

"And you, Gavin," he continued without looking at the man, "I trained and fought beside you for over a decade, yet you still can't give me more than a judgmental glare."

He let himself look and caught Gavin's deep-set frown. The Hillsidian Blood let out a frustrated grunt and turned his stare out the window.

Braeden leaned back in his chair again. "I can accept what I am, now. But my focus isn't on killing you. I don't care about any of you. I still don't think you're capable of peace, but it doesn't trouble me anymore, either. I have only two goals in this war, and you will help me achieve both of them. In exchange, I will help you win."

Ithone grimaced. "Pray tell us these goals of yours."

"I want Carden dead and Kara safe. If any of you interfere, I will end you. If you help me, I will give you the full layout of the Stelian castle, including secret entrances. We will take the war to him, and we will end it."

The Bloods shot sidelong glances to each other. Braeden turned to Gavin and stared even after the Hillsidian looked to the floor.

"You concern me most of all. I know what you asked Kara to do," Braeden said under his breath, so quietly he doubted anyone but Gavin could hear.

Gavin held his gaze this time. "It was my last means of protecting her."

Braeden shook his head. "It was your last means of getting what you wanted."

Frine cleared his throat. "We betrayed you, Braeden, several times now. You must despise us. How do we know you won't get your final revenge once we enter the Stele? Once we're in your home?"

"All you have is my word," Braeden answered.

"Then, why—"

"I told you why. We want the same thing. You want Carden dead, but you can't kill him without the element of surprise. I want Carden dead because I want to be free from him forever, but I can't do so without your numbers."

"And when he dies? What will you do once you are Blood?" Ithone asked.

"Stay as far away from the lot of you as I possibly can," Braeden admitted.

"Everyone wins," Gavin said with a dry laugh.

Braeden stole a glance out the window without looking at anything. How shameful to think he'd once called that man a brother.

"All in favor?" Aislynn asked.

"Yes," Gavin said.

"Blood Ithone?" Aislynn asked.

"I will keep an eye on you, boy," Ithone said.

"I would expect nothing less, old man," Braeden answered.

Aislynn interrupted. "I assume you're in favor, then. And you, Blood Frine?"

"Yes. And you?"

"Yes," she said.

"Shall we begin?" Gavin asked.

"I have another matter to attend to first," Braeden answered.

Frine laughed. "But of course. Tell us, where did you stow the Vagabond?"

"Far away from Ayavel."

"ENOUGH!" Aislynn's voice ricocheted off the walls and windows, echoing many times over in the small room.

Everyone went silent and stared at her.

She took a deep breath and caught Braeden's eye. "I apologize for jeopardizing Kara's safety. I did what I thought must be done. We all did."

Braeden leaned in. "What made you think attacking a drenowith would help you win a war? You're insane if you really think it was a good idea. It only gives you another enemy. A terrifying one. Garrett is no minor threat. If Adele survived, she will be after you as well. If not, Garrett will be out for blood. He loves her."

"You have more experience with these drenowith than we thought," Frine said, his eyebrow lifting in surprise.

"I trained with them. Adele was my tutor, but Garrett also critiqued me. The way he studied the sparring matches..."

That drenowith was not to be trifled with.

Aislynn arched her back, but she would only ever look like a broken child to him. "We had a reliable source—"

Braeden laughed. "I'm fairly certain your source was Deidre. She played all of you!"

"How could you possibly—?"

"Deidre found me while Carden was, uh…"Braeden shuddered at a sudden memory of the horrific pain, "while he was interrogating me. She told me you used Kara as bait to capture a drenowith and laughed at how stupid you were to do it."

Aislynn's quiet voice broke the tense air. "You're wrong, Braeden. My most trusted general told me he found an ancient book describing the table. He even showed me."

"And when was the last time you saw this general?" Braeden asked.

"This morning."

Braeden leaned back, still unconvinced. Deidre could be keeping up the façade, continuing in the general's everyday life to use him at some later time. More likely, she was slipping in and out of his life, making excuses to leave and returning in his guise. Or perhaps the general truly was fine and had found something. He would have to find the general and see for himself to be sure, but it didn't seem like Aislynn would even entertain the idea.

Braeden sighed. Isen made everything so complicated.

Aislynn stretched a hand toward him on the table but didn't come close enough to touch. "Even if Deidre had overtaken my general, what would she have to gain from lying to us?"

He sat back, away from her outstretched palm. "We can't know for certain unless we ask her, but I have my theories. It could have been a plot to divide you all further when it backfired, or make Kara vulnerable, or..."

Braeden's lungs deflated. He forgot the rest of what he'd meant to say. Kara was alone. Without the Grimoire, she was absolutely vulnerable. His attempt to keep her safe had probably only put her deeper into harm's way.

He was an idiot.

"I have to go," he said. The chair grated against the stone as he pushed away from the table and stood.

"Where to, Prince?" Frine asked, smirking.

But Braeden didn't answer. He tore from the room and down the hall. He ran until he found Iyra. She'd been isolated in a field far from the rest of the mounts, left to lie in the shade and stare holes into the barn wall as she waited for him.

He jumped the fence. Iyra turned her giant head in his direction. She stood and trotted toward him, but he climbed on without a moment's hesitation.

"To Scotland, Iyra," he said.

She nodded. He could have sworn he saw a grin twitch at the edges of the beast's mouth before she tore through the field and jumped the fence with ease.

To her, this must have been an escape into action. She would run as fast as she could if only to feel alive again after being crammed into a field, waiting for him to grow as bored as her and leave.

Braeden's heart raced for another reason. His life had become very simple: kill the man he hated and protect the woman he loved. The panic bubbling in his gut told him he had failed at the latter.

BRAEDEN

It took concentrated effort on Braeden's part to not break open the bed and breakfast's door when he arrived a few hours later. He'd left Iyra safely hidden beyond the lichgate he'd used to reenter the human world.

The inn's door was locked, and no one answered at first. He checked for signs of forced entry. No broken windows. The door seemed intact. None of it really mattered to an isen, though. They could snake their way into any building.

He was about to smash in the front door when he heard a familiar Scottish voice behind him.

"Ah, good to have you back!"

Braeden turned to see Lori standing on the sidewalk. She had a plastic grocery bag in one hand and a smile on her face.

"Is K—er, Anne here?" he asked breathlessly.

"Well, no, actually. She should be back soon, though. She went into Glasgow to spend time with one of the local girls. I suspect she felt a bit lonely, what with you gone—"

"How long ago did they leave?" he asked.

"A few days ago. I left a voicemail the other day and was just about to call again to check in. Is everything all right? You're pale."

Braeden's head swam. He wanted to vomit.

"Don't worry. Let's give Bonnie a call right now. She'll be with your girlfriend, and you two can hash out whatever's really going on here."

Lori left the door ajar. Braeden pushed through after her. He turned for the stairs and took them three at a time.

"You want some tea?" Lori asked.

"No, thanks. I'll be right down."

He needed a moment.

Glasgow? He wanted to scream. So much for Kara lying low. But could he really expect her to fly under the radar? No, it wouldn't be fair. So, she'd gone into the city. He wanted to think she would be fine, to think no one would find her. The human world was a big place, and even isen couldn't find her in just a few days.

Right?

He opened the door to Kara's room. His jaw tensed as he confirmed it was, in fact, empty. Daylight streamed through the bay window. The room hummed with a serene glow he wanted to absorb. Only, the panic in his stomach boiled with a new fervor. It wouldn't stop until he saw Kara.

But the light also illuminated an envelope placed on the pillow. He walked slowly closer. His pulse raced when he saw his name written on the front in handwriting he didn't recognize. He ripped open the envelope.

Dearest, little Braeden—
  You should keep better track of your toys.
  —Deidre

Braeden crumpled the note and threw it on the bed. He ran from the room and barreled down the stairs. He heard Lori say something, but he didn't care.

Something had happened. Something bad.

He ran across the street, over the bridge, and

through the forest to the castle ruins. He gave a half-hearted look around to make sure no one watched him and ran into the ruins' old keep. Blue light flared around him as he walked through a long-forgotten lichgate.

It was only natural for Kara to figure he'd take her far from Ourea, so he'd put her close to an ancient lichgate no one remembered. She would be unlikely to look for it, and he could get back to her quickly. But had the portal been how she was found?

He cursed to himself and jumped onto Iyra's back. He had only one option left: find Stone.

Stone was an isen. Even though Braeden hated to trust an isen with something so crucial as finding Kara, he was out of better ideas.

Braeden couldn't lose her. He'd do whatever it took to get her back.

CHAPTER FIFTY

KARA

Kara's head rested on a pillow. Crickets chirped in some distant place, their chorus carried on a breeze that covered her skin in goosebumps. She opened her eyes but couldn't see anything at all.

"I told you she'd make it," a man said.

"I knew she would, but I'm not any less furious with you." This second voice, she recognized.

Her voice scratched in her throat. "Is that you, Vagabond?"

"Yes, Kara. I'm here."

"Where am I?"

Light blurred into her vision, and the room slowly came into focus. She lay in a canopy bed, its sheer white curtains pulled back to reveal a series of circular windows along the far, stone wall. The windows were gaping holes without any glass to cover them, and they let in the night air. A full moon hung low on the horizon, illuminating the dark forests below. She seemed to be high in the air, as if in a mountain.

A creature flew low over the woods, just far enough away that Kara could only see its long body and jagged wings. It dove into the trees, its dive followed by a blood curdling screech. The thing broke back through the canopy carrying a carcass in its claws.

Kara was definitely not in the human world anymore.

"How are you feeling?" the Vagabond asked.

Kara turned to see his ghostly outline standing beside her bed. Stone sat in a chair next to him.

She seethed at the isen. "You."

"It's good to see you as—"

Kara didn't give him the chance to say anything else. She lunged at him with a strength she had never experienced before in her life. It was as if her muscles had grown stronger while she slept.

She shoved Stone into the wall, pinning his neck with her left arm. In her right hand, she summoned the first spell she could think of: the red sparks she'd never been able to master.

"Kara, don't!" the Vagabond yelled.

"I'll kill you, Stone. I didn't want to be an isen! You never gave me a choice!" Kara screamed.

"The power is delightful, isn't it?" Stone asked, his voice calm. He sounded more like she'd made a comment about the weather, rather than threatened to end him.

The red sparks fizzled in her palm. They had been effortless to summon, as if she hadn't been struggling for ages without any sign of progress. Even as her hatred for Stone cooled to a simmering anger, the sparks pulsed in her hand. They took nothing to create nor maintain.

"You were powerful before, but now you're unstoppable," Stone said.

Kara released him and backed away, the red flashes still vibrating between her fingertips.

"Why?" Kara asked.

"When I awoke you, it built you to your full potential, both physically and magically. Next to the drenowith, isen are the strongest creatures alive, Kara. And you can tame the drenowith."

"You've said enough, Stone!" the Vagabond shouted.

"I merely stated it is possible, not that she should."

A dull pain pulled above Kara's right hand. The wrist guard Deidre had pulled from the old, wooden box still bit into her arm. Kara reached down to rip the vile thing off, but Stone grabbed her hand. She twisted in his grip but couldn't shake him.

He glared at her. "Never, under any circumstance, are you to take it off. Not until I say you are ready."

"Why the hell not? It hurts."

"It's supposed to. It's a training device, meant to teach you to control your new strength. Agneon wore it, and so will you."

The name rang a distant bell, but Kara couldn't recall how she knew it. "Why does that matter? Who is he?"

"Don't tell her, Stone," the Vagabond said.

"And how, exactly, will you stop me?" Stone asked, turning to look at the ghost.

The Vagabond tightened his hands into fists. "She doesn't need to know!"

Kara bristled. "You don't get to say that anymore! You've hidden important facts from me since I opened the Grimoire. If you had just explained things, I might not even be in this mess!"

The Vagabond held up a hand as if to placate her. "You've been to hell and back, Kara, but I need you to calm yourself."

"I'll calm down when I have answers!"

Stone let go of her arm. "How about this? We'll give you answers if you simmer down."

Kara took a deep breath but didn't move. Stone, however, walked back to his chair and sat.

Stone pointed to the bed. "Would you like to have a seat, Kara? This might take a while."

"I don't want to be anywhere near you. Get on with it."

He crossed his arms. "There is no need to be rude, child."

"You turned me without asking, and I'm being rude? Seriously? I should—"

"Kara, please," the Vagabond said.

She groaned. "Fine but tell me who this Agneon guy is and why his name sounds familiar."

Stone cleared his throat. "Kara, you aren't merely an isen. You are Agneon's granddaughter."

"I said she didn't need to know!" the Vagabond shouted.

Kara bit back a scathing remark and turned to Stone. "Who is this guy?"

"He was Niccoli's best soldier, with a natural ability to quickly master magic."

It clicked. When she had first arrived in Hillside, and the queen ushered her into a room to meet the generals, someone had mentioned Agneon. The drenowith had killed him, and everyone at the table had been grateful for it.

Agneon was a murderer. Kara never knew her maternal grandparents because they'd lived in Ourea.

She put her hand over her mouth and leaned back into the wall.

Stone rubbed his cheek. "Agneon was the most arrogant man I knew, but it was warranted. He was the best and knew it. He could go into a fight alone and leave nothing but blood and corpses. He was fierce. Such is the trait of his bloodline. Your bloodline, Kara. Your family is one of the most powerful isen families in the world. You'll be more powerful than me someday, no matter how hard I train."

Kara just shook her head. She didn't want power if it came from such an evil man.

Stone continued. "An isen is born an isen, but must be awakened at some point in his or her life to realize true power. You've already experienced it, of course, but some go their entire lives without realizing what they are. An isen can usually sense another of his kind, awakened or not, but it's not the case with you. Your isen nature was hidden, but you wouldn't have such a strong ability to control magic if you were merely human."

"I get my magic from the Grimoire," Kara said, cutting him off.

"Not really. You learn quickly, don't you? More quickly even than yakona?"

Kara didn't answer. Her mind raced. When Braeden had taught her how to make arrows out of the wind, she had picked it up in minutes, even though he'd taken months to learn the same thing. They'd attributed that to the Grimoire. No one but the first Vagabond really knew the book's true power. Still,

Braeden was incredibly strong. For her to learn faster than him, well—she sighed.

Stone leaned forward. "Your skill comes from your heritage, Kara. Agneon was a powerful fighter. He wore the training guard long after he outgrew it simply because it made his battles more challenging. His only thought for years was of the fight. But your grandmother showed him the value of life, rather than the thrill of death, and now you see why he couldn't live with himself once he killed her, accident or no. He took their only daughter to the human realm to live with his wife's relatives."

"My mom," Kara said under her breath.

"Yes, your mother."

"How could you possibly know that?" Kara asked.

"He was my friend, once, and I owed him a debt," Stone said.

Kara's face flushed with anger. "Is that why you changed me? You think you're paying him back?"

"I suppose in part, yes. But it was merely the logical option."

Kara resisted the impulse to punch something. Namely, his face. "You want to make a little more sense than that?"

"What did Niccoli tell you before you escaped?"

"Next to nothing."

"Sounds about right. He doesn't waste time. I'm surprised he didn't tell you about your mother, though. The truth would have been enough to make you hate him and virtually guarantee you would come back from facing Death."

A lump formed in Kara's throat. "Wh—what do you mean?"

"I may not live with Niccoli's guild any longer, but I will always watch everything the vile man does," Stone softly said.

Kara leaned against the wall, calmer. If Stone had lived in Niccoli's guild, then...

"Was Niccoli your master? He turned you?"

Stone nodded. "He did. If I hadn't awoken you, he wouldn't have stopped hunting until you belonged to him. He wants your power. With you, an experienced isen guild could overthrow the yakona kingdoms. Isen would become the dominant race in Ourea."

"Whoa, really? Just from me?"

He looked at her over the brim of his nose. "You underestimate yourself. Don't be so foolish anymore. It only limits you."

Kara glanced at the wrist guard. "But now you can control me. How is that any better?"

Stone looked at the floor. "I lived under Niccoli's control for one century. It was the worst hundred years of my life. I came close to ending myself several times just to escape it. I have awoken only a few isen in my time, but I never control them unless forced to. None should endure mindless obedience. I won't control you as long as you don't do anything stupid. Am I clear?"

Kara paused but eventually nodded. "Will you tell me what happened to my mom?"

"Ah, well… " Stone rubbed his neck. "No, I think not. I believe you don't truly want to know."

"Tell me. Please." She rubbed her arm and pinched herself to control the ball in her throat. She would not cry—not here.

Stone sighed. "Niccoli hunted her for thirty years, but Agneon told me where she was. I was supposed to look out for her. I did, as best I could, but she didn't need to know of my efforts. Kara, your mother was born with a unique gift. She didn't have the traditional isen scent. Hers was subtler, almost undetectable. And you—well, you didn't have it at all. For this reason, isen didn't know what you were. I personally think your grandmother had something to do with this odd, little piece of evolution, but we'll never know. Now, of course, you smell like any other isen."

Kara sniffed the air, but she couldn't detect a scent.

Stone leaned his arms on his knees. "But Niccoli is persistent. Last year, he found your mother—though I still don't know how. He stopped her in a parking lot and demanded she return to Ourea. She told him she would go with Death rather than be Niccoli's slave. He granted her wish."

Stone rubbed his hands together and stared at the floor but didn't continue.

"What does that mean?" Kara finally asked.

"He killed her, Kara. He poisoned her. She was slowly burning alive from the inside out when she went home to you. He followed her. He found you. But sometimes the isen gene skips a generation or two, and it must have been what he thought happened to you. It's the only reason I can think of for him to let you go then."

Kara's voice crackled. "Mom was sick that night because of Niccoli?"

Stone nodded. "I paid her a visit when she was in the hospital, but I saw Niccoli go in first. The car accident isn't what ultimately killed her. I suspect she would have survived the crash."

Kara's bubbling anger cracked. Massive flames erupted around her hands, but she barely noticed them. Tears pooled in the corners of her eyes, and her throat tightened around the words she tried forming. She blinked away a few tears. "Why didn't you do anything?"

Stone leaned back in his chair. "Now, wait a minute—"

"You were there! You could have stopped him! You could have saved her! How could you be such a coward if Agneon was really your friend? His daughter was dying, and you—"

Stone stood. "Enough!"

Kara's mouth closed on its own. The flames dissolved with a *hiss*. Her throat tightened until she thought it might implode. She leaned into the wall and buried her face into her hands. She couldn't fight. She didn't want to. All she wanted to do was cry. All these months of shame and guilt at her mother's death, yet it wasn't even her fault.

It was Niccoli. Niccoli had ruined everything. He had destroyed everything.

Kara bit back tears. For the first time in her life, she felt true hate. Red sparks fizzed across her palm. They sizzled the air and danced along her skin like she was a conductor. Anger churned in her stomach. She slid down the wall and crouched on the floor, her arms wrapped around her knees.

Stone knelt in front of her, but she wouldn't look at him. He lifted her chin until her eyes caught his.

"Anger is normal. Hatred is not," he said.

A few tears slid down her face, but she wiped them away.

Finally, she nodded. "You controlled me just then, didn't you? When I was yelling at you?"

"Yes."

"But you said—"

"Yes, and not listening to me was stupid. Don't yell at someone when you don't know the truth of the situation. It's childish." He stood and headed back to his chair.

"So why didn't you help her?" Kara asked with a sob.

Stone paused. "Everything dies, Kara. It's natural. Why should I have stopped him? She said herself she preferred death to being an isen. It's apparently what she wanted."

"No one wants to burn alive from the inside!" Kara punched the wall. The rock cracked, shooting veins up to the ceiling. It didn't even hurt.

"Your anger is misplaced. Control it if you want answers."

Kara shut her mouth. She couldn't look at him. She would scream if she did.

He continued. "I still hear Niccoli's commands, even if I don't have to obey. They are difficult to ignore. It's why I didn't fight for you at the bar. I couldn't let him know who I was, though he had to know I was another isen. I found a boy who looked enough like Braeden with the hopes their similarities would make you trust him—trust me—long enough to get you out of there."

"I was mad at Braeden, so that just hurt your cause."

Stone shook his head. "Your emotions confuse me."

Kara shrugged. Emotion in general probably confused Stone.

"Are you calm now?" he asked.

"Not really, but that doesn't matter. I want to know how you broke Niccoli's control over you."

"I—"

"He betrayed my trust," the Vagabond interrupted with a hint of disgust.

Kara glanced at the ghost. She'd almost forgotten he was still there.

Stone took another deep breath. "I have done so much for you, and you're still angry? After a thousand years?"

"He was my friend."

"Who?" Kara asked.

"I've heard rumors about you spending time with the muses. Are they true?" Stone asked her, apparently ignoring the question.

"Yes, but—"

"Have any mentioned a drenowith named Bailey?"

She glanced at the Vagabond. "Not the muses."

"They're still mourning, then," Stone said.

"Muses are slow to heal, Stone. A thousand years is nothing to them," the Vagabond said.

Kara crossed her arms. "Let's get back to the part where you two give me answers."

The Vagabond shook his head. "I want you to hear this from the muses."

"After what Aislynn did, I doubt I'll ever see them again."

The old ghost sighed. "Good point."

"I can tell her," Stone said.

"Absolutely not."

Stone raised his hands in mock surrender. "Carry on."

The Vagabond sighed. "Not long after I met each of the Bloods of my time, Bailey found me and brought me to the drenowith. Though Adele, Garrett, and several of the other muses taught me invaluable techniques, Bailey was my only friend while I was there. Once I left, we travelled together for a while, always looking to uncover new magic and the truth behind old myths. With his help, I finished the Grimoire.

"I introduced him to Stone not long after I decided to make more grimoires, though I only did so because I needed them both to successfully create the extra books. I thought he was safe with Stone, and I went alone to take the finished grimoires to the village."

The Vagabond's voice broke, and he didn't say anything more.

Stone continued for him. "I couldn't ignore a drenowith in my home. Because the drenowith are immortal, I had to wonder. Would absorbing a muse let me live forever without ever having to absorb another soul? It made sense. I was young for an isen, but I could still hear the voices of my victims rattling together within me. I didn't want to destroy myself someday because they drove me to madness. Cedric, you lulled him into such a sense of security that I would have been foolish to ignore the opportunity."

"No, I was foolish to think you were a stronger man than to betray me. And don't call me Cedric," the first Vagabond said.

Stone arched his back. A flash of anger sparked across his face. In that second, Kara became nothing more than a spectator.

"I barely won," Stone said with a huff.

"Hardly a consolation!"

"Cedric, Bailey's voice is the loudest of them all. I live in a mountain because it makes him comfortable. It's as far from Niccoli as possible, which also helps. I try to make him happy, but I don't think you care. You spoke to me only once after it happened."

"To ask you to put his soul in the Grimoire," Kara interjected.

It made sense. The Grimoire was all the Vagabond had left of a body. Stone, an isen, could move souls around. The Vagabond would live as long as the book survived.

"You were never supposed to know any of this, Kara, much less be involved," the Vagabond said.

"Did you know I was an isen?" she asked.

"Yes," both men said in unison. They each looked at each other and furrowed their eyebrows in surprise.

"Wait, you both knew? How?" Kara asked.

Stone cleared his throat. "Do you remember my comment on your smell when I first met you?"

Kara rolled her eyes. "You said I smelled funny."

"I believe I said 'strange,' but yes. You smelled familiar. Thanks to Bailey, I have a drenowith's heightened senses. I could smell the nearly undetectable isen perfume on you, even when Niccoli never could. I knew."

The Vagabond sighed. "And the Grimoire saw everything about you when you opened it, even that which you didn't know. That was part of its design, to decide if you are truly worthy."

"You knew and never told me?" she snapped.

The Vagabond nodded. "I hoped it would never be relevant."

Kara shook her head. She had to pick her battles, and right now, her new master was her bigger concern. "Can I talk to Stone alone, please?"

The Vagabond hesitated. "I suppose so, but you and I have unfinished business."

"Oh, believe me, I know. But I need to talk to Stone right now."

The Vagabond nodded. The smoky tendrils composing his body unraveled and dissolved until he disappeared into the air.

Stone leaned back in his chair and watched her for a moment. She didn't say anything. She wanted him to apologize and admit this hadn't been his choice to make, but her gut told her that wouldn't happen.

"Oh, I believe this is yours," Stone said. He reached into his pocket and pulled out the grimoire pendant by its chain.

Kara smiled and fastened it around her neck. "Why doesn't it burn you when you touch it? It burned Gavin."

"I simply know better than to touch the pendant. The chain is safe," he answered.

"Oh."

Stone nodded but didn't say anything further. He looked out the window, and Kara crossed her arms. She stared at the floor, the wall, the bed—anything, rather than look at him. Now that she had the man alone, she wasn't sure how to word any of the questions running through her mind.

She groaned after a while. "You're not going to apologize, are you?"

Stone smiled and rubbed his face. Deep bags lined the creases beneath his eyes.

"So how does being an isen work?" she asked.

"Show me your right palm."

Kara frowned, her question apparently ignored, but she obeyed. A thin purple barb slid out from the base of her palm as she turned it upward. She stifled a gasp.

"Controlling that reflex will be your first and

hardest chore. I don't want you to leave my home until you can manage it. Otherwise, you will scare away those you try to help."

She nodded and sighed. "Can I get your advice on something?"

"I suppose."

"Isen or no, I just can't believe the Grimoire isn't the source of my magic. I felt powerless and weak when Braeden took the pendant from me."

"Your power never came from the Grimoire, Kara. You aren't powerless without it. The notion was all in your head. There is nothing in the book you can't learn on your own—it simply makes life a bit easier to learn from others. As you improve, you might want to use it less. If you rely too much on others to tell you what to do, you will neglect your own natural talent and never realize your full potential."

"I guess."

"I know," he said. His eyes shifted out of focus.

She shrugged. "I should thank you. That fall from the steps hurt me, and I wouldn't have gotten away. Niccoli would have turned me if you hadn't interrupted."

"No, I suspect you would have escaped. Again, you underestimate yourself. But he would have caught up to you eventually. He would have found you, and you would have been his slave until he died. By then, everyone you knew would be dead. You would have lost all sense of reason and probably killed hundreds of thousands, maybe millions by that point."

"Thank you for that lovely look into what could have been."

"So, yes," he continued as if she hadn't said anything, "you're welcome. Please refrain from pinning me against walls in the future."

"I'll try."

The conversation died. Instead, they listened to the crickets outside. Kara toyed with her right hand, clenching and relaxing her fist to retract the barb.

Stone nodded to her wrist. "Would you like to know how it works?"

"Yes."

"A soul is a pool of energy that clings to the spine, blood, and brain. Our barbs, then, work in two ways, both piercing the skin and absorbing the soul from the body much in the way it leaves naturally upon death."

"How do I control the barb?"

"Meditation, mostly. You need to connect with the desire to steal a soul, with that reflex to let loose the barb, rather than suppress it. Acknowledge its existence but forbid the desire. Even you will not pick it up quickly, but we will practice together."

Kara looked at her palm and stretched her fingers. The barb moved with her, extending and retracting as she moved her hand. The sharp tip reminded her of the spikes at each end of the table where Aislynn had tried to drain Adele's blood from her. "Stone, how much do you know of what the Bloods did to me and one of my drenowith friends?"

"Only rumors, none of which are very flattering."

"To whom?"

"You."

Kara grumbled under her breath but described the table and what happened anyway. Stone listened, one finger on the corner of his mouth, and he didn't interrupt to even clear his throat.

She scratched the wrist guard. "The spikes on the table were curved like our barbs. Did an isen really help make it?"

"I can't say. Might I be able to see this table?"

"I don't know how to get back to it. All I know is that it's in Ethos."

"Which doesn't tell me much."

"I know."

"I've read documents about this table. It likely works in much the same way as we do."

"What do you mean?"

Stone rubbed his hands together. "Well, I'd imagine the barbs on the table tap into the soul's essence, connecting it to another's. Essentially, a bit of one soul is transferred to another. That is how this Evelyn girl was given the bloodline when she wasn't born with it —a piece of her aunt now lives within her."

"Now that is a scary thought."

"Evelyn isn't controlled by her aunt in that sense, but her aunt will essentially become her conscience, and she will rationalize in a similar manner. As for the table itself, I would imagine one of the seats is designed to give the small bit of soul, while the other is designed to receive it. I have to see it to be sure."

"Why would you want to be sure?"

"Everyone has a purpose in life. Mine is to learn as much as I can about everything I come across."

Kara didn't have a reply, so she stayed silent.

Stone got to his feet and stretched. "As I wasn't quite expecting you, I must restock my kitchen. Will you stay here and out of trouble?"

It was a legitimate question. A request. No compulsion tied her to the cave. He'd actually asked.

"Yes," she said.

Stone's dry voice fell into an even flatter monotone. "Splendid. Feel free to walk about the house. I'll find you if you get lost."

"It's that big?"

"I've had several centuries to carve it. Bailey doesn't enjoy being idle."

"What's it like, having souls inside you?" she asked.

Stone paused at the doorframe. "Before Bailey, my mind was merely busy. Full of thoughts, some of which weren't mine. But Bailey is louder, harder to ignore. I often feel like he's standing next to me, suggesting what we should do and nagging me when I ignore him."

"Has he forgiven you?"

"Long ago."

"Then, why won't the first Vagabond forgive you?"

"Because he blames himself for what happened, not me. His longing for peace blinded him to the truth of life for so long, yet it wasn't until he himself died that he even saw it."

Kara's shoulders tensed. The first Vagabond had shown her ages ago, when she first found the village, what his most influential memory had been: the night his followers and lover were murdered. He'd lost everything and realized too late what it meant to be a Vagabond.

But he had also realized too late what it meant to live. He hadn't lived at all but served those who rejected him by slaving after the near-impossible purpose of universal peace. His memory and his memory alone had fueled her into denying her growing love for Braeden, but she couldn't deny herself anymore.

Kara had nearly died, and now she wanted to live fully. Completely. And that life involved Braeden for as long as he would have her.

Stone opened the door. "I have a lot to teach you but use the next few days to rest. I'll be back in a couple of hours."

He walked into the hallway and closed the door behind him.

Kara listened for Stone's footsteps to fade away. She waited, standing in the middle of the room even after the echo disappeared. When a good ten minutes passed in utter silence, she took a deep breath to prepare herself.

"Vagabond, can you come out again?" she asked.

Nothing moved. Kara waited, hoping she could have a chance to talk to him alone, but no answer came. She sighed and turned for the door, only to jump back when she saw him standing in front of it.

"What is it?" he asked.

"We obviously have a lot to talk about—Cedric," she added with a grin.

He sighed. "I can't believe he told you."

"Sure, you can. I mean, come on, this is Stone we're talking about. And I think Cedric is a nice name."

"Perhaps, but it's part of my old life. I'm the Vagabond now, and using my old name is merely a distraction."

No, Kara wanted to say, she was the Vagabond. He was a ghost. He had every right to move on, to be at peace, to find Helen in the next life. But Kara kept that to herself. He could read her thoughts, and if he'd chosen to do so at that moment, her intention was clear: she just wanted him to finally be at peace.

"Are you still upset with me?" he asked.

She shook her head. "Dying makes it easier to forgive, I guess. I've said a lot of selfish things in my life and held too many grudges. As for you, I want your help and advice. You just can't threaten the people I love if I don't take it."

He nodded. "Fair enough."

"I'm sorry for everything I said that night you called me into the Grimoire," she said.

"As am I, my girl, for what I said."

"I was just so mad," she said with a laugh.

He grinned. "As was I."

Kara crossed to the bed and sat, though the first Vagabond didn't move from his place at the door.

"This is all so much to process, Cedric—er, Vagabond. Are you sure I can't call you Cedric?"

"Please, don't."

"Can I ask why?"

His shoulders sagged. "The man I was—Cedric—died with Helen. That name embodies all of my mistakes, my weaknesses, my distraction from my ultimate purpose. I will not let myself be free from this world until I make things right. When I earn that name, I can have it back."

Kara leaned back. "I'm sorry. I had no idea."

"No need to apologize, but thank you. It's why I never wanted you to have personal connections. I merely didn't want you to end up like me."

Kara sighed. "That explains a lot. But—and I'm not

trying to make you angry with this—it seems like not having personal connections is a weakness. If you don't have loved ones, who do you fight for?"

The Vagabond frowned. "Some people can't fight for themselves, Kara. They need heroes. You can't leave them behind simply because no one else will fight for them. I fought for them. I had hoped you would, too."

"I will. I do. But that doesn't mean I can't be happy as well."

The Vagabond looked at the floor.

A twinge of regret shot through Kara. After all, that's what the Vagabond had always deprived himself of—happiness. She wanted to apologize, but she'd meant what she said. She wasn't trying to be mean... just honest.

The Vagabond sighed. "I didn't handle our dispute very well. I'm sorry if I took it too far."

She shook her head. "It's all right, Vagabond. As mad as I was, I still wished you were there with me through everything that's happened since. How much do you know? I didn't have the Grimoire there for a while, and—"

"I never leave you, Kara. I can find you anywhere. I merely can't speak to you unless the Grimoire is near. I saw everything."

"I wish you'd been able to help me when Gavin

proposed or when I was running away from Ayavel. I felt so alone."

He sighed, and in that breath, he disappeared from the door and reappeared beside her. She flinched, but he didn't seem to notice.

"Kara, I'm sorry I was so arrogant as to force you to do things my way. I wish I could take back my threats. I would never have hurt Braeden. But if I've learned anything in all my time in this life, the past can never be undone. We must simply learn from our mistakes, however grievous, and swear to never repeat them."

She nodded and suppressed the urge to hug him. He wrapped an arm around her, though, and pulled her closer. She rested her head on his shoulder, surprised that she didn't fall through him. Frost spread across her skin wherever he touched her, but the hug was nevertheless comforting.

"Do you remember Aislynn's memory?" he asked.

Kara shuddered at the images that had flashed across her mind when she'd seen the queen's most influential memory. The pain had taken Kara by the throat, making it difficult to breathe. It seemed as though days had blurred into a single, painful moment Aislynn could never let go of. She was broken because of her time in Carden's torture room, and she would never heal.

The Vagabond pulled Kara tighter. "Her memory

told you that she hunted drenowith, even though she denied it when you made the accusation."

Kara sat up straight. "But why? Was she scared about her guards knowing?"

"Do you think she lied?"

"I was in so much pain I can't honestly tell you."

"I believe she spoke the truth as far as she understood it," he said.

"That doesn't make any sense. How can her memory tell me one thing and she honestly tell me another?"

"We often distort our memories, churning them to benefit us and vilify others. But the memories you see with your gift are always the truth. They will never lie to you."

Kara's shoulders drooped as yet another mystery of her life as a vagabond came to light. It was as if she would never learn close to what she needed to know to survive.

Cedric—ugh, Kara wished he'd let her call him that—lifted her chin with his finger. "Have faith in yourself. You are the strongest vagabond I have ever met in my life."

She grinned and looked down at the floor. The ice on her chin disappeared, and the room warmed. She looked around, but the Vagabond had disappeared.

She laughed and stood. It was fine; he didn't need

to say goodbye when he faded out like that. He never really left.

Kara debated a nap, but she couldn't resist the prospect of a house so large she could get lost in it. She walked to the door and opened it to the creak of squeaking hinges. Stone obviously didn't entertain much.

CHAPTER FIFTY-ONE

BRAEDEN

Braeden charged through forest after forest on Iyra, racing for Stone's mountain home. Stone was his last hope for finding Kara, but the pit in Braeden's stomach brought on an unwarranted sense of dread.

Wherever Kara was and whatever had happened to her was completely Braeden's fault.

🙵

KARA

Kara meandered through a few dozen hallways, explored twenty-seven rooms, and discovered a small, indoor waterfall before she wondered how much time had passed. It had to be at least four hours. Stone really should have returned by now.

After a half-dozen wrong turns, she managed to retrace her steps to her bedroom. She continued past it, though, and walked down a stairwell to a den. Moonlight inched through the open cave entrance nearby, while a small hallway in the back of the room led to the kitchen. Stools sat beneath an open counter. Even though Stone had centuries to build his home, he must not have slept during its construction. The house went on forever.

Paintings of places she'd never been and people she didn't know lined the walls. One particular painting of a familiar, blond man caught her eye, but she couldn't place who it was. As she examined it, she heard the crunch of gravel underfoot.

Stone must be back.

"Stone!" someone shouted from just beyond the cave.

Kara paused. Maybe not.

The man yelled again. "Where is she? Stone, you backstabbing son of a—"

Braeden rounded the corner and stopped in his tracks when he looked her way. Kara held her breath as she took him in. His black hair sat at an odd angle on his head. Dark circles under his eyes meant he hadn't slept much lately. Whatever Stone did had royally pissed him off, but Braeden's face went blank when she caught his eye. He swallowed so hard she could hear it from across the room.

Her heart fluttered… but not out of joy. Braeden hunted isen. That's what he did best. And Kara was now an isen.

Would Braeden kill her for that?

"Kara?"

"Hi," she said with a weak smile. Where could she even start?

"Kara, I'm so sorry," he said in one rushing breath. He rushed toward her, but she backed away.

She wasn't quick enough.

"What—?" He paused, probably smelling the telltale lilac and pine scent that only mingled together in such a way for one creature: isen.

His chest froze, as if he couldn't breathe. His eyes narrowed into a glare that sent a shudder down her spine, and he reached one hand for his sword.

She took a quick breath. "Braeden, let me explain."

"What did you do?" he asked, but it came out more like a breathy growl. His words grated against the air, loud and commanding. His form flickered, and for brief seconds of his rage, Kara could see the smoking gray giant that was his true self.

"I—"

"Answer me, isen!"

"Don't use that tone with me!" she snapped. She didn't want to fight him, but she would.

He drew his sword. "What did you do to her, Stone?"

Wait—Stone?

She hesitated. "What are you talking about? It's me. I'm an isen. I was born an isen. Stone just—"

"Don't lie to me!"

He stalked closer. Kara inched backward. Her magic pulsed at her fingertips, itching to break free, to fight, but she couldn't hurt Braeden. She wouldn't. She bumped into the couch and edged around it, slowly backing away from him at the same rate he came closer.

His glare sent a shiver down her back. She didn't want to hurt him, but he sure looked like he wanted to hurt her.

"Braeden, I mean it! It's me!"

Before Kara could react, he grabbed her neck and pinned her against the wall. The grip held her in place, just loose enough for her to breathe. Inwardly, she kicked herself for not seeing that coming.

Tension pressed against the wrist guard. Anger brewed in her gut, bubbling and hissing with a foreign rage she didn't understand. Every fiber of her being screamed for her to rip the wrist guard clean off, but she tensed her jaw instead. Stone had been pretty clear about leaving it on, and probably for good reason. She just needed to keep Braeden busy until Stone returned, which would prove Kara truly was an isen.

Braeden leaned in close. "I gave you the Grimoire to protect, but that wasn't enough, huh? No, you found her. You stole her soul because that's what you demons do. You destroy every good thing in this world. She was my one good thing, Stone!"

She tried to correct him, to point out that she certainly hadn't gone anywhere, but Braeden set the tip of his sword on her heart.

Isen were hard to kill, but she was pretty sure getting stabbed would still hurt.

Kara jabbed a fist into his throat. He gagged, and his grip loosened. She slipped out of his hands, but his blade slid along her stomach and caught the loose fabric of her shirt, trapping her. It pulled her back with a sharp yank. Braeden pinned her against the wall again with his left forearm.

"Change back, Stone."

"I'm not Stone!"

"Be a man. Change back!"

"Stop it!" Kara kicked him in the knee with everything she had.

He cursed and buckled under the blow. She didn't feel too guilty, though, as the sound of joints popping back together already resonated from his wound as it healed itself. She darted for the stairs. When Kara glanced back over her shoulder, he still leaned against the wall as if in pain.

She wished he would calm down for a second to

just listen. Maybe she could trap him somewhere, thereby leaving him no choice but to hear her. Or maybe she could—

Something grabbed her feet and sent her onto the floor, kicking the wind from her.

Braeden appeared overhead when the room stopped spinning. He grabbed her shoulders, lifted her to her feet, and shoved her into a wall.

He raised the sword to her throat. "This is your final chance, Stone."

She grimaced. "Braeden, I know this is hard to understand. I didn't want to believe it either. But this is who I am, and you have to accept—"

"STOP!" he yelled.

Kara's ears rang after his outburst. "Wh—"

"You aren't Kara! I would have known if she were an isen, even an unawakened one, and she wasn't! She was beautiful, stubborn, perfect, and the only reason I'm even fighting this useless war. And you took her from me!"

Kara's lips parted in shock. The sword tip slowly dug deeper into her skin, cutting her, but she barely registered the pain. A hot bead of blood fell down the arch of her neck. The low collar of her shirt absorbed it.

Braeden's eyes shook. He glared at her, his face a mask of hatred. As much as Kara wanted to reach out and touch his cheek, she knew she couldn't. He would probably cut her hand off.

He raised his arm higher, so that she could see the whole sword in her peripheral vision. Numbness ate into her body, freezing her in place. No amount of anger could shake the disbelief.

Even though she wouldn't let him do it, he actually *wanted* to kill her.

The clang of metal falling to the polished stone floor pulled her from her revelation as quickly as it came. Braeden released her and sank to his knees.

He stared at the tiles. "I can't kill you when you look like her. I could never hurt her, even if I know she's not really there. You win, Stone. But take me, too, and at least she and I can be together in some small way."

"Braeden—"

He glared up at her, full of hatred, full of disgust, radiating the most powerful loathing she had ever seen in her life, and she forgot whatever she'd meant to say. His eyebrows twisted. His fists tightened, and his strength dissolved into grief.

"I loved her, Stone. I still do, and I always will, even if we're nothing but souls."

Kara's heart fluttered and did a sickening *plop* into her stomach immediately after. Even though Braeden hated isen with every fiber of his being, he would let an isen steal his soul because he thought she was dead. He would sacrifice his kingdom. He would give up life and the control over his own soul because he couldn't be with her anymore.

Braeden *loved* her.

Kara dropped to her knees and lifted his face in her hands. He smiled and grimaced at the same time. There weren't any words to fix this situation, so they sat there in silence.

Stone walked into the room. "Oh, hello, Braeden. Lucky for you, I bought whiskey while I was out, since you two are nigh inseparable."

The old isen stopped a few yards off, a large picnic basket in one hand. A head of lettuce and the brown neck of a whiskey bottle stuck from one of the basket's open lids.

Braeden stuttered. Kara couldn't bring herself to look at him. She stood and tried to hide the gaping hole in her shirt from where the love of her life had tried to stab her.

"Then who—?" Braeden finally asked.

Stone headed for the kitchen. "Boy, you're smarter than that. Who do you think that is?"

Braeden pivoted, staring at her, and neither of them breathed. She couldn't hold his gaze, however, and looked to the floor as she spoke. "I know it's a lot to take in, Braeden. I didn't learn about any of this until Glasgow. I can tell you everything later, if you want. But if you can't handle what I am, you can leave. I won't bother you again if you do."

She headed up the stairs to her room. He didn't move. He didn't even come for her after she closed her bedroom door.

She slid against the wood paneling until she reached the floor, head in her hands. Braeden loved her. With a small, happy pang, she admitted she loved him, too. But after everything they had been through, he had waited until he thought she was dead to tell her how much she meant to him. Why would he have waited so long if he loved her enough to sacrifice himself to an isen? She had forced him away, yes, but she'd had no idea how far he would go to keep her safe.

Kara pushed herself to her feet, walked to the bed, and sat on top of the comforter. She didn't even have the heart to smile. If love was supposed to be a happy thing, why did she want to cry?

CHAPTER FIFTY-TWO

BRAEDEN

Braeden leaned into the hard folds of Stone's couch, mind racing. He was still trying to process everything.

He loved Kara. But she was an isen. A demon.

Was he any better?

He sighed deeply. *No.*

"You look like you could use a drink," Stone said.

A glass half-filled with brown liquid and ice slid across the coffee table. Braeden grabbed and downed it without a second thought.

"You love her, right?" Stone asked.

Braeden's jaw tensed, but he nodded before he could help himself.

Stone leaned back in one of the nearby chairs and took a sip from his own glass. "Then, what's the problem?"

"I thought she was you. I almost killed her, Stone."

"Right, and while I won't forget that gut reaction of yours, I'll excuse it for the moment. You tried to kill her. What does it matter? You didn't."

"Not for a lack of trying."

"Her new strength is impressive, but you're a fair match for her at the moment. I think if you'd wanted her dead, she'd be dead. She's powerful, but also exhausted and emotionally spent. She hasn't mastered her new gifts yet. She didn't want to hurt you and wouldn't have. You probably could have killed her. So why didn't you?"

Braeden considered it a rhetorical question. He didn't bother answering.

Stone sank back into his chair. "You're close to losing her, boy. Every second you spend down here, she loses a little more faith in you."

"Why do you care, Stone?"

"Irrelevant."

"It's very relevant."

The isen rubbed his cheek. "Fine, if you must know. Vagabonds aren't fragile. They're strong, heroic, and powerful, sure, but they are so often unhappy. It's the unhappiness that destroys them. I watched it happen to so many, right down to Cedric himself—the first Vagabond, if you don't know. You are the only thing left in this world besides her teleporting ball of fur that makes Kara truly happy, and I didn't go through all the pain of awakening her just to let her get her killed." He leaned forward, eyebrows furrowing. "Now go fix this, you stubborn twit."

Braeden stared at the floor. Kara couldn't be very happy with him at the moment.

"Her room is up the stairs, first door on the left. You're a prince, for Blood's sake. Be a man." Stone grabbed the glasses off the coffee table and disappeared into the kitchen, their talk apparently over.

Braeden took a deep breath and headed for the stairs. His boots tapped across the stone steps as he made his way to the hallway above. A sconce every five feet or so blazed with fire. The light illuminated a row of perfectly spaced, wooden doors disappearing around a corner farther off.

He leaned his head against the first door and set his hands on either side of the frame to brace himself. Two minutes passed before he could bring himself to knock. He still had no idea what to say.

No one answered.

He knocked again, louder this time.

Silence.

He twisted the doorknob. It turned, and the door creaked inward.

The room didn't have much furniture—only a bed and a dresser. Kara sat on the mattress with her back against the headboard. She stared out the window, most of her face hidden in the chamber's shadows. She didn't acknowledge him as he entered.

Braeden closed the door behind him. "I came to apologize, Kara. I want to understand all of this."

He sat on the other side of the bed. Her head remained in the shadow, but his eyes finally adjusted to the darkness. Dried streaks of tears stained her face, and she still wouldn't look at him.

He sighed and pulled her into a hug. She didn't fight him, but she didn't hug him back, either.

She shook her head. "What is there to figure out? I'm the thing you hate."

Braeden flinched. She'd quoted him from all those months ago, when she'd driven him to her father's rental house in her disgusting, multi-colored car.

He kissed the side of her head. "I could never hate you. All I ever wanted was for you to be safe. I only took you to Dailly to keep you out of the fray."

"You disarmed me. Without the Grimoire, I had no way of knowing how to get back to Ourea."

"Agreed. I'm sorry."

She pulled away and pushed him back against the headboard. "You didn't trust me. That's why you tried to keep me away from everything. I'm the Vagabond. I can't be protected."

He kept his voice steady. "Don't be a hypocrite."

"What?"

"You wouldn't get close to me because you didn't

trust me to take care of myself. We're both at fault here."

She didn't respond. After a moment, she looked at the floor.

Braeden inched closer. "Still, you're right. I made you vulnerable without realizing it. I only hid you because there were too many chances for you to get hurt. You always have to be in the middle of everything!"

She sat up, her back arching like a queen's. "That's not your call!"

Braeden nodded. "You're right. It wasn't, and I'm sorry."

"Don't ever make a choice for me like that again."

"I won't."

"I'll never forgive you if you do. Never."

"I understand."

"You left me, Braeden." Her voice shook. She stared at the comforter, eyes out of focus.

He leaned in and cradled her head in his palm. Her soft hair spilled over his arm. If they never moved—if he could hold her like this forever—he would be happy.

"I only wanted you to be safe, Kara. I knew you wouldn't like it, and maybe you'd hate me for it, but I couldn't lose you. After the Bloods openly attacked you, I didn't think I had another choice."

"You were one of the last people I could trust,

Braeden, and you abandoned me while I was unconscious."

He sighed and let go of her cheek, but she leaned her head against his shoulder and reached her left hand around his waist. Since he couldn't see her face from this angle, he kissed her head.

"Like I said in my letter, I hope you can forgive me someday. It doesn't have to be now. Doesn't have to be ever. But I do love you, Kara. I have for a while."

"Then, why did you wait to tell me until you thought I was dead?"

"I didn't want you to shun me in an attempt to keep me safe."

She didn't answer. He suppressed a smile. It was exactly what she would have done if he'd told her.

He wrapped his arms around her. "I believed there would be a better time to tell you, maybe when the war was over. I never thought I'd have to face losing you. To me, you're the last thing worth protecting in an otherwise broken world. Ourea doesn't deserve you. I don't, either, but I'll do whatever it takes to keep you alive. Even—"

"—even if it means I never speak to you again?"

He sighed and burrowed his cheek against her neck. Soft strands of her cold hair fell against his face, tickling him. Several minutes passed in silence. After a while, she laced the fingers of her left hand through his. Her right hand, which must have held the still-hidden barb, lay flat on the blanket.

"Braeden, I thought loving you would make me weak. That's what the Vagabond told me, that love is a weakness. He used you against me to create more vagabonds. I mean, I wouldn't have done it if your life hadn't been at stake. That scared me. Your life had more meaning than anyone else's. I didn't think I could help Ourea if one life was more important than the greater good."

She paused, lost in thought for a moment. She ran her finger along his palm, and he didn't interrupt.

"But I faced Death when Stone turned me. You have to have a reason to live, to come back, and you have to prove to him that you want it. You can't lie to Death." Kara looked him in the eye. "Braeden, I came back to make a difference, but I mostly wanted to come back for a chance to live a full life... and that includes you."

His throat went dry. He didn't know what he was supposed to say. 'Thanks' wouldn't exactly cut it.

She continued. "I love you, Braeden. After everything we've endured, I can't imagine anyone else I'd rather get into trouble with."

He laughed, and his grip on her hand tightened. He hugged her as tightly as he could for as long as she would let him. After several minutes, she shifted her weight and leaned into him.

"Can you forgive me, then?" he asked.

"As long as you swear to never do anything like that ever again, even if I am in danger. You can't shut me out."

He nodded into her neck. She hummed. Apparently, silence had been the right answer.

She lifted her lips to his but stopped a few inches from his face. Her gray eyes locked on him. His throat went dry again.

A wave of her new lilac-pine scent crashed over him. Panic flooded his body. The smell had a pleasant twist to it, but to him it meant danger. He wondered if he could ever get over the smell he'd been trained half his life to track.

For her, he would try.

She leaned in closer and brushed her nose against his. The touch sent sparks running through him and twisted his gut into a knot. He ran his fingers through her hair and held the back of her head. She smiled, and it took all of his self-control to not pull her toward him. He wanted her to initiate this one.

Kara ran her left thumb along his eyebrow and down along his cheek, until it brushed his lip. Finally, she closed the space between them.

She pressed her lips against his in a hot rush that sent streaks of heat through his neck and down to his fingers. His breath caught, but he didn't care. He didn't want her to ever pull away, not now that he finally had her.

The room faded. His stomach lifted. Happiness buzzed through him. He kissed her again and again and again, until they lost track of time.

He leaned back against the headboard and pulled her toward him, trapping her in a hug. He kissed her neck a few times more. She giggled and swatted his nose.

"So. what's the plan?" she asked.

He hesitated. "I should go back to the Bloods and try to talk some sense into them. I don't think you should come with me."

"Not yet," she agreed.

He sighed with relief. It had been easier than he'd thought.

She drew circles on his chest with her finger. He grinned, her touch nearly making him forget what they'd been talking about.

"What will you do?" he asked.

"Drag Stone to the village. I need to learn more about being an isen, but I also need to see how Twin and Richard are doing."

"Thank you for taking Richard."

"You're welcome. I think Twin was happy to have a friend with her."

"I'm not surprised you made her a vagabond," he admitted.

"Apparently, neither is Gavin."

"He knows?"

"He guessed and forgave me, but I think the forgiveness was a ploy to make me agree to his little marriage proposal."

Braeden tensed and pulled her into his chest.

She laughed. "I would never have agreed. You can relax."

He did, but he didn't let go. Her laugh faded into a smile, and he couldn't look away.

"I missed you, Braeden," she said.

"I missed you, too."

He lifted her chin and brought her lips closer. She teased him and brushed her nose against his cheek instead. It left a tingling trail of warmth on his skin. After a moment, she reached her mouth to his. Warmth coursed down his neck. He set a hand on her waist. She hummed again, the sound vibrating through him. It took all his effort to not pin her on the comforter. After what she'd gone through, she probably wanted a quiet night. Other desires could come later.

She buried her head against his neck and sighed. He relished the cold night coming through the windows, and neither spoke. Braeden's thoughts drifted to Iyra, who was no doubt hunting. In the morning, he would have to find her. He couldn't leave the Bloods alone for long.

His grip around Kara tightened. He didn't want to leave. He didn't want to face the Bloods or the responsibility of finally accepting his role as Heir to the Stele. He sighed, the breath stirring the curls on Kara's neck.

"Kara, could you ask the Grimoire something for me?"

She groaned. "Can I not be the Vagabond tonight? I'm tired."

He laughed. "C'mon. It'll be quick."

She adjusted and leaned back against him before summoning the Grimoire from her pendant. The book settled on her lap as Braeden wrapped his arms around her waist.

"Your question, my lord?" she asked with a grin.

His smile faded. "Is it possible for me to completely break my blood loyalty to Carden without becoming a vagabond? I disobeyed a mandate not to leave, and I've disobeyed his commands, but I'm always tempted to obey. I barely won my last fight with him, and I had the element of surprise. I won't get that again."

She sighed and turned to the book without prodding for more detail, for which he was grateful. She mumbled in a language Braeden couldn't understand, and the book's pages flipped to a page with blurred text. Braeden didn't bother looking—the letters would continuously shift if he tried to read them, just as they had the first time he'd watched Kara use the book.

She shook her head. "Sorry, Braeden. If there's a

way, the Grimoire doesn't know about it. It didn't even know you could resist."

Braeden suppressed a groan. "It's okay. I just thought I'd ask."

Kara set the book aside. They settled into silence and listened again to the crickets. After a few minutes, she lifted her right hand and began looking at the thin barb in her palm. Braeden flinched at the sight of it. She sighed.

Guilt churned in his stomach. "Kara, I'm sorry."

She shrugged. "You can't suppress instinct. I'm not going to pretend you haven't been trained to kill isen," she swallowed hard, "like me."

"No, not like you. I kill the isen who steal souls. You'll never steal a soul, right?"

She smiled. "No."

"Then, you're set," he teased, pulling her in tighter.

The night went on, and they barely slept. They stayed up talking and listening to the forest, pretending the whole time they wouldn't have to leave each other the next day. It was the happiest night Braeden had ever known in his life.

CHAPTER FIFTY-THREE

BRAEDEN

Daybreak came too soon.

The morning blurred by: Braeden awoke to Kara snuggled next to him; he nudged her awake; her lips pressed against his again and again; he caught sight of her leaning against the cave window as he mounted Iyra and ran off into the forest.

He fought the unyielding urge to turn around and go back to her for the entire trip to Ayavel. The hours flew by like minutes as he thought of her.

It wasn't until he started down the row of cherry blossom trees toward the Ayavelian court that he even acknowledged his surroundings. The world seemed to get worse each time he walked this road.

Braeden crossed through the Ayavelian gates and onto the empty streets. He wondered if the Ayavelian people ever left their homes, or if the empty streets were their way of welcoming him.

Once at the palace, he dismounted and let Iyra jog off toward the stables. She would find a patch of shade and wait for him. When she disappeared around a building, he ran up the stairs and into the castle. A few soldiers at their posts followed his movement as if he would start killing everyone at any second, but he didn't even acknowledge them.

Let them look.

After a few minutes of walking, he stepped into the throne room and paused. No one sat in the grand chairs lined along the platform at the far end of the hall. A thin Ayavelian woman stood in front of Aislynn's throne, her eyes out of focus as she eyed the empty seat. She turned at the creak of the doors opening.

Braeden locked eyes with Evelyn but turned to leave after a moment. He wouldn't bow or pretend he liked her. He didn't have to anymore.

"Wait," she said.

He paused.

"Please, come in. I was hoping you would come back."

"You were?" he asked, unable to mask his surprise.

"Yes." She sat on the stairs and patted the space beside her.

He neared, suddenly alert. There couldn't be much

for them to discuss. He stopped at the foot of the stairs, now eye-level with her.

"Where is Aislynn?" he asked.

"She left to run an errand. She does that a lot, lately," Evelyn said without hesitation. Her gaze didn't lift from the floor.

"Evelyn, what did—"

"I'm not ready for this, Braeden. To rule. I'm afraid I made a mistake in accepting."

He took a deep breath and sat beside her. "I don't think any of us are ready. We simply must do the best with what we have."

"Is that what you're doing?"

He didn't respond.

She shrugged. "You and I might never be friends. I knew something was off about you the moment I met you, but Aislynn would never let me voice my concerns to anyone. Even Gavin wouldn't listen. He truly loved you as a brother."

Braeden stared at the stone walls. "No, he didn't. If he did, what I am wouldn't have mattered."

"I suppose. But you still saved his life in the ambush. Even if I cannot love him, I do care for him. I cannot thank you enough for doing that."

"You were there?"

"No, I heard of it later. The Heirs remained here in case..."

"In case one or more of the Bloods didn't survive."

"We tried to convince Gavin not to go since he has no Heir, but he wouldn't hear of it. It was good of you to save him. No one expected you to do that."

"No one expects much of me, but I don't care anymore. I do what lets me sleep at night, Evelyn. I suggest you do the same."

"I had little choice in the matter of imprisoning your love interest," she said.

"It's funny you mentioned it."

"Why?"

"Because I didn't," he said, glaring at her.

Evelyn caught his eye and sat up straight in defiance, but he didn't let her speak. He stood and headed for the door without looking back. "Tell Aislynn I'd like to speak with her when she returns."

And good luck sleeping at night.

As Braeden reached the door, someone else opened it from the other side. Gavin stood in the hall, fingers on the handle.

"Oh," he managed.

"Gavin," Braeden said with an annoyed nod.

"I meant to find you, actually," the king said with a look into the throne room.

Braeden turned to see Evelyn stand and walk toward a side door, head held high.

He and Gavin waited in silence until Evelyn left. The door shut, and the sound thundered through the massive room. Neither of them spoke until the echo dissolved into the tense air.

"You didn't really come to find me," Braeden said.

"Of course not, but it is convenient. I need to show you to your study."

Braeden followed Gavin from the throne room and kept track of their path as they went. They walked in silence through the hallways and stairwells.

"How much time do you need, Braeden?" Gavin eventually asked.

"To do what exactly?"

"Plan this little coup."

"As much time as possible, though we don't have much. A few months at most."

Gavin nodded and opened a nearby door. The room had a wall of windows similar to the Vagabond's study. It reminded Braeden of the last, peaceful moment he'd had with Kara before the gala.

He caught Gavin watching him in his peripheral vision. Once, he'd envied the man, but Gavin had since lost everything: his family, his innocence, his lover, his power over the yakona Council. There was nothing left to envy. A new emotion replaced it: pity.

"I already set what maps I have on your desk," Gavin said.

"Liar. They're copies. You'd never give me everything you had."

"What I said was an omission of some of the truth, not a lie."

Braeden shook his head and walked to the desk. He confirmed that these were all of the maps he'd seen in the queen's—now Gavin's—study over the years. Stacks of empty paper also lined a second table nearby.

"Thank you," Braeden said with a nod to the door.

Gavin forced a smile and turned to leave.

"No one is allowed in here without my permission," Braeden added.

Gavin paused. "We'll discuss your request at Council tonight. You're invited, of course."

"It wasn't a request."

The king tensed his jaw, and Braeden marveled at his own audacity. Here he was, barely a year from thinking "all going right" meant Gavin would forever be his superior, yet Braeden dared command him.

"I wouldn't have hurt Kara," Gavin said after a moment.

Braeden sat. "I don't believe you."

"I needed her help. I wouldn't have made her unhappy, but it's not like I'm in love with her."

"No, you love Evelyn."

Gavin cringed and looked at the floor. "Never mind."

"Don't let Evelyn go if you still love her," Braeden

said. He didn't exactly like the princess, but she somehow made Gavin happy.

"She won't have me, so I'm afraid there's little choice left in the matter," Gavin softly said.

Gavin never looked up. He hesitated, but ultimately left and shut the door behind him. Braeden leaned his elbows on the desk and sighed.

The king's silence had been a moment of hope, if an unanswered one: hope for the way things were, for an old friendship to rekindle. Hope that, someday, Braeden might get his brother back.

Braeden stared at the maps, but his mind wandered. He turned in his chair and looked out the window without really seeing the view. He should have hated everyone—the yakona were barely united, their loyalties hanging by a thread; Gavin despised him for what he was, regardless of over a decade of brotherhood; Kara, the only love he'd ever known in his life, was an isen, of all things.

But Braeden smiled. Despite all the misfortune he had suffered in his life, he could only feel gratitude. Hard as it was to endure, it had finally brought him freedom.

NICCOLI

Niccoli heaved, gasping for breath, still furious, his office a mess of splintered chairs and ripped papers as he briefly paused to think.

He slumped into his only surviving chair, disheveled and furious, glaring at the pile of wood that was once his desk. Anger boiled in him, fueling him, and he considered another rampage. He needed to destroy something, to kill something, to vent this utter rage in any way possible.

I will have Kara. He balled his hand into a fist. *Whoever I have to kill. Whoever I have to flay. Whoever I have to torture to get her, Kara will be mine.*

Her mother was cleverer than he had given her credit for, but he wouldn't make the same mistake with the girl. And if Deidre failed him again, he would kill that devious isen once and for all and finish this himself.

CHAPTER FIFTY-FOUR

KARA

It took two weeks of meditation and Stone smacking her hard on the wrist before Kara could keep the barb in her right hand from moving without her telling it to. It was only a start—there was so much more for her to learn about being an isen—but thoughts of either Twin or Braeden filled her every waking moment. She couldn't stay in the cave any longer.

Kara and Stone left for the village the moment the older isen agreed that she could control the barb. Stone walked, which meant Kara had to as well—how annoying.

He knew the way without the Grimoire's guidance, but Kara should have figured as much. It seemed the first Vagabond still had secrets, and she suppressed her growing resentment for that. She would never fix Ourea without all the facts.

She sighed.

Since she spent most of the trip lost in thought, the time flew by. In what felt like mere moments, she stood in front of the Amber Temple. A low-hanging moon rose from behind the auburn curves of the temple's dome. A buzzing sound made her blink out of her thoughts.

"What's wrong with her?" someone asked. The speaker sounded as if his mouth was full.

She knew that voice.

The lyth curled up in front of the doors, blocking their way up the steps. It cocked its head back to her and grinned. "Have you gone deaf, little one?"

"No. Pensive."

It chuckled. "Ah, big words. You seem different. A new perfume, perhaps?"

"Can it!" Her sharp tone startled even her.

The lyth raised its furry eyebrows and mumbled something. It turned without another word and stalked off into the night.

"You should never aggravate a lyth, you know. It's kind of stupid," Stone said.

"I'm an isen. It didn't need to be dragged out like that."

"A little defensive, aren't you?"

"I didn't want this, Stone."

"It was the most logical decision."

"Then, logical isn't always the best choice."

He sighed. "Logic is the best choice, always."

They walked through the doors and into the temple. Their footsteps echoed through the rows of empty pillars. So much had happened since she'd last set foot in the temple, yet the world hadn't gotten any better.

The lichgate arched across the wall behind the amber pedestal. Light poured from it and onto the hourglass, where the grains of sand holding the temple's guardians at bay ticked in a slow stream to its bottom chamber. In a room as still as the temple's main hall, the motion hypnotized her.

Stone led the way through the lichgate. The familiar kick to Kara's stomach made her flinch. Blue light flickered across her vision. Seconds later, the forest on the other side snapped into its full color.

Kara's boots crunched on leaves along the trail as she and Stone ambled through the twittering forest. Birds hopped from limb to limb and occasionally flitted out in front of them. The trees swayed, their leaves clapping together in a hushed chorus of wind and branches.

"Will you tell them?" Stone asked.

"Tell the vagabonds that I'm an isen?"

"Yes."

"Of course."

"Some will leave."

"I would rather they leave than feel betrayed later."

"Wise. You must still be prepared. Some may even try to kill you."

"They won't get far."

Out of the corner of her eye, she noticed Stone smirk. "You're right."

The trail stretched on forever, and Kara wondered if they would ever find the village. But as the worry flared in her gut, warmth seeped through her. She slowed and eventually stopped. The landscape blurred, and a kaleidoscope of color danced along her vision.

A field bled into view. Trees farther off came into focus. Kara turned around, only to see the lichgate beneath the Vagabond's tomb. A shooting star whizzed across a night sky.

"Wicked," she said under her breath.

Stone headed around the tomb, and she ran to catch up to him.

Kara grinned as they rounded the building. The entire village bustled with activity. Yakona ducked in and out of cottages, bags or piles of maps in their hands. Some waved to others and shouted for them to go slower. It wasn't just Hillsidians running about the town, either. A Kirelm walked toward a house next to a Lossian. An Ayavelian helped a Hillsidian pick up a few dropped books. Everyone spoke with each other, and all of them wore silver clover pendants around their necks.

"Kara!"

Twin bounded around the corner of the tomb. Kara braced herself for the full-speed hug she knew would come next. She wrapped Twin in her arms and sighed with relief, but still focused most of her energy on keeping the barb retracted in her palm.

"I did it, Kara! All but seven of the grimoires are taken, and I have names for each of them. It's just a matter of getting to those yakona safely."

Kara pulled Twin into another hug. "You're amazing! How did you do it?"

"I wasn't—"

"Kara! Good to see you safe and sound," someone else said.

Captain Demnug neared and tugged Kara into an embrace that lifted her off the ground. It knocked Kara's breath from her body.

"Oh! Um, good to see you, Demnug. I wasn't expecting—"

He set her down. "I didn't ever want to be in the position where I'd have to kill a friend, especially not Braeden. He may be a Stelian, but he's a great fighter and an even better man."

Kara grinned. She'd been about to say that she wasn't expecting a hug from him, which seemed so informal for the captain. She wasn't surprised in the least by his presence. Instead of correcting him, she said, "I'm glad to have you, then."

Twin poked her side. "So, what's been going on? You've been gone for ages! We've gotten bits of news here and there, but not—"

Demnug's smile faded. His hand reached for his sword. "Kara, you smell—uh—different."

"I have a lot to tell you both," she admitted.

Demnug glared. "How do we know you're really Kara?"

"What are you talking about?" Twin asked.

"She's an isen," he said.

Twin screamed and took a step back. "What? Kara! No!"

Kara suppressed a sigh. "No one stole my soul. It's me. Like I said, I have a lot to tell you."

"Get Remy!" Demnug yelled over his shoulder.

"Remy?" Kara asked.

Demnug nodded. "He's an isen hunter, even better than Braeden. He once mentioned he discovered a way to show an isen's true form. This way, we'll know for sure."

"Bloody hell," Stone muttered.

A Kirelm with thick, black wings—this must have been Remy—trotted to them, eyeing Kara and Stone all the way. His hand rested on a sheathed sword. He sniffed the air.

"They're definitely isen," Remy said in a deep voice.

"Can you see if this is their natural form?" Demnug asked.

"If they behave," Remy said.

Kara rubbed her eyes. "What do I need to do?"

"Don't move," he answered.

She straightened her back and watched him, making an effort to contain the barb in her palm. If she could have her way, she'd rip the thing out.

Remy set his hands on either side of her face. She suppressed a shudder. The last thing she remembered was looking up at him with raised eyebrows, waiting for something to happen.

The next thing she knew, she was on the ground, retching. Pain racked every inch of her body, burning down to her bones as she coiled around herself.

"What the—" She tried speaking but retched again instead.

"That is truly the Vagabond," Remy said over her.

Soft hands held Kara's shoulders. Someone pulled her upright and swept away the hair from her face.

"Hush, it's okay," Twin said in her ear.

Kara opened her eyes, but everything blurred. It took several minutes of blinking away the water in them before Kara could regain any sense of composure.

"What the hell did you do to me?" she asked.

"It's the only way I know of to force an isen into its —sorry, his or her—original form. I subjected you to an intense wave of pain by separating your muscles from your bones in a manner that is then instantly healed to—"

"Never mind. I don't want to know," Kara said, waving him away.

"Very well. You're next," Remy said with a nod to Stone.

Stone grumbled a string of curses. "Look, if I have to do this, I want Kara to see what happens if the isen is not in his original form. I'm going to change form, and none of you are permitted to lose your minds over it. Are we clear?"

Demnug and Remy nodded.

Stone stood up straight. The skin on his face peeled and cracked, dripping away like wax to reveal the young man he'd become in the Glasgow club the night Kara discovered she was an isen.

Twin and Demnug gasped, but Remy didn't move. If he really was as good an isen hunter as Braeden, this was nothing new to him.

Remy placed both of his hands on either side of Stone's now-disguised face. Stone took a deep breath, but he didn't do it fast enough.

The skin on his face split. He screamed and grabbed Remy's hands, but the isen hunter didn't let go. Stone's borrowed face splintered like a damaged mask, breaking apart with the crack of shattering glass.

Remy released him. Stone fell to the ground, retching. He curled his arms over his head until his breathing returned to normal. No one went to comfort him, but Kara figured he'd swat her away if she tried.

"Now you know," he said without moving, his voice muffled.

Kara turned back to Demnug, who sighed with visible relief.

"Now can I tell you all what happened?" she asked.

KARA

An hour and a half later, Kara had explained everything to the small group which had assembled in the mansion's war room on the first floor. They all insisted she sit in the head chair when they first came together, but many now glared at her, having learned the truth. Twin and Stone sat on either side of her, while Demnug settled into the free seat beside Twin. Remy took the chair by Stone. A myriad of yakona she didn't recognize sat in the other seats around the table. The room's doors stood open so that Kara faced a crowd of vagabonds. Some sat on the stairs, others on the floor, but all of them stared at her with mixed expressions of fear and respect.

Flick sat in her lap, purring in his sleep as she scratched his ears. Richard was off trying to get a grimoire to one of Twin's names, and would be back in a few days. Kara wondered how he would react to her news.

"And he, too, is an isen?" a Lossian asked, nodding to Stone.

"Yes." Kara rested her elbows on the table so that her hands hovered just in front of her lips.

Remy piped up. "Have you stolen any souls, Vagabond?"

"No, nor will I ever."

"So, you say," quipped an Ayavelian standing along the wall.

"You can doubt me. I don't care. Deidre stole my father's soul, and I will never force anyone to endure that slavery. It's wrong."

"So, you would really lead a mortal life?" Stone asked.

"Yes."

Murmurs raced through the crowd.

"I still adore you," Twin said with a smile.

Kara hid a small grin behind her hands and mouthed a hidden "thank you" to her friend. She cleared her throat before addressing the rest of the table.

"If you don't want to be led by an isen, you are free to leave. It's been hard for me to accept, but it doesn't change what I'm here to do. I'm the Vagabond, and for one reason or another, Twin trusts each of you to share this responsibility with me. If you leave, I ask only that you leave your grimoire here so that we can replace you."

No one moved. But before Kara could let out a sigh of relief, a Hillsidian woman stood and made her way to the table. She unclasped the pendant from around her neck. Its stone glowed blue as she placed the necklace on its surface.

"I'm sorry, Vagabond, but I too lost someone to an isen, and I can never forgive your kind for my loss."

Kara nodded. "I think you're wrong to judge me, but I can't stop you. We'll miss you, but you're free to go."

The woman took a deep breath and walked out of the hall without catching anyone's eye.

"Who else? It's now or never," Kara said.

A Lossian stood, followed by a Kirelm and three more Hillsidians. Each laid their pendants on the table beside the first, spoke their apology, and left. Kara's jaw tensed more with each vagabond she lost. She hoped she wouldn't lose any more. She closed her eyes and rested her face against her closed fists.

"The rest of us will stay with you," someone said from the crowd.

Kara looked up to see the hall and war room still

full. She let loose a relieved sigh. "Thank you all for not giving up."

A Kirelm in the hallway stepped forward. He nodded to Kara in a respectful bow before he spoke.

"The first Vagabond's name was slandered in my town, but my parents always told me the truth of what he actually taught. He wanted peace, but he mostly wanted to remind us that we were once great. With our unity in Ethos came an era of power and understanding. I joined you to bring our united heritage back, and I will follow you to the death so long as you never waver from it."

A chorus of agreement rippled through the room in hushed voices. Kara sat up straight. She had no idea how to respond.

Another, homeless voice spoke from the crowd. "The rumors of the vagabond's army gave me hope that we could once again achieve greatness."

More murmurs. More consent.

Demnug grinned. "We'll follow you, Kara, because you still want to help the Bloods, even after all they put you through. You still want to mend Ourea when most would have left its people to their pettiness, and that is commendable."

A Hillsidian at the table nodded. "I'm here because the Bloods have lost their way. You can remind them this war they fight is for peace, not for glory."

"This war against Carden was never about peace," Kara softly replied.

The room hesitated. Everyone watched her in a lull that suffocated the sound from the room. But there was no use denying it anymore. Fearing the truth wasted time. She had to embrace it, warts and all.

"This unity between the kingdoms is temporary unless we do something drastic to change their minds. For Gavin, this is revenge. For Aislynn, this is a ploy. For Ithone and Frine, this is sport. Each has a different agenda, one that will dissolve once Carden is dead. If he dies. Their lack of faith in each other might be their biggest weakness. He isn't above exploiting that."

"So, what do we do?" Twin asked.

"I don't know," Kara admitted.

The room hushed, but Kara didn't try to fill the silence. She didn't know the answer yet, and she wasn't going to rush into one now. She would come up with something, but she needed time.

Eventually, a conversation began about training and supplies, but Kara couldn't focus. She stared out the window, lost in a string of dire thoughts.

Was there any point to this? Any hope? Her mind drifted to Adele and Garrett. They had been punished, possibly put to death for helping. And now, Kara understood why Verum opposed their intervention. They had trusted her, and that made them open targets. She doubted she would see them again.

"Kara."

The voice snapped her from her musing. No one sat in the chairs anymore. Twin pulled herself onto the table a short way off, a few wrinkles of concern around her eyes.

Kara laughed. "I really checked out there, didn't I?"

"What were you thinking about? You looked so sad."

"I don't really want to talk about—"

Twin laughed. "Seriously? You dragged me away from my home and assigned me with a next-to-impossible task of creating an army, which I achieved—with flying colors, might I add. I think I get to hear the answer."

"I seem to recall you begging me to bring you here, actually."

Twin shrugged. "Details."

Kara grinned, but it faded. "I don't know if this is worth the effort, Twin. Everything—and I mean everything—seems so hopeless. The Bloods turned against the muses and tried to enslave me. I really wonder why any of us should care anymore."

Twin stared at her feet, which hovered above the tiled floor, from where she sat on the table. Her eyes glazed over.

She furrowed her eyebrows as if she were deep in thought. "Ourea has always been a dark place, Kara. I've never felt safe. I've never known what it meant to live without fear, not even in Hillside. I feel safer here in the village than I ever have anywhere else in my life, but we can still be found. You said Gavin knows where we are. We can use the lyth's powers to hide the temple for a while but not forever.

"We vagabonds are a part of this now, and we have a chance to improve things. Maybe we can make the world a little brighter before we die. At least, that's why I'm here. I've always wanted to see people smile. But, for the first time in my life, I'm powerful enough to do more than tell jokes. I can help change things. You empowered us, Kara. Don't give up. The rest of us need you to believe, or we'll lose faith completely. We may have grimoires, too, but there is only one, true Vagabond."

A smile crept across Kara's face—slowly at first, but it grew into a grin. She shook her head, stood, and gave Twin a Magari bear-hug. It made her think of her dad, so she hugged Twin tighter.

"Thank you," Kara whispered.

Twin hugged back. "Of course. We'll overcome."

"And we'll leave the world a little better for it," Kara agreed.

EPILOGUE
EVELYN

Evelyn pressed her back against a tree as her aunt disappeared into the forest yet again. She frowned as she lost sight of the woman, and Evelyn debated following her this time. She wanted to know where her aunt went on nights like this, why a queen as regal as Aislynn would slink off into the darkness, why she refused to tell anyone what she was doing or where she was going.

As far as anyone knew, Aislynn had retired early, tired from a trying day. She had looked Evelyn in the eye and said as much—that she needed sleep, and no one was to disturb her for any reason.

"It doesn't look like you're sleeping," Evelyn muttered under her breath, eyes narrowing with disdain.

Hands balled into fists, her stomach fluttering with

nerves, Evelyn leaned forward, debating her options: stay in the palace and let her aunt continue to hide whatever unsavory thing she was doing, or follow and probably discover yet another unpleasant truth about the Ayavelian Blood.

Evelyn took a wary step backward.

"You lie to everyone else," Evelyn said softly, staring at the now-empty woods. "Why should I be any different?"

The more Evelyn learned about being an Ayavelian royal, the less she liked her family tree. When she was young, becoming the Blood had been her greatest dream. She had hoped and prayed Aislynn would never have children, that the gift would somehow pass to her, and now she wondered if accepting had simply been a mistake.

She had lost Gavin. She had lost her freedom to choose. She now had to spend time with the wretched Bloods, and even worse, pretend to like them. To lie, to play the game, to pretend she didn't despise the lot of them.

All in the name of power—power she no longer wanted.

A sharp pain shot through her head. She grimaced and fell to her knees, cradling her neck, cursing the damned contraption that had given her the royal bloodline. These pains had begun the moment Aislynn hooked her up to the machine.

In her agony, thought had become more difficult. Sleep was almost impossible. Her magic fluctuated now, sometimes surging, sometimes so weak she could barely close a door.

Another excruciating twinge splintered through her head, and she couldn't help but scream. It felt as though her head were splitting, as though someone were trying to rip her eyes out of her body.

In her agony, she lost control.

A bolt of lightning shot from her body. The earth quaked. Wood splintered. Evelyn collapsed on the ground as the surge ended, barely able to lift herself as a thick log smacked against the soil in front of her.

She wished someone—anyone—would help. But no one knew she was out here, and she was utterly alone.

When Evelyn was finally able to open her eyes, only the charred remnants of the tree before her remained. The trunk had split open, the bark black and burned, the canopy lying around her, some of the thick branches having missed her by mere inches.

And in her chest, a void—a numbness that she couldn't shake, no matter what she tried. It blipped to life in an instant, and with every passing second, it seemed to grow.

Evelyn stared at her hands, astonished at what she had become—what she let her aunt turn her into. No lover. No freedom. Her vast power had come at a cost, and it was high time Evelyn accept it.

After all, there was no going back.

Truth be told, Evelyn had only one purpose left, and that was to serve her people, to be the last line of defense and the only surviving Heir with the bloodline. Without her, without someone to carry on the bloodline, the kingdom and its people would eventually die.

With the void in her chest growing ever larger, Evelyn merely sat in the debris, her skirts torn, staring blankly at the forest where her aunt had gone. Not much remained that Evelyn cared about, but she would protect what was left with her life.

DEIDRE

Deidre slunk behind a tree and held her breath. The fragrant scent of a bed of nearby hyacinth flowers swirled in her nose. Their scent would mask the lilac and pine aroma for which isen were known. She'd chosen this field because she needed cover.

The forest creatures carried on around her, oblivious to what she was about to do. And if that airheaded Ayavelian Blood would only show up, she wouldn't be stuck waiting.

But Deidre could be patient. She'd waited this long for her revenge, and soon—so soon—she would have it.

She adjusted the Hillsidian sword strapped against her back in a sheath to keep it from touching her. She shuddered, remembering what the hilt had done to Carden's hand. It hadn't healed completely, either. It never would, even for all his body did to counteract it. She didn't want to touch that sword until absolutely necessary.

"General Krik?" a soft voice asked from somewhere nearby.

Deidre let herself breathe. She grinned. Niccoli's lover was finally here.

Skin flaked and cracked as Deidre donned the appearance of the general Aislynn somehow trusted. She had no idea why; the man was an idiot. It only took a flirty eye and a few beers in a bar to lure him into a false sense of security. He belonged to her after four pints.

She huffed. Lightweight.

"Krik, you idiot!"

Deidre grimaced, remembering the way Aislynn had so freely used the word after the failed coup to steal the muse's blood. She hated living the general's life, mostly because Aislynn despised him. No matter. The queen wouldn't be alive much longer, and Deidre wouldn't have to worry about keeping up the stupid general's appearances afterward.

The last of Deidre's skin faded into the iridescent glow of Krik's body. Her spine stretched, and his white hair flowed down around her ears.

"My lady?" she asked in Krik's voice to buy time. Ayavelians were complex creatures. Changing into one took longer than other forms, but it would only be a few moments more.

"Where are you? Enough of this!" Aislynn snapped. Her voice wavered ever so slightly, the fear almost hidden by the curt tone.

Good. Be afraid.

The last of Deidre's façade pinched into place. She came out from behind the tree to find Aislynn eyeing the woods opposite. A billowing gown engulfed the thin queen's frame. How could she move in such a thing? Her feet, her arms—the rush of fabric hid everything.

What does Niccoli see in such a stupid, gullible creature?

"Ah, there you are, my queen," Deidre said, still using Krik's voice.

Aislynn jumped but recovered with a glare. "Why would you call me to the middle of the woods? What was so pressing that we couldn't speak in the palace?"

"We have a traitor, my lady," Deidre said, suppressing a grin. Yes, there was a traitor. There were several.

"What on Earth—"

Deidre rushed into her prepared lie. "How else could the Vagabond have escaped? She was drugged, my queen. She shouldn't have been able to open her eyes, much less escape. She had help. I have my suspicions, but with the other Bloods so close, there was no safe place to speak."

Aislynn's eyes narrowed. "Who was it?"

Deidre knew, but she wouldn't tell the queen. It wouldn't matter soon anyway, so she would lie to buy time.

She ambled toward Aislynn, so as not to raise suspicion. She only needed to be a foot or so away. Then, Niccoli's little queen would be hers.

She was so very close.

"I am uncertain, Majesty. I fear, though, that it is another Blood."

She walked behind the queen as if pacing and waited for Aislynn's eyes to fade out of focus. Deidre took one, painfully slow step after another, biding her time until the queen's defenses fell.

Aislynn crossed her arms and stared into the distant trees.

"No. Gavin's not foolish enough to—"

Deidre's heart stuttered in her chest.

Now!

She grabbed the sword from its sheath. It seared her hand, scorching Krik's palm to the bone in the few seconds it took to unsheathe the sword. But it was all she needed.

Aislynn turned too late. The blade sliced the skin from her right collarbone down and across to her left hip. Deidre summoned the wind into her palm and threw it into the queen's collarbone. The force propelled Aislynn backward into a tree. Bones cracked. The queen fell onto a pile of dead leaves.

Deidre groaned. Pain shot up her arm like fire and frost and lightning, all at once. She forced herself to slide the blade back into its sheath. White bone showed through the blistering skin on Krik's hand. Blood festered and popped in the untreatable wound. Deidre marveled at Carden's strength. She had underestimated him. Not only did he grab the Hillsidian Sartori, but he'd carried it back to the Stele.

She tried and failed to flex her hand. No matter. She wouldn't need Krik's face again, anyway.

Deidre let the façade crack and peel away. When the general's face disappeared, she examined her hands—smooth and flawless as ever.

She glanced back to Aislynn. The Blood's lips parted in horror.

"How? Who? Why?" Deidre cooed in a mocking tone.

"What have you done, Deidre? I have no quarrel with you!"

"Not directly, no. However, I am impressed you know my name."

"Every yakona does. You're a monster."

"Perhaps."

The queen's glittering blood trickled along the pale gown, almost identical in color. Deidre poked the skin beside the festering cut. The blood sizzled.

Aislynn stifled a scream. "Give me the sword. I will give you whatever you want if you let me make the antidote."

"And what is so precious about your life?" Deidre asked.

"What?" Aislynn asked.

"You said I could have anything. If you truly believe I'm a monster, you just gave me the reins to toy with your kingdom. With your people. With you. And for what? What makes your life so worth living?"

"A heartless thing like you wouldn't understand."

Deidre frowned and glared down at her prey. She set one hand on the queen's stomach. With the slightest of grins, she summoned magic to her fingertips. "That was the wrong thing to say, pretty, little queen."

Thin rays of black lightning danced up Aislynn's body. She froze. Only the occasional shudder broke through the paralysis. Her back arched. The muscles in her neck tightened until they threatened to pop from her skin.

Deidre didn't stop until she saw the thinnest trail of smoke billowed from the Blood's lips. She pulled her hand away, and Aislynn gasped for air.

"Think before you speak, yakona, and you might live a few minutes longer."

Aislynn gagged and coughed. "What do you want?!"

If the Ayavelian could barely handle that, this wouldn't be as much fun as Deidre had originally hoped.

"I want Niccoli to feel the same pain I have felt every day since he killed Michael."

Aislynn's eyes widened. "How—?"

"I once loved a man more fiercely than you and your heartless bastard could ever dream. Niccoli took him from me. I failed once in my revenge, but I will not fail again. It will devastate him to see how much you suffered before death. Though it is nothing close to what I have endured, it will be some small compensation to watch him mourn."

"You're insane," Aislynn whispered.

"We both are. Now, tell me. When you were with Carden, which of his tortures was your favorite? I've learned many things from that sadistic Blood."

Deidre sat with one leg curled beneath her and leaned her elbow on her other knee as she thought. She waved her hand through the air, summoning various techniques as she thought of them: icy blades flashed between her fingers; a current of yellow sparks snapped across her palm; hazy smoke coated her hand.

Aislynn sucked in a breath and stifled a quiet whimper.

Deidre laughed. "Is that it, then? You enjoyed the slivers. Am I right?"

The queen closed her eyes and held her breath.

"I am! Good. I just learned this one, and I need the practice."

Deidre summoned the shadows of the woods. They raced from their trees and twigs and pooled in her own shadow, deepening and darkening it until ribbons of black smoke rose from the mass.

She pointed toward Aislynn, and the tendrils slid over her fingers until they dripped off her. They wound closer to the queen, slithering over Aislynn's dress like thin snakes. They coiled and slunk, inching closer to her face with each of the queen's quick breaths. The occasional burst of white sparks running through the slivers illuminated Aislynn's face as she trembled.

Deidre brushed the hair back from Aislynn's ear. "Once you die, little queen, you should stick around for the show that follows. I am about to unleash a vengeance unlike any other, and my work has only just begun."

A sliver wound its way into Aislynn's mouth. She screamed. She shrieked until the slithering smoke filled her lungs, and then she writhed in pain. She cried. She moaned. She begged for mercy.

And Deidre did not stop until the queen's corpse began to fade away into dust.

DEIDRE

Two hours later, Deidre hung the Hillsidian Sartori, safe in its makeshift sheath, back on the wall in Carden's study. It hung alone, waiting to be joined by its long-lost brothers.

Carden might be insane, but at least he dreamed big.

"How was your trip, isen?"

Deidre glanced over her shoulder to find Carden sitting in the armchair by the fireplace. The room had been empty when she'd entered, but she was used to him simply popping up.

She shrugged. "All went well. Aislynn is dead."

"It worries me that you won't tell me why you were so willing."

She turned back to the sword on the wall and smiled. "You'll be rewarded for your patience."

A footstep warned her of his movement, but he lunged too quickly for her to do anything about it. He pinned her against the wall. She allowed it, for the time being. His frighteningly beautiful face hovered inches from hers.

Few men intrigued her like he did. He held a certain gift Deidre couldn't place. He could hypnotize and terrify those around him with a single look. Well, everyone but her. Deidre would never trust him, but he seemed to trust her enough. She tolerated his missions because, soon, he would give her everything she needed.

"What are you up to, isen?" he asked.

She didn't answer. He simply didn't need to know.

After a few seconds of silence, he ran his fingers along her shoulders. She tensed. Her fist tightened, but she resisted the impulse to punch him in the gut. She still needed his help.

His hands wove in and out of her hair as if they owned everything they touched. She closed her eyes, pretending the hands belonged to Michael. It worked. Her skin warmed. She faded back into a memory of an orchard filled with peach trees. Michael reached for one and said she could have it if she kissed him.

But Carden's voice in her ear ruined it.

"You betrayed your fellow isen, and I want to know why."

She stiffened, the unwanted memory of Michael's corpse lifting the careful folds of her mind. She stifled the thought and glared at Carden instead. He didn't move, but it was a look that would have sent lesser men running.

"They disgust me," she finally said.

She pushed hard against his chest, sending him backward several steps. He laughed at her strength, but she sneered.

"Good night, Carden."

"Good night," he said, offering an exaggerated bow.

Deidre pushed past him and threw open the study door. Once through, she slammed it behind her. She was nearly done with Carden—the thought rushed through her with a pang of joy. He would serve his purpose soon, as had Aislynn.

Deidre grinned. Niccoli would find the dead queen, half-rotten, in the weeds of their meeting spot tonight. If he truly loved her as much as he claimed, the agony of seeing her decomposing body would destroy him. He would see the scars. He would see the burns. In a few days, he would hear the fabricated rumors of how Garrett had come for revenge for what the queen did to Adele.

Niccoli's grief would be but a taste of what Deidre had endured. He did not yet know true pain. Deidre would show him. And she was so very close.

Read the sequel, HERITAGE, on September 3, 2018

IMPORTANT CHARACTERS AND TERMS

MAIN CHARACTERS

Kara Magari - Born in our world but dragged into Ourea by fate, Kara Magari was raised a human but soon finds out she's much more as she becomes the second Vagabond and master of the powerful Grimoire.

Braeden Drakonin - A Stelian Heir raised as a Hillsidian orphan, Braeden loathes his heritage and rejects his lineage. When he meets Kara he thinks he's found a way to officially leave behind his past and start a fresh life free from his cruel father.

OTHER CHARACTERS BY KINGDOM

HILLSIDE

The Hillsidian race is most similar to humans in appearance. Hillsidian blood is green.

Notable Hillsidian Characters:

Gavin - Heir of Hillside. Cunning, aggressive, and a bit of a womanizer. Raised as Braeden's brother.

Richard - King to the Blood Lorraine, ruler of Hillside and Gavin's mother. He and Gavin don't have much of a relationship.

Twin - A palace servant and close friend to Kara Magari.

Blood Lorraine - Ruler of Hillside. Mother to Gavin and adoptive mother of Braeden.

AYAVEL

The Ayavelian race is characterized by the triple irises in their eyes.

Notable Ayavelian Characters:

Blood Aislynn - Blood of Ayavel. She has spent her life brokering peace between the kingdoms and has, to some degree, succeeded. She has no children or Heirs of her own.

Evelyn - Blood Aislynn's niece and chosen ruler of Ayavel upon her aunt's death.

KIRELM

Kirelm people live high above the ground in a kingdom that floats over the Rose Cliffs and therefore have wings to travel.

Notable Kirelm Characters:

Aurora - Daughter to Blood Ithone and Heir to the kingdom, though she is the first female Heir in their kingdom's history. Their culture celebrates men as the leaders of the race, rather than women, and this has been a great shame to her father.

Blood Ithone - Ruler of Kirelm. Set in the ways of his culture, he has always been disappointed that he did not have a son to call his heir.

STELE

Stelians have grey skin and smoke steaming from their pores. They can change form to mimic other yakona races.

Notable Stelian Characters:

Blood Carden - A cruel ruler with a vendetta against the other kingdoms. He has worked tirelessly his entire life to get revenge, and he's so very, very close.

Queen Myra - Blood Carden's murdered wife and Braeden's mother. There's more to her death than meets the eye, and Braeden is determined to get his revenge.

LOSSE

Lossians can breathe under water which comes in handy since the kingdom of Losse is beneath the sea in a protective bubble.

Notable Lossian Characters:

Blood Frine - The careful, cunning, and manipulative ruler of Losse. He prefers to keep to his isolated kingdom and let the other kingdoms war with each other.

ISEN

Isen are soul stealers. By stealing a soul every decade or so they can stay young forever, but at a cost: the more souls they possess within them, the more likely they are to lose their minds. Isen can take the form of the souls they steal and impersonate their victims. A small retractable barb in their wrist is inserted into the neck of their victims in order to capture their soul.

Notable Isen Characters:
  Deidre
  Stone
  Niccoli
  Agneon

DRENOWITH

The Drenowith are also known as muses. These immortal creatures are very difficult to kill and have the ability to take the form of any creature, but they cannot reproduce. It's said they've been around since the first days of the Earth and prefer to be left to their own devices. Their magic is the cause of many, if not most natural disasters.

Notable Drenowith Characters:
Adele
Garrett
Verum
Mirrow

KINGDOMS AND NOTABLE PLACES OF OUREA

Hillside - A beautiful maze of trees. The castle itself isn't made from stone or dead wood, but is rather comprised of the five largest trees in the kingdom, all of which sit in the middle of the sprawling city. Those who live and work in the castle use the hundreds of rope bridges to cross between the rooms hollowed out of the trunks. It's a green paradise and a kingdom ruled by the Hillsidian Blood. Brilliant walkways span out from the castle like rays on a sun, the paths covered in shifting stones that take the shape of whatever touches them.

Ayavel - A kingdom of light ruled by the Ayavelian Blood. Ayavelians have the rare ability to shapeshift into any of the other yakona, as long as they practice early in life. Their natural skin is iridescent, glimmering like diamonds, and they possess eyes with three irises in them that can each convey subtly different emotions. The Kingdom of Ayavel is surrounded by a tall, white wall that protects the kingdom. The city is comprised mainly of white buildings trimmed with gold that have domed roofs and towering golden spires. The roads are lined with cherry blossom trees and their petals fly through the air with the breeze.

Kirelm - In the clouds somewhere near the Rose Cliffs of Ourea, the kingdom of Kirelm floats above the surface. Two layers of intricate and impenetrable wires keep intruders out while allowing the sunlight in. The silver-skinned people of this kingdom are equipped with massive wings in shades of white, gray, and black which allow them to travel throughout this kingdom in the sky ruled by the Kirelm Blood.

The Stele - A dark and dangerous place, the Stele is a home to many of Ourea's most terrifying creatures. Long ago banished from the other yakona realms, the Stelians are a culture of outcasts who resent their centuries of banishment. Like the Ayavelians, Stelians possess the ability to shape-shift, but their true form is the stuff of nightmares. Their ash-gray skin spews smoke when they're angry, and there are no whites to their eyes. The Stelian Blood rules over this kingdom.

Losse - This underwater kingdom is only accessible to those who can breathe underwater or those who are able to take the sting of the magical starfish that temporarily filters air from the water long enough to reach the kingdom's gate. Once in the protective golden bubble that encompasses the kingdom with air, the starfish is no longer needed . . . unless you want to leave, that is. Lossians have blue skin and large seaweed-green eyes. Most of them are bald, but some have black hair. Their thin form and webbed feet help them swim to their kingdom while breathing underwater. The Lossian Blood is the ruler of this kingdom.

The Villing Caves - Once a celebrated haven of caverns and lakes, the Villing Caves became the resting place for the Retriens. The long-lost yakona kingdom had claimed this place as their own after the fall of Ethos, but a dragon invasion soon thinned them out. In a last-ditch effort to protect his people, the Retrien Blood had no choice but to seal himself and the dragons into the caves. However, his Heir did not awaken as the new Blood, and so it's believed that the Blood still lives trapped inside the stone.

The Vagabond's Village - The Vagabond's Village is where the first vagabond and his followers lived. The Vagabond himself lived in a lavish mansion surrounded by the beautiful stone cottages his followers lived in, all of which was safely tucked away in a wooded valley. There is only one way to enter. First, visitors must get past the Lyth before attempting to pass through the terrifying Amber Temple, a place of worship which long ago opened a portal to deadly demons that took over the surrounding area. These creatures can only be contained by a glowing magical hourglass, but be warned: if the sands within are moving, the demons are trapped; but as soon as the last grain falls, they are free again.

Ethos - The abandoned city of Ethos is where all the yakona races once lived in unity and peace. There is little facts still known about its fall, but it's said the Stelians were at fault and that is, at least in part, the cause for their banishment. It was the First Vagabond's goal to reunite the kingdoms once more and rebuild Ethos.

GLOSSARY

Yakona - The yakona are one of the peoples of Ourea and known to be true masters of magic. Over eons, the six races have evolved to look quite different from each other: the Ayavelians, the Stelians, the Hillsidians, the Kirelms, the Lossians, and the Retrien.

Bloods and Heirs - Bloods are the rulers of each yakona kingdom, given the right to rule by unique magic in their blood that's passed from parent to child. The Bloods are connected to their subjects through a shared blood connection, which allows them to control the actions of their people via mandates and blood-bound orders. Heirs possess a lesser version of the blood magic, though Bloods and Heirs heal almost instantly from a wound. Upon a Blood's death, the Heir awakens and takes on the powers of his or her predecessor. The awakening is an incredibly painful process, thought to be the most painful experience known.

Sartori - Sword belonging to the Blood of each race. Only the Blood can wield the sword as touching the hilt will burn anyone else. The entire blade is coated with the only known poison that can kill a Blood, and each Sartori has a slight variation of the poison. An antidote can be made, but only from the blade that caused the wound.

The Grimoire - The First Vagabond created the Grimoire to document everything he knew about Ourea so that it could be passed down. The magical book can flip its own pages, make drawings come to life, and so much more.

The Vagabond's Necklace - The four-leaf clover pendant has a stone in the middle. It's able to hide the Grimoire from sight so that those who seek the power within cannot steal it. The stone can be clear, which means the Grimoire isn't magically hiding within the stone, or blue, which means it is. Only the Vagabond can call the book forward or wish it away.

Blood Loyalty - Each kingdom has a ruler called a Blood. The Blood can control the people in their kingdom through the blood loyalty. Anyone given a silent or spoken command must follow it. Cedric, the First Vagabond, discovers that he does not have a blood loyalty, and therefore does not need to follow commands given by his blood.

Lichgates - A lichgate is a portal that ties our world to the terrifying and beautiful world of Ourea. Lichgates can be found in remote places, and when you walk through a lichgate, the land you cross into is not what you would see if you'd simply walked around the portal. There are also lichgates within Ourea that can make traveling vast distances easier... if you know where they are.

Ethos - Ethos is an ancient city which once housed all the races of Ourea in one place. They lived in harmony until it was discovered that a Stelian figured out a way to steal the bloodline from other yakona royal families. After that, Stelians were banished and trust between the yakona races eroded. They all went their separate ways and abandoned Ethos.

YOU'RE MISSING OUT…

Boyce posts official artwork, updates, and random things that will make you laugh on Facebook, Instagram, and Twitter.

Boyce also created a special Facebook group specifically for readers like you to come together and share their lives and interests, especially regarding the Grimoire Saga novels. Please check it out and join in whenever you get the chance! Everyone in there is amazing, and you'll fit right in.

https://www.facebook.com/groups/Grimoire-Readers/

Sign up for email alerts of new releases AND exclusive access to the Grimoire Saga Fandom Encyclopedia: the official guide to Ourea exclusively for the Grimoire Saga's biggest fans. The encyclopedia is

ONLY available to Boyce's VIP email tribe, so sign up now to get access:

https://smboyce.com/email-signup-pages/grimoire-saga/

Enjoying the series? Awesome! Help others discover the Grimoire Saga by leaving a review at Amazon: **http://mybook.to/treason-by-boyce**

BOOKS BY S. M. BOYCE

The Grimoire Saga

Lichgates

Treason

Heritage

Illusion

The Misanthrope

The First Vagabond: Rise of a Hero

The First Vagabond: Fall of a Legend

The Demon

The Fairhaven Chronicles

Glow

Shimmer

Ember

Nightfall

Standalone Novels

Ari

ACKNOWLEDGMENTS

Thank you to my talented editors, Chase Nottingham and Allisyn Ma. Thank you also to my amazing beta readers: Dad, Nikki, Sylvalyn, Aly, and Adrienne. And of course, this novel wouldn't be what it is without my husband's incredible input and support. Thank you, Geoff.

ABOUT THE AUTHOR

S. M. Boyce is a lifelong writer with a knack for finding adventure and magic. Known for enchanting, expansive, and epic worlds, Boyce writes action-packed adventures with heroes who push boundaries to make their worlds better.

Word-of-mouth is crucial for any author to succeed. If you enjoyed this novel, please consider leaving a review at Amazon, even if it's only a line or two. Your review will make all the difference and is hugely appreciated.

Printed in Great Britain
by Amazon